Ripped & Shipped

AN ENEMIES-TO-LOVERS, FAKE-DATING ROMCOM

SAVANNAH SCOTT

(Spoiler Alert)

If you haven't read *Cruiseshipped*, Brooks & Gabriela's story, this book (*Ripped & Shipped*) contains a spoiler for *Cruiseshipped*.

If you think you will want to read *Cruiseshipped* someday, I recommend you read it before reading *Ripped & Shipped* first.

As for the rest of this *Getting Shipped* series, the books are truly interconnected stand-alone reads. You can read any of the other books in any order (though avid fans say the best experience comes by reading them in the order they were written).

Connect with Savannah

Visit Savannah Scott's website
www.SavannahScottBooks.com

You can also follow Savannah on Amazon.

For free books and first notice of new releases, sign up for Savannah's Romcom Readers email at https://savannahscott.website/romcom-reader-email/

Savannah is on Instagram at @SavannahScott_author

For Jon
Thank you for being the hero in my love story.
You've patiently stood by through it all.
I'm so grateful opposites attract.

For the bookstagram community and my faithful readers. This series has been the ride of my life.
Thank you for coming to Bordeaux with me.
Let's keep coming back here together,
and let's find new places we love just as much.

You make writing these stories a sheer joy.

You are worth it.

A note to you …

Welcome to the quaint and quirky town of Bordeaux, Ohio!

If you've already visited Bordeaux through any of the other *Getting Shipped* books, *WELCOME BACK*!

If you haven't been to our town yet, you're in for some fun times, heartfelt friendships, and sweet romances.

As Lexi said in *Friend(shipped)* …

We're talking about Bordeaux, Ohio, not the port city along the coastal southwest of France.

We don't pronounce our town name like our French sister city either. Some bright ancestor of mine who settled this valley in the 1800s pronounced our town name, ***bored ox****.*

Yep. Like some bull standing out in a field wondering what to do with his day. And, believe me, we have plenty of fields with plenty of oxen who, from what I've seen, look pretty bored.

So, welcome to Bordeaux … where the oxen might be bored, but you will not be!

Savannah Scott

CHAPTER 1

Ella Mae

"HELLLLLOOOO, my peeps!

It's me, Ella Mae, coming to you live from the quaint streets of my small town, which shall remain nameless. Yes. Yes. Yes. I know. Many of you have asked me for the name of this town. And, when I have refused to satisfy your curiosity, you cleverly asked for map coordinates, or begged to at least know the county where I live.

"And I love how much you want to visit and connect. I'd honestly LOVE to hang out with you! Love. Love. Love. I mean, you're my peeps for a reason, and this bond we share is beyond spesh.

"But let's be serious. Stalkers are real and I need to maintain my safety. Am I right?"

I smile a winning smile into my phone and walk toward our local coffee shop, Bean There Done That. I strategically avoid filming the name while walking in the door.

"It's time to get caffeinated!" I shout into the phone as I approach the counter.

Yes, I'm over the top. People eat it up. Of the nearly five billion individuals on the internet, only a select few make their living as influencers. It's a competitive, cutthroat world online, and I've carved out my niche by being trendy, bold, and a little eccentric.

Yes, I'm all those things in real life. But I'll be the first to admit I ramp it up for the camera. Not that I admit it out loud. A girl has her reputation to maintain. But in my heart, I know the truth.

"Hey, Madeline! Hey, Riley!"

I greet the baristas by name. That's how it's done around here. In Bordeaux, we're one big, happy, dysfunctional family of two thousand five hundred. I'm basically the black sheep of the family. A black sheep in knock-off Jimmy Choos, carrying a purse that looks like a tube of lipstick, and wearing a mini skirt that shows off the hard-earned results of my daily pilates workout. Not that you'd want to see a sheep wearing all that, but you get the gist.

As popular as I am online—and trust me and my bank account, I'm popular—I'm not so loved IRL (that's *in real life* for those of you who aren't up on the lingo). In fact, the only townsperson less popular than me is probably Cooter Shartz.

If he'd lay off the sauce and stop passing out in his neighbor's bushes, he'd move up the ranks in a hot minute, and I'd officially be the most disliked person in Bordeaux.

What can I say? Some people are born ahead of their time. I was born to live somewhere else—like New York, or Paris, or Milan. Maybe the French Riviera. Instead, I've got the muddy banks of the Mad River, and a group of people around me who mostly don't know the internet from a fishing net.

You're probably wondering why I never left Bordeaux. I've thought about it, trust me. But I do have my bestie, Meg, here. And, I've got my mom, who isn't always doing so great. I'm an only child, and basically one of the only friends Mom's got, unless you count my grams, who could probably drink

Cooter under the table. Maybe she's had a few or more with Cooter under a table or two in the past. I wouldn't doubt it.

Mom and Dad divorced years ago, when I was five. Dad runs the hardware store. He's one of those old-fashioned men who believed in providing for his family while the woman stayed home to raise the kids. So, even though he and Mom don't talk, he made sure she never had to work while I lived at home so she could stay with me. But other than that kindness, he's got nothing good to say about her and that runs both ways between them. Rumors tell me a lot more than I'd care to know about my parents' history.

Running a hardware store in a small town isn't ever going to make Dad a millionaire. It's probably barely going to provide for his retirement, but the store's his pride and joy, so he's never even given the option of doing a different job a second thought.

Basically, I'm here in Bordeaux because it's what I know. As avant-garde as I can be online, in real life, I'm a creature of habit. The idea of taking a big risk like moving to a new town overwhelms me. So, I live through my virtual connections. My online life is big, even if my real life is small.

"Caffeinate me!" I shout to the two baristas.

Both girls are home for the summer from their life on the west coast. Yes. These two local besties applied to get into UCLA and were accepted. They've been living it up in California for three years now and only come home for the summers.

"What do you want to drink?" Madeline asks me.

Her long blond hair has natural highlights from the time she obviously spends in the sun. She's adorable, and her fashion sense isn't half bad.

"I wish we could do a TikTok challenge right here. But alas, we can't. So give me your most requested drink."

I look at the camera.

"The beauty of big cities is you can do all the challenges. Here in the sticks, we have to make do. But there's all the sweetness of small-town life that makes up for the lack of fast-food chains and big box stores. Am I right? You know I'm right. Comment below with your fave way to caffeinate! I can't wait to hear what you've got brewing! And don't forget to put the *YOU* in fab-*YOU*-lous today!"

I'm about to turn off the camera when two of the hottest men in town walk into the coffee shop. I never can pass up an opportunity to showcase our stunning male specimens. I mean, we're in the midwest. People all assume we're buck-toothed and backwards. In reality, we're the dark horse when it comes to so many awesome things. And I aim to set the record straight as often as I can.

People think California boys are hot—all looking like buff surfers or the leading men in movies. And then you've got the hot lawyer types in Boston, or the gorgeous southern boys with their drawls from South Carolina or Texas. But we're not slouching here in Ohio. These men haul hay, aren't afraid of a hard day's work, and have the muscles to show for it.

"Ladies, Ladies, Ladies!" I say toward my phone. "I know I was about to sign off, but I have a treat for you. It's true, I'm in the coffee shop, but I may as well be in our sweet shop because … mmmm hmmm, I just found some suh-weeet eye candy. Get ready to fan yourselves, and not because the high will be ninety-eight today. We've got Duke Satterson and Chris St. James coming our way."

I turn my phone toward the door where Duke and Chris are walking in. They really are show-stoppers. Both of them are taller than six feet, blond, and ripped. They used to almost look like brothers until Chris went off to the Army. He came back with arms bigger than my legs.

Duke's married now, but Chris is single. If he weren't so reserved and moody, he'd be a great catch. But we're not talking about dating the man. I'm just trying to woo my audience with a little something to swoon over.

"Good morning, boys," I coo to Duke and Chris.

Duke hams it up, ever the charismatic charmer.

"Well hello there, Ella Mae," he says, "Hey Ella's peeps!" He waves to the camera and literally flexes his biceps so they pop. Hello, viral video.

"Have a … what do you say, Ella Mae?" Duke pauses, scratching his chin in an exaggerated way. "Oh yeah. Have a Fab-U-lous day!"

I chuckle. "That's Duke, girls. Of course, he's taken, so don't fill the comments with requests for his info."

I turn the camera on Chris. He turns away. His back faces me and the camera. Rude.

"So, girls, this is the back of Chris," I say, playfully. "What a back, though, am I right? Was it shoulder day today, Chris?"

He grunts like some neanderthal. Then his hand comes around, covers the screen of my phone and he powers it down. Mid-livestream. He just cut me off from my peeps.

"What the heck, St. James?" I ask.

"I think it's illegal to film people without their consent, Ella Mae."

"Not anymore, St. James. Keep with the times. If we're in public, I'm allowed to film. It's referred to as a no expectation of privacy contingency. I've done my research. And I'm not hurting anyone."

Duke, being somewhat of a peacekeeper by nature, jumps between us and looks at Chris. "She's just having fun, man. Don't be so hard on her."

"I'm actually doing my job," I say.

Yes, it can be fun, but social media is my livelihood. And Chris just cut me off from the people who butter my bread and keep a roof over my head. Not to mention, they think the world of me. In my world, reputation is everything. One turn of your image can mean disaster. The limelight is like a firefly, flitting around from person to person. You want to maintain your status and remain popular? Then you need to stay current and keep people coming back for more.

"Don't film me," Chris says.

"Ella Mae," Riley sing-songs from behind the counter. "Your drink order is up."

I turn my phone back on, staring Chris in the eye as I do. His eyes are bright and blue, they've got a depth to them, and they deceptively appear so much kinder than the attitude he's throwing my way.

I tap a few buttons on my phone. As soon as the screen tells me I'm live, I say, "Sorry, peeps! Technical difficulties are real!"

I glance at Chris. His arms are crossed over his chest like a nightclub bouncer. His face is an inscrutable mask.

"But I'm back! And we're about to see what the number one caffeinated drink for summer is here at the local coffee shop."

Shooting Chris a meaningful look, I tilt the phone slightly, and in a possibly overly-loud voice, I ask Riley, "Riley, do you mind if I film you?"

"Of course not, Ella Mae," she answers in her usually cheery tone.

I turn the camera toward my face, spin so my back faces the counter, and make sure the screen is filled with both Riley's and my faces.

"What do we have to drink today, Riley?"

"It's the chocolate coffee smoothie!"

This girl is gold.

"Ooooh. Sounds delish! Tell us what's in the drink!"

"It's almond milk, cold brew, chocolate syrup, and ice, blended to perfection. We add java chips at the end if we make it a chocolate chip coffee smoothie."

I pick the drink up, and toast the people watching. My on-screen counter says nine thousand viewers are watching me right now. That's a little low compared to my usual count, but it's midday on a summer weekday, and I didn't announce this live before I got on.

I take a sip, turning my eyes toward Chris, who looks like he's either constipated or ready to murder someone.

Then I lick my lips and say, "Mmmm. Now that's a drink you all have to try! This is me, Ella Mae, reminding you to put the YOU in Fab-YOU-lous ... and maybe put a little chocolate in your coffee while you're at it!"

Fab-U-lous_EllaMae

Comments on Livestream:
378 comments

@sparkle2shine123: You inspire me! Roll with those tech problems, girlie! And that drink looks scrumptious!

@beefitupfitnessdude: Ur hot. 🔥🔥🔥 R U Single?

@midwestcutiepie: Those men! Who was the one with his back turned to you? I'd love to see his face up close. If it's anything like his shoulders … Well, you know what I'm saying! 💪🥵🖤

@EllaMaeFan4ever: You're the best, EllaMae. Love you! 😘

@youdoyouboooo: Maybe the bro has it right. Should you really be filming people when they're just out for a cup o' joe?

> **@EllasSoBella**: Sorry, @youdoyouboooo, she's just sharing her life. She wasn't hurting anyone.

@DrakesDaMan: Let's collab! Love your energy.

CHAPTER 2

Chris

I WATCH Ella Mae saunter out of the coffee shop—that short skirt skimming mid-thigh, her blond hair swishing from side to side. She turns for a moment and catches my eye with a challenging glance.

If I were a different man, I'd shake my head at her antics. All those usual bodily reactions were trained out of me in the military. Instead, I stare after her with an expression I've mastered that appears to look past her or through her. Then I return my gaze to Duke, who's sitting across the table from me, leaning back with his legs outstretched.

Not a care in the world—ever—that's my best friend. And now he's my brother-in-law, a turn of events I still fight to wrap my brain around. So much changed while I was away for six years serving in the Army.

"You could lighten up," Duke says. "We're not in boot camp, Sergeant."

"Captain."

Duke mock salutes me, still leaned back like he's in a lounge chair, making the wooden chair beneath him look like a piece of child's furniture.

"All I'm saying is, you could go a little easier on Ella Mae. She's not hurting you."

"It's not me I'm worried about."

"Oh?"

"Can we change the subject?"

"Sure. Sure. Let's talk about those back muscles of yours. All the peeps want to know ... was it shoulder day?" Duke cracks himself up.

"Ha," I say, but I can't help smiling. "And, no. It was leg day. I'll hit shoulders and chest tomorrow."

My answer is serious, but a smile remains on my face. Duke's ridiculous, and his levity is contagious.

"Did you work out at the firehouse?" Duke asks.

"Why not? Ever since Brooks moved, someone's got to keep that rookie, Davis, in line."

"Pretty sure the rest of the firemen in town do that on the regular."

"He's new here," I remind Duke.

"Davis?"

"Yeah. It's not easy being on the outside of a tight-knit group of people who grew up more like cousins than neighbors. I figure it's our job to help him fit in."

"You're a good man, Chris."

"Don't let that get out to too many people," I joke.

"Your secret's safe with me," Duke says with an affable smile. "Speaking of secrets, I'm still not sure what you do on Wednesdays when you leave town."

I hum and then I take a sip of coffee.

"Is that your way of telling me to mind my own business?"

I just grin at Duke. Then I change the subject. My Wednesday excursions have been the topic of teasing and prodding in my friend group ever since I came home from my discharge over two years ago.

I've been trained to endure strategic interrogations. You'd think the inquisition from my closest friends would have nothing on a military shakedown. You'd be wrong. Relentless doesn't begin to describe a group of small-town citizens trying to unearth a bit of gossip.

"I just need to shake the dust sometimes," I supply.

"Shake the dust?"

"Yeah. Like when you take your bike out on the open roads to remind yourself this town isn't all there is to life."

Duke nods.

"But I always turn my bike around and come home. Everything I need is right here in this town."

Duke's voice rings with contentment. I envy him, and not in a way that means I'd take one thing away from him. I love seeing him so settled. I honestly never thought it would happen. He was far more restless than me only three years ago. Once he got serious with my sister, everything changed. Up until then, he had his weekly outings away from here too. I don't bring those up now. That's history. And he's more than proven he's committed to Shannon, and to being a responsible husband and provider.

I'm so far from that lifestyle it's almost comical. At thirty-two, I thought I'd be settled down, raising a family, coming home to a wife—whether she worked or not. Sharing our dreams. I'd be the safe place each of us needs in a life full of uncertainty and heartbreak. And trust me when I say this. The pool of candidates for my life's partner here in my hometown is shallower than a rain puddle in summertime.

Sometimes Bordeaux feels like a safe haven. At other times, it feels like an enclosure. A man could suffocate or shrivel if he never got out. It's a mystery to me how most of my friends never left here. Rob did. He even went to MIT, but then, like a homing pigeon, he flew back as soon as he graduated. Of course, he had a girl on the brain. That'll do it every time.

If it weren't for my family and friends living here, I'd have chosen to settle somewhere bigger. But my family needs me. And after traveling the world, I realized friends like the ones I've got aren't a given. So, I'm back.

Besides, this town is off the radar. I like that. I can get lost from the rest of the world here and blend in.

"What's your day looking like?" Duke asks.

He's the local history teacher and the co-owner of the gas station. But he's got mechanics running that business nowadays, so his summers are easy-breezy, consisting mostly of days that bleed together. If it were me, I'd be filling my time with some sort of structure and responsibility. Duke's fine letting all that go until mid-August when he preps for the coming school year.

"I'm popping by Dad's office, and then I'm helping Memaw clean her gutters." I tell him.

"Doesn't Bryan Dashwood do that?"

I shrug. "She asked me."

"Okay then." Duke chuckles. "Want some help?"

"If you're actually going to work."

"I bet you I'll clean more length of those gutters than you. Loser takes the winner to Mad River burgers Friday."

"I thought we all were going there anyway."

"Loser pays for the winner's double bacon cheeseburger with extra onions, large onion rings, and shake."

"That sounds like your order."

"Because I'm the winner in this scenario."

I chuckle. "Bet's on. And what's with you and the onions? Does my sister actually kiss you after all that?" I pause. "Nevermind. Please. Don't answer that question."

"Oh, she kisses me. I mean, look at me. How can she resist?"

He smiles and wags his eyebrows.

"It's a mystery what she sees in you. But who am I to judge? After all, she only had a few decent men to pick from in this town. Who can blame her for thinking you're awesome."

Duke shakes his head and stands to take his mug to the counter. From over his shoulder, he says, "You know I'm awesome. You're just jealous because you still haven't found the one."

He's laughing it up, completely oblivious to the bullseye in my heart. I smile a placating smile and carry my mug to the counter. Duke might be right, but I know better than bringing a woman into my life right now. For so many reasons that would not be a good idea.

CHAPTER 3

Ella Mae

"OH EM GEEEE!" I squeal as I run into our side of the duplex after reading my comment notifications on my livestream from the coffee shop.

My BFF Meg isn't home, but I plan to hop by her workplace and fill her in on my big news at her lunchtime. First, I need to do some editing on a few reels to post later this week.

But, OMG! DrakesDaMan commented that he wants a collab! He's HUGE. As in thirty-two million followers. I have over eight million. But I'm barely a blip on the screen compared to Drake. He started on YouTube doing product reviews, challenges, and just filming himself hanging out with friends. Before long, he grew, and now he's on Insta and TikTok too.

He's my age—twenty-nine. At our age, being an influencer gets precarious. People always want the younger, more hip vibe. We age out like pro athletes. And then what? At least sports celebs get to do ads for athletic shoes. I have exactly zero idea what I'd do if my social media gig dried up.

In case I'm dreaming, I check my Insta account again. Sure enough, not only did Drake drop a comment on my post, but he sent me a DM. I open my messages, rapidly shaking my hand in the air like I'm flicking something off my fingers. My nerves are all jittery at the prospect of a collab with Drake. This could be so huge for me. Exposure on his feed would bump my follower count exponentially.

@DrakesDaMan

Hey, Ella Mae. Just poppin in to say I loved your livestream today. A friend of mine suggested I check you out. Love your energy. Thought we might collab sometime.

As you know, I live half the year in California now, but what most people don't know is that I live another chunk of the year in Ohio. It's my home state. I keep it vague and chill, saying I'm from the midwest instead of naming a given state. I've had some psycho stalkers over the years. Stories to follow if you want to hear about all that cray action. What part of the midwest are you in? Let's hook up.

I place my hand over my heart. It's racing. Drake's in Ohio? Why would he be in Ohio during the summer when he could be in California? I'm going to ask just that. And he's acting like we're old friends. I can't even believe my life right now.

I take a deep breath, exhale slowly, and remind myself I'm a bad boss babe. My online life coach, Journey, would tell me to embrace the positive, envision myself as I want to be, and reject all small thoughts.

I close my eyes and remind myself I've worked hard to get where I am. I hear Journey's soothing voice saying, *Growth is natural.* And this is the growth I've been waiting for. Of course, Journey would tell me to imagine myself as a tree, growing with my ever-expanding branches reaching for the sun. She'd end that pep talk with her famous saying, *Yassss, QUEEN! Slayyyy!*

I've got this. I can be cool as a cucumber, a queen cucumber with ever-expanding branches. Whatever.

I look down at my knock-off Jimmy Choo fuchsia satin neon plexi pumps. These are the shoes of a woman who knows her own mind. They are the shoes of a woman who is going places. These shoes are a reflection of my vibrant personality and my bold presence in the world.

I take another deep breath. Shoes, don't fail me now. I'll just act like I'm texting Chris … only a nicer version of him. No. Not Chris at all. Why would I text him? Duke. I'll pretend I'm texting Duke.

@Fab-U-Lous_EllaMae

Hey, Drake! Nice hearing from you. I'm a huge fan. You've always made me smile. I'd love to consider a collab. Let me know what you have in mind. By the way, what are you doing in Ohio in the summer when you could be at the beach? I'm in Ohio too. Southwest Ohio.

That's good. Low key. Not at all fangirling. Just me and Drake. Pals from way back. Yep. I'm good. I reread the message a few times. It sounds good. Satisfied, I start to set my phone down, but it pings with a response.

@DrakesDaMan

I'm back home for some time with the fam. I'll only be here a few weeks. Then, because you're beyond right, I'm heading back to the Craze Shack in Malibu.

California calls to me when I'm not there—unless I'm in Europe or on an island, of course. I'm hosting a huge bash at the Shack two weeks after my return—my annual Surf, Sun, Social Shindig. Everyone will be there. You should come.

I should whaaa? Come to Malibu? To go to Drake's party? Is this a hoax? Maybe I'm being pranked. I double check the Insta account he's messaging from, and when I see it's the verified DrakesDaMan account, I squeal and do a little shimmy. Then I look down at my shoes.

"Thank you Choos! You made this day rock!"

Maybe it's not the shoes. But honestly, they didn't hurt. Well, they do hurt. But that's the price of looking fab-u-lous, as I always say.

@Fab-U-Lous_EllaMae

I'll have to check my schedule and see if I can make it to your bash. Thanks for thinking of me. Send me the deets on the collab whenever.

I'm so proud of myself. That answer sounds appropriately detached, while also giving the green light to all the things—a beach bash in California, a collab with Drake … and who knows what connections this will lead to. I raise my hands over my head and do a sexy dance even though there's no music playing in our house.

@DrakesDaMan

Sounds rad. My assistant, Genesis, will contact you with all the ideas I've got rolling around in my head, and with an official invite to the bash.

What would we do without our assistants? I don't even want to know. Looking forward to hooking up. Maybe even while I'm in Ohio. My fam is in Columbus, so that's my location for the time being. Keep that on the DL. ;)

My assistant? Yeah. Dream on. I'm my own assistant, my own social media coordinator, my own marketing rep, my own wardrobe consultant, and my own videographer and editor. Some of these hyped-up influencers have teams of ten or twenty people working for them. I have me, me, and, oh yeah, me. I'm not complaining. I like managing things. I might go bonkers trying to train someone to be my assistant. Still, it would be nice to be able to say, "Hey, my assistant will contact you with the details," just once.

@Fab-U-Lous_EllaMae

Sounds good. I'd love to hook up in Columbus if that works out. Keep me posted.

~

The weather is warm and humid by the time I climb back into my car to share my big news with Meg. By warm, I mean nearing eighty, and by humid, I mean not-quite-a-sauna. I pulled my hair up into a ponytail before I left the house just to keep things looking perky and on-point.

Besides, I did a hair tutorial while getting the ponytail set so it looks extra full. Two-for-one! My peeps love when I do makeup and hair tutorials. And keeping them happy makes me happy.

I park my cherry red Mazda in one of the diagonal spaces in front of St. James Common Cents Accounting Firm.

Yes. St. James. As in, Chris St. James—the man who turned his back on me at Bean There Done That this morning. Yes. The same man who interrupted my livestream without an apology. The man whose good looks are wasted on such a stern and unfriendly personality. That St. James.

Chris' dad is an accountant—*the* accountant in town. And Meg is the only other accountant in his office. Mr. St. James' daughter, Shannon, is the receptionist—-that's Shannon, as in Duke's wife. Let's just say that she and I don't run in the same circles.

Shannon's a super-sweet young woman—beautiful, graceful from years of dancing ballet. But like most of the town, I'm not her favorite flavor—at all. She usually barely tolerates my presence, and then she and her friends can't wait to titter on about me behind my back. It's okay. I'm used to it. What's a small town without a healthy dose of gossip?

I know my theatrics and larger-than-life personality have rubbed people the wrong way at times. But I'm of the mindset that we should all be ourselves. I'm not a typically demure midwestern girl. And I don't plan to start toning things down to win any popularity contests.

I walk into the modest storefront that has been home to all sorts of things over the years: a dry cleaner, a pet groomer, and even a photography studio. Shannon's desk is off to the side of the entryway. Across from her is a long couch and a coffee table with a few financial magazines stacked neatly on the surface. The little bell over the entryway tinkles as the door shuts behind me.

"Hey, Ella Mae," Shannon says with a smile that's not quite full, but is cordial.

"Hey, Shannon. Is Meg in? I thought I'd take her to lunch."

"She's just finishing up with Mr. Anderson. Do you want to have a seat?"

"I'm good."

A beat of silence hangs in the air. I glance around at the walls. They are a gray-blue. A few awards or certificates hang in frames, and on the far wall, behind Shannon's desk is a poster that says, *Spending is Quick, Earning is Slow.*

What a downer.

"Cute shoes," Shannon finally says.

I look down as if I don't know what's on my feet.

"Oh, yeah. They're knock-offs. But I still love them."

"You should. They're seriously awesome. And I'm glad they aren't real. Aren't real Jimmy Choos like six hundred?"

"At the least. They can run up into the thousands."

Shannon shakes her head. "Well, you rock those."

"Thanks."

This is by far the longest conversation we've had since high school—which was eleven years ago.

A door opens.

Shannon's dad's voice reaches the reception area. "Well, Chris. Let me know if you change your mind. And, if you have time, pop in on your mother. She's having a day."

Chris walks into the reception area. When he obviously notices me, his face turns from a semi-smile to what could be called a grimace. Except his eyes drop to my feet and travel upward toward my face. When he meets my stare … does he blush? It's not a really noticeable change, but I'd say he's busted and he knows it. That's right, St. James. I do pilates and yoga, and I've got the figure to show it.

"Chris," I say.

"Ella Mae," he retorts.

I smirk for extra emphasis. He turns away, tells his sister he'll see her later, and walks out the front door without another word in my direction.

Fab-U-lous_EllaMae

Hey, peeps!

You never know what good fortune will slide your way. Just remember that little nugget of truth during the down days, the slow days, and the days when you feel unseen and misunderstood.

Good things are always coming.

And today, well … Today I got a big invitation from someone HUGE! His name might rhyme with MakesMaCan. Shhhhh. Don't tell!

I'm not saying a thing yet, but let's just say a collab may be in the works. And maybe a trip … somewhere sunny and beautiful.

So, keep on believing in yourself. Never change for anyone. And most of all … say it with me … don't forget to put the YOU in fab-YOU-lous today!

CHAPTER 4

Chris

MY CHILDHOOD HOME is a pretty typical house in Bordeaux. We have a variety of styles common in the midwest around town—craftsman, ranch/rambler, and even some colonial and victorian.

Ours is a two-story home with a concrete front porch, a gabled roof, and an old-fashioned, solid-wood, craftsman door. I guess you'd call it charming.

The paint color has changed over the years. It's currently a light yellow with white trim and navy shutters. Dad keeps the yard and exterior looking good enough to be in a magazine. The picket fence has gone from brown to white. But otherwise, the property is the same as it was thirty-two years ago when my parents bought it to prepare to start their family.

I sit in my car, looking up at the two sets of bedroom windows visible from the street, and then I glance at the attic windows above them. Shannon and our middle sister, Bridgette, shared the left bedroom. As the older brother and only boy, I had the one on the right to myself.

If I close my eyes, I can see Bridgette and Shannon practicing dance routines in the front yard.

I take in a steadying breath. Dad said Mom's "having a day." Ever since we lost Bridgette in an accident when she was sixteen, Mom's days are clouded with chronic, relentless depression.

The night of the crash, I stayed home to play in a football game. I've always believed I could have made a difference. If I had just skipped that game, fate would have been different.

Alter one element, and the whole trajectory of a situation changes. My presence could have been that element.

Maybe I would have shouted, "Watch out!" at just the right moment. I might have made us run late, or more likely, kept us on schedule. I could have done something—anything—to avert the accident that took my sister from us. But I was home celebrating a win while my family endured a horrific car crash, and Bridgette breathed her last breath.

And we didn't only lose Bridgette that day, we lost Mom. She's still here in body, but she's never fully come back to us in spirit. Clinical depression set in, and she has far more hard days than good. Thirteen years have passed, but for Mom, it's like the worst kind of groundhog day. She relives the trauma of losing her middle child daily.

Squaring my shoulders, I get out of the car, open the front gate and latch it behind me. Then I continue up porch steps until I'm facing the front door. I don't need to knock, so I walk in.

"Hey, Mom! It's Chris!" I shout, even though I don't expect an answer..

Silence greets me.

I walk toward the sunroom at the back of the house. It's not too hot out yet, still early summer. In a few weeks we won't want to be outdoors in the middle of the day. For the time being, Mom can enjoy the afternoon breeze and the backyard wildlife from the comfort of her rocking chair here on the screened-in porch.

Mom always loved her garden and anything to do with nature. Dad sets her up here during the mornings before he goes into the office.

"Hey, Mom. How's it going on this beautiful sunny Ohio day?"

She smiles a wan smile in my direction. It doesn't quite reach her eyes, but it's better than no smile.

"I just went into Dad's office before lunch. Have you eaten?"

She shakes her head.

"Let's get food. I haven't eaten either. Maybe we could have a sandwich out here together. I promise to add lettuce just to make you happy."

Her eyes warm a little at my joke. I never wanted lettuce on my sandwiches as a kid. As soon as I got to school, I'd pluck the offending leaf off the otherwise perfect lunch, toss it in a hallway trash can, and repack my lunch bag. That was before Bridgette turned me in. As soon as I got home from school that day, Mom lectured me about vitamins, minerals, and roughage.

Mom's reprimand worked. I never let my sister see me pull the lettuce off my sandwich again. I made sure I went into the boys' restroom to do my disassembly and reassembly in private from then on.

I leave Mom in the sunroom and make us some sandwiches. We eat in silence. I tell her about Dad's attempt to convince me to join the accounting firm again. I'm not qualified. My background is in technology and personnel management. In the military, I learned coding and all sorts of skills related to fraud detection and espionage.

I'm equipped to lead people, or to use a computer to track

someone. I'm not a numbers guy. Dad merely wants me to be engaged in his business.

I appreciate Dad's heart, but he's not thinking straight. In business, you need someone suited to the job. As flighty as Meg is, she's a surprisingly good accountant. And Dad doesn't need another accountant.

"Your dad just wants you around," Mom says quietly. "He missed you while you were away."

"Then we should grab a bite together, or go on a bike ride. He doesn't need to hire me. I've got other work, Mom."

She nods. I haven't told my family everything I do in my job, but they know I make a living. I don't want Mom to worry about me more than she already does.

A chickadee chirps in the yard and Mom turns her head in the direction of the sound.

"I love those birds," she says.

"Me too. I understand the midday bird calls are the women wooing the guys."

Mom laughs lightly. "Girls always have to do the heavy lifting. It's not very fair, is it?"

"What's that supposed to mean?"

Mom pauses. She looks out in the yard where another bird is answering the first call.

Her voice is soft when she answers me. "We have to get all dolled up. It's up to us to get your attention. Then we have to worry you'll be distracted by the next pretty bird you see."

I hum, a smile spreading across my face. Mom doesn't usually talk this much. She might have been having a harder day this morning, but she's in good spirits now—even lightly joking about birds and women.

"So, us guys have it easy?"

"Maybe not. But Chris?"

"Yeah, Mom?"

"Don't make it hard on the women who want your attention. You're thirty-one. It's not good for you to be alone."

"I'm okay. I have my friends. If I want to date, I go out with someone."

Mom looks out across the back yard. I think she's done, but then after a few minutes, she says, "It's not the same, Chris. Having that one person is different. When you find the one, it's everything."

"Like Dad?"

She smiles a faint smile, but I can see the emotion behind it.

"I don't know what I'd do without him. I just wish I could be more for him."

"You're everything to him."

Her smile is sad, but sweet.

"I know."

"And you still have the rest of your lives together."

She nods.

We don't talk anymore about my singleness, or her depression, or Dad. Instead, I fill her in on some events coming up in town. Mom usually stays home, barely ever leaving unless it's for the evening walks that Dad insists she take with him most nights after supper.

We finish our lunches, and I take our dishes into the kitchen. Then I return to Mom, kiss her cheek, and tell her I'll visit again in the next few days. I should probably visit daily. But tomorrow's Wednesday, so I can't make any promises.

CHAPTER 5

Ella Mae

"WHAT IS ON YOUR FACE?" I ask Mabel when I walk in her door.

My seventy-plus-year-old neighbor is definitely hashtag-goals for senior life, but today, I'm wondering if she swallowed a few too many gulps of Listerine while swishing. She's standing in front of me in her fuzzy hot pink bathrobe and matching slippers with what looks like compost on her face—it's thick, and brown, and clumpy.

And is that … a flower petal sticking out near her cheek?

"Oh, heya, Ella Mae. Come in. Come in. This here's my facial anti-aging mask."

"It looks like dirt," I tell her, honestly.

"Well, partly, it is." She pauses, smiling.

A chunk falls off her chin and onto the carpet beneath her. She looks down, waves a hand dismissively, and smiles back at me.

"You put mud on your face?"

"Well, the gal on the YouTube said some sort of natural botox was found in hibiscus flowers. It's better than the fountain of youth!

"And, dontcha know? I've got a hearty hibiscus bush right out back. It's called the rose mallow variety. She said I needed the hibiscus powder—hers was all ground up like baby powder, but I figured the more natural, the better. So, I just plucked a flower and brought it in. Then I tore it up into little bits and chopped it on my choppin' block for good measure.

"The next two ingredients for the mask were some sort of clay or other. And I didn't have clay powder like the YouTube girl. I mean, who has that just sittin' around unless they're one of those potters? Right? So I got to thinkin'. I know my Ohio geology, and our dirt is mostly clay anyhow. So, I dug up some mud while I was out there gettin' my hibiscus.

"Then I put all that in a cereal bowl. All I needed to do was add yogurt and … Well, the YouTube girl said some other oil. Rose or somethin'. But all I had was vegetable, so I put that in. Come to think of it, I'd think Crisco would do the trick in a pinch, but since I had the jumbo jug of vegetable oil, I used it. Gotta save the Crisco for my biscuits.

"Anyway, this here mask feels pretty amazing. Wanna slap some on and join me?"

"I have makeup on already," I say, secretly glad of the fact.

"Well, next time." Mabel smiles big, and the now-drying part of the mask cracks a little under her eyes.

"I'm guessin' you won't even recognize me in a few weeks with the way this is going to tighten up all the wrinkles. Won't Walt just be tickled to have a girlfriend who looks so young at our age? I only wish I had known of this treatment when I was in my twenties like you. I've got plenty of the mixture left. I could put some in a tupperware and send it on home with you."

"Oh, that's okay. I have a clay mask I already use. Thanks, Mabel."

"I shoulda' figured you did, as pretty as you are."

"Awww, Mabel. You're too sweet."

Another clod of the face mask falls onto the floor.

Mabel tracks it with her eyes and says, "Don't you worry none about that. I'll get to it later. It's sweepin' day anyhoo."

Mabel had asked me here to help her with her booming TikTok channel. Yes. She's got an account at @bordeaux-grannysgotback. Even though I got everyone in town onto social media a few years ago to help a struggling local author gain exposure and get a publishing deal, Mabel's the only one who's treated her account seriously and grown it. Most of the people in Bordeaux have long since left their accounts as neglected as a graveyard in a ghost town. Mabel's got an honest-to-goodness following. Every so often she asks me for help, and I'm glad to give it.

"Do you want to take care of your skin care regimen? I can come back later?"

"Oh, no. That won't be necessary. I'm about to wash this off with vinegar. Then I'll be ready to collab with you, as you say."

"Vinegar?"

"Apple Cider Vinegar," she clarifies. "The stuff smells like the devil's spit, but my girl on the YouTube said it has some healing properties. Though, I forget quite what it's supposed to do for me. I'll give it a go since I can use all the help I can get."

"I think you look amazing. And your followers think so too," I assure Mabel.

I wonder at what age a woman is allowed to just let go and be herself without trying so hard. I'm already half-exhausted from managing my online image, and I'm only twenty-nine.

Mabel forgets herself and steps toward me to draw me into a hug. I feel bits of dirt, and probably dirt-coated yogurt clumps, crumble off her face and into my hair. I'd tell you it bothered me if it did, but it's so rare I get a hug that I actually don't mind a bit.

Mabel changes into a red dress that's more like a mumu. Then she and I film two dance videos based on trending dances she memorized the moves for. She tags me in the one she posted, and I accept the collaboration invitation. The comments rack up in no time. Everyone's saying how cute Mabel is, and how sweet I am to spend time with the seniors in my town. People love Mabel—as they should. She's a hoot.

Mabel's account has our town name in it, but I'm ninety-nine percent sure most people think she's either talking about the wine or the city in France, since some people in Dayton haven't even heard of Bordeaux.

Allowing my followers to see Mable's TikTok handle is the closest I've come to disclosing my whereabouts. Back when I was a wannabe, just starting out and only dreaming of coming half this far in popularity, I openly filmed around town, never hiding any of the shop names, and hardly thinking twice about anyone finding me. Even though I aspired to greatness, I never imagined making it this far—to the point where people want to know exactly where I live.

But the world's a crazy place. And as fun as my followers can be most of the time, I don't go a day without some stranger saying something inappropriate, propositioning me, or making phony offers to help my account soar. Most of it's relatively harmless, but I don't want to take my chances.

I finish helping Mabel. The air conditioning of my car blasts my face while I sit in the driver's seat in front of Mabel's house making sure each comment on the video she and I just cross-posted has a reply. This kind of personal touch is what keeps people coming back to me. Responding to my peeps consumes hours of my time each day, but it's worth it.

I'm about to drive off when I get a notification of a DM

(that's Direct Message, for those of you still living in the stone age. Not knocking you, of course. You do cavegirl you, boo, just do it as fab-YOU-lously as you're able. Rock that prehistoric life, you know?).

The handle of the account is @GenesisAssistsStars. Drake had mentioned that his assistant's name was Genesis. I'd be lying if I didn't tell you my heart rate kicks up a notch as I open her message.

@GenesisAssistsStars

Hey, Ella Mae! Drake asked me to reach out for him to plan a time for the two of you to meet. This month he's doing a retrospective focus on his early days as a YouTuber. Drake's hoping you could do a little collab in the style he used in the old days.

Maybe subscribers can pick your meals and you two can eat what they pick and rate it? Does that work? He's itching to get this filmed. His plan is to collab with a few less-known influencers like you. It's going to be a whole series of "throwback" collabs. He said something about it being his way of giving back and supporting small accounts. So sweet, right? His followers will love this return to his roots, and the generosity vibe always gets great ratings.

I take a deep breath and reread the message. Why do I feel slightly insulted? This is a great opportunity. And Drake's reach is massive—nearly four times larger than mine. He would naturally see me as small. That's normal. This *is* generous of him.

It's never easy hearing someone else refer to me as a *less-known influencer*. Try telling my eight million followers and superfans I'm less known. To them, I'm as big as it gets.

And I don't like the term *generosity vibe.* Either you're being generous or you aren't. To call it a vibe makes it sound selfish and manipulative. While I can be a bit overzealous, and even outrageous, my generosity never has been, and never will be a "vibe."

But this isn't my initiative. And it's not my place to drive this project. It's Drake's. He's been on social media for years, making a name for himself and consistently growing. If I'm going to do this collaboration, I'll have to let him use whatever terms and approaches he wants.

@Fab-U-Lous_EllaMae

Hey, Genesis! Great to meet you! Thanks for reaching out. I've got a slightly flexible schedule. Let me know when Drake wants to meet. I love the idea of a follower-engaged collab. If they're the ones picking the food we'll eat, they're going to be invested. Let me know when and where Drake wants me.

I wait a minute. No response. Tossing my cell onto the passenger seat, I take off. My brain races with thoughts about Drake, this collab, and my strategies for the coming month of my own posts.

I push the bluetooth on my steering wheel. Calling Meg should distract me from the flurry of ideas and emotions this collab is dragging up. She's always good for me—especially when I'm spiraling into overthinking mode. Even though we live together, we don't always make time to hang out. She started dating this older guy, Joe, about a year ago. They don't seem super-serious, but they are consistent. If I want some of Meg's time, I need to get my name into a slot on her calendar.

"Hello, Ella Mae," Meg answers in her professional, I'm-at-work tone of voice.

"Hey. I was wondering what you're doing for dinner."

"I don't have plans, but we've also got nothing in the kitchen but a few frozen burritos and some bananas that have seen better days."

"Want me to pick something up at the grocery? I feel like cooking."

"Do you think I'm going to turn down someone buying groceries and cooking for me?"

"Good point. I'll see you at home."

I almost hang up, but then Meg asks, "Are you okay?"

"Yeah. I'm fine. Why?"

"You sound a little off. And you want to cook."

"I love to cook."

"Yes. And you also offer to cook when you're trying to distract yourself from something."

"I think I'm just nervous about this collab with Drake. I want things to go well."

"You're a sensation for a reason. He might have more followers, but I've seen his videos. You've got ten times the personality he has. He's lucky to be collaborating with you."

"Awww. Thanks."

Meg has no idea how much I needed to hear those words. She may not know social media. And she's definitely biased where I'm concerned. But her encouragement still takes some of the edge off what I've been feeling since that DM from Genesis came through.

"See you at home, you rock star," she says. "Go put the YOU in fabulous."

"Thanks."

I chuckle as I hang up. Nothing like having my tagline thrown in my face at a key moment of self-doubt.

CHAPTER 6

Ella Mae

THE KROGER PARKING lot is relatively packed. I guess I'm not the only one out hunting for supper last minute. I put the car in park and grab a cart on my way in.

I'm hunched over my phone in the produce section, typing in a short list of items we probably need when a certain deep voice catches my attention from somewhere over near the root vegetables.

Chris.

He hasn't seen me yet, so I grab my cart and make a beeline to the center aisles. I'm pretty sure that man never eats junk food, so I'm relatively safe hanging out next to the Pop-Tarts and Fruit Loops.

I finish my list and start to push my way down the aisle when a notification pings from my insta account. I wheel the cart off to the side of the aisle and pull up my app.

I talked to Drake. He wants to meet you next Wednesday at Frisch's Big Boy in Columbus. I'm attaching a file link with the details of what you should post on your account leading up to the collab. Feel free to hype this up however you want. You'll meet Drake at 5:00. Filming starts at 5:30. His local crew will be with him. Dress as cute as you always do. And, I'm quoting Drake here, be sure to bring that "vibrant" personality of yours.

My cheeks hurt from the smile that stretches across my face. Drake thinks I have a vibrant personality. I've been called a lot of things over the years: loud, obnoxious, outspoken, wild, free-spirited, crazy, flamboyant, and even self-absorbed. I don't think I've ever been called *vibrant*.

I like it.

"This calls for steak!" I say out loud to no one but me, just as an overly-muscled torso turns the corner and enters the cereal aisle, taking up more space than a man should be allowed to occupy.

His eyes narrow in on me. He doesn't smile. As a matter of fact, his face could be on a statue for the lack of expression. It's an objectively beautiful face. Breathtaking, actually. He's got this combination of softness and hard lines that make him seem like he could be your best friend while simultaneously protecting you in a dark alley. It's an overwhelming juxtaposition of features on one man. His jawline and nose have sharp, angular edges, while his eyes, cheeks, and forehead all have a roundness that give off a more approachable look. Not that he's approachable. He's anything but.

To top this off, he's wearing the heck out of a faded, navy

blue T-shirt and he's topping off the scrumptious sundae with a backward baseball cap, which somehow makes his steely blue eyes more pronounced and his full lips more of a focal point. Not that I'm thinking about his lips. I'm totally not.

I'm half-tempted to whip out my phone to film Chris, just to get a rise out of him, but it's been a long day, and my next few posts need to stay strategically focused on a slow reveal of my collab with Drake.

Just the thought of that project brings another smile to my face.

Chris looks like he's in a debate with himself. Or maybe I'm just reading into things. The man is like a blank canvas, people could project all sorts of misguided interpretations onto him. He leaves so much to the imagination.

Would it hurt him to be mildly friendly? I'm not saying we should be actual friends. We're obviously not about to plan a day trip to the reservoir together. But would it kill him to grin?

"Steak, huh?" Chris nearly grumbles as he slowly ambles toward me.

His voice is so quiet and low I almost wonder if I imagined him echoing my dinner menu.

"Yes. I'm celebrating."

I do a little shimmy of my hips, accompanied with jazz hands, mostly because I know my over-the-topness gets under his skin. I don't know why I want to get under Chris' skin. Maybe just because he's so cantankerous and outwardly judgy. He ought to shimmy in the grocery store a little more. It would do him some good to let loose and have a little fun for a change.

Why do I care?

I don't.

Chris tips his chin in acknowledgement of my celebration.

A small smile almost cracks onto his face. I saw it whether he'd ever admit it or not. News flash: he won't. But I saw him get a kick out of my antics and I'm counting it as a win.

"What are you celebrating?"

"Am I so interesting to you?" I ask, poking the bear even further. "You want to know what I'm celebrating?"

Don't ask me why I like shoving a stick into the hornet's nest where he's concerned. It's like he's got one of those signs on his back that boys used to tape to girls' shirts in elementary school saying, *Kick me.*

"I don't know if interesting is the word I'd use," he says in such a blasé tone, I almost believe he couldn't care less.

Chris shakes his head and starts to move past me. But then he stops, directly across from me. We're less than a foot away from one another. I can see the green ring around the iris in his eyes. Huh. I never noticed that before. But have we ever been this close? I don't think so. Chris' hand reaches out toward my face. Is he going to touch me? Oh. My. Gosh. What is going on?

Before I can think another thought, Chris reaches past me and grabs a box of instant oats—the kind with no flavoring or sugar—and then he plops that box into his cart.

His scent lingers behind him. He smells musky, like a hike in the woods on a fresh spring day. But then there's this hint of oranges and coffee, like we're eating breakfast around a campfire. I'm curled up in a warm flannel blanket without a care in the world while he adds another log to the fire and leans back in his canvas chair. His morning hairdo is mussed and unruly, and he smiles across the flames with a look that says he's been wanting me for years.

Whoa. Whoa. Whoa.

Hold that mental stagecoach. Get off at the next station and run. No one's going overnight camping with the emotionally constipated soldier. And the day he'd look at me like he wanted to kiss me would be the actual end of the earth, involving a scenario where we were the last two people on the planet and our entire species depended on us dating for survival. It would sort of be a zombie-apocalyptic situation, hopefully minus the zombies. Even then, Chris would probably rather die than entertain the idea of getting friendly with me.

Which, for the record, is fine by me. More than fine. The last thing I need in my life is an attraction to a man who mostly hates me.

I probably just need a date. Or steak. Definitely steak and potatoes. And oranges. No. No oranges. I'll bring home cherry pie filling and vanilla ice cream—two things that distinctly do not smell like Christopher St. James.

"Plain oatmeal," I tease, trying to regain my equilibrium and exit my little fantasy woods excursion once and for all. "Aren't you quite the breakfast chef?"

"It's a great quick breakfast. Throw in a protein shake and you're good to go."

"And a Pop-Tart," I say, grabbing a box of the ones called *Wildlicious*—a jelly filled tart with blue and purple frosting—and tossing it into his cart.

Even I can admit they look so artificial they must be gross. Though: Can you really go wrong with Pop-Tarts?

"Man can not live on oats alone, Soldier. You need a little color in your diet. A little fun for fun's sake."

"Fun, huh?" His lips spread into a thin line as he smoothly removes the box of offending Pop-Tarts and places them in my cart.

"Yes," I say. "Fun. It's when people let loose. Laugh. Take a breather from constantly standing guard and following all the rules. You know?"

Chris chuckles. It's not a real laugh, but it's glorious in its own way. His eyes crinkle just the slightest, and I feel the same rush I would if my follower count jumped up another five thousand in one day. He's a hard sell. That's all I'm feeling. It's a rush to get a man like Chris to crack a smile, let alone chuckle.

"I wouldn't know," Chris says, his face returning to its resting impassive state.

"I'm guessing you might be more fun than you let on. But as I always say, you do you, boo."

"Were you the one who made up that ridiculous saying?"

"No, and no. It's not ridiculous, and I didn't make it up. It's a fantastic encouragement to be exactly who we each are —a celebration of uniqueness. I only wish I coined it. But even though I didn't, I still say it all the time."

"Well, what if being me is just not a lot of fun?"

He almost seems serious. But I'm mostly sure he's mocking me. It's getting late and I'm cooking supper—a supper to celebrate my upcoming rise to greater notoriety. I'm not going to let some local, small-minded, small-town, wet blanket of a man ruin my happy mood.

"I've gotta run. Steak and potatoes are calling my name," I say with a wink.

Winking bugs Chris. I've watched him cringe every time I do it.

He doesn't gratify me with a reaction. Instead, he just says, "Yeah." And then he pushes his cart past me without another word. Not a goodbye, not a grunt, not a look back over his shoulder to check out how amazing I look in this skirt—which is ah-maze-zing, in case you wondered. I know you didn't. You knew. I'm rocking this skirt.

But does Chris appreciate the gratuitous view of my retreating curves and long legs? No. He. Doesn't. Chris just pushes on as if I'm as insignificant as the bug he swiped off his windshield on the way over to the grocery store this evening.

Forget him.

Frustrating, stoic soldier.

Who needs men like him when I've got eight million people who hang on my every word and action?

Not me. That's for sure.

Fab-U-lous_EllaMae

Well, my sweet followers and fans, I've got a huge HUGE HUUUUGE announcement!

As some of you noticed @DrakesDaMan commented on my post last week. Holla! And, while I'm always growing, having a huge influencer like him here on my page gave me all sorts of warm fuzzies.

You know ladies. I know you know. I mean Drakes-Da-Man for sure!

Anyway, he and I have been in touch and he's actually here in the midwest for a visit with his family.

So … are you sitting down? Well, maybe you should be if you're prone to fainting. Or if you like jumping up and down when you hear big news, then get outta yo' seat, girl. Because … drum roll … Drake and I are doing some throwback collabs!

Yes! You heard me!
The first collab will be this Wednesday at 5:30pm.
What are you waiting for? Grab your phone and set an alarm.

Drake and I have put together a poll on his site where you can actually pick the food you want us to eat at a certain restaurant.

(Shhh. I'm not telling where). I'll be traveling to meet Drake on Wednesday and we'll be livestreaming right from the restaurant! (That's filming live for those of you who don't know what livestreaming means).

We'll eat what you picked for us and rate our meals. So, go on over to DrakesDaMan.Website and cast your vote for our meals, appetizers, drinks, and desserts.

This should be tons of fun.
And yes, @ariapilatesgoddess, don't you worry your cutie patootie. I will be doing extra yoga and pilates and drinking only green drinks the day before and after this massive, epic, amazing collab.

So … go now! Mark the time for 5:30 pm on Wednesday on your calendar and JOIN US!

Comments:

@always_wearing_prada_gurrrll: DrakesDaMan! Shut the front door! You're so lucky! Drake is soooo 🔥🔥🔥. Are you two an item?

> **@Fab-U-lous_EllaMae**: He is all that. And no. We're just friends. Thanks for your support, girly!

@beefitupfitnessdude: So you're near Columbus?

> **@EllasSoBella**: Stalk much? That's not appropriate to ask, bruh.

> **@beefitupfitnessdude**: I'm just curious. You never know,

we could be soulmates. I'd treat @Fab-U-lous_EllaMae so right.

@EllasSoBella: Just no. She keeps her private life private for a reason.

@EllaMaeFan4ever: Squeeeeee! OH MY GOSH! YOU AND DRAKE. I JUST CAN'T EVEN. DEAD. I'M DEAD. Marked on my calendar and set two alarms on my phone. I jumped up and down, btw. A bunch. My roommate had to come ask me what all the screaming was about.

@midwestcutiepie: I still want more of that hot man from the coffee shop. Do a collab with him. 😉 But this time have him face the camera, alright?

@KeepingItFabu: I can't wait! This is epic! Heading to the website to pick some scrumptious food for you now.

@ariapilatesgoddess: Thanks for the shout out, Ella Mae. I know you're committed. 80-20, gurl. 80-20. And go slay the day with Drake! I'll see you in our virtual classes this week.

CHAPTER 7

Chris

"THAT'S a double bacon cheeseburger with extra onions, large onion rings, and shake—make it chocolate today, Georgia." Duke smiles at the waitress and then smirks in my direction.

Yeah, yeah, so he cleared more leaves out of Memaw's gutters than I did. I'll get him next time.

Our waitress, Georgia, collects the menus from everyone and turns to leave. "Put mine on this guy's tab, Georgia," Duke says, pointing at me. "And that color looks fantastic on you."

Duke flashes the woman one of his charming smiles. Georgia's close to our parents' age, but Duke's charm knows no age limits. She looks like she's about to fan herself. A blush rises up her cheeks, and she smiles at Duke like a groupie at her favorite concert. I simply nod to let her know that, yes, I'm paying for this overgrown toddler's meal.

"Hey, Aiden," Duke shouts down to the other end of the group of tables we've bunched together. "Did you know Chris is paying for my dinner?"

"I heard."

"I cleaned more of Memaw's gutters than him this week. That's all it takes to get a free dinner around here."

Aiden shakes his head. The three of us were thick as thieves growing up. Only, Aiden and I were more subdued most of the time. Not that we didn't do our fair share of stupid stunts. It's just, compared to the two of us, Duke was the one always pushing the limits and constantly making us laugh.

"I can be fun," I blurt out without thinking.

"What was that?" Duke asks.

"Nothing," I mutter. But then I notice Duke still staring at me, so I repeat myself. "Nothing. Okay?"

"You can be fun?" Aiden asks with a smile that says I'm in for it.

Trevor, Aiden's younger brother, walks in and pulls a chair up to our table. Thank goodness. I'm saved from the humiliation of explaining my momentary lack of inhibition. I never blurt. I'm a non-blurter. I barely talk half the time, preferring to observe and listen, giving myself time to consider my responses to situations. I don't know what came over me.

Ella Mae, that's what. That woman. She's like a splinter—a loud, outspoken splinter in a mini skirt, outrageous heels, and lipstick.

I know better than to let her teasing get under my skin. Most of what she says seems solely intended to get a rise out of me. I rarely give her the satisfaction of a reaction.

Rob, another friend of ours, follows behind Trevor. He grabs a chair and greets everyone. Then he adds, "Grant's not coming out tonight. Said Jayme wanted a quiet night, just the three of them."

"Ahh, the life of a family man," Duke says almost wistfully.

He's got another look on his face that seems like he's

itching to say something. I watch him, but he turns the tables on me and eyes me with a purposeful stare.

"And speaking of family men," Duke says, "Chris was just announcing how he can be fun. Fill us in, Chris."

"What do being fun and being a family man have to do with one another?" I ask innocently enough.

"Family life is plenty of fun," Aiden says. "I've had the most fun in my life laughing with the kids … and that doesn't begin to match the fun Em and I have after they're in bed."

"Fun times over here," Trevor echoes.

"Nothing but fun," Duke chimes in.

"Ditto," Rob adds. "Well, not nothing but … But yeah. Fun. And so much more."

"I need new friends," I grumble.

"Who would bring the fun factor if you found new friends? We need you, man," Duke says with a lightly taunting laugh.

"What's new with the goats?" I ask Aiden in the lamest attempt ever to shift the topic.

"Nope. Not taking the bait. Why are you questioning if you're fun?"

"I'm not. At all. Can we just drop it?"

Duke displays one of his rare moments of sincerity. "Seriously, Chris. You want to know if you're fun?"

"Not really."

Duke ignores me.

"You're not as fun as you used to be. I'll give you that. But maybe you've been through more than the rest of us. I take that back. You definitely have been through more than the rest of us.

"After seeing whatever you've seen, I'm sure it's hard to let yourself go. Or maybe the military trained some of the spontaneity out of you." He pauses, giving me a warm smile. Then he goes in for the kill. "It's like something invisible's always got you in its grips. I'm not complaining. Just answering the question. But you're still fun. It's just not the first word I'd use to describe you."

I think he's finished, but he adds. "... or the second. Or third. It's a bit down the list, really."

Duke seems to forget he's even talking to me as he rambles on about how far down the list my fun factor rates in my overall qualities as a human being.

But then he obviously remembers I'm here. And he stares at me, unflinching. His face softens and his eyes refuse to leave mine. I've had years of being stared into by drill sergeants and other officers, learning not to crack, not to look away first. This stare-down feels far more intimate. I shift my gaze toward Aiden.

"You've been through a lot," Aiden affirms. "You're still fun. You just dole it out in rations. You laugh. I've seen you. And you smile. You're just not free with it like Kevin the Minion over here."

"Seriously, man?" Duke asks. "I'm a minion?"

I look over at my best friend, turned brother-in-law. Then I picture Duke with a yellow face and blue jean overalls on, talking in that nonsense language, saying, "Papoy! Papoy!"

I start to chuckle.

Duke *is* a minion. He's a mischievous, silly sidekick. He laughs at everything, and he turns life into a party. I never saw it before and now I can't unsee it. The image of Duke wearing goggles, with his eyes wide and a crazy smile on his yellow face turns my smile to laughter. I laugh hard, tears even coming to my eyes.

"See," Aiden says. "You're plenty fun."

"Yeah." I say, wiping the tear from my eye. Then I mutter, "Kevin," and start laughing under my breath again.

Duke shakes his head. He mutters, "That nickname's not going to stick."

"Wanna bet?" I ask, chuckling again. "It's sticking, Kevin."

Rob speaks up, drawing the group's attention away from me and Duke the minion. "Laura and I have been doing a lot of talking lately. Speaking of family fun …" He pauses and looks at each of us. "We've decided to adopt a baby."

And just like that, the conversation around the table shifts from my residual insecurity after bumping into Ella Mae at the grocery, to the logistics of Rob and Laura's adoption. All the guys chime in with thoughts about fatherhood, and I sit back, knowing I've got nothing to offer on the subject.

Duke looks over at me and nearly whispers, "You ready to be an uncle?"

"To Rob's adopted baby?"

"Nope," he says with a smile that won't quit. "To *your* new niece or nephew."

"To my …" I can't finish the sentence because Aiden obviously overheard us.

"Is Shannon …?" Aiden asks.

Duke smiles and I swear his chest puffs out with pride. "She is. Eight weeks along. We agreed I could spring the news tonight, but then Rob stole my thunder."

Rob smiles. "Our kids will grow up together."

Duke nods, his joy palpable.

"Do the girls know?" Aiden asks.

He's talking about all of their wives. It would definitely not be okay for us guys to find out before the women.

"She's telling them tonight. But she's waiting on telling her parents." Duke gives me a knowing glance. "She wants to hit the three month mark before she tells her mom."

I nod. Makes sense. Mom will be over the moon about being a grandma, but we need to be careful with news like this. Any loss could send her spiraling into dark places again.

I don't know how Duke and Shannon expect to keep their

pregnancy under wraps. This town isn't known for its ability to conceal secrets, especially not ones of this magnitude. Mom's not in the information food chain, but if word gets out, it will definitely make its way to Dad at his office. I sure hope Shannon gets to him first.

The table erupts into congratulations for both Duke and Rob, and I sit back, unable to hold in my smile. I always thought I'd be a dad before I became an uncle, but I'll take this. Heck yeah, I will.

~

I usually work remotely from home, but on Wednesdays I check in with the main office. I also have ulterior motives for making my way to Columbus once a week. The fact that our office is headquartered there gives me an easy excuse.

The drive along the two-lane highway starts with farmland on either side of me—wide open fields with parcels of property scattered here and there. The world is full of people who have chosen to live an agrarian life—like Aiden—only he's nearly in town compared to the folks out here. These farms are remote, set apart from prying eyes and annoying social media celebrities trying to turn their small town into a spectacle.

Why I can't get Ella Mae off my mind is a mystery. I usually rule my thoughts, discarding the ones that distract or disable me. Last night I had a dream that I was being chased by all manner of Pop-Tarts—sprinkled, rainbow, and even s'mores flavored. They had little cartoon smiley faces, and out of their small, illustrated mouths, they were taunting me by yelling, "You're no fun!" "You're no fun!" "Have some fun once in a while!" "Do you even know what fun is?" "It's letting loose." "Let loose, Chris!"

Do you know what it's like to wake to images of Pop-Tarts

in miniskirts and high heels chasing you? Trust me. You don't want to know. I woke up shaking my head, and craving processed food with neon-colored toppings.

This day away from Bordeaux will do me good. No way I'll bump into a self-proclaimed star with a phone camera aimed in my face.

The scenery shifts from rural farmland to smaller cities, and before long, I see the skyline of Columbus come into view.

CHAPTER 8

Ella Mae

MY FACE TRULY LOOKS RADIANT. I used my clay mask—not Mabel's—last night before bed. Then I hydrated this morning before coming downstairs to film. I am looking fierce, if I do say so myself.

"I've been living on nothing but green drink for the past twenty-four hours in preparation for tooooonight!"

I nearly trigger the automatic exposure settings to readjust on my phone when I flash my smile at the camera. Home tooth-whitening system for the win!

Yes. Today is the day. As in, *the* day. I am meeting Drake tonight at Frisch's Big Boy. I personally never thought I'd be excited to be meeting anyone at a cheesy family diner, but never say never, am I right?

I turn back to the camera.

"Okay my peeps! I have to sign off. Time for yoga, and then I'm going to steam my face. After I open my epidermis and moisturize, I'll chill my pores shut with a cold cloth I just set in the freezer. I've got the best outfit picked out—it's the one that *you* selected for me to wear! The patchwork herringbone dress has such a vintage Bob Mackie feel to it. Well done, to those of you who voted in the poll in my stories. You are literally the best! The. Best.

"Okay. This is me, Ella Mae, telling you to put the YOU in Fab-YOU-lous today. And for sure, for sure, be here on my channel when we go live at five-thirty Eastern Time tonight!"

I click the phone camera off with my tripod remote, and pause to read the stream of comments already flowing in beneath the live video. I can't afford to get swept up in everything everyone's saying. People are so hyped for my evening with Drake, but I have to stay focused and on schedule. I've set aside time later this afternoon to respond.

Yes. I've got eight hours to kill until we meet at Frisch's Big Boy. But that's not idle time, I'm going to the salon for a style, then I'll take my time getting dressed and doing my makeup. After an afternoon green drink, I'll recite my affirmations, answer comments, and finally, I'll hit the road with time to spare. My drive to Columbus should take under an hour.

Meg walks up to the kitchen entryway and pauses. She's dressed for work, looking very professional. Sometimes her traditional line of work, being all nine-to-five, makes me feel like an imposter. But truthfully, we both know I work loads harder than she does. My job as an influencer has no schedule or guaranteed paycheck, so I have to bust my chops far more diligently than she does in so many ways.

Meg mouths, "Is it safe?" to me.

She's asking if I'm filming. And yes, living with me means you can't just stroll through the house in your skivvies. You never know when I've got a camera on. Meg's used to our home being the backdrop to my social media presence.

"Coast is clear," I say, lifting my green drink in a mock toast.

"You're going to turn green," Meg jokes.

"I'm only drinking these until tonight when I let loose and

eat whatever the followers have chosen for me and Drake. Then I'll have another green day. After that, you and I are going to celebrate by eating out wherever we like Friday night. My treat!"

"We already had steak and potatoes to celebrate."

"True. But that was to celebrate me getting invited to do the collab. This is to celebrate us actually filming the first segment."

"You won't find me complaining about celebrating your successes anytime soon. But Friday I'm going out with Joe. He said he's got a surprise for me. I'll have to take a raincheck. How about Saturday?"

I try not to let my disappointment show. Of course she has a date with Joe—which she deserves and should go on, it just means I'll be home alone, trying to forget my singleness instead of celebrating with my bestie. I could always pop in on Mom. But more than likely, I ought not take that gamble on a night when I want to feel positive.

"Is it weird that I don't even know Drake's last name? I don't even have his phone number. I'm not sure where he exactly lives in California, except that he's in Malibu. But I've got the confirmation message about this evening from his assistant, Genesis. And he's been posting on his feed daily about the throwback collabs he's got planned—including this kick-off to the series with me. So everything's good, right?"

"It's a little weird," Meg agrees. "But this is your world. No one knows anyone else's last name. And yet, you all seem to connect somehow."

"You're right. I just don't know how I'd reach him if something were to happen. Like, what if I get a flat tire, or get stuck behind an Amish cart somewhere between here and Columbus?"

"Why don't you message him your number."

"Hmmm."

I consider the option. Do I want Drake to have my number? He did invite me to his party in California. Our worlds are going to overlap more completely soon enough. What's so different between him reaching me through social media and him having my phone number? It's not like he's a stalker. He's DrakesDaMan. If anyone would be considered a stalker in this scenario, it would be me. Besides, it would kind of be cool knowing my number is in his phone.

"Yeah. I'll do that," I tell Meg.

I pluck my cell out of the tripod on the counter and type a quick message to Genesis and Drake leaving them my number in case they need to reach me for the collab. Genesis answers almost immediately, thanking me.

Drake has been a little quiet this past week. In fact, I haven't heard from him since the day we connected to confirm everything. But he's a busy guy, and he told me he's here in Ohio to catch up with his family. I can't expect him to stop everything just to reach out to me. This is business. Besides, he's never met me. I make a good impression—memorable and unique—in person. After we meet, he'll probably interact with me more.

"You've got that look on your face," Meg says.

"Which look?"

"The one where you're worrying, but you don't want to tell anyone you're worrying, so you hide the expression as soon as I call you out on it."

I don't answer her.

"Don't fret," Meg says. "I'm not going to force you to admit you're nervous about tonight. I'm just going to remind you that you're awesome. The whole world outside Bordeaux knows it too."

"Not the whole world."

"Whatever. Details. Eight million people know. And more than that, if you do the math."

I'm sure she's doing the math.

"You've got to figure for every follower, there are one or two people who know about you, but don't follow you. You've got eight million followers, so probably at least twenty million people are very aware of who you are. And even more know of you in some vague way. It's just statistics. And, after tonight, more than fifty million will know about you—-just because you ate dinner with Drake."

"No one would ever guess you're a math nerd."

"Because I don't come across all brainy."

"Well, for the record, Rob and Jayme aren't the only geniuses in town."

Meg makes a noise that sounds like, *humph*. Her intelligence won't ever be widely known because she's not one of Bordeaux's favorites.

Our town has dividing lines worse than *Mean Girls*. We don't wear pink on Wednesdays, but still, there are those who are in, and those who are not. The Capulets and Montagues have nothing on us. We're like *West Side Story* met Old MacDonald. And while no one's drawing pitchforks to run me and Meg out of town, we aren't included, welcomed, or appreciated. Opinions in this town are rigid. Friendships and romances stay on defined sides of an invisible barrier.

Of course, Meg dated a guy from the other side in high school—Trevor. But at the end of the day, he married his best friend, Lexi. I'll be the first to admit, Meg was a bit *extra* when she came back here after her job tanked in Pennsylvania seven years ago. Maybe a better word is *unmoored*. The way she went after Trevor scared even me. She was like a piece of Saran wrap, the way she clung to him.

It's for the best that didn't work out. Meg spent much needed time getting herself on track, and now she has Joe. He didn't grow up here, so he's neutral when it comes to Meg and me. He doesn't treat us like pariahs.

"I'd better run," Meg says. "Good luck! Not that you'll need it. You're going to have so much fun and people will love you."

She steps over toward me and pulls me into a much-needed hug.

Meg leans back, grabs my cheeks so I have no choice but to look her right in the eyes, and says, "Besides, who cares what the world thinks. Right?"

"Right."

I say the word. I mean it. But a part of me is so conditioned to seek the approval of my followers and fans, I don't know how deeply I believe that the world's opinions don't matter. Their judgments and reactions drive my popularity.

Without the approval of my fan base, I don't really know what I am. Broke, for one thing. And a little aimless too. But that's not going to happen. I've got a mission and a focus tonight. And I'm living a life where fifty million people care what I'm putting in my mouth at a family diner. Life's good.

I hear the front door shut behind Meg.

I know I scheduled my affirmations for this afternoon, but as Journey always says, "It's always the right time to kick things into the positive."

I'm a bad boss babe.

I'm a stunning boss babe.

I'm a fierce. Boss. Babe.

I feel like Rocky in those old fighting movies. I throw a few punches in the air. Online kickboxing classes have given me some stellar moves. I look like a pro. Punching the air always feels gratifying and empowering. I punch while I recite affirmations with more oomph, starting with a modification of one of the lines from that movie.

I'm gonna eat lightning and crap thunder!

No. I'm not. I'm definitely not crapping thunder. Can you imagine? Back to my regular, non-digestive-related affirmations. I'm gonna drink green drink, and my bathroom habits will remain non-explosive and somewhat silent.

I take a deep breath and focus.

I built my empire from scratch.

I have what it takes.

People love my brand.

People love me.

Drake sought me out.

I will slay this day.

I inhale slowly and let the air out on a count of four. Squaring my shoulders, I walk upstairs to do thirty minutes of yoga. Then I finish my skincare routine, dress in a mauve velour tracksuit that looks like the ones Kim Kardashian and Paris Hilton wear out and about when they're going for a sexy-but-carefree vibe, and head to the Dippity Do, our local salon.

CHAPTER 9

Ella Mae

"WHAT BRINGS you here for just a style?" Laura asks as she spins the salon chair around so I can take a seat. "Big date?"

"Something like that," I supply.

Most of this town doesn't have a clue what I do with all my filming. They look at me as if I'm simply a poor form of local entertainment. Most of them have probably never heard of DrakesDaMan. Considering Laura's husband Rob is a YouTuber, she should know. But I'm not going to be the one to break my good news to her. She'd probably think I was bragging.

"Someone I know?" Laura presses.

"Maybe. His name is Drake. We're meeting in Columbus."

Laura gives me a blank stare in the mirror, as if I'm being difficult by insisting she might know a man named Drake who is forty-five minutes away from here.

"He's a YouTuber." I cave when her look borders on irritation.

"Oh. A YouTuber?"

"Yeah. DrakesDaMan? Do you know of him?"

"Rob probably would. How did you meet him?"

Laura grabs her hot tool and starts running a brush through my hair while juggling the brush in one hand and the curling wand in the other. It's a talent, and I only flinch a little at one point when it looks like the iron will slip and burn me. It doesn't. She's a pro.

"We're doing a collab tonight."

"Ahhh."

"That's where the two of us get together to film a segment, and that video goes out to all our followers on all our social channels."

"I know what a collab is, Ella Mae. I'm not completely at a loss when it comes to social media."

"Okay. I didn't know since you shun the modern world so vehemently."

"I just prefer friendships where we can go out to dinner regularly, raise our kids together—you know, actually see one another in the flesh. I've never understood the appeal of building relationships with a bunch of random strangers—most of whom you'll never meet face-to-face."

I have no answer for her.

"Mind if I film you doing my hair?"

"You don't usually even ask."

"I'm asking now."

"Be my guest."

Laura's not a mean person. She's actually really loyal and fun. She's just not a fan of me or what I do, obviously, so her snarky side comes out more often than not during my appointments. But alas, she's the only really talented hairdresser in town, so I endure the scoffing while I get my coiffing.

I chuckle at my little rhyme.

"What's funny?" Laura asks.

"Nothing. Inside joke. With my imaginary friends, you know."

"Whatever, Ella Mae."

"Yep. Whatever."

I turn on the camera. I could use the boost of several thousand people watching me and chiming in on how they love my hair right about now.

"Hey peeps, sweet followers, and anyone new to my page! Today is the BIG day! I'm going to have dinner in Columbus with DrakesDaMan and you are all invited. But first, a girl's only as confident as her hair, as I always say. And today, my stylist, Laura, is going to work her magic on my tresses to make me beee-YOU-tee-ful. We all have bad hair days. But why have a bad hair day when you can have a great hair day, am I right?"

I turn to Laura. "Say hi to the peeps, Laura."

"Hey, peeps," she says, in a voice with such flat affect I might just call a psychiatrist to have her evaluated.

"Well, that's Laura, friends. What she lacks in exuberance, she makes up for in sheer hair genius. Sheer. Hair. Get it? Okay. Enough with the dad jokes. I'm going to get this done, and I'll post pics of the after in a bit. Why don't you go out and treat yourself to a little self-care today? Or take a little extra time in front of the mirror. Post the results in your stories and tag me! See you tonight!!"

I turn the camera off. Laura rolls her eyes at me. She doesn't even try to hide her judgment. I do respect that about her. She's a what-you-see-is-what-you-get kind of gal.

"This is my job, you know. You cut hair. I entertain people. It's not a crime."

Laura pauses. Our eyes meet in the mirror. A long silence stretches between us. She doesn't raise the brush or the curling iron. She just stares at me from over my shoulder.

She finally says, "I never thought of it that way."

"You, of all people, should. Rob does this same sort of thing. Of course, he's blowing things up, and I'm not, but still —we're both entertainers. We use the same platforms. Entertaining people on YouTube is how Rob carries his weight as a provider for your little burgeoning family. And congrats, BTW. I heard you're adopting. That's one lucky baby."

"Thanks."

She releases the eye-lock and returns to doing my hair. Neither of us says anything else while she gets down to the business of making me look fab-u-lous.

The bell over the door of the salon tinkles. We've got those quaint bells over every shop entrance in town. They're like little alerts for us to stop gossiping until we see who's joining the conversation. At least, that's what I think they're for.

Maybe they are there to make sure we greet one another, though, that's sort of ridiculous. We're Midwesterners. If we do anything well, it's greeting people. We greet people to death. *Heya! Oh, hey there! Well, now, good to see ya'!* And then we talk your ear off for another hour or so. It's just how we are. And don't even try to make a quick getaway. We've mastered the art of the prolonged farewell better than the vonTrapp family children at bedtime, minus the harmony.

When I look up to see who entered the salon, Jayme and Shannon are walking in together. Lexi brings up the rear of this happy little gathering.

The salon fills with chatter among Laura's friends. Only Shannon has the decency to greet me at first, but then Jayme looks up and smiles warmly.

"Hey, Ella Mae. Your hair looks great!"

"Thanks, Jayme. Laura's a genius with a curling iron."

Jayme's been nicer to me than the rest of her friends ever since I helped her author career skyrocket. Of course, she doesn't ask me to lunch and I'm still never a part of these elusive girls' nights they have almost every week, but she doesn't duck behind a bush at the sight of me, which is saying something.

"We missed you at girls' night," Lexi tells Jayme.

Girls' night. Yep.

"I was tired," Jayme says. "Sorry I missed."

It doesn't escape my attention—the way her hand travels to her abdomen and rests there for a moment. Her friends seem to overlook the obvious tell.

I mutter, "It must be in the water."

"What's that?" Laura asks me.

"Fertility. It must be in the water. Though, only Shannon and Jayme are expecting and your situation isn't exactly the same. Even though adoption's amazing in its own way."

I realize I'm babbling. Watching all the women who graduated from high school with me pair up, get married, and now prepare for motherhood obviously opens my verbal floodgates.

Shannon looks at me.

Then everyone looks at Jayme.

Shannon mouths, "How did you know?"

I mouth back, "Bordeaux."

The rumor mill is alive and churning. Meg heard the guys were out talking about it at Mad River Burgers. She came home and told me. That's how anyone knows anything around here. No need for a local paper when you've got the locals themselves.

Shannon turns her eyes from me to Jayme. Her eyebrows are raised and her eyes wide.

"You're pregnant too?"

Jayme blushes. Then she looks at me. "How did you know?"

"Lucky guess."

"Um, yes," Jayme says, looking each of us in the eye. "We're ten weeks. I was going to tell you all this week. That's why I missed girls' night. I'm so wiped out these days. The first trimester is no joke. I plan to cook supper most nights, but I usually curl up on the couch, thinking I'll just lie down for a few minutes. Before I know it, Grant's nudging me to tell me it's time to move this party up to our bed."

"You're pregnant!" Lexi shouts as if the news just registered.

I sit in Laura's chair like one of those life-sized Barbie heads, as if only my hair were present. I'm as good as a fly on the wall. A blond fly with a killer velour sweatsuit, mind you, but just as invisible and insignificant as a resting bug. Laura continues to expertly wrap my hair around the wand and release the curls while the four friends all gush about babies and pregnancy and how their kids will all grow up together. Eventually, Laura finishes curling and brushing out my hair. She gives me a dousing of hairspray, and I'm on my way.

The rest of the afternoon flies by between responding to my followers' comments and posting a photo of myself in my rockin' dress with my hair and makeup done.

At three forty-five I leave my house. I arrive at the Big Boy on the outskirts of Columbus an hour later. It's not really mealtime, so the parking lot is less than a third full. My heart rate kicks up when I think of the magnitude of this collaboration. I take a cleansing breath, letting my grip fall from the steering wheel.

Supreme boss babe. That's me.

I know I am. It's still intimidating facing a dream like this —knowing everything will change after this one night. Either people will love me or they won't, and their reaction to this video will definitely impact my rankings. Either tonight will open up doors for future collaborations and more exposure, or it will be social suicide. No biggie.

It's just a meal. Have fun. Ignore the cameras. Be your best self —the online version. Like Meg said, people will love you.

Okay. Here goes nothing.

My little inner pep talk would make Journey so proud. I'll have to tell her how I grabbed a hold of my thoughts and rode them like a steed until I tamed that wild horse and it was eating out of my hand. She taught us that equine metaphor about a week ago. Look at me, already implementing it. I'll have to share that technique with my peeps—after this whole night is successfully over.

Journey comes up with the most interesting analogies. I guess that's why she's the guru and I'm not. Well, I'm not the positive-thinking guru. I'm the go-to-girl for skin care, and for being boldly, unapologetically, and uniquely you.

CHAPTER 10

Ella Mae

I SHUT the car door and look around. I wish I knew what Drake drives. It might quell my nerves if I saw his car. Or maybe it wouldn't help at all knowing he beat me here and is sitting right inside that restaurant. DrakesDaMan in person.

I smooth my dress down in the front even though it's not even wrinkled. I'm wearing these chunky wedge sandals that match the green in my dress. It's all very retro and throwback to go with the vibe of Drake returning to his roots. My blond hair falls in beach waves down my back and over my shoulders. I definitely look more suited to a night at Hyde Park Prime Steakhouse, not an outdated Big Boy, but hey. *Dress for the life you want to have,* I always say.

I walk into the restaurant and look around. I don't see Drake or anyone but a few families and an old man sitting at the counter on a barstool eating a bowl of soup. The hostess walks up to me.

"Table for two. But could you make it a roomier booth? We'll tip well, I promise."

"It's not that busy right now. Pick wherever you like," she tells me.

"Thanks, Amber," I say, reading her name tag.

She gives me a polite smile and I walk toward the back of the restaurant, selecting the largest booth in the place and sliding onto the bench seat.

I have a straight view to the front door from our table. I'll easily see when Drake arrives.

Five o'clock comes and goes. No Drake.

I check my messages and his page almost obsessively. My followers start to message me that they're looking forward to my livestream with Drake. I send back short answers like, *me too*, or *thanks*.

My waitress, Shawna, comes by to ask if I'm ready to order. I explain to her that I'm waiting for someone. She brings me an ice water and sets it down on the table, smiling a smile I'm sure she gives out over one hundred times a night, whether she feels like it or not.

I check my social media account again, quickly flipping over to Drake's page. There's no mention of the collab on Drake's posts for today. His previous posts this week mention all the collabs he has planned. But he hasn't hyped this one specifically since two days ago.

That's okay. I don't mind doing the heavy lifting of promoting. He's bigger than me. It makes sense I'd do some grunt work to earn my spot as a collaborator with him. His followers aren't so interested in me that announcing a partnership with me would give him any sort of traction. I understand him being low-key about tonight.

Drake said we start filming at five thirty. Maybe he's just going to show up with a few minutes to spare. It's fine. We're just eating a meal, filming, and posting. Life will go on either way.

Shawna comes by again, filling my water and looking at me with that waitress look that says, "Are you sure he's showing?" It's not busy enough for her to be worried about me occupying her station without ordering, but a few more patrons have filtered in since I arrived.

I snap some photos of myself sitting in the booth—alone. I can add them to posts later. I resist the urge to message Drake or Genesis. I don't want to seem overeager.

Five fifteen comes and goes. Drake still isn't here.

Okay. I'll message Genesis. Just to check in. Nothing crazy. Just touching base.

@Fab-U-lous_EllaMae

Hey, Genesis. Just checking that we're good for tonight. Anything else you need from me? I'm here at the Big Boy. I can do any pre-filming needed. Looking forward to meeting Drake in person.

The minutes drag by until it's finally five thirty.

Still. No. Drake.

The restaurant fills a bit more now that it's actually nearing a usual supper hour. It's a Wednesday, so it's not like a weekend crowd is rushing to eat here, but a significant number of tables are filled now and the noise level has gone up a bit.

I'm starting to literally sweat. And I don't sweat. On the other side of my phone, my peeps are waiting for me to go live.

I don't know what to do.

Over the past quarter hour, I have responded to comments and I've checked the message thread with Drake once a minute. That's fifteen times since five fifteen. Genesis hasn't answered me. Drake still hasn't shown or messaged. It's time to think on my feet.

Shawna comes by. "Just checking to make sure you still want to wait to order."

"Yes. Sorry," I tell her. "I need to wait. But I will order something eventually, whether my friend shows or not, and you'll get a tip worthy of the amount of time I've filled your booth. Don't worry."

"Oh, I'm not worried, Sugar. I just want to make sure I check in on you."

Sugar. She's probably only two or three years older than me. The term feels out of place, but also somehow comforting.

"Thank you so much, Shawna."

"I love your dress, by the way," she adds.

I smile as I thank her. I needed that compliment more than she knows.

My messages ping as Shawna walks away to take an order from customers at a nearby table. It's Genesis.

@GenesisAssistsStars

Ella Mae! I just got off the phone with Drake. He totally spaced out. He went to the new action movie with his sister and her kids. Says he needs to reschedule. Sorry for the inconvenience. If you end up eating at the Big Boy, send me the receipt and we'll cover your meal—of course.

I'll be in touch to get a new date planned when I hear from Drake. Soon. It will have to be soon since he's on his way back to Cali in a week.

. . .

Damage control. That's what I need to do — and stat. I have thousands and thousands of people waiting for this live with Drake.

I take one of the deepest breaths I've ever taken and blow it out slowly.

What would Khloé Kardashian do?

She would not have to do a thing. She can literally mess up royally and still be in the spotlight, start a cosmetic line, a clothing brand, or whatever she wants. She's a flipping Kardashian. I'm just Ella Mae from Bordeaux. Miss Corn Husk once a year, a passing trend the rest of the time.

But people are counting on me. So, here goes nothing.

I press my camera button on to record, and smile wide. Feigning a level of cool and excitement I don't remotely feel, I start talking to the camera.

"Hey, my peeps! And a special welcome to all of you who showed up to watch me eat a meal with Drake! You are the reason I lived on green drinks for the past twenty-four hours. If you could hear my stomach growling, you'd know how very, very much I love you!"

The count on the screen says 5k. Five thousand people are watching me and the number keeps growing. Comments roll in so fast it looks like a ticker tape. I shout out to a few people, calling their name and welcoming them before I get back to the business at hand. People are saying how much they love me, but also how excited they are for tonight's meal.

I take a breath, securing my confident smile.

Then I say, "There's been a slight hitch in our plans. But do not fear. The show must go on! Am I right? Sooooo … Drake had to tend to some family stuff. Everyone's fine. Don't stress. But he was detained and that means we have to reschedule this awesomeness for another week.

"We will bring you a meal between me and the fab-u-lous DrakesDaMan in the coming seven days. It will be twice as epic. Trust.

"But I'll tell you what I'm going to do! Since you all showed up to watch me and Drake and we had to postpone, I've got a few special things I'm going to do for you!"

I'm scrabbling here, but desperate times call for desperate measures. The viewer count is at 7k now. That's seven thousand people watching me try to salvage my reputation.

"I'm going to do five giveaways! That's right! Five twenty-dollar Amazon gift cards will be given away tonight to five lucky followers. All you have to do is like this video, tag a friend, and follow me. For an extra chance to win, put your choice of what I should eat tonight in the comments. I'll scan the first hundred comments that come in and choose my feast from your suggestions.

"And while we're at it, what do you think of this amazing dress? The full pic is in my stories, and also in the post before this video. Life may have its ups and downs, but we can always dress the part. Am I right? So, go like, follow, comment, tag, and don't forget to pick my meal.

"And most of all, put the YOU in fab-YOU-lous tonight!"

I shut the camera off and sag back against the cool vinyl of the booth. I'm staving off the tears threatening to run down my cheeks. I did the best I could. Now all I need to do is scan my comments, order what they choose, and then drive home to tally entries in the spontaneous giveaways.

Looks like I'll be pulling an all-nighter. I close my eyes and squeeze them shut to help myself keep it together in public. My job here isn't done. I still need to make it through a meal—alone.

When I open my eyes and straighten from my slumped position in the booth, I see him.

No. No. No.

Of all the people, at all the places in the world, what is Chris St. James doing at a Big Boy outside Columbus tonight?

CHAPTER 11

Chris

IT'S BEEN A LONG DAY. Wednesdays always are. I've gotten into the habit of popping by this diner whenever I'm out this way, unless a friend asks me to stay for dinner or I'm not that hungry. Being single and working from home, there's a strange comfort in eating out, even if I'm still technically alone.

Amber greets me at the hostess stand. She bats her eyelashes almost imperceptibly. I smile back with a reserved grin that hopefully lets her down gently.

"Shawna's station?" she asks.

"I'm a creature of habit," I confess.

I glance toward the back of the restaurant. Casing my surroundings is second nature. I'll never lose some of the instincts I developed in the Army. I sit at the back of the room, my eyes capable of seeing every exit. My own escape strategy mapped out before I settle in. I look for suspicious people whenever I'm in an unfamiliar setting.

I don't expect to see what I see when I look at the far corner booth.

Ella Mae.

What on earth is she doing here? As if my day hadn't been draining enough.

I don't even realize I'm stopping dead in my tracks until Amber pauses and looks quizzically over her shoulder at me.

"Are you okay, Chris?"

"Yeah. Yeah. I'm just going to make a pitstop. I'll find a table for myself after I wash up in the restroom."

"Okay. Whatever you want. Just let me know if you need anything. I'll be right here. You know where to find me."

She smiles at me—an invitation written all over her face.

"Thanks," I say, turning toward the men's room near the entrance.

I don't actually have to use the restroom. I just went a half hour ago before I left to head home. Stepping up to the faucets, I turn on the cold water, scoop a handful and splash it on my face. After I dry myself off with a tan paper hand towel, I stare into the mirror.

I could leave.

Curiosity seems to get the better of me. What is Ella Mae doing here? She looks like she's dressed for a date. But not a date at a Big Boy. This is definitely not her speed. She'd want to be wined and dined at some Michelin two or three star restaurant. Her face looked—weary. Or maybe disappointed. And she was dressed up—even for her.

Yeah. I can't just leave.

I'm having a solid stare down with myself when a man opens the door.

"Evenin','" he says.

"Hey," I answer.

He walks to the urinals, and I know hanging out in here will seem more than creepy. My time is up. I have to face the music.

Amber smiles at me when I step into the foyer of the restaurant again. I return her smile, and then I glance over at

Ella Mae. Her face turned toward her phone, as usual. Her finger runs up and down the screen, scrolling, obviously. She types something into the cell.

Ella Mae's by far the most beautiful woman in our town. She always has been. She's also the biggest pain, and the one who never has seen herself as more than a fashion icon and social media guru.

Most days, I can't be bothered with her and her antics. She's all fluff and try-hard. Whatever else she's got going on is hidden under layers of makeup, and lashes, and those outrageous outfits.

But since I've been back from the army, I've watched her from a distance. The military taught me to watch people—really watch them. And something's changed in Ella Mae. There was never any guarantee it would. Sometimes a ball starts rolling downhill and it just picks up speed. But sometimes it hits an obstacle. And that's just enough to slow the roll and change the trajectory.

Two years ago, Ella Mae threw herself and all her hard-earned knowledge into blessing Jayme. That group—my younger sister, Shannon, and her friends—never gave Ella Mae the time of day before she set aside her life to pitch in.

And I get it. Ella Mae's an acquired taste. Off-putting. Maybe too direct and outspoken. Too showy, for sure. But Ella Mae didn't let the cliquishness in our town stop her from saying yes when one of them needed her help. She jumped right in with both feet, and Jayme got a huge book deal that put her on the map as an author as a direct result of Ella Mae's efforts.

At the time, I had asked myself if any of them would have done the same for Ella Mae if the tables were turned. Sadly, I don't think they would.

I approach Ella Mae's table, still not sure why I'm here, but unable to stop myself. She looks up.

"Chris?"

"Yep."

"I thought that was you. But then you disappeared. What are you doing here?"

"I could ask you the same question."

Her eyes look a little red, like she's either been crying or fighting tears.

"May I sit?"

"Suit yourself."

Her tone is flat. Guarded.

She's got walls up. Defensive. I feel like telling her I don't represent my friend group. Not here. We're on neutral ground. But I'm aware she's got grudges against me that have nothing to do with my friends.

I slide into the booth, taking a seat directly across from her.

"What has you so far from home?" I ask.

She snort laughs. "Grove City? A real road trip, huh?"

"Well?" I ask.

"I was meeting someone."

"A date?"

She tenses. Her lips draw into a thin line. She looks at me out of the side of her eyes and crosses her arms across her chest.

"Not a date. A work meeting."

I lean back, extending my arms out to each side of myself on the back of the booth. It's a posture that leaves me intentionally wide open. If we were in combat, I'd be simultaneously acknowledging my capacity to hold my own, while also indicating a clear surrender.

I'm not here to fight.

"What happened?"

"He had to cancel."

"So, why'd you stick around?"

I gesture around the room with one hand and then bring it back to rest on the back of the booth. Ella Mae studies my arm muscles. Gotta love how unabashed she is about objectifying me. I huff out a light chuckle.

"What's so funny?"

"You looking me over like I'm a cow up for auction."

"More like a bull," she says, regaining some of the color in her cheeks. She wags her eyebrows playfully. That's the Ella Mae I know.

"So, he canceled, and you stayed here?"

She sighs, looks down into her lap, and when her eyes meet mine, there's almost this silent plea in them.

"Truce?"

"With me?" I ask.

"For tonight only."

"I wasn't aware we were at war," I say.

"Talk about bull, St. James. You're smarter than that. It's full-on war between us, Soldier. And you know it. I just need one of those nights when everyone lays down their weapons, comes out of the foxholes, and sings Christmas carols together. You know?"

"The Christmas Truce of 1914?"

"Yeah. That."

I shake my head in amazement. Just as I suspected, there's more to her beneath the surface than she lets on.

"Cease fire," I agree.

"Truce."

"So …" I ask, hoping she's going to tell me everything now that we've agreed to lay down our invisible weapons.

Shawna steps up to the booth right then. It's this gift most seasoned wait staff have. They can sense when your mouth is overly full, or you're about to confess your undying love to the woman you're out to dinner with, and right then, they approach the table. It's like impeccable timing, but in reverse.

"Do you want to order?" Shawna asks me, looking at Ella Mae and then me, and back to Ella Mae with a questioning expression on her face.

"The usual," I tell Shawna.

"Have you decided what you'd like?" she asks Ella Mae.

Ella Mae looks at her phone screen. "I'll have the … Nathan's New York Cheesesteak. … and …" She looks at her phone again. "The Grandma's Banana Pudding Shake."

"What are you looking at there?"

"My followers are ordering for me tonight."

"Huh."

Ella Mae shakes her head, looks down, then looks up at me, and over at Shawna. Something shifts in Ella Mae's expression. A sort of steely resolve takes over her features. And then the floodgates open.

"So, I was supposed to meet this guy, Drake, here. DrakesDaMan?" She looks at Shawna, like Shawna should know him.

Shawna shakes her head and shrugs her shoulders.

"Well, he's huge on YouTube and he asked me to collaborate with him. Our followers were all hyped up for it. We were going to meet here, eat what our fans chose for us, and rate each item. We'd ham up the dining experience, film the whole thing …" She stops and looks down.

"And he didn't show?" I fill in.

"He blew me off. Went to see *Sloane: Secret Agent* with his sister and her kids. I spent the whole day prepping for this. I only drank green drink for twenty-four hours leading up to it. I even got my hair done."

The fire in Ella Mae's eyes dims. She looks up at Shawna and then reluctantly looks at me, like showing her weakness is the worst thing she could do in front of me. She doesn't know me well enough to know it's my kryptonite. I can't stand to see a woman hurting. Jilted's even worse. I want to hunt down this Drake guy. Ella Mae should be furious. Instead, she's a shrunken version of her usual self.

"So, you were supposed to eat what your followers picked?" I ask.

"Yeah. I know you think what I do is stupid. But it's my job. And this collaboration was a big deal for me."

She won't even look at me.

"Ella Mae."

"Hm?" She looks past me, not at me.

"Look at me."

"What do you want, St. James?"

"Truce," I remind her.

Shawna shifts a little, obviously unsure if she should hang out or flee.

"Can you give us a minute?" I ask Shawna. "Hold our orders for just a bit. I'll wave you over when we're ready."

"Sure, Chris," Shawna says.

She practically bolts from the side of our table toward the kitchen.

"So, you were ready to do this food thing and film it. And Drake canceled."

"Seven thousand people were online when I went on without him. And I don't even know how many more tried to join in after that. It's kind of a disaster, but I'm rolling with it the best I can. I've set up some spur-of-the-moment give-aways to offset the backlash from letting everyone down. Drake said we'll reschedule."

"He talked to you?"

She shakes her head. "His assistant messaged me."

"And you're giving him a second chance?"

She looks at me like I'm failing kindergarten.

"He's DrakesDaMan. A chance with him would boost me to the next level so fast. These kinds of things don't just come along every day. If he wants to reschedule, I'm rescheduling."

"Okay," I say, not wanting to question her right now. It's obvious she thinks this guy is amazing. He sounds like a jerk, if you ask me.

"Why don't we just do it instead?" I offer.

"Do what?"

"Order what your peeps want you to eat. Film ourselves. Rate the food. Whatever."

"You'd do that?"

"It's our Christmas Truce."

"In June."

"Yeah. In June."

"I don't need rescuing."

"I can see that. You were already bouncing back when I got here."

"You'd really do this?"

"Why not? I need to eat anyway."

Ella Mae studies my face. The corner of her mouth tilts up the slightest bit. Her eyes sparkle. She really is stunning. And she looks way too pretty to be hanging out in a Big Boy tonight in that dress with her hair all wavy and her makeup done to perfection. But here we are.

"Okay, St. James. Brace yourself. I don't think you know what you've gotten yourself into."

CHAPTER 12
Chris

I DON'T THINK I've ever seen someone go from distraught to elated so quickly. Ella Mae is a woman on a mission. And, yes, her annoying persona is securely back in place. But weirdly, I'm not as bothered about that transformation as I usually am. She's like an actress, gearing up for a role. I'm not saying I want to watch this show on a regular basis, but anything's better than seeing her downcast.

"So, here's what we're going to do," Ella Mae says, nearly bouncing in her seat. "I'm going to introduce you. I'll say you just happened to walk into the diner …"

"Which I did."

"Yes. Right. You did."

She pauses like it just occurred to her that it's as odd that I'd show up at her collaboration location as it is that she'd be in my favorite weekly spot for dinner.

"Well, anyway, I'll say you just walked in, and I was about to order. But then you agreed to do the challenge with me."

"Challenge?"

"It's a challenge. Because we'll eat whatever they say."

"And, that's a challenge?"

"Chris."

"Ella Mae."

"Can you leave the ridiculous inquisition until after we film? We're already experiencing attrition. People have gone on to their regularly scheduled lives. We're only going to have a fraction of the viewers engaging at this point. Time's a wastin'."

"Gotcha. No more questions."

"Okay. So, I'll show you off. And then we'll have people pick what you're going to eat. Shawna will take our orders. I'll tell everyone to wait until the food comes and then, when it arrives, I'll film us eating."

"And people will watch this?"

"They so will."

"Wow."

Ella Mae shoots me a look.

I hold my hands up in mock surrender.

"Okay. Are you ready?"

"As I'll ever be."

"Show some spirit, Soldier."

For some reason, I wink at her. At Ella Mae. As much as I will never admit this to her or anyone, I'm having a lot more fun than I usually have on a Wednesday night. I came in here feeling weighed down by my hard day. Right now, I'm occasionally smiling, and actually enjoying myself.

Ella Mae looks at me and nods. I nod back. She pushes the button on her phone, and we're live.

Usually, I'm very cautious about my online exposure. Tonight, I'm feeling uncharacteristically reckless. I'm still going to be careful. Ella Mae and I discussed her not mentioning the location of this restaurant and not using my last name. I can rest assured that none of my friends in Bordeaux will be watching her. I'm ninety-nine percent sure that the majority of Ella Mae's followers have no clue who I am, and also have no interest in me at all.

Ella Mae smiles into the camera. "Well, peeps! Do I have a surprise for you!" She talks right at the screen, as if she's actually talking to someone. "Remember the man who turned his back on me in the coffee shop? Some of you have taken to calling him Mister Shoulders?"

They have? Oh crud.

"Well, here I was, sitting by my lonesome. Just a girl, ordering a sandwich and a shake in a diner, even though she was way overdressed for the atmosphere."

She looks down at her dress and does a little shimmy of her shoulders as she gestures to the dress with the hand not holding her phone. "And in walks Chris. When I told him about the change in plans with Drake, he volunteered to take Drake's place for the night. Now, don't you fret. Drake and I will still do a collab. Stay tuned for all those details later this week. But onward and forward, as my life coach, Journey, always says!"

She has a life coach? Named Journey?

"My stomach's growling and Chris here's a big boy. Big Boy! Oh my gosh! He's a big boy in a Big Boy! Anyway, he's massive. I mean, look at those arms, ladies."

She turns the phone so it's aimed at my chest and arms. I see only my chin along with the wide expanse of my torso on the screen. She pulls the phone back toward herself.

"Girls. Girls. Girls. Chris' arms are as big as my legs. If I had a measuring tape we could measure my thigh circumference, and then measure around Chris' bicep. He'd win, hands down."

Thank God for the lack of a measuring tape, is all I can think right now.

"And what does that have to do with tonight's challenge? It means the man has got to be hungry. A big boy like Chris has to work up an appetite just sitting around. So, let's feed him."

She's not wrong. I do get pretty hungry by supper time. I'm not quite sure how to feel about being called a big boy, but the look on her face feels somewhat worth it. And since when did I care what look Ella Mae has on her face? Since I saw her dejected and nearly broken by that jerk, Drake. That's when.

Ella Mae continues to carry on to her followers. I wonder how many of them are actually watching.

"The menu's in my stories. Pop your thoughts as to what Chris should order in the comments. We'll be back in five minutes to tell you what he got served. And then Chris and I will rate our meals for your entertainment."

Ella Mae beams over at me. "Say hi to my peeps, Chris."

She aims the camera at me. And this time it's my face, not my arms, that is the focus.

"Hey," I say with a little wave-salute motion to the camera.

Ella Mae holds the camera in front of me for a few more seconds, so I sit there smiling like an idiot. Then she moves back into the screen.

"What's more yummy? The burgers or this man? I'll let you know in a bit." She winks. "Now go pick our meals and we'll be back shortly."

Ella Mae turns off the camera and collapses back into the booth.

I sit in stunned silence.

"Okay," she says, sitting up and getting right back into business mode. "Now we just wait for the comments. Then we'll order. Let's see if Shawna will let us film her."

Meanwhile, my mind's still trying to process that introduction.

"How many people were watching you—us—just then?" I ask as Ella Mae waves her hand to flag down Shawna.

"Only three thousand or so."

"Only?"

"I was at seven K before. Maybe it will pick up for our actual dining experience."

"Three thousand," I mutter, shaking my head. "Three thousand people want to watch you eat dinner?"

"Chris. I know I'm worse than the muck Jed White gets on his boots back home, but elsewhere, people actually want to watch me. I even *inspire* people."

"Inspire? With a sandwich and a shake?"

I'm not picking on her, I'm just baffled.

"Inspire. I'm here for them. I encourage them to be themselves—the best version of themselves. And, yes, I entertain."

"You do that," I admit.

Shawna arrives at our table. Ella Mae asks Shawna if we can film her while we order, promising her a big tip. Shawna looks thrilled that she'll get to be on the video. Ella Mae scrolls the comments. When she says, "Ready," she turns the camera on, asks me to pick a number between one and three hundred eighty-two. I guess that's how many comments there were. Then I pick another. And another. And that's how I end up with Anne Burrell's Double Smashed Burger with a side of mac-n-cheese, and hot fudge cake for dessert.

Shawna's so serious and overly friendly as she takes our order, I start to wonder if she's one of those waitresses who aspires to be an actress. She's not likely to get discovered on the outskirts of Columbus, but stranger things have happened—like me sitting here having dinner with Ella Mae.

Our food arrives. Ella Mae records Shawna announcing each item as she sets them on the table for us and graciously asks if she can get us anything else.

Then Ella Mae says, "Shawna, ladies and gentlemen! Isn't she just the best?"

Shawna beams.

I even inspire people. Yeah, Maybe you do.

I shake my head.

It feels like I've entered an alternate reality where Ella Mae doesn't annoy me so much, and I can actually see the value in her ridiculous social media obsession.

I'll willingly camp out in this reality for a while because the smell of this meal—two patties, cheese, shoestring fries on the burger, onions and all the fixin's—is rising up from my plate and nearly making my mouth water. The thing is probably five inches tall.

I'll manage.

Ella Mae turns the camera and does a sweep of our table to show off the feast in front of us. Then she whips this little bendable, table-top tripod out of her purse and props the camera in it. She's like Mary Poppins with her carpet bag, only way sexier and far more eccentric. And you've got to work hard to be more eccentric than Mary Poppins.

She pats the seat next to her. "Move over here, Big Boy. The peeps need to be able to see both of us in the same frame. Not that you'll fit a frame, but we'll do our best, won't we?"

I'm speechless, so I just scoot over, dragging my plate and shake with me, and reaching for my bowl of mac-n-cheese once I'm situated.

Ella Mae runs the show. It's a meal, but we have to elaborate about each thing we're eating.

"Okay, Chris. Let's watch you dig into that scrumptious burger. It's about as big as my head!"

I laugh, and then I face down the massive stack of meat, bread, and condiments. Grabbing it with both hands, I bring it up to my mouth and take a substantial bite. Something hits my chin, and I know there's food on my face. On camera.

Ella Mae giggles. It's this sound that's so natural and unmanufactured. It's just her, having fun, losing herself in the moment.

She grabs a few napkins from the stack between us and reaches over.

"Here, Soldier, let me get that for you."

Then she wipes across my face so carefully. When she pulls her hand back she announces, "Clean!"

I don't get touched all that often. Duke, bless his crazy heart, hugs me every time he sees me. My sister does too. But other than those two people and Aiden's kids, I go long stretches of time without anyone else's hands on me. It shouldn't matter that Ella Mae wiped my face. And it doesn't.

She's smiling at the camera, singing a song about women wishing they were her. "Oh, yes, girls. I know you wish you could wipe that face. Sorry, Charlie. The privilege is mine alone tonight."

She winks at the camera. Then she turns to me and says, "So, rate the burger, Chris."

"Okay."

I consider this a job now. What would I rate this burger?

"Taste, I'd give it an eight out of ten."

"Only an eight?"

"Well, I've been eating fresh burgers cooked over a fire pit for years. It's not really fair to this burger, but those beat this one. As far as a restaurant burger, this one's pretty good."

"How about the overall experience?"

"Well, I did spill half the meal on my face."

"A-dor-able. And no one's complaining. Do you see these comments? Everyone wants to wipe your face, Chris."

Um. Okay. That's a lot to take in. Total strangers want to wipe my face?

"Anyway," Ella Mae continues without missing a beat. "Overall experience."

"I'd say nine of ten."

"There you have it, peeps. Flavor is an eight; experience is a nine. And Chris?" she asks, leaning in so our faces are close together and the camera can capture us both. "What do you usually eat here?"

"The spaghetti with chili, and a side salad."

"Is that a ten?"

"Compared to Skyline in Cincinnati? No. Definitely not. But compared to a lot of other diners, yeah."

"Okay. My turn," Ella Mae says.

She holds her sandwich up and takes a healthy bite of it.

She hums, "Mmmm."

When she pulls the sandwich away from her mouth, she's still got a bit of a bite left in her mouth.

She talks around the bite, somehow managing to come across cute instead of disgusting. "I can't say if this is a ten because I haven't eaten anything in thirty-six hours, or if it's actually this good. Chris? I need you to chime in."

Before I know what's happening, Ella Mae is holding her sandwich in front of my mouth and I'm taking a bite—while she feeds me.

I pull back and smile with my mouth full, lips closed. Once I've swallowed, I say, "Ten. That's a definite ten."

Ella Mae turns to the camera. "It's official peeps. This sandwich is the winner!"

We eat the rest of our meal. Ella Mae shows me how to tell how many people are joining us live by watching the counter in the top corner of the screen. The number goes up the longer we're on.

We eat and banter. And finally, we get to dessert. Ella Mae has a banana pudding shake that has to be at least three thousand calories. And I've got this chocolate cake dessert with whipped cream and a cherry.

I'm so relaxed now—more relaxed than I've been in longer than I can remember. So strange.

We swap bites. Ella Mae sticking her spoon in my mouth, and me returning the favor to feed her a bite of cake à la mode. We agree the combination of flavors is actually the best taste.

"So, the moral of the dessert story?" Ella Mae says to the camera. "Bring a friend and share these two scrumptious treats."

She smiles over at me.

"And that's it for me, Ella Mae, and my dining companion, Chris. Don't forget to put the YOU in Fab-YOU-lous today, and share a dessert with a friend if you can!"

She pushes the button for the live recording off, but the comments continue to stream in. Her phone looks like that bar that runs under the NYSE showing the prices of all the stocks.

"Whew," Ella Mae says, sticking her spoon back into the shake and taking out a bite.

She pops the spoon in her mouth and drags it back out through her lips. Objectively, I know why she's single. But right now, it baffles me. She's beautiful, fun, and resilient as all get out.

"Look at you," she says, taking another scoop of her shake, and then reaching over for a bite of my cake to follow it. She swallows and smiles. "These desserts should be illegal! And I'm so glad they're not."

"Look at me?" I ask, harping back to her comment.

"Having fun and all. Who knew? Chris St. James can be fun."

"I knew." The defensiveness in my tone is thinly veiled.

"Welp. I didn't. So, now I do."

Her face morphs a little. Softer. More vulnerable.

"Seriously, though. Thanks, Soldier. You didn't have to do this for me."

"It was fun," I admit.

"Well, I'll get Shawna to bring us the check before our cease fire turns into a pumpkin."

Does she think we're still enemies? Not that we ever were actual enemies. She just got on my last nerve. And I avoided her and her camera, with good reason. I'll probably still avoid her camera. Tonight was just a one-off to help her out in her time of need. I still have plenty of reasons to keep a low profile and avoid being seen online regularly.

"What happens now?" I ask.

I feel like I need a DTR talk, and we're not even in a relationship.

"What do you mean, Big Boy?"

I chuckle. "You can ditch that nickname, anytime."

"Not happening. I like it. Besides, you earned it."

"And I'll get supper. It's on me," I tell her, waving Shawna over.

"Nope. This is a business expense for me. And you did me the favor. My treat."

"I'm used to paying when I'm out with a woman."

"Well, get used to not paying tonight."

Shawna arrives at our table. "I'll be covering the meals, Shawna," Ella Mae says. "And thank you again for your help with our segment. Are you on social media?"

"Yes. I sure am."

"Give me your handle and I'll tag you if you like. Only, please don't give this location away. I need to keep myself a little removed from some of my followers."

Shawna rattles off a name to Ella Mae, and Ella Mae's fingers fly over her phone.

"I just followed you!"

What does that mean that Ella Mae has to keep herself

removed from some of her followers? My spidey-senses go on alert. I'm trained to watch and listen to things most people overlook. Is Ella Mae in danger? Has someone tried to stalk or harass her?

"I didn't know who you were at first," Shawna says. "But when you started filming, I looked you up."

She dutifully hands the check to Ella Mae.

"Oh, I'm so glad you found me."

"My niece was dying with jealousy. She loves you. You're her inspiration."

Ella Mae looks over at me with an *I told you so* look.

"Well, do you have something I could sign? I'd be glad to give her an autograph."

I watch as Ella Mae graciously signs a paper napkin, and then pulls out something from her purse to hand to Shawna with her signed paper goods.

She pays and we walk out together.

"Well, St. James. Thanks again. I'll see you around Bordeaux."

"Yeah. See you."

We both stand there by our cars when we should be getting in and driving home.

"Don't make this weird, Soldier. It was sweet what you did, but you don't owe me anything. The lines remain the same. We're good. And by good, I mean, all's fair in love and war."

She gives me a coy finger wave and I watch as she turns and slides into her car. I stand there, watching her drive off, and trying to make sense of the last three hours of my life.

Comments on Livestream:
1253 comments

@lifes_a_beach123: I loved that live! You did great. Bounce back from adversity, girlfriend. We're with you.

> **@Fab-U-lous_EllaMae**: Thanks so much for the support! And you're so right. Drake had something come up, but we still made it happen.

@allthatsazz: I honestly like this guy Chris more than Drake. Do more filming with him. He's hotttttt.

> **@Fab-U-lous_EllaMae**: Chris is something alright. So glad you enjoyed our segment!

@beefitupfitnessdude: I'd eat dinner with you any day, Ella Mae. Say the word. And you won't find me taking you to a Frisch's either.

> **@EllasSoBella**: Like I keep saying *stalker vibes.* Get yourself a girlfriend IRL. Are you even her age?

> **@beefitupfitnessdude**: I mean no harm. What's ur problem? Ella Mae and I are obviously in the same part of the midwest. I've followed her forever. I'm a good looking guy and I'd love to treat Ella Mae like the queen she is.

> **@EllasSoBella**: Again. Creepy. On what planet do women date men they randomly meet online?

> **@beefitupfitnessdude**: Um. This planet – earth. If that's

where ur from. Ever heard of online dating? Catch up with the times, EllaSoBella.

@midwestcutiepie: Oh my gosh! Mister Shoulders is so much hotter than I even dreamed. You have got to be kidding me! Ella Mae! Tell me you're going to date him! If not, please, please, please bring him back. What's his Insta handle? I want to follow him (to the ends of the earth, obviously, but at least on social media for starters!) And you two were so cute together, so if you're into him, I'm totes jelly, but he's all yours.

@KeepingItFabu: TBH I was a little bummed when I saw you weren't with Drake tonight. But you pulled off a great segment. Love the guy you were with. He's so sweet. Do more collabs with him!

@EllaMaeFan4ever: No Drake 🙁 I was so sad. But you and the new guy were great! Loved it. The way you mixed desserts was #relationshipgoals. SO sweet. I'm totally shipping you two. He's so ripped! #rippedandshipped #ChellaMaeBae #DessertFor2

@sparkle2shine123: Oh my gosh! What a fun live! At first I was like, no Drake? What? But then I saw Drake 2.0 sitting with you and I was like, that's what I'm talking about. You two made it work. That shake looked delish!

@Fab-U-lous_EllaMae: Thanks, Sparkle! The shake was scrumptious. I'm so glad you loved our live!

@ohiogirl4evah: I don't know what I'd rate that burger, but I give that "big boy" eating with you a ten out of ten.

@fashion_beauty_lifey: O.M.Goodness! When you wiped his

face! I was dead. Stick a fork in me. I'm done. Who needs Drake? #rippedandshipped #ChellaMaeBae

@healthy_greengoddesssss: I need that smoothie recipe, Ella Mae. I'm making a cookbook of only green smoothies. Promise to give you 100% credit for your concoction. That shake you drank on the livestream would put me in a sugar coma.

> **@Fab-U-lous_EllaMae**: I DM'd you the recipe. Thanks for the shout out in your cookbook! Let me know when you put it out and I'll promote it here. The shake was worth the coma, trust me.

CHAPTER 13

Ella Mae

MY PHONE PINGS with notifications all the way home from Columbus. It's sweet music to my ears. After Drake blew me off—forgot, overlooked, whatever—I imagined losing followers, word spreading, and then my mind spun into all the worst-case scenarios.

I mean, all it would take is one person saying I made up the collab as a publicity stunt, and people could stage a mass exodus from my account. Everything I've worked so hard for would easily slip down the drain.

But now, after tonight's dinner with Chris and the obvious popularity of our livestream, I'm enjoying a leisurely drive home, chilling to the sounds of Pink's soundtrack and the constant dings of my cell—each one a chime of validation.

They loved it.

They loved it!

My mind replays our dinner. Chris surprised me—not only with his heroics, but also with the way he rolled with everything. I never did find out what brought him into a Big Boy on the outskirts of Columbus on a Wednesday night.

When I get home, I bump the door open with my hip and

shout, "I'm home!" and then I promptly pop off these wedge shoes and wiggle my toes.

Meg and I rent an older home in the middle of a typical neighborhood in Bordeaux. Our front hallway runs down the center of the house, with a room off to the left when you walk in that we use for my filming and our yoga. Well, my yoga. Meg only joins me occasionally these days.

The staircase leading upstairs is to the right along the hallway. The kitchen and living room are at the back of the first story. I see the light on in the living room as I walk further into the house.

Meg's sitting sideways on the couch with her legs outstretched, reading something on her kindle. She looks up when she sees me walk in.

"So, how'd it go?"

"Stellar. Simply stellar. And weird. And ... wait. Didn't you watch?"

"Sorry, I had a headache, so I came home and went straight to bed. I only got up a half-hour ago. I just grabbed a bowl of soup and snuggled up here on the couch. I figured I could watch a replay with you later, and you would fill me in on everything."

"Are you okay?"

"Yeah. Just a stressful day at work. I'm good. So? Tell me everything."

"Well, Drake didn't show."

"He *what*?"

"Yeah. He blew me off. Or forgot. I was sort of freaking out until—well, you're not going to believe this."

I barely believe it myself.

Meg's eyebrows are raised, obviously I've got her attention.

"Chris walked in."

"Chris ... St. James?"

"The one and only. Of all people."

Meg looks stunned. But then she gives me this inquisitive stare.

"It was crazy. Chris walked up to my table. And … Well, long story short, he did the live with me."

"Chris St. James?"

"Mm hmm."

"Did a live? With you? On Insta?"

"Yep."

"Are you sure?"

"What do you mean, am I sure? I'm sure. I think I'd know if someone did a live with me. Check my account. It's up there."

Meg picks up her phone, taps the app, and pulls up my account. Her mouth literally pops open as she watches the beginning of me and Chris at dinner. I haven't even rewatched it, so I sit down next to her.

"Keep watching. You may as well."

"Okay. Just … wow. I'm speechless. Chris St. James filmed with you."

Meg shakes her head in disbelief and pushes play. The two of us sit through the announcement, the clip of me and Chris eating, and the rest of the night through the part where I film Shawna and then say goodbye to my peeps for the night.

The comments are still flowing in, over one hour after we finished filming.

I think about Chris. If he drove straight back to Bordeaux, he's only two blocks away from us right this minute. He's settling into his home, just like I'm settling into mine. I wonder what thoughts he's having about tonight, or if he's even giving it a second thought at all.

It's so surreal. Nothing could have prepared me for what

happened over the past four hours. It almost feels like a dream. I get why Meg just questioned me.

Meg looks over at me. "So, what does this mean? Are you two, like, friends?"

"No." I shake my head. "We're not friends. We had a sweet night. He was able to flex that hero complex of his, but at the end of the day, we're still who we are. I bet he won't even talk to me in public here in town."

I'm actually fine with that. Chris got me out of a pinch. He doesn't owe me anything. And considering all the facts of our life here, and what's gone down in the history books, there's no reason we would ever be anything but what we were before this little blip of an event.

"You think he's going to ignore you?"

"Hasn't he always?"

"He's a reserved person. I don't know if it's personal just to you. He only gives me one of those dude head tips when he sees me. He's not super-chatty to anyone."

"Sorry. You're probably guilty by association—by being my roommate. I've seen him be kind, and even talkative to other people."

I think of tonight. Chris seemed to genuinely care about what I was going through. He stepped in voluntarily. Yes. That's his default mode. Damsel in distress? Soldier to the rescue! But it felt like more at times. Like he was actually enjoying himself. And like he wanted to be there—with me.

"Well, to be fair ..." Meg trails off, a look of apology in her eyes.

"What?"

"You do often have the phone camera aimed in his direction."

"Can you blame me? He's pure eye candy. My fans love when I show off local guys. Chris is massive, and super-attractive—objectively speaking. Plus, he's got that whole mysterious, broody thing going for him. Women lap that up like a kitten at a bowl of milk. You should see my feed. At least five hundred comments of my over twelve hundred on that live are about him. And that was just the total the last time I checked.

"Everyone's saying things like, *Who's the hottie?* and *I ship the two of you!* Some people even said, *Forget Drake, go for Chris*. Guys who follow me are not just commenting on me, like they often do. They're asking Chris for workout and nutrition tips. He could probably start his own account and go viral tomorrow."

"I totally see that happening," Meg deadpans.

"Do you?"

She looks at me with a modified eye roll and chuffs out a laugh. "No. I most definitely don't. He avoids social media and cameras like he's allergic to them. Which is what makes this whole night so out of left field."

"Yeah," I agree. "But he seemed to be enjoying himself."

"That's what it looked like to me too."

Meg's eyes meet mine. She looks at me with this particular expression she gets when she's going to spear me with a hard truth or make me hold a mirror up to myself.

"So, you like showing off the men, but that still begs the question: Do the local guys love being props on your posts?"

I pause. Maybe five years ago I'd have been able to dismiss that sort of inquisition. But I'm getting older. Maybe wiser. For sure more sensitive.

"Maybe not."

Meg's eyes soften. "You are awesome. I hope you know that. You've built something most people like you strive to achieve, and the majority of them never do. You've poured your heart, soul, and talent into creating your platform. I get that you have to play things up to be where you are and keep growing. I really, really get that. I'm just saying, maybe

Chris isn't avoiding you as much as he's avoiding your camera."

"Maybe."

Meg's an optimist. She's been as over-the-top as I have in the past. When she tried to get back with Trevor, welp, that was an epic disaster. And when the new doctor moved into town, she came onto him in a way that made even me cringe.

Okay, I'll admit I tried to film my medical appointment during his first month here. He was having nothing to do with that. And he gave my poodle purse the evil eye. I'm still not completely over that. Trust me. That purse is epic. But I didn't out-and-out flirt with the man.

Anyway, that's all water under the bridge. Meg's stable now. She's barely a shadow of her old self—and that shadow's nothing but sweetness and encouragement when it comes to me and my work. It's amazing what having a supportive man in her life has done for Meg. I don't know if Joe's the one she'll settle down with forever, but there's no doubt he's been good for her.

No matter how hard I try to sop up Meg's positive outlook on what could happen between me and Chris, I just can't quite get there. Friendship is a far cry from having a night out on neutral ground where Chris was merely helping me because he saw how desperate I was.

Chris and I are what we are. I'm not about to waltz into town thinking we're going to meet up for coffee and hang out, or assume I could just call him if my car stalls out so he could come give me a jump.

It's not happening.

I made it clear that I knew the score, just to save myself from hoping, and to save Chris from any sense of obligation he'd feel to suddenly act differently around me.

Social lines around here are more firm than Aria Pilates Goddess' glutes. And that's firm, let me tell you.

After Meg goes up to bed, I stay awake reading and answering comments. People loved us—loved Chris. I mean, there's the usual, *Hey, you're hot,* stuff from guys who act like they've never seen a woman who takes care of herself before. They're mostly harmless. If they get out of hand, I block them. End of. As always, there are a few haters in the mix too. *Who wants to watch you eat? Get a life.* That kind of thing. I ignore the creeps and the negative comments.

Before I go to bed, I decide my ego can handle rejection if it comes to that, so I reach out to Drake and Genesis to try to reschedule.

@Fab-U-lous_EllaMae

Hey, you two, I'm just reaching out to see what might work for a reschedule. Let me know what you have in mind and I'll check my calendar to see if it works on my end. Peace, Love, and Positive Vibes ~ E.M.

I like what I wrote. It says I'm someone who should be considered. I have a life. I shouldn't be brushed off so easily. It's not a confrontation, but it's a statement of my worth. And, I leave off with all the good. No hard feelings. I smile at myself for taking the high road.

I'm about to put my phone on *do not disturb* for the night so I can go start my skin care routine, when a message notification pings.

@DrakesDaMan

Hey, Ella Mae.

My sister asked me to the movies and I completely spaced on the collab. I hope Gen reimbursed you for your dinner. Here's what I'm thinking. We do a segment where we call uber drivers and have them take us to the fast food restaurants our followers pick, and then we let the uber driver order for us. We can eat/rate the food. What do you think? And how about Saturday? I've gotta blow out of the midwest sometime next week.You're still coming to Cali, right? For the big bash at my pad? Gen, make all this happen. Peace out - D

Technically, not one bit of that message contained any sort of an apology. Drake reiterated what I already knew happened, but he never took ownership for leaving me high and dry. Still, this collab is just what I need to go next level. And people do forget commitments sometimes. I'm big enough to move on if he is.

Saturday, I was supposed to be going to dinner with Meg—to celebrate this collab and the obvious windfall of popularity it will be bringing me. She's already asleep upstairs. I'm not waking her to make sure it's okay to reschedule. I'm just going to say yes. She'll understand.

And, am I going to California? That's something I'm not even going to answer right now. Considering how nonchalant Drake is being about this whole collab, I'm going to need something a bit more concrete than *Come to Cali* to start me making official plans. Though, that party is the place to be. I really should try to make that happen somehow.

I shoot back a short and sweet response.

@Fab-U-lous_EllaMae

Saturday works. Thanks.

Genesis chimes in right away.

@GenesisAssistsStars

Drake, I've got all this. I'll arrange the deets from here. You arrange showing up, mkay? Ella Mae, thanks for being flexible. We'll get you everything you need. And if Drake stands you up again, I'll make his life miserable. Send me your dinner receipt. I saw your live. Genius. And that man. Whew.

I chuckle. Genesis obviously has job security. She told Drake. And she watched my live? Hmmm. She's another fan of Chris. Whatever spikes my popularity. And tonight it was definitely Chris' presence with me at the diner.

Drake gets back in the thread after Genesis' response.

@DrakesDaMan

Gen, please save your roasting for our private message thread.

I know I blew it, k? And I'll be there Saturday. Ella Mae made something good of the night with that friend of hers. No harm. No foul. All a W. See you Saturday, E.M.

Well, well. He actually knows he messed up. I have to keep in mind the power of Genesis for future reference. I reread Drake's last message. I smile at him calling me E.M. I think we're going to have a blast when we finally do film together Saturday.

Don't ask me why my mind travels to a soldier who's probably crawling into his well-made bed right about now. I bet he bounces a quarter off the sheets before neatly untucking them and slipping in.

Did we have a blast? I don't know if I'd call it a blast. But it was way more fun than I'd ever expect out of someone who can't be bothered to eat Pop-Tarts.

CHAPTER 14

Chris

SWEAT BEADS on my forehead and neck, drenching my shirt as I push through another set of reps with the barbell. I thrust the weights up and onto the rack, and grab for my towel.

"Something extra on your mind today?" the rookie fireman asks.

I'm a creature of habit. Our friend, Brooks, moved to Bordeaux a few years back and he, Duke, and I used to work out here in the firehouse. It's a decent weight room. When Brooks quit his job here and Davis joined the squad, I just kept coming to the firehouse to do my workouts.

"Nah. Nothing's on my mind, Rookie. Something on your mind?"

Truth is, I've got too much on my mind. But I'm not one to spill my guts, especially not to someone I've only known less than a year.

I can usually easily command my thoughts to fall into formation. I learned that mental discipline in the military. Daydreaming can get you killed in the wrong setting. Sure, I'd let my mind drift at times, but I chose the time and place, how far it wandered, and when to call it back in line. Over time, I learned to primarily focus on the thoughts that helped me get the job done.

Today, my brain is as unruly as a bunch of new recruits on the first day of boot camp when an attractive female officer walks by. Only, the focus of my wayward attention is on one loud, quirky, blond social media influencer. I can't seem to shake images of her smile, the sound of her laughter, or the way it felt when she wiped my face.

She.wiped.my.face.

And as surprising as our night together was, the most humiliating thought is how I let my guard down. I went on social media, of all things. If anyone I know at work or in my personal life finds out I was on that live video, I won't live it down. I might even be in trouble, though it wasn't TikTok, so I'd probably only get some sideways glances, and maybe a warning. The nature of my job means I need to keep a low profile. Yesterday was anything but.

What was it about Ella Mae that caused me to abandon all usual rational thought and throw caution to the wind?

I'm almost angry as I think about it. Not at her. She has no idea the restrictions I live under. She didn't even ask me to film with her—as per her usual M.O.

I offered.

I'm angry at myself. I know better than to go soft like that.

I'm meeting Duke for coffee again today, even though we've got a guy's night planned at Aiden's farm in two days. Duke's in vacation mode, so he asks me to meet him for coffee most mornings. I oblige him a few times a week. I know it's good for me to get out and spend time with him. He balances me. We're usually good for one another—an anchor and a sail on the same watercraft.

After I hit the shower, I walk into town. It's still that time of year where it's comfortable outdoors before lunchtime. As

I pass through the neighborhoods on my way to the coffee shop, I walk down Ella Mae's block. I'm not trying to see her. It's just one of the ways to get from my house to Main Street. I glance at the two-story she rents with Meg. No sign of life.

Probably for the best.

Being a civilian has obviously caused me to drop my guard. I'm trained to use situational awareness, and constantly hone my mental acuity. *Think ahead of what you see. Double check your perception. Consider all possible outcomes. Never allow yourself to be caught off guard.*

As I walk, I run myself through some all-too-familiar practice drills for my mind. The brain is a muscle. If it's weak, it merely needs consistent exercise to become strong again. When I pass a few people, I size them up, reminding myself what I know about each one, and pushing myself to imagine what each mannerism or facial expression could be hiding. Before I've even made it downtown, I'm already feeling more control over my thoughts and feelings.

Townspeople wave and shout out greetings. I'm not outgoing by nature, but I'd be a fool to ignore someone when they say, "Heya, Chris," or "Beautiful day!" or "How are ya?" Talk about an instant way to drag the town spotlight right over my head and turn the beam on high. The last thing you want to be known for around here is being the one person who doesn't respond to a greeting.

So, I wave, say things like, "Hey, Joe," and "Mornin'," and make my way to the coffee shop, free of all thoughts of Ella Mae and the unexpected night we shared.

Except that thought.

But I push it down.

There. Free. I'm free now.

"Chris!" Duke shouts from his spot in line.

I saunter over to him slowly, drawing out his anticipation

because it's fun to toy with him. He's way too easy. Like a cat with a laser beam.

"Hey, Duke."

"Hey! What a day. Am I right? This day. It's so beautiful it makes you want to sing or something."

"Yeah. Or something."

Madeline calls Duke's name. He steps up to the counter and flashes her a smile.

"Hey, Maddy-waddy. What's going on today? How's vacation treating you?"

He asks the question like he's her personal purveyor of sunshine. Madison giggles as if Pico Alexander just walked in and asked her on a date.

"It's good. I mean. We're in Bordeaux, so it's basically work, hanging out at the Res … and yeah. Not much else. But it's actually good to be home."

"Nothin' wrong with Bordeaux, Maddy. And you know about that chip, don't ya?"

"What chip?" Madeline asks.

Her face is innocent and wide-eyed.

I cross my arms. Ready for the line to move forward so I can get my coffee and find a seat. Apparently, I'm the only one with a clock or watch around here.

"The chip they put in you at birth," Duke teases. "It's got a magnet that always pulls you back to this town. You might go to UCLA, but mark my words, you'll be back to Bordeaux."

"That's just creepy," I murmur while Madeline giggles.

"What can I get you, Duke?" she finally says, glancing at the short line of people behind us and smiling.

"The usual, Mads. And I'll get this guy's coffee too."

Duke smiles over at me.

"Just a house coffee, black. Thanks," I say.

Duke pays and shoves a five dollar bill in the tip jar.

"What's got you acting so extra-Dukeish today?" I ask as we grab a table for two in the middle of the room.

The shop is busier this morning because it's summer. Everyone's out of school. Some businesses even open a little later through the summer just because they can. Hours of operation tend to be sketchy around here as it is. If the fish are biting, you might not find Ella Mae's dad at the hardware store until ten that morning. But someone will warn you he's out on the river if you come into town, so there is that. It's no secret what anyone's up to—ever.

Ella Mae. There my mind goes like a soldier gone AWOL, traveling back to thoughts of her. Well, to her dad, but still.

"My wife's pregnant. That's what's got me walking on sunshine," Duke answers, interrupting my disturbing thoughts. "Shannon's having our baby. If that's not something to make a man smile, I don't know what is."

I can't help but grin. "Yeah, she is. I can't believe you're going to be a dad. I mean, do they just let anyone do this parenting gig, or what?"

Duke chuckles. "Apparently."

My two best friends are married and settled—one with kids, the other expecting. One married to my baby sister, of all the things. I still feel like Rip Van Winkle most days. I left as a kid out of high school, went to college, entered the Army, and by the time I came back, people had married, started dating, or moved. Life went on without me.

Riley walks over with our coffees.

"Awww, thanks Rye-Rye. I could have stepped up and gotten those at the counter. You're the best," Duke says as Riley sets the two mugs in front of us.

She gives Duke the smile most people give him, full of admiration. Must be nice to have charm to spare. And, with Duke, it's genuine. That's the clincher.

"What's up with you?" Duke asks, taking a sip of his coffee and looking at me over the rim of his mug.

"Me?"

"Yeah. You look more constipated than usual."

I shake my head. "Nothing's up."

"So you say. You've got that one dent right here." Duke taps a spot over his eyebrow. "It always comes out when you're thinking too hard. So, what gives?"

I study my best friend. How he notices those kinds of details when he seems to be constantly distracted by every shiny thing is beyond me. But that's Duke. He'll surprise you every time with his depth and loyalty.

"I just had a weird night in Columbus. Nothing major."

"Far as I'm concerned, every night in Columbus is weird for you, since you never tell me where exactly you're going or what you're up to. I'm good with it. One day, you'll crack, and I'll find out what you do every Wednesday. Maybe I'll tail you sometime."

"I'm sure you've got better things to do than stalk me."

"You've got that right," Duke says with a laugh.

The air literally shifts. I feel a change as if all the molecules ionized around me. I don't even need to look. I know she's here.

Duke glances up from his coffee and smiles. I keep my eyes on my mug. I'm seated so I can watch the door—an old habit. Place yourself where you can see all exits and entrances. Size up the environment before sitting down.

I drop my eyes before Ella Mae catches me looking at her. Something about the way she invaded my mind this morning sets me off. I feel the chink in my armor and it's not acceptable.

Even with my gaze trained on my coffee cup, I can feel Ella Mae make her entrance. Out of the corner of my eye, I catalog what she's wearing: a pink top that looks like someone did origami with the fabric. It has little straps over her shoulders, but folds across her waist and flows out into these angel sleeves. Pink. So pink.

And she's wearing these shredded cut-off shorts that show off her impossibly long legs. And then she's got some sort of strappy sandal with a heel on her feet. Sunglasses are perched on top of her head—the kind that look expensive. And her blond hair is pulled back into a ponytail that must be meant to look effortless, but I'm guessing took her a while to fix up.

She looks as high-maintenance as she is.

She's got this tourist vibe, and not like she's exploring this town, for sure. Her whole appearance is more suited to somewhere on the French Riviera, hanging off the arm of an up-and-coming movie star.

I look around the room at everyone else in T-shirts and jeans or shorts, with tennis shoes or farm boots as their footwear of choice. Ella Mae stands out, even before she opens her mouth.

"Yoo hoo, Madeline! Good morning, beautiful girl!"

Ella Mae looks straight at me. She wiggles her fingers in a wave, and then promptly turns away. I don't smile. I barely acknowledge her. Here I was last night, wondering what came next when we were back in town. And now, I'm the one acting aloof.

She called it.

If it's possible, I'm even angrier with myself than I was earlier this morning.

Ella Mae grabs her drink and strolls over to our table. "Good morning, Duke. Chris."

She keeps her eyes trained on Duke and barely glances at me.

"Hey, Ella Mae," Duke says, his tail practically wagging like the overeager puppy he is.

"Congrats, by the way," Ella Mae says to Duke. "That's going to be one cute baby. Between you and Shannon, we're talking about winning the genetic lottery!"

Duke thanks her, beaming like the proud dad he is.

Turning to me and taking a long sip from her frothy frozen coffee drink, Ella Mae says, "My peeps ate you up like ice cream on a hot summer day, Christopher."

I've been studying my coffee like it holds the secrets to all life's mysteries. My eyes snap up to meet Ella Mae's at this announcement. I shoot her a subtle warning glance. Maybe I should have laid out parameters before we redrew our lines last night—no discussing our little filming session with anyone in our zip code.

"How would your peeps know about my man, Chris?" Duke asks, obviously salivating for any juicy detail he can get.

He's as bad as the seniors at the salon when it comes to gossiping.

"Oh, Chris didn't tell you?" Ella Mae asks.

She turns and winks at me. "I guess it's just our little secret, then."

"By the way, I rescheduled with Drake," she adds.

I grunt. I know it sounds like a grunt, too. I don't think that guy deserves a second chance to film with her, but it's really not my business.

Ella Mae seems to read my thoughts.

"Not to worry, Big Boy. He's DrakesDaMan."

Big Boy. She went there. In front of Duke.

"Yeah, well. Now that you put it that way," I say, glancing up at her again.

The pink of Ella Mae's shirt draws my eyes to her lips and cheeks. They're both shaded a light, bubble-gum pink. Her lips are glossy and frosted, like a glass of pink lemonade with sugar crystals around the rim. My gaze travels up to her blue eyes. They're so blue, like a swimming pool with the sunlight glinting off it in the middle of July. And they're sparkling with challenge right now.

"I'm not in need of a bodyguard, Soldier." She smiles a cat-ate-the-canary smile, and turns to walk away from our table and out the front door. "Have a great day, guys!" Her voice trails off as she steps outside. "I know I will."

"What was that about?" Duke asks before the door even swings shut behind Ella Mae.

"Nothing much. She and I bumped into one another in Columbus. She caught me on camera."

I'm not actually lying. Just keeping a bulk of the details to myself. The last thing I need is Duke looking up Ella Mae's video and sharing it with anyone who has a minute to check it out.

Duke studies me as I sit silently drinking my coffee. I change the subject by asking him what he and Shannon are thinking of in terms of baby names. Duke's easily redirected to other subjects, especially ones involving him, my sister, and my new niece or nephew. I only wish my mind could be so easily coaxed to focus on something other than Ella Mae today.

CHAPTER 15
Ella Mae

I STEP out of Bean There Done That with a winning smile on my face. Did I plan the timing of my morning frappuccino run just right? Did I leave the house hoping to land smack dab in the middle of one of the usual coffee dates between Chris and Duke? And did I put just a tad extra effort into my hair, makeup, and wardrobe today so I could be a fierce force of femininity and take charge of the narrative?

Mayyyybe.

When it comes to diffusing potentially strained situations, I always say, better sooner than later. Chris and I were bound to see one another. More than likely, he was going to dodge me, ignore me, or simply make this awkward. I merely got a jump on things by showing up looking ahhh-maze-ing and acting cool as a cucumber. I actually did Chris a favor, even though he was squirming like bait on a hook from the moment I entered the cafe until the second the door swung shut behind me.

He could have been more friendly. That choice was completely up to him. But as I told Meg, we're not friends.

I'm not going to let a rejection from Chris get me down. There's too much good mojo going on from our livestream.

I slip into my car, still smiling over how well I nailed letting Chris know he doesn't affect me. I walked into the coffee shop like a boss babe in pink, and I walked out head held high. I didn't even have to reapply my lip gloss. Take that, Soldier.

I'll always be grateful to Chris for bailing me out, and for causing my followers to go into a frenzy over him. But I'm not going to pause my life to fret over this small-minded town and the way people can't get over themselves. It's a beautiful day. And I've got a coveted collab on Saturday.

The next two days, I focus on pre-recording social media posts, answering even more comments on the livestream from Wednesday night, and doing my usual routines of exercise, skin care, and mindfulness practice.

By Saturday, I'm in top form, ready to meet Drake and make one more move in my quest for social media domination. I pull into a Burger-in-the-Box parking lot at noon. We'll be getting Uber drivers to select our food over a five-hour period, pausing between going to each next stop.

The plan for today is more detailed and intricate than our original collab. I'm wearing a pair of cotton shorts with an elastic waistband and an off-the-shoulder top over a tank. It's not the dress I wore to Frisch's. I also didn't drink enough green drink over the past twenty-four hours to pass a small marsh out my other end. I've been eating smaller portions, but I didn't go all out to prepare my body for an onslaught of junk food.

It's a different day for me. I feel more like Drake owes me one, even though I'm still a little starstruck about getting to film with him.

Drake's here. When I pull up, I see him leaning on his car in a pose that's so young James Dean. He's tilting back on the hood of his sports car with his legs casually crossed at the ankles. Well, hello.

I check my lipstick in the rearview mirror, and hop out.

"Ella Mae! Good to see you. Glad you could make it."

I'm glad he could make it, and I don't want to sound bitter, so I just say, "Thanks."

"Come on over here and give me a hug," Drake says, extending his arms, and popping up off the hood of his car. He's tall, muscular, dark hair, cut mid-length and wavy—the kind of hair that makes a girl want to run her fingers through it. He's got that "it" factor thing going for him. He oozes confidence and comfort in his own skin. But he seems pretty smitten with himself too.

I lean in for a quick hug, and he holds onto me like an old friend. A little too long for having just met one another. I don't meet his eyes as I step back out of the hug, causing his arms to drop to his sides.

He casually runs a hand through his hair. It falls out of his fingertips, the ends feathering in different directions. Drake's got a Timothée Chalamet or Bradley Cooper look, and I'm not complaining.

"So, my camera guy is meeting us here. He'll ride along next to you in the back seat, but he's got a dash-mount camera too. He'll put that in each Uber so he can capture shots from all angles."

"You have a camera guy here in Columbus?"

"My cousin, Andy."

"Nepotism. I love it."

Drake laughs a little too hard at my lame joke. It's one of those laughs that feels like he's auditioning for a studio audience.

"You're even more beautiful in real life. I can't take my eyes off you, Ella Mae."

I'm spared answering the awkward compliment by the arrival of Andy.

He hops out of his truck shouting, "Uber number one's on its way!"

Sure enough, right behind Andy, a car pulls into the parking lot and parks right next to Drake's car. Drake introduces himself, and then me and Andy, to the driver and tells him our plan. We all load into the Honda Accord and Andy sets one camera on the dashboard. Then, we get ready to film.

I pop open my phone.

"Heyyyy, my peeps! I'm here with DrakesDaMan!" I turn the camera toward Drake who's in the front passenger seat. He does a little two finger salute and a wink into my camera. "And this is Andy, Drake's camera guy. Say hi to my fans and followers, Andy."

Where Drake seems to come to life for the camera, Andy definitely is more comfortable behind a lens. He gives a shy glance into my phone and then looks down.

"And with us is Stan, the Uber driver! Say hi to everyone, Stan!" I stretch my hand around the front seat so the camera can capture Stan. He smiles and says, "Heya, all the people in TV land."

I pull the phone back to myself, laughing at the cuteness of Stan. I explain to the over eight thousand viewers watching me right now that Stan is going to pick our meal, and we'll eat whatever he orders for us.

The first stop isn't too bad. We get potato wedges loaded with gooey nacho cheese topping and bacon, a giant burger to split, and jalapeño poppers. I'm dying to ask for a diet Coke, but I'm following the rules. I can grab one on the way home if I still want one after a day of binging on junk food. Stan didn't get us drinks.

We park the car and dig in, Andy filming us, and me turning my camera on sporadically to catch bits of the day to share live with my followers. The counts continue to climb as Drake posts on his socials. He'll put a final edited video on his YouTube channel this week.

Drake plays it up, even leaning around the front seat to hold a jalapeño popper out so I can take a bite while he feeds me. He's being playful. Not as fun and harmless as Chris, for sure. But this is all for the ratings, and to give our followers something they want to see.

Chris. He has no business slipping into my mind right now.

Comments start streaming in as Drake pays Stan. I catch him sliding a fifty dollar bill into Stan's hand too. That was unexpectedly sweet. Then I notice Andy filming the exchange. I hope Drake's generosity isn't merely for show. But that's his business. After all, I'm here for the exposure, so I'm not one to talk.

I check my phone while we wait for the next Uber to arrive.

@allthatsazz: Ella Mae! New to your channel. Love the chemistry between you and Drake! Those wedges made me hungry. But when he fed you that popper! Talk about hot and spicy! Whew!

@Fab-U-lous_EllaMae: Glad to have you here! Hang around for life hacks, beauty tips, and lots of fun content. And yes! That popper was spicy! Drake's super fun.

@beefitupfitnessdude: You're letting too many men feed you, @Fab-U-lous_EllaMae. Let me feed you.

@EllasSoBella: Ella Mae should block you.

@beefitupfitnessdude: I'm not talking to you, @EllasSoBella. Let Ella Mae answer me. I'm only offering her the chance of a lifetime—to be with a man who will treat her so right. Check out my page. I take good care of myself. And I'd take good care of her too. Such good care.

@EllasSoBella: Cringe. I saw your page. You seem pretty into flexing. Good for you working out. Why don't you find a girlfriend at the gym and leave EM alone?

@beefitupfitnessdude: Shouldn't that be up to Ella Mae? Or are you jealous?

That guy, *beef it up fitness dude*, has been a bit forward lately. Maybe I'll ask Meg what she thinks I should do. I don't like blocking people when they're showboating or throwing compliments my way if they aren't hurting anyone. Lots of guys do this. It never amounts to anything. I just ignore him and answer other comments.

I keep reading my thread. Lots of people are speculating about whether there's something going on between me and Drake. Just like last week had hashtags about Chris, now there are hashtags #DrellaMae and #DrakeAndEllaMae. It's good press. I don't confirm or deny. And there are a few "What happened to Mister Shoulders?" and "Where's Chris?" comments in the mix. He sure was popular with my followers.

We hit three other restaurants in four hours, eating tacos, fried chicken, curly fries, shakes, and finally, hot dogs loaded with all the toppings, and a soft serve cone.

Thankfully, we pause for an hour between each stop.

When the last Uber driver parks next to Drake's car to let us out, my hand is on my abdomen.

"I've got a food baby," I tell my followers, with a crazy

grin on my face. "I think I'm going into a food coma any minute."

Drake chuckles from up front. He's got a nice laugh. We got along pretty well as the day wore on. He got more comfortable with me and let down some of the façade. But he also got more touchy-feely, feeding me at each stop and saying things about my lips or asking his followers to rate me 1-10. I rolled with it all.

When I last looked, I have gained over fifteen thousand followers in four hours. There's nothing like a collab with a super-influencer to boost someone like me. And I'm riding that high. Well, as much riding as I can do, when I really feel like someone needs to roll me out of this car.

"I'm heading home now, my sweet peeps. If you're new here, check out my other content and come back tomorrow for my, *What to do when you've overdone it* post. And remember to put the YOU in Fab-YOU-lous tonight!"

I hit the record button to end filming.

Drake looks back at me, slumped in the back seat, rubbing my belly like an old man in a white tank top and house slippers.

"You did great, Ella Mae! Just amazing. I haven't had this much fun in a while. Tell me you're coming to the bash in Cali."

Andy looks over at me with a look of concern. Or maybe he's just being shy again.

"I'll think about it. Thanks again. Can I split the cost of the food with you?"

"No way. My treat. All these collabs are for my channel, so I foot the bill. You can consider this our first date. Next time I won't make you eat so much, and it can just be the two of us."

He looks over at the driver, Mildred, who's quietly watching all of us like we're the latest episode of *Gossip Girl*.

I sit still, trying to dissect what Drake just said. Did he just ask me on a date? Or was he joking?

"Welp, Mildred, this is where we part. Thanks for driving us around today. Here's an extra fifty for your troubles."

Andy's not filming right now. Maybe Drake's not as cheesy as he occasionally seemed today.

"For me?" Mildred nearly squeals. "You don't have to! Thank you! Oh my gosh! You're the sweetest! Can I just hug you?"

Drake chuckles and says, "Sure," while Mildred's already unbuckling and practically hauling her fifty-plus-year-old self over the console to hug Drake. That's some hug. Mildred's squeezing Drake, and Drake's patting her back, saying, "Okay, then. You're welcome, Mildred."

I'm grateful she's not hugging me. I might blow. I'm like that girl who insisted on eating the gum in Charlie and the Chocolate factory—until she turned into a blueberry from chewing, chewing, chewing all day long. You could definitely enter me in the county fair right now. If you could get me there.

Mildred finally releases Drake, and we all get out of the car. I'm nearly dizzy from all the fast food, and I'm definitely ready to get home, take off my makeup, and put on some cozy summer pjs.

"Come 'mere," Drake says, holding out his arms. "I'm so glad we did this together."

Andy makes a show of packing up his equipment and loading it into the trunk of his car.

"Me too," I say to Drake. "People are going crazy on my Insta account. I'd better hit the road. Thanks again."

"I'll be in touch. And I *will* see you in Cali, beautiful."

"Maybe. I'll let you know."

I'm not playing hard to get. I still need to think through what it would mean to go to the effort to take a trip out to

California. There are a lot of details involved in making a trip like that.

Drake moves toward me and pulls me into a hug. He smooths his hand down my hair and holds me to his chest. His strong arms wrap around me and he bends down so his chin is resting on top of my head. It feels good to be hugged, but I'm not sure what he's thinking, so I gently push back and say goodbye to him and Andy.

CHAPTER 16

Chris

IT'S BEEN SUCH a weird week ever since Wednesday. My mind has settled the more time has passed since that evening with Ella Mae. I kicked myself a few times for not being more friendly when I saw her at the coffee shop. But it's probably for the best. It's not like we're about to start hanging out.

I park my car on Aiden's gravel driveway and walk up his porch steps to join my friends for guys' night. Nothing could have prepared me for what I see on the big screen in the living room when I pop open the front door.

It's me.

Ella Mae is wiping my larger-than-life face.

On an infinite loop.

As soon as she pulls back, smiling warmly, the scene begins again.

I turn to leave back the way I came in. Maybe no one heard me enter the house.

"Hey, hey, hey!" Duke shouts. "It's the man of the hour, our own social media influencer, Mister Shoulders, the Big Boy himself, Chris St. James!"

I shake my head, chuckling. I've been on the other end of pranks like this, doling out the humiliation by shovels full. No one pulls pranks like a bunch of midwestern guys who've grown up together their whole lives. We don't have many alternatives for entertainment out here. So, we play sports, and we excel at cornhole, gossip, and pranks.

And this one is the mother of all pranks. I can't escape it now, I may as well ride it out with a smile that says they didn't get to me—not at all.

"Hey, guys!" I say, walking into the kitchen as if I can't see a gigantic version of my face filling the screen of Aiden's monstrous living room TV.

"Oh, here he is!" Trevor shouts. "The man of mystery. But now. Now! The mystery is solved. What does Chris do when he goes away on Wednesdays? Well, folks, he goes to Frisch's with none other than Ella Mae Lindstrom."

Aiden's arms are crossed over his chest. He's leaning back on the counter eyeing me suspiciously, like someone abducted me and inserted an alien into what formerly was my body. It's plausible. I was there, but I still don't have any good explanation for what happened that night. Rob chuckles softly from across the room.

"Yep. You caught me. I'm on a weekly dinner date with Ella Mae. Now, do you old ladies have anything more interesting to do than scope out Ella Mae's social media?"

"No, we actually don't," Trevor says with almost a pouty tone to his voice.

"Sad. Pathetic, actually," I say, shaking my head in an exaggerated way.

The sound of Ella Mae and me talking continues to filter in from the living room. The infinite loop has ended and the actual post is being streamed through the TV at a not-so-quiet volume.

"Let's go watch the show and maybe you can run us through it like a sportscaster," Aiden suggests. "I cannot wait to hear your thoughts on this."

Grant leans in, "I had nothing to do with this lynching, in case you wondered."

"I figured you didn't. These guys are capable of far worse. They don't need any help to humiliate one of their best friends. Trust me."

Davis shows up. He's not Brooks, but he's alright, and I'm glad we're including him in our guys' nights. Being new to town can't be easy. Heck, coming back here hasn't been what I'd call a walk in the park.

And guys' night is a great way to form friendships. We wouldn't even have a designated time to get together if the women these men married didn't have a staunch insistence on having their girls' nights. We're lame enough that we wait for them to schedule their plans, and then we're all immediately texting one another to figure out what we'll do while the women hang out.

"Why is Chris on your TV with Ella Mae?" Davis asks.

His brow furrows and his lips draw thin.

"We've cracked the Wednesday mystery," Duke says. "We're about to get our own personal viewing of the segment Ella Mae filmed this past week—with a play-by-play breakdown from our own star of the show, Chris. Grab some popcorn and join us in the living room?"

"Popcorn? Seriously guys?" I ask, shaking my head again.

"It's a show. We popped corn," Aiden jokes.

It's the first time he's smiled since I walked in.

"I even whipped up this seasoning mix to sprinkle on it …" Rob says proudly, but then trails off when he sees the look on my face. "Never mind. You'll appreciate the finer points of gourmet popcorn another night."

"It's not what it looks like," I say to Aiden as we move side-by-side toward the living room.

"Oh, it never is, is it?"

I might as well face it now. I'm doomed.

I'm trained to think on my feet. Ever since my sister passed, I've been what my therapist called hyper-vigilant. The Army capitalized on that weakness and made it a strength. I live on high alert. And, yes, I saw a therapist. For a while. She helped. But she didn't fix me. Some things just can't be fixed.

Right now, I'm rolling options through my head. How much do I say? What explanation do I give?

I remember something from my training on enduring enemy wartime interrogations. *Say as little as possible.*

When I walk into the living room, the screen is paused with Ella Mae's giant, beautiful face smiling into the camera. Our whole evening together flashes through my mind like a montage. I had fun with her. Infinitely more fun than I'm having right now, that's for sure.

Duke takes the floor in front of the TV, standing like the emcee of a WWF match.

"Well, peeps! Let's get the fun going! Without further ado, I bring you The Chris, aka Big Boy, and Ella Mae, aka Chin Wiper, Show!"

I shake my head and chuckle. Duke plops down next to me on the couch facing the TV.

"Payback is such a bear, my friend," I warn him.

"Oh, it'll be so worth it," he whispers back, as he hits the play button on the remote. All eyes are glued to the screen as Ella Mae's voice rings through the room.

"Well, peeps! Do I have a surprise for you! Remember the man who turned his back on me in the coffee shop? Some of you have taken to calling him Mister Shoulders?"

Duke looks over at me and wags his eyebrows.

Ella Mae's voice continues. "Well, here I was, sitting by my lonesome. Just a girl, ordering a sandwich and a shake in a diner, even though she was way overdressed for the atmosphere."

On screen, Ella Mae does that shimmy. I remember when she did it that night. She looks down at herself and then over at me. It's so weird watching it on TV. She'd freaking love this. I chuckle to myself. I should call her and invite her to *The Ella Mae Show*. She lives for this kind of thing. I'm not going to, of course.

She continues, "And in walks Chris. When I told him about the change in plans with Drake, he volunteered to take Drake's place for the night. Now, don't you fret. Drake and I will still do a collab. Stay tuned for all those details later this week. But onward and forward, as my life coach, Journey, always says!"

Duke hits pause.

"Okay, there's just so much to unpack there. Chris, you'll need to help us out. So far, it looks like Ella Mae got stood up, and my boy here stepped in and agreed to film with Ella Mae. Am I right, Chris?"

"Pretty much," I say.

"Who is this Drake dude?"

"He's another social media influencer. He was supposed to meet Ella Mae, but he was a no-show."

"I see, I see," Duke says with a voice that's eerily like one of the guys on who announces Sunday NFL football. "And why would her *peeps* be calling *you* Mister Shoulders?"

I shake my head at Duke. "Seriously?"

"Do tell. There's a roomful of men waiting to crack this mystery. And you know you're not getting out of this, so …"

I sigh. He's right.

"I turned my back on Ella Mae when she tried to film me

at Bean There Done That, so some of her followers created a nickname."

"And yet, here you are, willingly filming with her later that same week."

"Seems like it."

Duke smiles this smile that says more than I can explain. It's this brotherly, *I've got you,* smile. As if all this is somehow for my good instead of their twisted version of entertainment.

Duke hits play. Ella Mae's facing the screen telling her viewers, "My stomach's growling and Chris here's a big boy. Big Boy! Oh my gosh! He's a big boy in a Big Boy! Anyway, he's massive. I mean, look at those arms, ladies."

Duke pauses. "A demo, please. Could we see those arms, Big Boy?"

This I can do.

I shove my T-shirt sleeves a little to expose more skin and flex up, and then down.

The room of idiots I call friends erupts in cheers like a group of teen girls at a Harry Styles concert. I laugh and brush my sleeves down.

This next part causes me to run a hand down my face. Ella Mae says, "Girls. Girls. Girls. Chris' arms are as big as my legs. If I had a measuring tape we could measure my thigh circumference, and then measure around Chris' bicep. He'd win, hands down."

Duke pauses, "Aiden? Measuring tape?"

Aiden shakes his head. "Nah. We're good. We all know Chris is massive."

Aiden's face is a combination of what looks like frustration and confusion. Is he upset that he didn't know about me filming with Ella Mae before Duke brought this situation into the spotlight? I hold his gaze, a question in my expression. He tips his chin toward me. Okay. We're good.

Ella Mae goes on to talk about me being hungry. She puts

the menu in her stories. Her followers pick our meal. Duke's smiling through it all, glancing over at me. I have to wonder what the point of all this is besides the usual humiliation of a good friend for fun.

Ella Mae has me talk to her followers.

"Say hi to my peeps, Chris." And there I am, filling the big screen, saying "Hey," with a little wave-salute.

Then she asks, "What's more yummy? The burgers or this man? I'll let you know in a bit." She winks. "Now go pick our meals and we'll be back shortly."

Duke pauses the video.

Then, in a falsetto, he says, "I'm going with this man. So yummy! Am I right, guys?"

A chorus of high-pitched, "SO yummy!" fills the living room until we're all laughing hard.

Duke fast forwards through the meal until the part where Ella Mae reaches over and wipes my face. I relive the experience watching it as if I'm a nosy fly on the wall at the diner.

"Here, Soldier, let me get that for you," Ella Mae says, her tone flirty, but I know she wasn't intentionally flirting with me. It was all for show. But on the screen, it looks so real. I remember she had just let out this giggle that felt so unguarded and natural.

My friends and I look on as Ella Mae grabs a napkin, wipes across my face and announces, "Clean!"

You can literally hear a pin drop when Duke pushes pause.

He looks over at me with one eyebrow raised.

"She wiped your mouth."

"Yep."

"You let Ella Mae wipe your mouth. You two look awfully cozy there. I mean, there's filling in when a woman gets stood up, and then there's sharing dessert and wiping one another's mouths."

Duke waggles his eyebrows. The rest of the room looks on like jurors in a murder case. These guys are the worst. I don't want to throw Ella Mae under the bus. She already went through enough that night. And I've been more confused than I've ever been since then.

I cross my arms over my chest.

Duke looks at me. I glare back at him. Wall-of-Chris. That's what I am right now. Nothing gets through this impenetrable fortress.

Duke knows it. He finally breaks our little stare-down.

"Welp, gentlemen! That was fun! Let's grill some burgers."

"Instead of grilling me?" I mumble to Duke only.

"Yeah, man. Instead of grilling you. But you and I are still going to talk. That's a bit more than *we ran into one another and she caught me on camera*. Why didn't you say something on Thursday when we had coffee?"

I look over at the big screen—exhibit A. "Um, I wonder."

The rest of the guys are filing out through the kitchen toward the back yard.

"Yeah. Good point. But I only went to these measures because you didn't tell me. I mean, I had to go hunting when you mentioned she filmed you. And when I saw that motherlode of a live video, welp. You know I had to share."

"You didn't have to share."

"Oh, but I did." Duke chuckles. "I so did."

I shake my head. It's not like I don't want my friends knowing I ate dinner with Ella Mae. I just like to figure things out without a lot of interference. And I haven't figured this out. So, I wanted space to do my own sorting.

"So, what gives? Are you two ...?" Duke asks, standing from the couch.

"Nah. We're just ..."

"Friends?"

"Something like that."

Duke hums.

"Okay, Big Boy, let's go get some burgers."

"Kill that nickname."

"Not happening," Duke says with a chuckle. "Definitely not happening."

Fab-U-lous_EllaMae

Sweet, fab-you-lous peeps!

This day was so special. 🩶

I just want to get on here and thank all of you for coming along for the ride while DrakesDaMan and I did our taste test live!

For those of you who are new to my page–WELCOME! You're going to love hanging out here. I do a lot of beauty and wellness vids, but also, this is a lifestyle page, so you'll get fashion tips and awesome life hacks.

I'm always here to give you positive vibes and remind you to be the best version of yourself—because there's only one you, am I right? So be you, boo.

Tonight, I'm curled up on my couch in my summer jammies. I'm STILL answering comments on the video collab with Drake.

Did I eat dinner? Are you kidding me? I don't even want to think about food ... blech. I'm drinking ice water and a ginger lemon cayenne drink that might just possibly put hair on my chest, but will also give me allllll the gut health after a day of indulging like a contestant who entered both the pie eating and hot dog contests at the county fair. Whew. Give me all the cleansing. All.the.cleansing.

Comment below with your fave way to get back on track after overindulging. If you're new, tell me something about you.

And don't forget to put on your coziest jammies and put the YOU in Fab-YOU-lous tonight.

COMMENTS:
137 Comments

@midwestcutiepie: I'm still team Mr. Shoulders. He's got something about him that draws me in. Drake's awesome, of course, and you two were so cute today. I'm just saying—#ChellaMaeBae

> **@Fab-U-Lous_EllaMae:** I'll pass on your compliment to Chris. Thanks for watching!

@always_wearing_prada_gurrrll: I don't know how you ate all that food! But—hear me out—if DrakesDaMan popped a jalapeno in front of my face, you know I'd be taking a bite, so I get you. Drink lots of water, girly.

> **@Fab-U-Lous_EllaMae:** It was for fun, but yes, I have a food baby! Maybe that baby is TWINS! Lol. And yes, I'm sitting here with my half-gallon sipper cup full of agua like it's my new bff.

@ariapilatesgoddess: That ginger shot sounds like the ticket. And water. Hydrate, hydrate, hydrate! I'll send you a cleansing smoothie recipe in your DM's. And show up for our virtual classes next week. You're a trooper!

@Fab-U-Lous_EllaMae: Thanks, Aria! I'll do all the things you tell me—all day, every day. You're the B-E-S-T!

@.Muscle.mindset. I'm new here. I work out twice a day. Lifting, cardio, extreme sports. I also do triathlons twice a year. Fitness is life. Loved your live, but man, your body's a temple. Yours especially ;) … Take care of it and it will take care of you.

@Fab-U-Lous_EllaMae: Awww. Thanks, @.muscle.-mindset. I don't usually eat like this, obvi! I'm impressed with your dedication. I'll be taking good care from here on out. Just the thought of a potato skin makes me turn into that green emoji with the puffy cheeks.

@beefitupfitnessdude: I watched you ALL day. It drove me nuts seeing you with Drake. But after rewatching the videos a few times, I can see there's nothing between you two. Just friendship, right? Save yourself for me Ella Mae. And I'd come nurse you back to health if you need it.

@shoe_luvr_babe: New here! Followed you after seeing you with Drake today. You're adorbs. Can't wait to check out your beauty tips.

CHAPTER 17

Ella Mae

I'M HOME on my couch. I just posted a welcome post and status update, and now I'm answering comments on today's live videos and tonight's post. Whew.

Growth always means more dedication to my followers. But since I'm for sure, for sure not eating anything tonight, I saved time not having to cook. I can spend that extra hour online.

I hear the front door open. Meg's quiet at first. She's obviously not sure I'm awake, so I shout out to her.

"Back here. I'm up! Just answering comments."

She walks into the living room with a smile bigger than any I've ever seen on her face.

"Good date?" I venture a guess.

"Great date."

Her voice is dreamy.

"Best date ever, maybe."

"In Bordeaux? Did you fall and hit your head?"

I'm having a hard time imagining any date in our small town that renders a woman all wistful and moony.

"In Bordeaux. With Joe. Joe Deitrich."

"I know your boyfriend's last name. Sit down. You seem light-headed."

I'd offer to get her water, but moving around upsets my already overworked stomach. Remind me not to binge fast food ever again.

"I don't need to sit down. But I do have something to show you."

"Okaaaayyy."

Meg holds out her hand. Her left hand. On the ring finger sits one of the most beautiful diamond rings I've ever seen.

"Is that what I think it is?"

"Mm hmm." She smiles big, her eyes glassy, cheeks lightly flushed. She even rocks lightly from side to side as if she can't stand completely still and manage to contain her joy.

"Joe proposed. Can you believe it?"

Her hands fly up to her cheeks and she looks like that emoji that's half blue, half yellow, with a screaming face. Only, happy. Really, really happy.

"You understand saying *yes* means being his wife—forever—right?"

"Duh. You're so silly, Ella Mae. Of course I know that."

I'm confused. Really confused.

"But ..."

"But what?" Meg's tone holds a slightly huffy edge to it, even though she's still beaming.

She's right. What is this reaction of mine? She's my best friend. And she just got engaged.

"I'm super super happy for you! That's what! Oh my gosh! You are getting married! Married! You! And Joe! Meg Deitrich! You'll be Meg Deitrich. Because you're getting married. To be his wife. His lawful wedded wife. To have and hold. For better or worse. In sickness and health. Til death do you part—that wife. That's you."

"Yep! That's me! Maybe we'll have you marry us since you know the vows so well."

"Ha! Yeah. No. Oh my gosh, though!"

I didn't see this coming. Obviously. I mean, I knew they liked one another, but I didn't even know they had said they loved one another. And marriage. Wow.

But Joe is really good for Meg.

"He's really good for you. He loves you, obviously."

"He does. And I love him."

"You do?" I take her in. "I mean … you do! Of course you do. You love him. He loves you. Love and marriage. Then comes the baby in the baby carriage."

"Are you alright?" Meg asks.

"Me? Yeah. Yes. Of course. I'm just shocked. Were you? Shocked, I mean."

"I was surprised, but not shocked. Joe's it for me. And when you know, you know."

"And you know?"

"I do."

"Those two words."

"Yeah. Those words. I do. I really do."

"Well, congrats! I'm so happy for you both. Sorry I was … weird. Probably all the junk food I ate short circuited my brain."

"Oh my gosh, yes! The junk food with Drake! How did it go?"

"I'll fill you in, but first, go get cozy. I want to hear all about this proposal." I pause, smiling up at Meg. "You're getting married."

"Yeah. Yeah, we are." She turns to head upstairs and shouts back over her shoulder, "And I want you to be the maid of honor, of course!"

Meg comes back down in a pair of sweats and a loose T-shirt. I'm still carefully sprawled on the couch, feeling like a mama sloth who just raided a Taco Bell.

No. More. Junk. Food.

Meg sits on the loveseat across from me and pulls her legs up under herself. The ring is still on her finger.

"I'm happy for you. You know that, right?"

"I know you are, even though that was definitely one of the weirdest reactions to an engagement I've ever heard of."

"Sorry. It's me, not you."

She laughs.

"Oh, I know. It's you. All you."

Meg tells me all about the proposal. She and Joe went to get a steak dinner. Then he drove her out to watch the sun set. He had a picnic blanket laid out under twinkle lights strung in the trees on a friend's ranch. He served her dessert there, on the blanket, while the two of them watched the sun go down. Just before it dropped behind the horizon, Joe turned to Meg, raised onto one knee, and pulled the little black box out of his pocket. The things he said to her almost brought tears to my eyes. Though I'd probably cry ketchup and nacho cheese sauce after today's eating frenzy.

Meg said yes before Joe even finished asking. Then they stayed out there under the stars, holding one another and talking about their future together and how lucky they were to have found one another.

After hearing Meg describe the proposal, I'm certain she and Joe are right for one another—in love, and ready to commit for life.

This old song by Queen runs through my head: *Another One Bites the Dust*. I can't remember what that song was really about, but in my life, it's about people moving on and finding their happily ever afters while I remain here on the island of one that is Ella Mae. At least it's a fashionable island with great taste. I'll always have my knock-off Prada and my poodle purse. And my followers. I'll always have them.

"So," Meg asks. "What about this day with Drake? Tell me everything. And how are the responses from your followers?"

I fill Meg in on Drake, the weird way he complimented me, his hugs that lasted a little too long for comfort, the fun we had with the drivers. I tell her about Andy, and the way Drake tipped each driver a little extra. No wonder I'm exhausted. After a while, Meg moves to sit next to me so we can watch a few clips of the live videos together. Then we scroll comments.

"What's with this guy?" Meg asks, reading a comment aloud from beefitupfitnessdude.

"I don't know. He's probably harmless, but he makes comments like that every post lately—about how he wants to meet me, be with me … How he'll rub my feet if they're sore … He'll take care of me. You know. I get that from guys who don't know me. Once they know me, well … You know how that goes."

"Okay, no. Most guys we know don't really know you. They know the Ella Mae that parades around town making videos and being over-the-top to please her followers. They don't know this side of you—at home, Ella Mae. Though, they should. It's not like you've hidden your huge heart from everyone.

"You've always stepped in when asked. If they could see past the age-old lines in this town, they'd realize you helped Jayme get her contract with Heracles Publishing. Jayme probably wouldn't even have a book deal if it weren't for you. You stepped in to shoot the photos for that fireman calendar and didn't even ask to be paid for a full day's work.

"You always pitch in. You're never mean or catty. You build people up. You may be an acquired taste for a bunch of provincial small-town people. But you're awesome."

I can't help smiling. I wish I saw myself the way Meg sees me.

"You're sweet."

"I am. But that's beside the point. I'm telling you the truth. If those men, well, most of them are married now, but if they knew you—the real you, which includes your over-the-top, super-fun side, but so much more—they'd be lining up to get a chance with you. Plus, you're drop-dead gorgeous. All the fire emojis, girl. And you know I mean that. Besides, Jimmy Shaller always wanted you."

"Oh my gosh! Do not bring him up!"

We both devolve into a fit of laughter.

Jimmy had been obsessed with me since junior high, or maybe even earlier than that. He used to follow me around like a lost puppy. His mom is the whole reason I'm nominated Miss Corn Husk every year. Yes. *Miss Corn Husk.* I used to think that was an honor, but the older I get, the more I dread wearing that itchy costume and riding on that float down Main Street in the Fourth of July parade while everyone stares at me—and I try not to scratch myself silly.

Thankfully, Jimmy met a girl when he was showing livestock at the State Fair in Columbus. Word has it, they were the top two finalists in the hog competition and, well, the rest is history.

"But back to this Beef It Up guy," Meg says. "I don't like the way his comments are escalating over time."

She's holding my phone, scrolling through posts and finding different times he commented.

"And go, EllasSoBella! This girl tells him to back off the stalker vibes. She's awesome."

Meg keeps scrolling, reading comments aloud. And, I do have to admit, hearing her read them makes them sound worse than I thought they were.

"He's probably harmless," I say, for some reason.

"You should totally block him."

"He hasn't done anything. I mean, he compliments me. Says he wants to take me out. Lots of guys say that. They put fire emojis or hearts or that face that looks like it's on fire, or they say I'm their dream girl. I'm used to it. It comes with the territory. Check out any female influencer and you'll see the same thing."

"Doesn't make it right," Meg says plainly. "If this were any other workplace, which this *is* your workplace, these kinds of comments could get a man fired. It's harassment."

"I hadn't thought of it that way. I guess I've just gotten used to blocking it all out."

"Well, I think you should block him. That's my vote. And please, let me know if this gets more intense."

"I will."

"And that EllasSoBella named her whole account after you. She reposts your stuff all the time. She's just as obsessed as this Beef It Up guy, but she's respectful about it. Can you imagine naming your whole account after another person?"

"It's probably just her fan account. She probably has another account that has nothing to do with me."

"Face it. You have rabid fans, roomie. I'm in the presence of greatness!"

"You're in the presence of a woman who can't get off the couch because of all the food she ate today."

Meg laughs hard. I smile watching her. She's still riding the high of her engagement, as she should be. I push down the fact that life is going to shift within a year. I'll need to move someone in here or find another place to live. Maybe I'll finally leave Bordeaux and reinvent myself somewhere else—somewhere I'm not seen as a puffy pink pariah.

I could have a fresh start anywhere.

If it weren't for Mom.

CHAPTER 18

Chris

I PULL up to Alex and Courtney's house. It's a modest brick and clapboard, ranch-style home on the outskirts of Columbus. Their large front yard is framed with some pine trees and other deciduous trees, and a long driveway leads to the garage.

I bet my car would drive here on autopilot if I didn't navigate. I've been coming every Wednesday for the nearly two and a half years since my discharge from the army. As soon as I finish up at the main office downtown, I head to Alex's home like clockwork.

Alex and I served overseas together. I was the captain of our company, and Alex oversaw one of the platoons in my company as a first lieutenant. He was due to be promoted to captain when the accident happened that changed everything.

The front door is open, so I shout through the screen door before I walk in.

"Hey, hey! Look what the cat drug in," Alex jokes as he wheels into the front living room. "Courtney," he shouts. "I've got a surprise for you."

"Let me guess," her voice rings through from the back of the house. "It's Chris!"

"The woman's a psychic, I tell you. One of her many talents." He waggles his brows.

Alex is a lot like Duke. Maybe that's why I was drawn to him in the first place. Within a week of us meeting, it already felt like we'd known one another forever. We both entered the Army straight out of college, ROTC completed, ready to take our roles as commissioned officers. I'm two years older than Alex, so I rank higher because I started serving sooner.

Nothing could prepare a man for his best friend being injured on his watch. Even though we conjure up all sorts of scenarios to ready us for the worst in combat situations, when an actual tragedy happens, it's beyond anything any training or indoctrination could have equipped us for.

And that's what happened. Alex took a hit to the back that altered his life forever. I still have nightmares of that day. I thought he might not make it. But he did. He received an honorable medical discharge for his partial paraplegia, and a purple heart, along with his electric wheelchair and a few years of emotional and physical therapy at the VA hospital.

Alex's four-year-old daughter, Kassie, comes running out and jumps up at me. I catch her midair.

"Uncle Cwiss!"

"Hey, princess!"

I lift her up and pop her on my hip.

"I'm not a pwincess, Uncle Cwiss. I'm a dwagon!"

"Ohhhh. You're a dragon, are you? What color dragon?"

Kassie nearly rolls her eyes at me, giving us all a foretaste of her teen years. "I'm gween. But I actually have very, very red eyes!"

She widens her eyes and stares at me with the most serious expression.

"Oooh. Those are red. Do you breathe fire?"

"No."

She puts her hands on her hips as I hold her. I'm obviously getting this all wrong.

"I'm not breathing fire. I breathe marshmallows."

"Of course. That makes total sense."

I look over at Alex who is beaming at his daughter, and then laughing at me.

Courtney walks in, kisses Alex on the top of the head, and places her hand on the back of his wheelchair. He reaches up behind himself and puts his hand over hers. They're one couple that makes me think about my future and having a family. I should feel that way every time I'm with my friends back home, but for some reason, it's Alex who brings out these wayward thoughts every single week.

I set Kassie down and make my way to the couch. She runs out of the room shouting, "I'm going to play dwagon now! Where is dat magical, magical wizard?"

We all exchange a knowing smile. Kassie's a miracle. Alex and Courtney got pregnant a year before the accident one weekend he was on leave. They still could have more children, since it was only Alex's leg that was impacted in the accident. But with all his therapy, and the long road from then to now, it wouldn't have been likely. Kassie's buoyant personality and vibrant imagination brought life to this house at a time when everything seemed nearly hopeless.

"So, what's new in cybersecurity?" Alex asks.

"I'd tell you, but I'd have to kill you," I joke.

"I'm trained to avoid being killed. I'll take my chances."

Courtney shakes her head. She turns to leave us alone, but Alex reaches around and pulls her onto his lap.

"Where do you think you're going, beautiful?"

"Nowhere now," she says with a warm smile.

Their eyes lock, and they share a private exchange. The blatant flirting should make me feel awkward, but somehow it has the opposite effect. Knowing all Alex endured, and seeing him bounce back to embrace life the way he has, gives me a comfort I can't even put into words.

"I should get dinner started," Courtney says, looking into Alex's eyes with a teasing expression.

I see his arm muscles tighten as he holds her in place.

"I say you stay right here and we order out. Chris, can we finally talk you into staying for a meal, or are you still dead set on eating that diner food?"

I only stay occasionally, even though they offer most weeks. I don't want to be an imposition. Stopping in and catching up, seeing that Alex is okay, that's all I need.

The mention of the diner brings images of Ella Mae rushing uninvited into my head. It also reminds me of something I've wanted to ask Courtney. She's outside my circle enough that I can be sure of no repercussions to this request.

"Actually, I had a question for you, Courtney. Do you have a minute?"

"You finally want my wife to fix you up with one of her hot friends? Man. Took you long enough to ask."

I shake my head. These two are constantly joking about trying to get me a date.

"I date."

"By date, do you mean hanging out with your friends for guys' night?"

"I date women."

"When was the last time you took a woman out? You know, had a meal with her, shared conversation, and laughed together."

"Last Wednesday."

Okay. That wasn't a date. But for the sake of Alex's criteria, and for the benefit of getting him off my back, it fits.

"Really? You were here last Wednesday. And, you left and went on a date?"

"Yep."

Before Alex can pry more details out of me, I look at Courtney.

"Do you know anything about Instagram?"

Alex coughs out a laugh. It's an admittedly out-of-character question for me to ask.

"Sure," Courtney says. "Doesn't everyone?

Alex scoffs. "Hun, Chris here is such a throwback, it's like a dinosaur had a baby with a caveman, and out popped Chris. He'd use Morse code, smoke signals, or chisel in stone if it could get his point across efficiently."

Courtney laughs.

I shrug. He's not wrong.

"Why do you need to know?" Alex asks me.

I sit still, silently staring at Alex.

He studies me and then guesses, "It's a woman."

I blink slowly, willing my face to remain placid.

Alex's eyebrows raise and I know he knows he hit on something, so I concede with a small nod.

Then I clarify. "Not like that, though. She's a girl from my hometown. Woman. Yeah. I guess she is now. Anyway, it's not anything romantic."

Alex looks at Courtney. "That's Chris for you. He's so busy protecting some hometown girl, he didn't even notice she's a woman."

"I think that's admirable," Courtney says.

"Who said anything about protecting anyone?" I mutter.

"When did blindness to the opposite sex become admirable?" Alex asks, nuzzling his face into Courtney's neck.

She shakes her head. "Think about it. He could be like the other guys in your platoon."

Alex and I both laugh.

"No woman goes unnoticed in their presence, whether she likes it or not," Alex says.

"I can help you get on Instagram," Courtney offers. "It's really easy. But she'll know you're on her page if you follow her. Everyone can see their followers. Of course, anyone can look at her posts if she's got a public account. She won't be able to track that. I'm assuming you want to remain anonymous?"

"Definitely."

Alex releases Courtney, and I hand her my phone. She sits on the couch next to me and walks me through creating an account. I don't add a profile picture. I call myself @got.your.six.now.. It's an Army saying, meaning I've got her back. I don't explain that to Courtney, but Alex watches me like a hawk, and when he hears me say that phrase, his gaze narrows like he's trying to ferret out something deeper going on here.

Once I have an account, Courtney helps me look up Ella Mae.

"Oh my gosh! She's the one? Ella Mae? I follow her! She's adorable. Such a character. Is she in danger?"

"She's safe," I say.

I don't mind them thinking my motive is protecting Ella Mae. It makes sense they'd assume that's what I'm up to. I am in cybersecurity for a living, and it's my nature to protect vulnerable people. But that's not why I'm creating this account. I just want to assess the fallout of our filming last week in case I need to do damage control. Ella Mae's probably fine, I'm the one who might need protection.

"Wait!" Courtney exclaims. "That's you!"

Before I can control the situation, Courtney's scrolling and tapping on one of the videos of me and Ella Mae from last Wednesday.

"What?" Alex asks, pushing the control on his electric wheelchair to maneuver closer to us.

"Oh. My. Goodness! Chris St. James. Ella Mae was your date last week?" Courtney's nearly giddy.

Awww, heck. Now what? I already said it was a date. What was I thinking?

"Looks like it," I say.

Technically, I'm only saying what it looks like, not admitting or denying whether it was an actual date.

Courtney flashes the phone to her husband. Alex lets out a low whistle.

"Apparently, you don't need to date one of Court's hot friends. This woman's way above your pay grade, Cap."

"Insubordination," I mumble.

Alex chuckles. "Nothing to be ashamed of. You look like you're having fun. And if she's half as sweet as she is nice looking, I'm happy for you."

"She's …" I don't even know what to say. How do you explain Ella Mae to someone who hasn't experienced her first hand?

Courtney steps in. "She's amazing. Bright, positive, full of energy, always trying to inspire people. She's the whole reason I started yoga again."

"Well then, I owe her a personal thanks," Alex says with a chuckle. "When are you bringing her by, Cap?"

"The twelfth of never," I say loudly.

Both Alex and Court laugh. Then Courtney says, "Don't rush him, Alex. This seems new. Let him get settled with her. Then we'll have them to dinner."

Um, no. No, I will not be bringing Ella Mae to dinner anywhere, especially not here.

Courtney grabs my phone back from Alex. She hits play on the video and starts watching it. I don't even try to stop her. She's got a phone. As soon as I leave, she'll be looking this up anyway.

"You two are so cute."

She continues watching, then looks up at me. "But this was an impromptu date. You stepped in when another guy canceled?"

"Yeah. This guy, Drake, was supposed to meet her there. He didn't show, so I stepped in. She's from my hometown. We've known one another forever. She's Shannon's age."

"A younger woman. Look at you go."

"Alex," Courtney playfully warns with a smile on her face.

"What? I think it's great."

Courtney scrolls through some comments.

"Lots of people are trying to ship you two."

"Ship?" Alex asks.

"Oh, sweetie," Courtney says with a laugh. "Ship. It means to try to get two people together romantically."

"Oh, yeah. I knew that. I was just seeing if Chris knew."

Courtney looks at me and rolls her eyes.

"You so didn't know," I joke, even though I only found out the meaning of ship last week because of all the comments on Ella Mae's post.

"Awww," Courtney coos, still watching the video. "She wiped your chin."

I don't blush. I just feel a little prickle rise across my skin.

Alex busts out laughing.

Honestly, is there nowhere I can go without someone highlighting that moment between Ella Mae and me?

"This I have to see," Alex nearly shouts.

"I've gotta run. It's been great seeing you two."

"Okay. Okay. We'll stop," Alex says, holding his hands up like he's innocent. Then, to Courtney, he says, "Babe, you can show me later."

Courtney laughs. "I promise we won't lie in bed watching this over and over tonight, Chris."

"Yeah. We'll just watch it a few times. We've got better things to do in bed."

"Alex! My word, you're on your worst behavior whenever Chris is here."

Courtney's still smiling at her husband with those adoring eyes, reminding me of what I wish I had.

Kassie comes running in.

"Mommy! The wizard turned the pwincess into a toad. But I breathed all my marshmallows at him. I told him, you stop it. Don't you turn the pwincess into a toad. But then she was a toad. And I was holding her. And she was smiling at me even though she was a toad!"

"That's amazing, Kass. Want to help me make the salad for dinner?"

"Dwagons don't cook."

Courtney chuckles. "If you help with salad, I can help you make a potion to turn the princess toad into a princess again. How does that sound?"

Kassie stares at her mom, twisting her lips to the side. "Otay. You can do that. I'll make salad."

"Deal. Let's go wash our hands. Give Uncle Chris a hug goodbye."

Kassie loops her arms around my legs and I bend down to press my hand to her back, holding her to me until she pulls away and skips off toward the kitchen.

"We'll see you next week, Chris," Courtney says, leaning into me for a side hug.

She follows Kassie into the kitchen.

"You sure you don't want to stay for dinner?" Alex asks me.

"Nah. Maybe next time."

"I'm glad you went on a date, Cap. In all seriousness,

having Courtney by my side these past few years has saved my life. I still had to do the hard work, mentally and physically, but she's the whole reason I pushed through—her and Kassie. If you find something like that, well, you'll know when you do. And the only way to find it is to put yourself out there."

"Thanks, Yoda."

Alex makes his voice a little nasally and scratchy and says, "The greatest teacher, failure is."

"I'm not about to fail."

"I sincerely hope you don't. You deserve the best, Cap."

CHAPTER 19

Ella Mae

"HEY, MOM," I say out my rolled-down window as I park on the driveway of her property—the home I grew up in, even after Dad left us. At least he had the decency to leave Mom the house.

She looks up from the flowerbed where she's pulling weeds. Her floppy sun hat keeps me from seeing her eyes.

"Oh, hey, Ella Mae. I've been wonderin' when you'd come out here."

Mom doesn't live on the ranch side of town. Her property is on one of these older, larger lots down the pike that leads southbound from the outskirts of Bordeaux. The flat, grassy landscape is dotted with houses and only one or two trees on each property. It's pretty common to see a well-used plastic swimming pool in a front yard, or a swing that looks as old as my grandma hanging from a branch of a tree off to the side of the house. Other homes have dilapidated cars that someone meant to repair and just never got around to, or an old washing machine set out for who-knows-why and left to rust. It's not the slums, but it's not a place someone would aspire to wind up living out their later years of life.

The people out this way either want to be left alone, or they can't afford the house they'd really rather own somewhere else in town. My mom qualifies for a bit of both those reasons.

The morning already feels a bit muggy. And mom's guilt trip only adds to my sense of suffocation.

"You've been on my mind," I tell her as I step out of the car and walk toward her.

My words are hopefully a gesture of penance, making up for me living my own life and leaving her partially in the dust.

Moms. Am I right?

On one hand, she's the most precious person in my life, the one who unequivocally believed in me, who always pushed me to grow, who stuck by me when so many around here haven't. On the other hand, my mom gives me the most messed up mixed messages, and because of who she is in my life, they sink to the deepest recesses of my heart and take hold.

Growing up, Mom always told me I was exceptional.

You're so special, Ella Mae. You're not like these other people around here. You're beautiful. You've got spunk. You're made for something great. Get yourself out of this town and take all those qualities that make you fabulous and go get your big life. The only life you can have in Bordeaux is a small one. And no matter what, never let anyone relegate you to second place.

I felt like a prizefighter at the side of a boxing ring—pumped and ready to take on the world.

But then she'd turn and say, *Never leave me, baby girl. You're really all I've got. After your dad left, you were the only thing that kept me pushing on. If you left Bordeaux, I don't know what I'd do. You're my sunshine, Ella Mae.*

That second layer made me feel like I stepped in the ring

and went down on a one-two punch before the fight even started.

Logically, I'm smart enough to see the mind trip my mom laid on me. I know this is all about her issues, not mine. But for some reason, the part of me that makes choices always factors my mom into every move I make. I may be her sunshine, but she's my gravity—pulling me to earth, holding me back, yet also strangely keeping my world together.

"I saw that live video last Wednesday."

As I walk toward Mom, I notice how badly the grass needs mowing. I know better than to wear my good shoes out here, so I'm sporting a pair of red converse all-stars. They're old and comfy. I'm wearing a vintage red T-shirt and jeans shorts. It's sort of a Hollywood starlet going to the market on Saturday and caught off guard by the paparazzi look.

I kneel next to Mom and start pulling weeds with her. It's something we did when I was growing up. Ironic how I never do yard work around Meg's and my place. But with Mom, it just feels right.

"Did you hear me?" Mom asks.

"Yeah. I heard you."

Usually, Mom's a fan of everything I do on my channel. She doesn't comment on any posts, but she follows me almost as religiously as she watches *Days of Our Lives*, a soap opera she's watched since before I was born. But I know what's coming, and it's not a rave review of the live I recorded at Frisch's.

"Chris St. James?" Mom asks with the same tone of distaste she uses anytime that family's name comes up.

Mom stops pulling weeds and looks over at me. I keep pulling weeds to avoid meeting her gaze.

"Ella Mae, what on earth would prompt you to include that young man on your platform? And now your followers are trying to get the two of you together?"

She's not yelling. My mom can surely yell. Thankfully, there's plenty of room between us and the next property over, so no one ever heard her lose it over the years. Though, I wouldn't be surprised if her voice carried a half-mile when she really got going. Even without raising the volume, Mom's agitation carries clearly in her tone.

"So?" I mumble.

"So? That's all you have to say?" She huffs. "So? You could have had anyone in that video. Heck, I would have driven to Columbus to sit with you and eat a big ol' burger. Why him?"

"He showed up. Drake didn't."

"You expect me to believe you were sitting in a Frisch's outside Columbus and that man walked in out of the blue?"

"Believe it or don't, that's up to you, but that's what happened."

She shakes her head. "You still didn't need to put him on the camera with you. And then you wiped his face. What a moment. It looked so tender and intimate. Have you rewatched that video?"

I have. And she's not wrong. I'm not giving any thought to what it looked like. I'm a good actress. I was lost in the moment, swimming in the emotions of being ditched—and rescued.

"I saw the look in your eyes, baby girl. You had more stars than Orion flashing at that man. The way you went on and on about his muscles. Really, Ella Mae."

"It's not personal, Mom. He's eye candy. And my viewers love that stuff. Part of what I do is hype. You know how it works."

"I know your methods, and I know you. And what I saw in your eyes wasn't all hype. I'm sure I don't need to remind you, that man is off limits."

"I know. It's not like we're actually dating. Chris came to

the restaurant. I was freaking out. He stepped up in my time of need. He was great on camera. My followers and likes exploded. People are still talking about Chris a week later. He's a gimmick. Don't worry."

She looks over at me. I meet her eyes this time. I hope she sees that nothing could ever happen between me and Chris.

"Okay then. If you say so." She sighs. "Now tell me about this Drake. That looked like one fun afternoon."

Mom and I finish up in the garden while I detail the day with Drake. We laugh at how full I was at the end of the night. We drink lemonade on the porch after we're satisfied with our work in the yard. Then I drive back into town on a mission—to put a little space between me and my mom, yes. But also, to touch base with Riley. I've got something important I need to talk with her about. After my time at Mom's, talking to Riley feels more pressing than ever.

Bean There Done That's pretty empty when I step through the front door. Riley's wiping tables and Madeline's in the back. She steps out to man the register when she hears the door shut behind me. A couple sits near the front window. Jayme's off by herself in a booth, Airpods in her ears, her face a mask of concentration as she stares at her computer screen, deep in thought. Otherwise, the cafe is empty.

"Just an ice water with lemon, please," I tell Madeline. "I ate my way through half the town of Columbus Saturday, and I'm still feeling it."

"I saw! How fun was that?" Madeline says.

"Super fun. Thanks for watching."

"I love your channel, Ella Mae. You're so engaging and positive."

"Thanks."

I don't know what else to say. I'm not used to people complimenting my channel in person. Maybe there's hope for the future generations of Bordeaux.

"I'll get your water."

I slip a dollar into the tip jar and walk toward Riley.

"Hey, girl."

"Hey, Ella Mae. What's up?"

"I wanted to talk to you. Can you sit for a minute?"

"Sure. It's slow." She tucks her towel into her apron and shouts over to Madeline. "I'm taking a break with Ella Mae for a few."

"No problem," Madeline says as she walks toward us.

Madeline sets my water in front of me and smiles the smile of a college student on summer break. I wouldn't know. I never went to college. I've taken a few courses online—photography and marketing, mostly. But I'm a self-made woman. Educated through high school and the school of hard knocks, or something like that.

"What's up?" Riley asks.

"Well, I wanted to toss an idea at you."

"Shoot."

"You know how I've always been Miss Corn Husk?"

"Everyone knows that. I'm pretty sure they should put a statue of you as Miss Corn Husk in the town square."

"O.M.Goodness. I sure hope they never do that!"

We laugh.

"Anyway, I've been thinking about this year's float since the Fourth of July is only a few weeks away. Did you know I'm twenty-nine? I've been Miss Corn Husk for fourteen years —except two years I was sick over the week of the *Red, White, Blue, and Corn Too* celebration"

"You're *twenty-nine*? I thought you were *way* younger. Like twenty-five. But, yeah. It makes sense. I mean, you're much older than me, of course."

Old. I usually don't feel old. Put me around a perky co-ed and I definitely feel my age.

"Anyway, I think I'm outgrowing the role. And I'd like to nominate you for Miss Corn Husk this year."

"Me?"

"Yeah. You grew up here. You're adorbs. You have personality to spare. I think you'd make a great Miss Corn Husk. I will warn you, that costume is scratchier than bathing in a bale of hay, but it's an honor to be selected. I'd like the honor to be yours this year—if you want it."

"Oh my gosh! I would totally want that. I know it's crazy —wanting to be Miss Corn Husk in a town as small as ours. But you've always worn that sash and crown. And I always watched you every year, thinking how amazing it must feel to ride down Main Street as Miss Corn Husk."

"It's special alright—and itchy. Don't forget itchy."

"How do you know I'll get it?"

"Well, let's just say Mrs. Shaller has always had a huge say in the outcome. And she wanted Jimmy … Well, let's just leave it at that. Anyway, if I tell her I am nominating you, I'm pretty sure that will make you a shoo-in. And you deserve it. She'll surely see that."

"I'm so honored!" Riley puts her hand over her heart.

"I'm so happy you want to carry on my legacy. You have no idea."

"Thank you, Ella Mae. You're the best."

The door to the shop opens and shuts, and of course, Chris St. James walks in. He looks preoccupied as he approaches the counter. His eyes scan the room and lock on mine.

"Well, I'd better get back to work," Riley says.

"Yeah," I answer Riley, my eyes still caught up in Chris' stare.

"Can I get you anything besides that water?" Riley asks.

"I'm good. Thanks," I say, breaking eye contact with Chris to look at Riley.

Riley follows my line of vision when I look back at Chris, and in a conspiratorial voice, she says, "I loved the live you did with him. I'm all for team #ChellaMaeBae."

I chuckle. "Yeah. Well, don't believe everything you see on social media, Riley."

She smiles and walks toward Chris to take his order while I take a long sip of my water and wait to see what he'll do next.

CHAPTER 20

Chris

WELL, this is either highly convenient, or about to be a massive train wreck.

I take my coffee from Madeline, pop a five dollar bill in the tip jar, and slowly turn to check whether Ella Mae is still looking at me. She is. Our eyes meet again, and for some reason, neither of us looks away.

I walk slowly toward her table, as if I'm looking for somewhere to sit, not like I'm planning to join her. At the last minute, I turn toward Ella Mae.

"Ella Mae."

"Chris."

"Water?" I tip my head toward her drink.

"With lemon."

"Coffee?" She tips her chin toward the hand holding my coffee.

"Yep."

She stares at me, a look of challenge in her eyes, like she's daring me to sit, or talk, or leave, or do a dance in the middle of the room. Anything I do will be a win for her because she's daring me with her gaze.

I lift my eyebrows once, not making a move. Daring her in return.

I dare you to ask me to join you.

I dare you to wipe my mouth again.

What? No. I don't dare you to do that.

All this teasing from my friends is making me crazy.

"Want to sit, Soldier? Or do you plan on standing guard all afternoon?"

Well, if I wanted a segue, she sure handed me one on a platter.

"I might just stand guard."

"Suit yourself."

She takes a sip of her water, looking at me over the rim of her glass. Her bright blue eyes sparkle. She's not wearing fake lashes or thick eyeliner today. She's got this whole girl-next-door thing going for her—worn T-shirt, jean shorts, even Converse.

I'm a fan of this look on her. Not that I'm a fan of hers. Objectively, she looks great. That's all. Speaking as a guy, admiring a nice looking woman, not as Chris looking at Ella Mae, specifically. Whatever.

"I can stand guard while we talk." I pause to gauge her reaction. "If you want."

She tips her head toward the seat across from her.

I nod and slide into the chair, setting my coffee in front of me and crossing my arms over my chest.

I just came from Aiden's house.

When I got on Instagram last night, I never expected to see what I saw. The sheer volume of comments about me was overwhelming. It felt like that time my costume pants fell down during the class play in fourth grade, and instead of being the woodcutter, I stood on the stage of Bordeaux Elementary with my yellow boxers exposed for all to see.

No one cared if the Big Bad Wolf was about to eat Little

Red Riding Hood when my little yellow boxers stole the show. I've never been a fan of all-eyes-on-Chris, let alone, all-eyes-on-Chris when he looks like a half-dressed version of the man in the yellow hat from Curious George—assuming his commitment to yellow goes all the way to his undergarments.

Whenever Duke runs out of things to tease me about, he'll bring up that memory. *Hey Chris, flashed any crowds your golden undies lately?* Or *Chris, I'm in the market for some new underwear. Know where I can get some the color of a school bus? You know, something that says, yield, or caution in the bedroom?*

Don't feel too badly for me. I have plenty of ammo to use on Duke too. And I don't hesitate to use it when the time's right.

But it wasn't the number of comments on Ella Mae's posts, or the way people were saying they wanted us to date that got to me.

It's this one guy.

There's more than one guy commenting on every post about how beautiful Ella Mae is, proposing things they'd like to do with her, or trying to get her to respond to them.

I noticed she never does answer those types of comments. She lets the flattery or advances sit there unattended. I respect that.

But this one guy, beefitupfitnessdude, seems to be more aggressive in his efforts than most of the others. He's obsessed. What's most concerning is the pattern of progression. He's escalating.

So, I went to Aiden's to see what he thinks. After he did a little teasing of me for being on Instagram at all, and then taunted me as to why I'm so interested in Ella Mae, I was able to convince him I'm just concerned for her safety. Aiden and I both work in the cyber world.

I'm employed by the Department of Defense. The restrictions of my position make it so I can't just go fishing into anyone's background. I *could*. But I also could get into a heap of trouble, and maybe even lose my position if anyone found out. So, the next best thing is to get my best friend to go digging for me. He'd never let anyone know I asked him. And this way, I'll know what's going on at a root level with this guy who's giving off stalker-vibes.

Aiden can hunt and remain undetected.

So, he did.

We found this guy's IP address. An IP address identifies a network or device on the internet. Every interaction online has a source and the IP address is like a physical street address, only it's online.

And we found it. The follower who keeps making inappropriate comments to Ella Mae lives here in Ohio. We saw his city, zip code, and area code. Looks like he's somewhere in the Columbus area. Just our luck. It would be nice if he were in somewhere like Greenland, or Antartica.

Needless to say, I'm concerned.

"Why are you looking at me like that, Soldier?" Ella Mae asks.

"Like what?"

"Like you want to smash something—hopefully not me."

"I don't want to smash you."

I smirk.

Ella Mae knows I don't want to smash her. She's just doing what she does. Trying to get a rise out of me.

"Okay. So, what's up?"

"I saw the comments on your posts from last week."

"Oh? And how did you see those?"

She's smiling, looking up at me through her lashes.

"I um … I got online."

"On Instagram?"

"Yep."

"With an account?"

"I got on. Okay? And I saw the comments."

"People love you, Soldier. You could even start an account. Do fitness stuff. Film yourself working out. Share some tips. You'd get so many followers."

"Not a goal of mine."

I take a sip of coffee, trying to buy myself some time and figure out how to broach this subject with her.

I set my cup back down. "Lots of guys say things to you."

"They do."

She looks the opposite of rattled.

"They all comment about your looks, and say they want to go out with you ..."

"Does that bother you?"

"Why would it bother me?"

"Just asking. I mean, you seem bothered."

"I'm not. But there's one guy I wanted to ask you about."

She looks at me and raises one eyebrow in another dare.

I plow forward. "That guy, beefitupfitnessdude. He's pretty out of line."

"Says you."

"Yeah. Says me. I noticed he's ramping it up over time. What do you usually do about guys like that?"

"I might block them—I try not to. They're good for gathering comments and a little drama, which never hurts."

Drama never hurts? I'd beg to differ on that one.

"Why haven't you blocked him?"

"I'm actually thinking about it. He's been a little extra. You know? Like he wants to rub my feet—which face it, from the right guy would be amazeballs, but from a creepy guy I never met ... no thanks. He's said things that would be sweet if we knew one another. But we don't. So, I told Meg I'd block him. I will."

"Go ahead."

"What?"

"Go ahead and block him."

"Bossy much?"

"I'm just concerned, Ella Mae. I'm trained to look for danger. This guy gives me all the warning signals. You need to block him."

Ella Mae leans forward, so her face is halfway across the table. She lifts her well-manicured hand and points at me.

"You don't get to tell me who to block on my account. Just because we ate a meal together doesn't make you my guardian angel or personal bodyguard. I've been doing this for years. You don't think I've had creepy guys along for the ride the whole time? I have. I know how to handle this. I don't need some overgrown, hot, muscly guy acting like he's my new wall of defense."

Her finger remains pointed at my face.

Hot? She thinks I'm hot?

Not important.

CHAPTER 21

Ella Mae

I STARE CHRIS DOWN, my finger aimed at his face. I don't need someone man-splaining how stalking escalates or what I need to do to protect myself on social media—especially not a man who just got on Instagram for the first time this week.

"I looked up some stats," Chris says, talking around my pointer finger, and looking me straight in the eyes.

I study that green around his iris. My gaze drops to those lips. They're so beautifully carved and defined. Manly lips. Firm, but full. And then I drag my focus to his jawline. He didn't shave today. He's still clean-cut. God forbid he'd be disheveled for once. But that slight shadow along his jawline looks like he's possibly considering growing in a beard. His stubble's a bit darker than the sandy-blond hair sticking out from under his backwards ball cap.

Why does this man have to be so attractive and simultaneously so infuriating?

Chris continues his infomercial about online predators.

"If an influencer appears to be in a relationship, the incidences of stalking decrease greatly. It's human nature. Men are less likely to pursue a woman they think is committed to another man."

"Not every man backs off so easily," I say shrewdly.

I've been around long enough to know. Besides, both Chris and I are well aware of what it's like to witness the ugly fallout of a love triangle. Some men don't know when to back off.

Chris stares at me. A world of unspoken understanding passes between us.

"True. Not every man backs off when he should. But an obvious romantic relationship does tend to dissuade guys from pursuing a woman online if they think there's another guy who might come after them if they do."

"Your point?"

"You need to give the illusion that you aren't available."

"But I am available."

"An illusion, Ella Mae. You need to convince your followers you are in a relationship so these creeps will back down."

"And how do you suggest I go about doing that, Soldier?"

I take another sip of water, pretty sure I know where he's going with this, but needing him to be the one to spell it out.

"You should make it appear like you have a boyfriend."

"And how will I do that?"

"Have someone pose as your boyfriend. Go on social media together. Post pictures of the two of you that look believably romantic."

"Did you have someone specifically in mind?"

I stare at him, half sure of what he'll say, yet doubting he ever would go that far to ensure my safety.

"I'd do it. If you don't have anyone else in mind."

I nearly do a spit take of my last sip of water. But somehow, I'm able to keep my drink in my mouth and swallow slowly enough to regain my composure.

Did Chris St. James just say he'd fake being my boyfriend online so that my over-the-top, slightly obsessed followers would chill out?

I pause, holding his gaze. Then I say, "If you want to date me, just ask me out, Big Boy."

I wink and look over at Chris through my lashes. He's almost visibly squirming. It's delectable.

"Is that what it would take?"

He's dead serious, his face an unreadable mask, except this one little dent over his eyebrow I never noticed before. It makes him look more rugged or stern.

"I'm joking!" I tell him, letting him off the hook.

"I'm not," he says. "I said I'd be willing to pose as your boyfriend online, and I meant it. I'm trained to watch for danger. And this situation has me concerned."

"Obviously, if you're willing to ask me out. Those are some pretty drastic measures, even for you."

"It would be a farce. For your safety. I'm offering, and I think you should consider the offer. "

"No need. Sheesh. I'm telling you. I think you might benefit from some lavender essential oil. I wish I had some in my purse. You could put it on your pulse points. It would relax you. Maybe you should also drink some passion flower chamomile tea. Yes! That's definitely on tap for you."

Chris scrunches up his face like a child being forced to eat brussels sprouts with a side of mushrooms.

"I don't need any of that woo-woo stuff."

Chris takes a sip of his coffee and sits quietly, studying me.

After a minute or so of not-so-comfortable silence, he says, "At least block him."

He's got this pleading look in his eyes, like he truly cares about what happens to me. I know better. Chris is a hero—the type of guy that runs into situations that don't concern him just to save the day. He sees what he thinks is danger, and he wants to rescue me. I could be anyone in this scenario. It just happens to be me he's targeted as the distressed damsel du jour.

"Fine. I'll block beefitupfitnessdude. But only because I told Meg I would, not because you're getting bossy."

"Good."

"Great."

I pull out my phone and it buzzes with a notification.

"What's that?" Chris asks.

It's kind of adorable how much of a neanderthal he is when it comes to social media.

"It's a notification. It means someone messaged me on Instagram."

Chris nods, but I can tell he's holding back from saying something.

"Got something you want to say?"

"Who messaged you?"

"Oh my gosh! You are so nosy." I tease him.

I look down. Great. It's from beefitupfitnessdude. I almost want to fake that it's someone else and deal with this when Chris isn't watching me like a hawk.

"It's him," I say, handing my phone over to Chris.

I may as well let him read what the guy wrote. He'll ask to see it anyway.

Chris reads the message aloud. "Hey, Ella Mae. I've been waiting for the right time to reach out to you. I think I recognize that Big Boy where you ate with that guy, Chris. If I'm right, it's near Columbus. I didn't want to say anything on your posts since I know you're private about your location. I appreciate you being that way. You don't want guys inappropriately reaching out to you. I don't either.

"I just want you to know I'm in that area. What's the likelihood? I've been telling you how good we'd be together. I know you don't answer me on the post threads because you don't want to expose our connection to everyone. I respect that.

"Just answer me here and we can make plans privately. I want to treat you like the queen you are. You are so beautiful. I can't stop thinking about you. When you answer, I'll tell you my real name. Meanwhile, check out my latest post. I made it just for you."

Chris looks up from my phone and his face looks—dangerous. Not that he's a threat to me, but man, oh man. He's got this whole protective vibe going that is hotter than hot.

I'm not one to let a man defend me. I've been taking care of myself on my own my whole life, thank you very much. And, as Mom says, *If you never count on a man, then they won't be able to let you down*. I know that's her baggage, but there's some sage wisdom tucked in between her unfinished business.

If I were into that whole hot gladiator thing, Chris would be so doing it for me right now. An image of sweaty Chris, shirtless, wearing one of those Roman belt things with dangly scraps of leather and metal studs flashes in my mind. His face is fierce, and he's roaring while he stands over beefitupfitnessdude with a sword outstretched toward his opponent's neck. The sun gleams off Chris' rippling muscles. He's the epitome of masculinity, defending my honor and saving me from online trolls.

Nope. No gladiators for this girl.

Definitely not the angry gladiator across the table from me, wearing a backward ball cap and a too-tight white T-shirt. I almost see steam pouring out his ears.

"Down, boy. This is just a message. I am blocking him. Watch me." I add a joke to diffuse some of the tension wafting off Chris. "I mean, you should see the messages I get from foreign princes."

"What? What messages?"

Oh. I forgot Chris is a newb when it comes to social media. I flash him my phone to confirm that beefitupfitness-dude is officially blocked.

He smiles.

Then I pull up a message from some random guy posing as a prince and read it to Chris.

"Elllozzzz, my beauty beautiful queen. You are so fine to look at. I wish you all the prosperity this glorious day. I want to tell you I have many fine things. And those are all for you. Even the 5,000 dollars a month you can spend any way you like. You are meant to be my queen. Only say the word, my beauty. Have a highly beneficial day!"

I look up, a big smile on my face. I'm lightly chuckling until I meet Chris' stony glare.

"Guys send you this kind of stuff?"

"Chris. Oh my gosh. This may not even be a guy. I mean, look at his picture."

I tap the profile and a photo fills the screen of a middle-aged man with a poodle and a bouquet of roses. He's sitting outside in front of a yacht.

"He looks like a guy to me."

"This is just some random picture." I explain like I'm teaching preschool. "Look."

I show him the other photos. The same man posing in front of a sports car. Another one of him sipping wine somewhere near an ocean.

"These aren't photos of the guy sending that message, I'm sure. And who says, *Elllozzzz?* What even is that?"

I can't help but laugh.

"Did you block him too?"

I don't want to even give Chris the satisfaction, but for some reason, I have mercy on the man.

"Yes. I blocked him. But I saved the message because it makes me laugh."

Chris nods, satisfied that I'm not being hotly pursued by a foreign prince.

"I sure could use that five K a month, though," I joke.

"Who couldn't? Maybe I need to find a foreign prince."

"Right? He'd treat you so well with all his fine things. They would give you prosperity on this fine day."

"So beneficial," Chris jokes back.

Oh, girls. If you could see this man smile. I can't even. It's so rare when he lets one loose. My goodness. Women would be in danger of spontaneous ovary combustion if they saw that smile up close.

I'm doubly relieved because Chris seems to have regained his sense of humor. All this talk of stalkers was bringing too much negativity into my day.

CHAPTER 22

Chris

MY PHONE IS SITTING on the kitchen counter ringing when I come in from mowing the back yard. I grab it. Aiden's calling.

"Hey, Aiden. What's up?"

"Do you have a minute?"

"Yeah, sure."

"It's about our little surveillance project."

"Our what?"

I walk to the fridge and pull out a cold bottle of water. Holding the phone between my ear and my shoulder, I twist the cap off and take a long pull. *Surveillance project?*

"You know, the favor you asked me to do because you can't do it?"

"Oh. Yeah. Yeah." *Ella Mae*. "What about it?"

"Well, I was fiddling around after you told me Ella Mae blocked that guy. It's sort of addicting knowing I can keep tabs on him. I did some gray hat hacking. Do you want to know what that entailed?"

"No. I definitely don't. It's best if I can claim ignorance if any of this ever comes to light."

"It won't. I'm not messing with the guy. And I know how to cover my tracks. But I can see every keystroke from his home computer now. And that's why I'm calling."

When I approached Aiden, I told him everything about what I do. He's the first person to whom I've fully disclosed that I work for the Department of Defense. I had no choice but to come clean. Aiden needed to know why I couldn't be the one hacking into this guy's internet fingerprint.

"What did you find?"

"Well, only a few hours after you told me Ella Mae blocked this guy, I saw that he got onto Instagram again—and he's using a different account name. It's one she hasn't blocked because she obviously doesn't know it's him."

"What's the name of the new account?"

"I'll send it to you." Aiden chuckles.

"What?"

"It's just ..." he laughs some more.

I wait. Aiden keeps almost regaining composure and then laughing again.

Finally, he says, "ImSOBeefy."

"His account is I'm so beefy?"

"Yep. And the *so* is capitalized. You know, in case his beefiness level were up for debate. Well, that capital SO settles it. He's SO beefy."

"Man." I chuckle.

Ella Mae's got a winner on her hands. Winner winner chicken dinner. Or beef dinner, in this case.

Aiden laughs some more. "Obviously confidence is not this guy's issue."

"Who knows what his issue is. He just needs to stay away from Ella Mae, that's all I know."

"I still find it intriguing that you're so invested in keeping her safe."

"Loyalty, Duty, Respect, Selfless Service, Honor, Integrity, and Personal Courage," I recite.

"What is all that?"

"It's our values—the Army core values. I might be discharged, but once a soldier, forever a soldier. I spent countless hours memorizing those values and their meanings, and learning the importance of living them out in everything I do. Selfless service. That's all this is. She's a citizen in danger. I'm a soldier. It boils down to that."

"I'm sure it does, Soldier. Her legs in a mini-skirt, and the way she challenges you have nothing to do with it whatsoever, right?"

"Right. Absolutely right."

"Well, carry on, Captain St. James."

I can almost imagine Aiden mock-saluting me. Not that he ridicules my time in the service or my devotion to the values I learned. He's just doing what we do—irreverently teasing one another.

At least Aiden got my rank right. Duke's forever promoting and demoting me, or changing me from a commissioned officer to non-commissioned status simply by calling me Lieutenant, or Sarge, or Major General.

"Keep an eye on the situation with this guy, would you? I know it's a lot to ask of you. What you're doing isn't exactly above board."

"I'm not a soldier, but you know I'm a sucker for someone in need of a little help. I'd hate to see something happen to Ella Mae. I'll keep you posted if anything looks suspicious."

"Thanks."

"And Chris?"

"Yeah?"

"Think the CIA might want to hire me as a spy?"

"I'm pretty sure that'd be a hard no."

"Really?"

The note of disappointment in Aiden's voice makes him sound like a pouty child who missed his nap.

"Yeah. I'm ninety-nine percent certain they're not looking for small-town hobby goat farmers with an IT consulting business to sign on as agents. And trust me, government work isn't nearly as glamorous as 007 makes it look."

"MacIntyre … Aiden MacIntyre," Aiden says in a very Sean-Connery-as-James-Bond style voice.

I chuckle.

"I've always wanted to say that," he says.

"Welp. Now you did."

Aiden and I hang up. On my way to the shower, I fight the urge to hop in my car and drive to Ella Mae's to tell her about *I'mSOBeefy*. Not that I'm so beefy. Well, I am. But I'm not headed to Ella Mae's to tell her that.

I want to warn her about this guy. The fact that he made another account and started following her again shows a concerning level of persistence on his part. But considering the way Ella Mae's hackles were up about my suggestions yesterday, I'll wait. Better to watch this guy behind the scenes, and then step in when she can clearly see I'm right. Not that I want to be right. This is one instance where I'd love to be proven very wrong.

I put Ella Mae out of my mind—mostly. I've got errands to run today. First stop, Mom and Dad's.

I take the route that happens to pass Ella Mae's home on the drive toward my parents' neighborhood.

Is that the town fire truck?

It looks like … Davis.

Is he uncoiling the hose?

Is that smoke coming from Ella Mae's or the neighbor's?

Other trucks and cars pass me, pull up in front of the house, and park. Men are jumping out of vehicles quickly. I park a few houses down and hop out of my pickup.

A small plume of smoke is wafting off the front porch of Ella Mae's home.

In theory, civilians should avoid stepping into any official situation. Any time a civilian gets in the mix, it enhances the danger and makes it harder for those trained to be involved to get their job done. But I'm not the average civilian. And, this is Ella Mae.

By the time I reach the yard, Meg is running frantically back and forth in front of the house. Davis and the other firefighters, EJ and Mack, have started spraying a stream of water across the porch. Whatever fire there was is out, and the residual smoke makes the fire look more dramatic than it probably was. A charred black spot remains where they are spraying one spot of the porch.

"Where's Ella Mae?" I ask.

Meg points to a spot on the curb where Ella Mae is sitting with Champ, another one of the firefighters. Her head is down, and it looks like he's checking her vitals.

I don't even stop to think. I run toward Ella Mae and Champ and plop down next to her on the curb. A confused look passes over her face. I look up at Champ.

"Her vitals are fine. She was outdoors. She got off the porch pretty quickly and the fire was small."

"What happened?" I ask Ella Mae.

Champ says, "Neighbor called to report fire coming off the front porch."

I look at Ella Mae.

She smiles a sheepish grin. "I was filming myself doing salamba shirshasana."

"You were filming *what*?"

"Salamba shirshasana. It's a headstand in yoga."

"Why didn't you just say a headstand?"

Ella Mae might be experiencing shock, but she's still able to dish out the sass. She spears me with a look.

"It's not just any ol' headstand, Soldier. It's more beautiful. And it requires more strength. It's a part of my yoga practice. Anyway, I had candles out on the porch to set the ambiance for my live."

"You were filming yourself doing a headstand? And let me guess, thousands were watching?"

"Yes." She rolls her eyes. "Only around nine thousand, but yes, people were watching. All of a sudden, I saw a large rat or a squirrel or a small rodent of some sort come skittering across the porch.

"He knocked into a few of the candles, and I think my scream scared him, which sent him bolting in the other direction. A few candles fell onto my mat. I didn't know what to do. I tried picking the mat up to shake it out, but it was already on fire and the flames were climbing up it. And this other candle caught a corner of the welcome mat on fire. It was all happening so fast, so I dropped the mat and ran off the porch, still screaming. Meg was in the garden in the back yard. She heard my screams and ran around front. By then, the flames were higher. The neighbor ran out of his house saying he called Davis. And then all the firemen showed up and started spraying everything."

Champ clears his throat. "Are you feeling alright now, Ella Mae?"

"Yes. I think so," she says. "But could you stand on the other side of me, behind Chris, so the house is behind you?"

Champ looks confused, but he does what Ella Mae asks and walks around so he's behind me.

Before Champ or I have a chance to figure out what's going on, Ella Mae brandishes her phone and snaps a selfie, making the duck face and everything, with the smoke drifting off the porch in the background.

"Thanks, Champ! I needed that shot to show my peeps."

"Seriously, Ella Mae? You nearly burn your house down

and you're taking selfies?" I can't help myself. I have to question her.

"Relax, Soldier. I didn't burn the house down."

Her voice has a topnote of bravado, but I hear the quaver beneath her words. Ella Mae's shaken up. She just doesn't want me to know it.

"Hey," I say quietly to her while Champ walks over to talk to the other firefighters.

"What?"

"I'm glad you're okay."

Ella Mae looks into my eyes. She drops her guard for a moment. Her whole expression softens and her fear shows through. I don't know what comes over me, but I wrap my arm around her shoulder and tug her to me.

Then I ask a question I never thought would exit my mouth. "Did you catch the headstand on film?"

"You know I did!" She's full of her usual spunk, but her body softens into a slump and she nearly whispers, "I'm so stupid."

I'm quiet. She's not stupid. Far from it.

I know better than to speak up when she's finally confiding in me. I wait.

"I set my house on fire. Who does that?"

"You want my thoughts on this?"

Ella Mae looks at me. "Why not? I'm going to hear about this from everyone for months anyway—maybe even years."

"You're not stupid, Ella Mae. You're pretty smart, actually. You started your own business. You support yourself with this … stuff you do. You're not stupid. A bit misguided at times? Maybe. But you're definitely not stupid."

I pause, waiting for her to jump on me and argue. When she doesn't, I say, "You'll find your way. We all do. Well, not all of us, but I believe you will."

"Thanks." She tilts her head and smiles up at me.

"Anytime."

Ella Mae gives me this impish grin and then she says, "You can take your hands off me now, Soldier."

I look over. My arm is still around her shoulder. It's not like I didn't know, but it felt so … natural. I just forgot.

I drop my arm.

Once I'm sure Ella Mae and Meg are alright, I take off for my parents house. I turn up the radio to drown out my thoughts. No use trying to make sense of why I seem to be drawn into Ella Mae's orbit lately.

Some things are better left alone.

Fab-U-lous_EllaMae

Oh, my peeps!

You know those days when you're just doing salamba shirshasana on your front porch and some runaway rodent knocks your ambient candles over so you end up setting your porch just a teensie-weensie on fire?

No? Just me.
Yeah. Well ... so ... *THAT* happened.

Thankfully I have amazeballs neighbors. And our town, being as small as it is, shouldn't have such a big fire team, but well, let's say certain people had repeated needs for some dousing over the years. Truly yours included now. ❤

If you want to see the yoga practice in full BEFORE I scorched the porch ... check out the photos in my yoga post. And yes, Chris did happen to show up to lend me a shoulder to lean on. Shoulders! Those shoulders. I can attest that the nickname "Mr. Shoulders" fits him to a T ... because can he fill out a T or what?

Friendly shoulders, girls. Nothing else going on there.
Comment below with your most embarrassing moment.
And don't forget to put the YOU in Fab-YOU-lous today and,

maybe keep a fire extinguisher handy in case your version of fabulous is smokin' hot like mine apparently was today.

COMMENTS:
1143 Comments

@allthatsazz: So crazy, girlie!! Be safe. Love your yoga moves.

@always_wearing_prada_gurrrll: I would have freaked out like nobody's business. A fire! No more candles for you, missy. And yassss. That man. Drool.

> **@Fab-U-lous_EllaMae:** Agreed. No more mixing candles and yoga, for SURE.

@EllaMaeFan4ever: So glad you're safe! Hope your house is okay.

> **@Fab-U-lous_EllaMae:** Thanks! Kisses! Looks like it's only the porch, thankfully.

@youdoyouboooo: Candles and yoga – that's a no-go for me. But glad you're safe.

@ImSOBeefy: How can you still be so beautiful after enduring such an ordeal. Well, easy. It's you. But babe, that guy again? I sure hope he's your brother. I don't like sharing. I know you understand me. Let's meet up. I'll kiss your boo-boos.

@KeepingItFabu: Totally did this … not this, but yeah. Set my house on fire using a wok once. Grabbed the extinguisher and sprayed like a madman. That white stuff was everywhere. End of the day, I ruined my beef and broccoli and our stove top. But everything else survived.

CHAPTER 23

Ella Mae

FOR THE NEXT WEEK, it's like I have a shadow named Chris St. James. I get it. The fire was scary, even though it was small. In hindsight, I really was stupid. I probably could have stomped it out, or turned on the garden hose and sprayed it. But I freaked out, and my brain locked up. It all happened so fast: Skittering critters. Tipping candles. Flames in more than one location.

These daily appearances of Chris' aren't even stealth. He will "just happen" to show up in front of the house, or at the coffee shop, or around town wherever I am to check up on me. He always asks, *How are you, Ella Mae?* with this sincere look that cuts through all my layers and wraps around my heart. I tell him I'm fine. Then I make a joke, or ask him if he has nothing better to do than follow me around like a stray dog. He either lingers or leaves. I'm not sure if I'm annoyed, flattered, or just confused.

And now, my big, burly shadow is just beyond our front porch doing whatever he has to do to replace the burnt floorboards. I guess he's a handyman? I don't know. I've seen him doing odd jobs around town. I get the feeling he does something else too, but it's obvious the details of his life are kept intentionally hidden, at least from me they are.

The owners of the house said their insurance covers the repair. They informed me they hired someone to come this week. And, there he is. Right outside my front room window, bright and early this morning, his shirt stretching over his muscles as he saws wood he has placed over two sawhorses in the front yard.

I'm doing yoga. Not filming. I'm still a little rattled. Not that I'd tell anyone besides Meg. I've apologized to her at least a hundred times. She finally put an apology jar on the counter, saying, *If you apologize again, you have to drop a dollar in the jar for every 'I'm sorry' out of your mouth.*

Meg walks into the front room and looks out the window. "I've seen worse views first thing in the morning."

"Are you ogling Chris?"

"Not exactly. Joe has my heart. But admit it, Chris is someone you can't easily ignore. I'm just appreciating his hard work."

"What hard work is that?"

"All the effort he obviously puts in to stay in peak condition."

"That's so objectifying." I chuckle.

"Okay. And, he seems to be doing a very good job measuring and cutting boards."

"As if you'd know."

Meg yawns and places the back of her hand over her mouth. "I have to get ready for work. Make sure Chris has what he needs."

"And what do you mean by that?"

"You know. Like if he needs food or something to drink, or has to use the restroom while he's here."

I stare at Meg. "His house is only a few blocks away."

"Be neighborly. That's all I'm saying."

"The man has practically shown up everywhere I've been all week."

"That's sweet, right?"

"In a way, I guess. But it's also a bit much."

"You don't even know when a guy's into you."

"He's so not into me—at all. He's just a hero on a mission. And I guess I'm grateful he's looking out for me, but it's also …"

"Also?"

"Suffocating."

"I don't know why you wouldn't want a man like that to suffocate you."

"What? That's just weird."

"Okay. Yeah. It is. What I mean is, you don't always have to be the only one on team Ella Mae. Let some other people care for you sometimes. I think it's sweet that Chris is popping up all over town checking on you. Why can't you just let it be what it is. Stop trying to make it into this awful, annoying thing. What woman wouldn't want a man like that purposely crossing her path all day long? If I weren't with Joe, I'd say, sign me up."

"There's so much wrong with what you just said, I can't even. But yeah. I'll try to see it as sweet."

If it weren't so confusing.

But it's not really confusing. I meant what I said to Meg. Even if she doesn't want to see it, this is a classic case of a hero latching onto someone he thinks needs saving. Cut and dry. Nothing more.

Meg's and my attention shifts as Chris sets down the saw and walks up onto the porch. His knock causes Meg to wiggle her fingers at me and hightail it up the stairs in her matching pj tank and bottoms, leaving me to answer the door.

Chris rubs the back of his arm across his brow.

"Hey."

His voice is deeper and more rumbly in the morning. It sends an unwelcome chill through me. A visceral reaction, that's all that is. There's nothing like a raw, manly voice to set the hairs on my arms and the back of my neck on edge—in a way that isn't so awful. But it is awful. It's Chris, after all.

"What can I do for you, Soldier?"

Chris' eyes scan my outfit. I'm wearing hot pink yoga pants that have a lace panel up the side of each leg. My feet are bare, and conveniently, my toenail polish matches the pants. I have on a hot pink, white, and lavender flowered, cropped yoga top that's form fitted. Chris lifts his eyes to meet mine.

I cock an eyebrow.

Yeah, Soldier. You're so busted.

"Um. Could I … uh. Could I use your restroom?"

I stand back and wave Chris in with the gesture of a butler. "In the back, off the kitchen."

He toes off his boots, which earns brownie points, and also reminds me he's a grown man who lives alone, taking care of a house, cooking, cleaning, doing all the adulting. Something about that makes me see him differently. Maybe even admire him a little.

Meg comes down carrying her satchel for work. That woman can shower and dress faster than Superman changes from Clark Kent.

"What's with guys who have *Beefy* in their username?" she asks as she heads toward the kitchen.

"What do you mean?" I ask, following her.

She pulls cereal out of the pantry, opens the fridge, grabs the milk, and turns to pull a bowl down when Chris steps out of the half-bath and into the kitchen.

She gasps. "Oh! Chris! I didn't know you were in here! You scared me!"

"Sorry," I say. "I was listening to whatever you were saying about beefy guys. I forgot to tell you he came in."

"Anyway," Meg continues, as if Chris isn't here. "You and the beefy guys."

"What?"

I look over at Chris. He's leaning against the door jamb, his arms crossed across his chest like he's got all day, and like whatever Meg has to say is his business too. It's not.

"Don't you have a job to do?" I ask him.

"I'm on break," he says to me, a smirk on his face. "What were you saying, Meg?"

"I was saying Ella Mae's got some guys on her account that are always crossing the line in their comments. Ironically, two of them have *beefy* in their username. Crazy, huh?"

Chris has that look again—the dangerous one. "Someone's bugging you again?" he asks.

"No one's bugging me."

"It should bug you," Meg says. "I think you've gotten numb to it. Right after you blocked beefitupfitnessdude this new guy shows up: ImSOBeefy. Who even names themselves something like that?"

"He's harmless," I say.

"How do you know?" Chris asks.

"We've been over this before," I warn him. "You aren't my personal online bodyguard. I've got this."

"I say, block the beef!" Meg shouts.

Chris chuckles. "Yeah. Block the beef, Ella Mae."

I shake my head.

Meg's phone buzzes in her satchel.

"That's my cue to head to work," Meg says. "Be good you two."

As if anything would go on between me and the soldier.

The snick of the front door causes the air in the kitchen to suddenly feel slightly compressed and warm. I look over at

Chris. He's still leaning on the doorframe like a model for Hot Guy in Doorway magazine. I seriously need a subscription to that, and pronto. And here I was chiding Meg for objectifying him.

"Are you ..."

"Do you ..."

We both speak at the same time.

"Go ahead," he says, tipping his chin in that way guys do.

"I was going to ask if you do home repairs for a living now. I honestly don't know what you do besides being an unpaid bodyguard."

He chuckles, drops his arms, and runs a hand through his hair.

All.the.moves. He's got them all. It's a darn shame. A man who looks like him and has those moves without even trying to muster them should be nicer, or less ... Chris. Not that he hasn't been nice, lately. Oddly, he mostly has.

"I do some odd jobs around town when needed."

"And then you live the secret billionaire life the rest of the time?"

"Exactly. I'm secretly a billionaire." He winks. Then his voice drops to a quiet, raspy rumble. "I hope my secret's safe with you."

He ends that little display with a brow quirk. And ... that's my cue to leave.

"Well, I've got posts to answer and things to do. Show yourself out, mkay? And help yourself to whatever while you're here working. You don't have to knock. Just come get water, or there's stuff in the fridge. And use the restroom. Whatever."

I finish babbling and gesturing around at the fridge, and the bathroom, and the faucet. And then I turn and leave the kitchen. The sound of Chris' amused chuckle follows me up the stairs.

CHAPTER 24

Chris

WAS THAT FLIRTING? I wouldn't know. I don't even know if *I* was flirting, let alone whether Ella Mae was. I'm sure she wasn't. It's Ella Mae. And I'm me. Yeah. We just play our version of verbal tennis. That's all that was—sparring, because we both love to have the upper hand in situations.

I picture Alex, Duke, and Aiden standing in a line, mocking me. Why not throw Trevor, Rob, and Grant into that peanut gallery? A man who doesn't know if someone's flirting—that's what I've become.

Ever since the fire last week, I've felt an extra layer of concern for Ella Mae. She puts on a great act. Always has. But I saw her eyes when she let me close to her on that curb. And she was scared. I just want to make sure she's moving past the incident and not carrying around unnecessary guilt—hypocrite that I am. But my guilt isn't unnecessary. Both Alex and my mom are living testaments to my reckless decisions and selfish choices.

I glance around the kitchen. On the counter next to the sink there's a jar with a label that says, *No more apologies*. A few dollars sit at the bottom. I wonder what that's about.

I walk down the hall and out the front door, not wanting to encroach on Ella Mae's privacy more than I already have this week. But then I open my phone to the Instagram app as soon as I'm outside. Meg must have had a reason to mention ImSOBeefy.

I tap Ella Mae's account and flick through her posts, scanning the comments under each one. There are hundreds of comments. Nearly a thousand under the live of her doing yoga on the porch last week, and over a thousand under the one of her with me and Champ in front of the smoking house.

How does she keep up with all this—and more importantly, why? It's so draining. At least for me, it is. I feel the life being sucked out of me as I read comment after comment saying how amazing she is, or giving sympathy, or commenting on her body, or her looks.

I don't even realize how tight my jaw has gotten at first. I'm actually grinding my molars as I read some of the things these guys say to her. Who says this stuff to a total stranger? To anyone for that matter? Slimeballs.

The comment from ImSOBeefy on the yoga fire video jumps out at me. *Hey, babe. I hope you're okay. If you need a hero, I'm here for you.*

She doesn't need a hero. Especially not you, SOBeefy. And, babe? He doesn't get to call her babe. As usual, Ella Mae didn't answer him. It seems like her approach is to hope he'll take a hint if she ignores him. He's not taking the hint.

His next comment under the pic of me, Champ, and Ella Mae is, *That guy again? I sure hope he's your brother. I don't like sharing. I know you understand me. Let's meet up. I'll kiss your boo-boos.*

Uh. No. You won't kiss anything. And I'm not her brother. I'm her … Not relevant what I am. I'm *your* worst nightmare, that's all you need to know, BeefyDude.

I scroll through a few more comments. Each one is more

aggressive and forward. In one he says, *I'm so glad you're single. Keep some room in your life for me, Ella Mae.* Why don't these comments bother Ella Mae? The fact that this guy is actually beefitupfitnessdude, back again, unwavering in his pursuit, makes him more of a threat. Ella Mae needs to know.

I pace the porch, considering my options. Ella Mae's so quick to shut me down whenever it seems like I'm pushing her to take action on her own behalf. She's far too independent to take direction from me. So, I have to make this feel like it's her decision. She really should consider faking the appearance of a relationship. That would probably send a strong message to this creep.

All we'd have to do is post a few photos online together. She could say whatever kinds of things she says ... something ridiculous and over-the-top about how much she loves her boyfriend. That would send the message to all these guys, not just the meathead.

The air is getting warmer. I need to finish the work on the porch before it's too hot to be comfortable doing physical labor. Once I'm done, I'll figure out what to say.

It takes a few hours to cut out the burnt section of the porch and replace the framing, measure the replacement boards and secure them. I'll come back tomorrow to paint everything. I pack up my tools and throw them in the back of my truck. While I was working, I had a brainstorm. I'm hoping it will work.

Instead of going in to talk with Ella Mae, I drive into town and park in front of Dad's office. When I walk in, Shannon greets me. I haven't seen her in a few days.

"Hey, Chris. How are you?"

"Fine. Just doing a little work for the Graynors on their rental."

"Yeah. Meg told me about the fire fiasco."

"It was an accident. Could have happened to anyone."

"I know. I wasn't going to come down on her."

By her, we both know she means Ella Mae.

"Good."

My sister gives me a look that feels like she can read my mind. I sure hope not.

"How are you feeling?" I ask her.

"Why does everyone ask pregnant women that question?"

"I guess we just want to make sure you're okay."

"I'm great. I get a little queasy in the morning, but so far, so good."

"That's awesome."

The smile that takes over my face feels deeper than my usual grin. I'll admit, I can't wait to be an uncle.

"I'm going to tell Mom and Dad soon. Duke and I talked about it. It won't be fair if they hear our big news from someone else."

"Good call. I'd love to be there when you break the news."

"I'll make sure we tell you when we plan to go over there. Were you here to see Dad?"

"Actually, I want to talk to Meg for a minute. Is she with a client?"

"No. She's free. Let me tell her you're here."

Shannon stands up, walks past me, and heads behind the dividing wall between the reception area and the offices. I hear the knock on Meg's office door and the sound of their voices, and then Shannon returns to the waiting area telling me I can go on back.

I step into Meg's office, shutting the door behind me. I hope my hunch is right and coming here is a good call.

"What can I do for you, Chris?"

I get right to the point.

"It's about Ella Mae."

Meg looks at me with a knowing look. What she knows, I

can't tell. Maybe she could enlighten me. I've never been as confused as I have been in the past few weeks.

"May I?" I ask, pointing to a chair in front of Meg's desk.

"Sorry. Yes. Have a seat."

"So, here's the thing. I'm concerned."

I practiced what I want to say. I'm going to present this in a way that doesn't give away Aiden's identity, and doesn't reveal my profession.

Meg nods, indicating that I should go on.

"After that night Ella Mae and I were on her live together, I got on social media. I just wanted to see who was saying what about me after that evening we spent together."

"Makes sense."

"When I went on her page, I saw that BeefItUp guy's comments. They were over the line."

"That's what I kept telling her!"

Okay. Good to know.

"Well, I tried to tell Ella Mae to block him. She resisted, but she finally listened to me."

"You've got the magic touch when it comes to her, Chris. She wouldn't listen to anyone but you."

What? I have a magic touch? Hardly. Ella Mae fights me more than the town's rogue cow, Lulabelle, fights a team of men trying to get her into her trailer.

"Well, anyway. She listened to me, but I still thought that guy might be a threat. His comments escalated in intensity. He seemed to be more than a fan."

"A stalker, if you ask me," Meg says plainly.

"I don't use that term loosely, but yeah. Probably something of a stalker."

Meg nods.

"So, I have some friends who know how to track people."

Meg does this little bouncing thing in her seat. She actually rubs her hands together like she's excited. "And you got them to track this BeefItUp guy?"

"Basically."

"That's so hot. So amazing, I mean. I mean, that's … wow. I knew it!"

"What did you know?"

"Nevermind. That's so sweet of you, Chris. Looking out for Ella Mae like that."

"I'd do it for anyone."

"I'm sure you would."

She looks like she doesn't mean that. Whatever. I would do it for anyone.

"So, while my friend was monitoring BeefItUp, and Ella Mae blocked that account, he saw something. So, he called me. And he told me that BeefItUp started a new account."

"ImSOBeefy!"

"Bingo."

Go Meg. That was great deductive reasoning.

"I knew his creepy vibes were all too familiar," she says.

"Well, here's the thing. We could try to get Ella Mae to block ImSOBeefy. But obviously this guy is going to keep creating new accounts and following her under each one."

"Yeah," Meg says. "ImSirLoin, ItsTheFlank, HeresThe-Brisket, APoundofGround …"

I laugh. She keeps going. "TheMostPotRoast, RibEyeGuy, BoneInRumpRoast, RawhidePride …"

"Right," I say, cutting off Meg's recitation of all things beef. "So, blocking him isn't the answer, obviously."

"Obviously." Meg nods. "He's not going to give up. Blocking him doesn't keep him from coming back."

"I had made a suggestion to Ella Mae after I did some research on stalkers and online threats."

Meg looks at me, obviously ready to go all in on whatever suggestion I make.

"I told her she should give the impression that she's in a relationship. Stalkers or guys who make inappropriate comments on influencers' pages are less likely to do so when they perceive the influencer is committed to someone."

"But she shot you down?"

"Basically."

"Bet you're not used to that."

"To being told no?"

"To a woman saying she won't date you."

"How did you know I volunteered?"

Meg crosses her arms over her chest and looks at me from under a raised brow.

"Okay. I offered. Only because it makes sense. I'm available. I know the situation. I've already been in her posts."

"Makes perfect sense to me."

"Only, she said no. And you know her."

"She's stubborn."

"I was going to say independent."

"It's stubbornness. She's always so good about looking out for others. But when it comes to herself, she won't let anyone close enough to do the same for her."

Wow. I sensed it, but I thought it was about me. At least Meg sees how Ella Mae's always doing for others. It's surely not the thing she's known for around here, though it should be. Ella Mae's partly to blame for that. She acts so eccentric and over-the-top. She alienates people with that false persona. But if you look beyond all that surface stuff, she's got a giving heart.

"So, what do we do?" Meg asks.

"I need you to convince her to fake date me—just online. We'll take some photos. She'll post them. She can spin a story about how we got together, and she can convince her followers—especially these creepy guys—that she's taken."

"You'll have to post pictures of the two of you too. The

relationship will need to look corroborated if anyone goes digging."

She's right.

"I can do that."

I really, really don't want to post anything online. But if it means Ella Mae will be safe, I'll do whatever it takes.

"Okay," Meg says. "Are you free tonight?"

"Yeah. Why?"

"Come by after I get off work. I'll tell her I'm buying pizza to thank you for fixing the porch. I'll have Joe there too—to back us up. We'll do an intervention and get her to agree to fake dating you—or making it look like you two are together."

"You sound so sure she'll go along with this."

"I'm not even the least bit sure. But we'll give it our best shot."

CHAPTER 25

Ella Mae

"NO. JUST NO."

I cross my arms for emphasis.

"Ella Maaaaeee," Meg pleads from her spot across our living room. "You need to think this through."

I turn my eyes on Chris like twin laser beams. If I could set a man on fire with a glance, I'd do it right now. He's sitting adjacent to me in our overstuffed chair, looking a combination of guilty and self-righteous.

"I can't even believe you, St. James. You stalked a guy that follows me?"

"For your safety. And it's not stalking, really," he says. At least he has the decency to look a little contrite. "I wouldn't normally … Well, *I* didn't, technically."

"Right. Right. You had your henchman do your dirty work. Whatever. You were the mastermind behind this unnecessary sleuthing around. It's so humiliating. Like you don't think I can handle myself."

"That's not at all what this is, Ella Mae."

Chris' eyes meet mine, and it's like the whole world disappears, and it's just the two of us locked in this odd stare-down. Only he looks … compassionate, or concerned. Ugh. I hate when he pulls that soft, caring approach on me. It gets me every time.

"I'm not falling for that puppy dog thing you do with your eyes, Soldier. Just because you're able to make your face look like that doesn't mean I'm giving in."

"What does my face look like?" Chris asks, a playful smirk taking the place of the tenderhearted look that was there a moment ago.

"You know very well what it looks like. And it's not fair to use your charm to try to distract me."

His eyebrows waggle briefly, the corners of his eyes crinkling. But then his face softens again. He leans his elbows onto his knees and rests his chin in his hands as he tilts closer to me.

"I'm not saying you're not capable. You're more than able to handle your business. This situation concerned me. So I had a friend check into the guy. Now, we see he's come back under another account. If this happened to someone you know, what would you think?"

I'm quiet. Chris keeps his gaze on me. I take in his coarse sandy blond hair, the depth of his eyes, the scruff on his jaw. I was right. He's growing out his facial hair.

"I like the beard."

Chris chuckles.

Oh. I said that out loud.

"Good. Take some pictures with me and my beard. Tell your followers you like my beard. Didn't you say they love me? They are going to eat up our fake relationship. And my beard."

He lifts a hand and runs it over his jawline. He's totally not playing fair, and he knows it.

"Low blow, Soldier."

He's quiet. Calm. Waiting for me to make the next move.

Joe speaks up. He's been on the sideline, sitting next to Meg on our loveseat, holding her hand. The hand with his ring on it.

"Do you want my opinion, Ella Mae?"

He's asking. A man who respects me enough to ask. Maybe the soldier could take some notes from my roomie's fiance.

"I'd gladly entertain your opinion, Joe."

"I think making the impression that you have a boyfriend can't hurt, and it might help. And whenever something can't hurt and might help, it's good to give it a shot."

"Lying to my followers," I mutter. "I've maybe exaggerated things at times—you know, occasionally made things look better or different than they are to show off my life, or to help them see what I want them to see. But I've never outright lied to them."

"I'm sure most of them would want you to do what it takes to stay safe," Joe says.

At his side, Meg nods.

I glance at Chris. He purses his lips and tips his head like he agrees, but he's silently conceding that it's up to me.

Finally, it's up to me.

I sigh, collapsing back onto the couch.

"Okay. Okay."

Chris awards my choice with another smile. This one isn't full, but it feels special, like the last chocolate in a Godiva box.

"And for the record, I'm only saying yes because the pizza's going to be here any minute. I'm starving, and I don't want to sit here debating this while the pizza goes cold."

"Good reason," Chris says, all smirky and gloaty, and full of himself.

My boyfriend, Chris St. James.

I laugh out loud.

And the laughter won't stop.

I double over in hysterics.

"What?" Meg asks.

"Me and St. James!" I snort and then cover my nose for making that sound, but then I laugh some more.

"Dating!" I shake my head, lightly gasping for breath between my laughter.

"Me and him!" I keep giggling and point at Chris.

I'm the only one laughing.

I start to regain composure, but then I lift my eyes, look straight at Chris, and I start laughing again.

"Man, you are good for my ego," he says with a smile. Yes, girls. *The* smile. That's the smile. The one that sends my internal organs on a level-five roller coaster ride. Only because he's such eye-candy, nothing more than that. But man, oh man, that smile.

~

Saturday, I wake to the sun coming through my bedroom window, and the first thought I have is that Chris St. James is my fake boyfriend.

Chris St. James.

My boyfriend.

Fake. Of course. Totally fake.

After I fell apart laughing, the pizza arrived. The four of us hung out eating and talking as if Chris usually just comes over for a meal. What is my life?

He hung around so we could figure out some details. He has to come paint the porch sometime today anyway. Apparently, he has some other work he has to catch up on this morning since he spent time fixing the porch yesterday. He'll be here later this afternoon.

We'll take a few photos. I'll upload them to my page and caption them with a story about how we've started dating.

We'll do a few more photo shoots in the days and weeks to come. He and his hacker friend will keep an eye on this ImSOBeefy guy to see if he backs off.

I guess if I had to have a fake boyfriend, I could have done worse than Chris. If he were going to have to pick a pretend girlfriend, he definitely could have done better than me. But for some weird reason, he's volunteering to do this, and Meg and Joe think it's a good idea, so I'm going forward with it.

I get ready for my day, checking in with Journey for my weekly coaching session. I can't tell her a thing about how Chris and I are putting on a ruse. Journey's active online and she always follows my posts. I need to keep this secret tucked away. But I do tell Journey my life has taken a surprising turn over the past few weeks.

She says, "Turns are good. Without turns, we only go in a straight line. Boring, unending, unchanging. Embrace the turn, Ella Mae."

Um. Okay. I almost feel like I opened the wrong fortune cookie when I hear her response.

I continue to mull over Journey's words after we hang up. *Embrace the turn.*

Maybe that just means to accept what's going on and try not to fight it. Okay. Here goes me … embracing the turn.

I promised Meg and Joe I'd take engagement photos for them today. We pile into Joe's car, and I direct them to various spots around town—the flower shop, where Joe hands Meg a bouquet and I snap the moment from different angles; the sweet shop, where they feed one another bites of a dessert; Main Street, where they walk holding hands; and finally, we go to the river.

I love taking photos out here. The lush green of the trees along the bank, the way the light plays off the water, and the occasional wildlife in the background all lend to the perfect shot. I have Meg and Joe sit on a fallen tree, looking into one another's' eyes. Then Meg sits between Joe's legs while they both stare out at the water. I lead them to the river's edge, so I can capture the perfect shot.

After a few serious poses, I call out, "Silly faces!"

They both stick out their tongues.

"That's great! Now face one another and stick out your tongues!"

They do and then they burst into spontaneous laughter. I catch some great shots of them laughing, staring into one another's eyes. In my favorite one, Joe's holding Meg's forearm in this unspoken gesture of care and protection. It's everything.

"Okay, Meg, step behind Joe. I'm going to have you wrap your arms around his waist from behind. Joe, you're going to sort of look over your shoulder and behind you at Meg. Right. Just like …"

Before I can finish my sentence, Meg squeals and then she shouts, "I'm slipping!"

She wobbles, slides, tips, and starts to drop away down the mud that lines the edge of the river. Her arms spin like pinwheels. Her back arches and bows as she tries to gain balance.

"Oh! … Aghhhhh! … Joe! … Oh, no! … Help! I'm going down!"

Joe turns and lurches for Meg. She grasps for his hand.

"I've got you, babe!" Joe says, preemptively.

There's more shrieking and flailing. Joe definitely has a hold of Meg, and he's trying to secure his feet on the top of the embankment, but the ground's too soft and slippery.

"Oh, no!" Meg shouts.

"Oh, no. No! Not good!" Joe agrees.

Meg disappears and I hear the splash. Joe dives in right after her, shouting, "I'm coming in, babe!" I step toward the edge, but stay far enough back to ensure I don't join them.

Meg's got her arms around Joe's neck. Her dress is clinging to her like she's clinging to Joe—for dear life. Joe's trying to grasp at the muddy slope they slid down, while balancing Meg in his other arm. She's clinging to him like a baby spider monkey. He makes headway getting up the embankment, and slides back down … makes headway, and slides back down.

I lift my camera and snap a few shots.

"Did you just take our picture?" Meg shouts up at me.

"I wanted to capture the moment for you. You'll thank me later."

We finally figure out how to get them up. I grab a larger broken tree branch and extend it to them. Meg grasps the branch and makes her way up first, with a little shove from behind from Joe. Then Meg and I hold the branch so Joe can climb up. They're soaking wet and muddy. The three of us collapse onto our backs in the grass a safe distance from the river.

As soon as Meg's eyes meet mine, we devolve into a fit of laughter. Joe just chuckles and shakes his head.

Meg turns to Joe and says, "You jumped in to save me."

Joe props himself up on an elbow and looks down at Meg. "I'll always jump in after you, babe."

I carefully lift my camera and capture their moment.

CHAPTER 26

Chris

MY PALMS AREN'T SWEATY. That would be ridiculous. I wipe them down my jeans anyway before I knock on Ella Mae's front door. She told me Meg was out with Joe after a photo shoot they all did earlier. So, we'll be alone. In her home. Just the two of us. Which is fine. We're just taking pictures. And I need to get a grip. Somehow this woman is the one person on earth who unnerves me and takes down all my defenses.

Ella Mae opens the door. She's wearing yoga attire again. This time it's leopard print with this criss-cross weaving of fabric down the sides of the pants and another top that shows her midriff. I look her squarely in the eyes. Eyes, Chris. Eyes.

She's oblivious to the fact that her outfit caught my attention, or that I'm coming apart at the seams on her front porch.

"Heya, Soldier. Come on in. I've got everything ready in the front room. Do you need water?"

Ella Mae turns to walk ahead of me.

"I'm good."

My voice comes out a little more sternly than I wanted. Ella Mae looks over her shoulder giving me a questioning look. I smile to let her know I'm fine. It probably looks like the smile of a deranged lunatic, but hopefully when he's doing fine.

Nothing could have prepared me for the next words out of Ella Mae's mouth.

"I thought we'd do yoga."

"You thought we'd do what?"

"Yoga. It's something my peeps are used to on my channel. And it gives us something to do in the pics. Then we can cuddle on the couch and take photos afterward."

She's saying this all so calmly. I'm wondering if I just should have called some guys I know in special ops to handle this BeefItUp guy.

"I'll go easy on you, St. James. Don't worry."

I laugh. Again. It's forced. What the heck is wrong with me?

I toe off my shoes and leave them by her front door. Ella Mae did tell me to wear something comfortable. Now I know why.

I join Ella Mae in the front room. She pushes a button on a remote she's holding, and some sort of music that sounds like an orchestra is slowly warming up comes through a bluetooth speaker. There's a guy in the background of the soundtrack on a didgeridoo playing the longest notes ever in the history of music. Dude's got breath control, that's for sure. Ocean noises and birds mix in with this cacophony of sounds.

"Here's your mat," Ella Mae says.

Two mats are on the ground side by side. She's got a couple towels on a loveseat near the window, and bottled waters on the side table.

"I'm actually more of a weightlifter. Or a runner. Or a cyclist. I'm not sure yoga's my thing."

"You'll be fine. Let's start with some warming up," Ella Mae says, completely ignoring my protests.

"My phone is there." She points to a spot across the room where her phone is on this tripod. "So look at it when you can. Or look at me. Those shots will be good too. And mostly, just relax and have fun. Yoga's good for you. You may surprise yourself and keep coming back for more."

I nod, biting back the words, *not likely*.

Ella Mae stands at the front of her mat.

"Come on up here, Big Boy."

I'm not blushing. I'm sure it's nerves, or maybe my testosterone is surging.

I step up to the front of the mat. Ella Mae clicks the remote in her hand when I look over at her.

"What was that?" I ask.

"The remote links to my phone for photos. I can shoot pics without having to fiddle with the cell itself."

"Oh. Huh."

She continues on, more focused and calm than I've ever seen her. It's a different side to her—one I knew was there. I've just never seen her so uninhibited and open.

"So, we're going to start with Mountain pose."

"Mountain pose?" I repeat.

"Yep."

I picture myself bending over to form the shape of a mountain, but instead Ella Mae walks me through standing straight, being aware of what she calls the four corners of my feet. Then she tells me to press out through my feet like I'm trying to rip the yoga mat apart with the strength radiating down through my legs.

"Only, don't rip it. A big guy like you could probably tear through yoga mats all day long."

She smiles over at me. Again. I do not blush. I just focus on not tearing her mat and keeping my eyes on her face. That's all I can handle at this point. I'm multitasking like a boss. Eyes on her face. Don't rip the mat.

The camera remote clicks.

"We're basically just standing," I point out.

She giggles. "It's more than that, Soldier. You're focusing on body awareness."

She puts her hands like fists in front of her hips. "Focus here. On your pelvis. And then lengthen your spine gently. Feel where your feet are. Feel the earth beneath you. You don't usually do that when you stand around with your bros, do you? Or just hanging out doing whatever it is you do with your time. Yoga is about awareness."

I take her seriously, copying her stance, and some of my nervousness seems to drift away.

"Now slowly bring your arms into a superhero pose. This one should be easy for you."

"Because I'm a superhero?" I joke.

"You'd like to think so."

This woman never gives me a break, that's for sure.

I mimic her movements again.

"Now, raise your arms overhead, into the volcano pose, shooting all your energy out through your fingertips."

I do what she says. Another click of the remote.

After a few more standing poses, Ella Mae gracefully drops to her mat and crosses her legs with ease. She's flexible. I'm ... not.

I take a seat on my mat, struggling to cross my legs.

"It's okay," she assures me, even though she captures my struggles on film. "No one is flexible at the start. You'll get there with practice. Just do the closest thing you can without injuring yourself."

We move through a few seated poses, and then she has us on our hands and knees like dogs. Although, apparently we aren't dogs, we're cat-cows. What the heck? Who names these positions?

Mountains aren't standing. That should be called a tree

pose. Volcano, well, okay. But I think a volcano should have spread legs at the bottom so it looks more like an actual volcano. And this, Cat-Cow? Who came up with that? Dr. Seuss?

We arch our backs, and then we drop our lower backs down, and again, and again. And then, the most embarrassing moment of my life happens.

Alone. With Ella Mae. In the very silent space that is her front room.

I fart.

It's not a quiet little something either.

This gas came without warning, and let itself be known. And now I'm redder than a beet. All that not-blushing I was doing before, well, that doesn't matter. Because now I'm blushing, and also planning to re-enlist in the military just so I can never be seen in this town again.

Ella Mae looks over at me, obviously hiding her reaction, though there's a light in her eyes that tells me she's dying to crack up, big time. I can't believe I have the courage to meet her eyes.

"Don't worry, Soldier. It happens to the best of us."

"What does?" Am I really trying to deny that very obvious and explosive intrusion to our workout?

Ella Mae spears me with a look. I can't take it. I start chuckling. She sees this as the green light it is, and laughs with me. Our heads fall forward, all yoga poses abandoned. She flops onto her mat, doubled over in laughter.

"Your face," she says between laughs. "You were horrified!"

I just laugh some more, sitting back on my heels and taking in the exquisite sight of Ella Mae curled up in laughter on her yoga mat.

People get her all wrong. They have no idea the heart behind the facade she dons just to face the world and gain whatever it is she's after—approval, maybe. Her livelihood, for sure. But I get to witness this unrehearsed, unscripted side of her.

Her laughter dies down.

"We'll never speak of that again," I tell her.

"Oh, you wish," she says with that same spunk that keeps me on my toes every time we're together. "I'm so bringing that up. It was classic! You were all serious, arching your back, and then bffftttt, and you looked like you were ready to move to a remote village in the Andes."

"I did consider reenlisting for a minute."

She laughs some more. "Chris, join the human race for once. We all fart. And we all mess up. You get to be just like us. You don't have to hold yourself to these incredible and unattainable standards, you know?"

She's sitting now, staring at me like she didn't just expose me down to my core.

I take her in. No one has ever seen me like this. Not even my family. Maybe Alex. Maybe.

"Okay. Well, I think that killed the mood," she says. "We'll do more yoga tomorrow. Let's get our savasana on."

"Our what?"

"Chill, Soldier. It's just the wind down. We lay on our backs and breathe. You've got this."

I lie down next to Ella Mae, every so often I sneak a peek over at her. She's got her eyes shut and she's breathing peacefully. I wonder if this is what she looks like when she sleeps. She's got such a gorgeous face. Today, it's mostly make-up free, my favorite look on her. It's unguarded, just like she's been with me today. No mask. No pretense. Just the two of us hanging out while I pass gas. Yeah.

I close my eyes and breathe.

Yoga. Who knew?

After a few minutes, Ella Mae tells me to stand up.

"Let's go get the rest of our pictures taken. Drink some water first."

"Bossy."

"Always." She winks at me.

I barely remember that the reason we're doing this is to put on a charade for that creep online.

"Sit on the loveseat," Ella Mae says.

She grabs her camera and tripod, and rearranges it so it's facing us on the couch. Then she plops down next to me so our thighs are touching.

"Ready?"

I don't know what I am. Ready seems to be the farthest thing from whatever it is I'm feeling.

"Okay. I'm just going to fawn over you, and you can be all broody or you can respond, or fawn over me, or whatever. I'll capture pictures and we can pick which ones sell the concept best."

The concept? What concept? My brain has exited the building. Our legs are touching and I feel every spot of contact. Ella Mae smells good—citrus and cinnamon or cloves. Her face is mere inches from mine. I'm overwhelmed by her. When was the last time I was this close to a woman? My last date? That was over nine months ago, and I felt nothing like this, not even when we were kissing goodnight.

Ella Mae shocks me out of my thoughts when her hand reaches up and cups my jawline.

"Oh, this beard!"

She actually said that.

"I've been dying to touch your beard."

What? She has?

Her hand caresses my cheek and chin.

"Relax, Chris. You look like you're going to the dentist, not hanging out with your adoring girlfriend."

She laughs this carefree laugh. I look at the phone screen

to see the picture of us. She's right. I look tortured. She looks —beautiful.

"Okay," I say, recommitting to the mission.

I'm going all in. This Beefy guy needs to see that Ella Mae has a man in her life, and that man could flatten anyone who tries to hurt her.

I turn my face toward Ella Mae's, intending to look in her eyes to give the camera a show. But her eyes are right there, staring back at me, wide and blue, and full of playfulness. It's like a punch to the gut. I hear the remote click.

Ella Mae's still looking at me. A smile graces her lips. She looks over at the phone. "Oh! These are pure gold! Do more like that, Chris!"

"Okay," I say, regaining focus again. Photos. For Instagram. Yes. Photos for Instagram. Okay.

I look at her and then I cup her cheek, allowing my thumb to caress her soft skin. She gets this serious look on her face, but I hear the click of the remote.

"Enough looking in one another's eyes!" she announces. "Though, I could look in your eyes all day. That green around the blue is something else. It's just an extra dash of color that's so unexpected."

She just says things like that so easily. There's no hidden motive. She's obviously unaware of how intimate her words are, or the impact they are having on me.

Ella Mae turns her head toward the camera.

"Kiss my cheek, Soldier."

"What?"

"Kiss my cheek."

"Kiss you?"

"My cheek. Pretend I'm your grandma and kiss my cheek."

She's not my grandma.

Not even close.

I clear my throat.

Ella Mae looks over at me like I'm ridiculous. "I'm not asking you to actually kiss me, Chris. If this is so distasteful, we can skip it."

"No. It's not that. I just had to … I wasn't … Yeah. Let's do it."

She shakes her head lightly, and looks directly at the camera.

I take my hand and gently brush her hair over her shoulder, so her face is completely exposed to me.

Click. I hear her remote capture that shot.

Then I bend in. Click. And I feel my breath as it fans across her cheek. Click. And then I brush a featherlight kiss on her cheek. Click. My lips hum, and my head feels light. Maybe it's the yoga. Maybe it's just Ella Mae. I suddenly feel heady and overwhelmed—from barely kissing her cheek.

CHAPTER 27

Ella Mae

DANGER, danger, forest ranger!

I pull back from Chris. Who knew he was capable of this kind of tenderness? Oh.my.lanta. Is this what they mean by swooning? His touch. And the way he looked at me. I need a minute here to regroup.

I'm passing things off between us like they're fun and we're easy breezy here.

And we are.

I feel so relaxed with Chris, like I can be myself in ways I never am. Sure, I let my guard down with Meg, but we don't usually laugh like this, and she doesn't send chills up my spine by cupping my cheek and caressing it with the pad of her thumb like we're the two main characters in some romance novel. Thank goodness, she doesn't. That would just be beyond awkward.

I can't even look at Chris right now.

I have to keep this light—for both our sakes.

Chris is doing me a favor, and he's obviously uncomfortable showing this much affection. That kiss to my cheek. Whew. His newly-grown beard had just the right amount of bristle to tickle my face and leave my skin buzzing when he pulled away.

Speaking of buzzing, my phone vibrates with a message notification.

I look over at Chris. He's sitting back on the loveseat next to me, chugging from his water bottle.

I open my messages. It's from Drake.

@DrakesDaMan

Hey, Ella Mae. I really loved our time together, beautiful girl. Genesis is sending all the details about the bash to your inbox. Plan to come. I'd love to see you again.

Lots of big names will be there. I'll make sure they know who you are. You could stay here at the house with me. I've got plenty of room.

I feel Chris' warm breath tickling across my neck and shoulder. When I turn my head, his face is right there, and he's reading Drake's message from over my shoulder.

"You're not going out to see him."

It's not even posed as a question. He states it like some sort of directive. Um. No. I thought I made it clear, I'm not a lowly cadet he gets to order around.

I arch my brows, give Chris a haughty look, and turn my attention back to my phone. I know Chris is still reading over my shoulder. Fine. Let him get an eyeful.

@Fab-U-lous_EllaMae

Thanks for reaching out again, Drake.

I loved our time together too. Got plenty of traction out of those lives and my follow up posts. I'm seriously considering coming to the bash. Thanks for reaching out again. I'll have details to coordinate, but it's a great opportunity, as you said. I'll keep you posted on my plans for accommodations. Thanks for the offer to stay at your place. SO sweet! Send my love to Andy! ~ EM

I have no intention whatsoever of staying at Drake's. I'm not a complete idiot. I know plenty of women would jump at that invitation. Yes. Drake's gorgeous, and he should check all the boxes, but I don't know him well enough to stay at his place. He probably offered rooms to a bunch of influencers. His home will be a madhouse that weekend.

But do I want the overbearing soldier who is literally breathing down my neck right now to know I'm not staying at Drake's? No. That would be a heck-to-the-no. Chris doesn't get to boss me around. I choose where I go, why, and when.

Chris is my *fake* boyfriend, not my real one. And even if he were real …

If he were real.

Well. If our relationship were real, I wouldn't be sitting here answering Instagram messages after a session of couples yoga and that kiss to my cheek, so there's the answer to that.

"I'd better go paint the porch," Chris says in his usually gruff, detached voice.

I haven't heard that tone from him in a while.

"Yeah. Good idea. I'll just go through these photos and choose the ones to upload without you."

"Did you need me to …"

"Nope. No. That's fine," I say in a not-so-huffy, but yes, a little huffy tone. "I'll send you a few too—you know, in case you want to post them."

"Yeah. Meg said I should."

"Welp. Thanks."

I stand from the couch, putting much needed space between me and Chris. The distance doesn't do a thing to erase the feeling of his beard on my cheek, or how it tickled the palm of my hand in the most delicious way, or the sensation of his lips on my skin when he kissed me oh, so softly.

"And, you know, use the restroom or help yourself to whatever while you're working here. Mi casa es su casa!"

I'm a little overly animated with that last sentiment.

"Just like Drake's casa is your casa?" Chris mumbles as he stands from the couch.

Is he jealous, or just being an overbearing jerk? I'd really like to know. But I won't ever know, because I'm not opening a can of worms with my fake boyfriend. He did me a favor today—I've come to see it as that, especially after talking with Meg again today before she and Joe took off for the afternoon. And, as always, Chris doesn't owe me anything.

Chris walks out without saying another word. Nice. He's so hot and cold I feel like I'm doing the polar plunge with him. One minute I'm cozy. The next I'm frozen, numb, unable to catch my breath.

I take my phone with me to the kitchen. I'm going to make a recovery shake. Not because we worked out—just because I need to recover.

I pour orange juice, a banana, ginger, blueberries, greek yogurt, and chia seeds into the blender and turn it on high. While my smoothie is whirling away, I look through our photos. I am not prepared for what I see. We look like a couple madly in love with one another.

My breath hitches when I see the one where Chris is about

to kiss me. I can't stop my smile from breaking free at some of the yoga ones. These are fantastic. They definitely meet the intended goal. Chris and I look like a power couple doing yoga and then enjoying a little cuddle time on the couch.

I select ten pictures and upload them with a caption.

Fab-U-lous_EllaMae

Well, peeps! This is a big announcement!
I've been single, and not-so-ready to mingle for a while now, as you know. I embrace my independence.
No men needed! I'm complete as the woman I am.

But sometimes, out of the blue, a handsome man with a heart of gold steps up at just the right moment. Maybe you knew him your whole life. But he was never (and I mean never) the one you had your eye on.

Of course, you knew he was good looking. I'm pretty sure blind women can see the beauty of this man. Whew-eee.

But one night, when you've had the biggest plans of your life and they fall through, well, that's the night he shows up. And yes, those of you who've been around here, you guessed it. You shipped us. Chris is the one. Mr. Shoulders, whatever you want to call him. He's the guy who literally came into my life like a dark horse and won my heart.

So, here I am, sharing with you the best thing that ever happened to me. This man. He's ex-military, stubborn, funny, a jack-of-all-trades, my latest yoga partner, and surprisingly sweet. And yes, his kisses are to die for!
So, as of this week, he's all mine. And, I'm his.

So, let the hashtagging begin #rippedandshipped #ChellaMaeBae #myguy #hesthebest #thatbeardthough #couplesyoga #hemakesmelaugh #hemakesmesmile #hegetsme #militarymenarethehottest #mysoldier

I look over what I wrote, scroll through the photos one more time, and hit *Post*. My words feel a little too raw, but my followers won't know that, and neither will that bull-headed soldier who's out front painting my porch right now.

The comments stream in almost instantly. So many people are saying how happy they are for me. Others comment that I'm a lucky girl. A lot of them say how cute we are together. Other hashtags I didn't think to use pop up, like, #relationshipgoals, #powercouple (I knew it!), #couplesofinstagram, #EllasFella, and more. I keep scrolling, writing responses like, *Thanks, girlie!* and, *Yep! He's amazing*. All the while, I'd like to go hit him over the head with one of the floorboards he's been using to fix the porch. Why does he have to be so infuriating?

I guess that's a man for you.

Mom's voice chooses this moment to chime in. *You can't count on a man to fill your needs or complete your life. They're fickle creatures, never to be fully trusted, especially not with your heart.*

I know that's some messed-up, dystopian relationship advice, but it's served me nonetheless. And it will do me well to remember the essential truths hidden in my mom's dysfunctional wisdom. I can't really count on Chris. I can only count on myself. And, in a way, that's good news. Because I can't control that unpredictable man on my porch, but I've got all the power of choice in my own hands when it comes to how I live my life.

I nod my head as if I'm agreeing with myself.

I'm going to have to share that nugget with Journey next weekend. I won't tell her about us faking, but I'll share the wisdom in self-reliance, I know she'll eat that up with a spoon. As long as I keep my eyes on the prize, treat these photo shoots with Chris like fun times and nothing more, my heart will remain safe and sound.

CHAPTER 28
Chris

I FINISHED my work for the day and I'm sitting here flipping channels on the television, finding nothing worth watching—or at least nothing that could hold my attention. It's late afternoon, and Duke's coming over in a little bit. I'm not really in the mood for company, but like the bloodhound he is, Duke sensed I'd gone into full-blown hermit mode, and of course, that made him insist he's popping by.

It's been two days since I've seen my "girlfriend." That invitation from Drake shouldn't have mattered to me. Ella Mae's a free woman. If she wants to fly to LA to see him, why should I care?

The guy's obviously a complete tool. He stood Ella Mae up. I'll never forget the look of dejection in her eyes that night. Maybe I owe him a thank you for doing me a favor. If he hadn't skipped out, I never would have sat with her, and things wouldn't be … whatever they are right now.

I've been on my account and posted the pictures Ella Mae sent me. I also posted a few of me working out so my account doesn't look like I'm this guy just sitting around pining for his girlfriend.

That would be pathetic, right?

Thankfully, no one here in town has a clue I have an Instagram account. Ella Mae got on my post of the yoga pictures and commented the same day I posted. She put all these kissy-face emojis and said, *Luv you, Big Boy*. That comment cemented the fact that she's all in for the fakery. Not so much for anything other than that. Which is fine. Totally good. I mean, when we're in her front room, or at Frisch's Big Boy, we can have our moments that end up making me delusional. But in real life, we can't ... and shouldn't ... and won't.

Then Meg commented, *You two are perfect for one another.*

They also both commented on my workout pictures. Ella Mae's comments made me chuckle. *Definitely shoulder day today*, and *Oooh la la. That's what I'm saying*, and *Give me all of that and a side of fries*. She's crazy.

The most important outcome of all this effort has been the reaction from ImSOBeefy. He wrote a comment under Ella Mae's post that said, *You should have picked me, Ella Mae. I'm still here if things don't work out.* What a jerk. But still, it seems he got the message that she's taken. Hopefully that sticks after a few more posts from us.

I pick up my phone like a complete masochist and scroll over to Ella Mae's account. She's got a new reel up. I check it out. She's talking about thinking positive, and then she transitions into presenting the best shoes for this summer's wardrobe. The rest of the video is devoted to multiple images of her feet flashing in rapid succession with various sandals and shoes on. Why does this spark a desire to go see her feet in person? Well, not just her feet—her.

Maybe it's for the best that Duke is coming over here. Otherwise, I'd be likely to do something foolish like show up at Ella Mae's without a reason or a plan.

I have to come out of hibernation this evening anyway. Duke and my sister are announcing their pregnancy to Mom and Dad over dinner. Duke and I will head that way after we hang out here. Being with my family for such an important event should distract me from everything else in my life.

The screen door opens and shuts, and I look up from my spot on the couch to see Duke smirking at me.

"What's up, loverboy?"

I stare at my best friend. Yes. We always joke around. But he's never gone so far as to call me loverboy.

"Come in."

I ignore his greeting on purpose.

"Aren't you going to fill me in on the latest developments in your love life?" he asks as he flops down on the other end of the sofa.

"Yeah. Here are the developments in a nutshell: nothing."

"Hmmm."

"What's that supposed to mean?"

"Well, rumor has it you were at Ella Mae's the other day alone with her while Meg and Joe were out. In her house, not outdoors. Yes. You worked on the porch, but then you spent more than an hour inside."

This town. And Duke.

"Don't believe everything you hear."

"Seriously, Chris? Are you going to sit there and tell me you weren't inside Ella Mae's house?"

"I was inside her house."

"And?"

"And maybe that's not your business. Or anyone else's, for that matter."

Duke crosses his arms over his chest. Then he pulls out that good-ol'-boy charm of his.

He gets serious and says, "Look, I know I came in teasing you, but really, I want to know what's up. Are you interested in Ella Mae?"

"I don't know. Okay?"

I blurt out the words in aggravation before my brain even gets a chance to consult about the wisdom of saying anything. But this is Duke. Aside from dating my sister in secret, he's always had my back. And when it comes to Shannon, I can't really blame him for how they went about things. He was in love. And love makes a man crazy—apparently. Not that I'm in love. But I'm in something. Deep, murky, relentless something.

"Okay," Duke says, gently.

We sit together, looking around at nothing in particular, saying nothing in particular. We're just letting my truth bomb sit undetonated between us.

Finally, I speak. "Ella Mae was in need of some help that day out at the Big Boy. I go there sometimes on Wednesdays. I work downtown, and I stop in on an army friend after I get off work. Then I usually go hit Frisch's to sort through all the thoughts and feelings of my day."

I look over at Duke. He's as still as a statue—as if he knows any sudden movement might force me back into secrecy. But I've hit some sort of limit. And it's not really fair that Aiden knows I work for the DOD and Duke's still in the dark.

"I'm in cybersecurity. It's not glamorous, but it's private, and a lot of what I deal with is classified. So, I figured it's better you—and everyone—didn't know what goes on in my work life. I do odd jobs around town because I can flex my hours, and also because it gives me a little cover for what I really do. And the friend I visit, his name is Alex. He was wounded while we were serving together. I go each week to check up on him and his family."

"Man. I'm sorry."

"About Alex?"

"Yeah."

"Believe me, if you met him, you'd be amazed. He's got

such an indomitable spirit. Bounced back after a lot of therapy. He's one of the most positive dudes I know."

Duke scoffs and points to his own face.

"Yeah, yeah. Next to you. Okay, Captain Positive?"

Duke smiles with satisfaction.

"And I want you to meet him. I'm not sure why I kept my worlds so compartmentalized. But I do want you to meet Alex. And for him to meet you. You two will be dangerous together—in the best of ways."

"I'd love to meet him."

"So, back to Ella Mae."

I'm on a roll, and now it's like I just have to get this all out.

Duke nods.

"Well, I walked in on her crying that night at the restaurant. She wasn't actually crying when I got there, but I could see she'd had some tears, so I stepped in. Even though I hate social media and I have real reasons for keeping a low profile. But seeing her like that, well, I couldn't help myself. I had to do what I could."

"You and Aiden, man. Hero complexes all day long."

"Nothing wrong with being a hero."

"I guess not. I just never got that gene. I take care of Shannon. Always will. But as far as feeling like the whole world's going to fall apart if I don't step in? Nah. I've got none of that. The way I see it, most people figure things out on their own if you leave them to it. And if they really need help, they ask."

I shake my head. This is why Duke and I make such good friends. He's the polar opposite of me.

"So, you stepped up at the Big Boy."

"As you well know."

We chuckle. That video on guys night still is one of the better pranks any of us have pulled on one another. Not that I'm telling Duke that. It's way too easy to puff his ego up, and way too challenging to deflate it once it's gotten larger than life.

"This next part is between you, me, Aiden, and God. You can't tell a soul. Not even Shannon."

Duke nods. "Got it. Whatever it is, it goes to my grave."

I know he's serious. He may be a gossip hound, but when he says he'll keep my confidence, he will.

"Anyway, there's this guy who keeps commenting on Ella Mae's posts. He seems harmless at first. Just inappropriate—really skeezy. But then he escalated. So, I got Aiden involved. And I talked to Ella Mae. And Aiden put a little tracker on the guy, since I can't due to my job. But that didn't slow this putz down. So, Meg and I decided it would be good if Ella Mae had the appearance of a boyfriend online."

"And who better to pose as her boyfriend than you?"

"Exactly. I'd already been in her posts. She trusts me. At least, I think she does. And she's got to send this guy a message. He's got to see she's with someone who could kick his butt if it came to that."

"Well, that would be you, for sure."

"So that's where we're at. I'm posing as her fake boyfriend."

"And catching feelings."

Duke says it like it's a fact and no big deal.

"I don't know."

I look over at the man who's as good as a brother to me. And that was long before he married my sister.

"I've never been so confused in my life. I'm on my ear half the time around her. She makes me frustrated. She doesn't put up with a bit of anything from me. She never listens to me. And then I can't get her off my mind no matter how hard I try. I wake up to thoughts of her. I randomly wonder how she's doing. I think of her whenever my mind is idle. And don't get me started on her post about her feet. It's driving me nuts, if you want to know the truth."

Duke smiles this grin that's so giddy I almost want to get up and punch him.

"Oh, yeah. You've got it bad."

Thankfully, he didn't pursue that whole line about Ella Mae's feet. I can't even believe I said that out loud. I'm losing it.

I look at Duke, then I drop my head into my hands. He's right. I probably knew I had feelings for Ella Mae all along. But it's like those days when you feel this tickle in the back of your throat and you just know you're getting sick, and the timing couldn't be worse. Besides, who wants to get sick ever? So you down some extra vitamin C, lay off the sugar, and get to bed early. But the next morning, you feel a bit worse. You still hold out hope. Maybe this is as bad as it will get. Maybe it will pass in a day. That night, you're under the blankets shivering with a fever and a raspy cough, and your throat feels like you swallowed nails.

Yeah. I just compared falling for Ella Mae to catching a cold. Let's keep that between us.

"I think I might have it bad," I admit.

"You and Ella Mae!" Duke slaps his knee like he won the lottery.

"No. Man. You know that can't be a fact. We live here. There's no possible way two people from our families can ever, ever be together. It's a miracle we've even been able to talk to one another without a riot breaking out and a full-blown war ensuing between our families."

"That's all in the past. And it's not your battle. That's got nothing to do with the two of you."

"Maybe not, but it's real, and you know it is. We may want to rise above it, but this town won't. All hell would break loose if we started to officially date."

Am I honestly talking about dating Ella Mae, for real?

"And then there's another issue. A big one. I'm ninety-nine percent sure she's not feeling a thing for me besides gratitude and a little appreciation for my hard work in the gym. Maybe we're friends now, but that's all. She's thinking of going out to LA to see this other guy—a big influencer who's an even bigger jerk. He's the one who stood her up that night at Frisch's. But she's considering flying out to the west coast so she can stay at his house with him and attend some big party he's throwing.

"So, yeah. Even if I am having feelings for her …"

"You are. You definitely are."

"Okay. Whatever. Even if I am, she's not. And that's all she wrote."

Duke sinks back into the sofa, laces his fingers behind his neck, and turns his head so he's looking right at me.

"Do you know how long I wanted to date your sister?"

"No. And don't make me kick you out of my house by telling me."

"She was six, on that little pink tricycle …"

Duke looks at me, serious as a heart attack.

I think steam comes out of my ears. He would have been nine. And that would have been so not okay with me.

"I'm kidding, man! She was fully legal and then some. All I'm saying is I wanted her for a long time before she ever let on that she felt anything for me. You don't just throw in the towel on a hunch that a woman doesn't reciprocate your feelings. Besides, I hate to break it to you, but all signs point to the fact that you're at the point of no return."

"The point of no return?"

"Yeah. You've been bitten. You've got the bug. It's not like you're going to just shake these feelings. Even you, the master of self-discipline, able to withstand all torture and keep a straight face. Whatever you learned in the Army, it's of no use here. You're in a new playing field. Love is not war. And you are not going to outwit your own emotions, my friend. You may as well wave the white flag, because once you start feeling things—really feeling things for a woman, you are done for."

CHAPTER 29

Chris

DUKE KEEPS the conversation lively over supper, asking my dad all sorts of accounting questions like the big brown-noser he is.

I shoot him a look when my mom asks my dad to pass the mashed potatoes.

"Kiss up much?" I tease.

Duke just shrugs and Shannon giggles. She thinks everything he does is adorable. I'm glad she's happy, even if it is because she's blind to any of his faults.

After dinner we move into the living room. Dad offers everyone coffee or tea. He never does that. Then again, it's not like we're all here together that often. We should do this more. I look over at Mom. She's got a faint smile on her face. It's not full. The underlying pain of her chronic depression seeps through like a stain. But she's smiling, and that's something.

Shannon clears her throat.

"Mom. Dad. We have something to tell you."

Dad's perched on the armrest of the big chair Mom's seated in. His arm is around her shoulder and I notice how his hand makes gentle strokes of comfort on her upper arm. Duke and Shannon are on the couch, and I'm in this wingback that feels too small for me, but I'm making do.

"What is it, hunny?" Mom's brow creases.

I wonder if her default setting will ever be anything more positive than worry and dread.

"It's good news," Duke adds in a soft voice that makes me remember why he's one of my closest friends, and truthfully the only man I'd want married to my sister.

"Oh?" Dad asks, hopefully. "You hear that, dear. It's good news."

Shannon smiles over at me. I bob my head, encouraging her to go on and say it.

"Well. Duke and I. Well, we're pregnant!"

Mom's eyes go wide.

Dad's smile breaks out as if Warren Buffett just walked into our home to hang out and talk investment strategies.

A slow smile makes its way across Mom's face.

"I'm going to be a grandma?"

"You are," Shannon says. "It's still early. We don't know the gender yet."

"And we don't care," Duke says easily. "Girl or boy, we're going to love this kid. We already do."

"Oh my goodness," Mom says. "This really is good news. Oh, Shannon. You made me so happy!"

Mom stands up and walks over to Shannon, and Shannon stands so Mom can wrap her into a hug.

"My baby's having a baby," Mom whispers into Shannon's hair.

"And me. I'm having a baby too," Duke says from his seated position on the couch.

"Well, of course you are," Mom says, completely avoiding the obvious need for an anatomy lesson.

Dad walks over to Duke and shakes his hand. "Well done, son. We're so happy for you both."

I sit behind everyone in my wingback chair, feeling like a kid on the bench during the homecoming game. It's all good. I'm just glad to be here. This isn't my moment. It's theirs. And they chose to share it with me, or at least allowed me to witness it. It will be a long, long time before I forget the smile I just saw on my mom's face.

The oddest thought passes through my mind.

I mean, it's *odd*.

I wish Ella Mae were here.

Of course, she couldn't be. And that's the worst of it. Even if it turned out she'd want to be, it would be a long shot to picture the scene unraveling before me comfortably including Ella Mae in the room.

Then I have an even odder thought. What if sometime in the distant future, Ella Mae and I were the main focus. I almost chuckle at the thought of Ella Mae sitting on that same couch, her hand encased in mine, her other hand on her pregnant belly. I picture her saying, "We're pregnant."

Yeah. That would go over like a turd in a punchbowl.

Dad interrupts my bizarre daydream with an announcement. "This calls for a celebration! Let's all go get ice cream!"

I figure Mom will bow out. She's never one to go into town these days. Not if she can help it. But tonight, she's the first to say, "A scoop of Rocky Road sounds wonderful."

I sit in the back seat of Duke and Shannon's car on the way to the ice cream parlor. Duke drove me over here, so they'll just drop me home after we get our dessert.

"Did you get an invitation to Brooks and Gabby's reception?" Shannon asks.

"I did. Just yesterday."

"Are you going?"

"I plan on it. Brooks is a good friend. He and Duke and I

hung out pretty regularly before Gabby stole his heart, and ultimately stole him away from us."

"I wish we could have been at the wedding," Shannon says. "But a local reception's a great way to celebrate with all their Ohio friends and family. Are you bringing anyone?"

"Who would I bring?" I ask, innocently.

Duke looks at me in the rear view window like he's trying to use his jedi mind powers to make me think of Ella Mae. He doesn't realize it's not that complicated. I'm already thinking of her. As a matter of fact, I could use a jedi to help me stop thinking about her so much.

"Aren't you dating anyone?" Shannon asks.

Her voice has such a note of concern in it.

"Not really," I say, trying to be vague.

Duke's eyebrow raises for a brief moment. Only I catch the movement. Technically, I'm not dating anyone. Would I like to bring Ella Mae to the reception? Yeah. I really would. Will I? That's a whole other story.

~

Three days. I literally have never counted the days between seeing a person. But I am counting now, and it's been three days since I've seen Ella Mae.

I'm so out of my depth here. Usually, dating is easy for me. If I like a woman and I know we're attracted to one another, I flirt, or maybe she flirts. We decide to go out. We date until it doesn't work anymore.

I don't usually get serious. Plenty of guys in the Army had wives and girlfriends. In my typically cynical way, I called all those significant others, *distractions*. I know. I know. Once I met Courtney, I took all that back. Alex loved every repentant minute of that experience. Courtney's amazing, as you know.

But I figured that committed life was for other guys, not me. My mind was on the mission.

Whatever has me in knots over Ella Mae is so different than anything I've ever experienced. Distracting doesn't begin to define it.

Today, we're taking more photos. When I get to Ella Mae's she opens the door before I knock.

"Hi, Soldier. Long time no see, boyfriend."

No kidding. Was I supposed to come around?

"Yeah. I've been working. And we had a family dinner last night."

"That sounds nice."

"It was. Duke and Shannon broke their big news to Mom and Dad."

Ella Mae walks into her house and I follow her down the hall.

"I bet they were out of their minds with happiness when they heard they were going to be grandparents."

"Mom was so happy. They both were. Mom even let us take her to ice cream."

Ella Mae pauses just before we reach the living room, turns, and looks me in the eyes.

"Chris. That's so awesome."

Everyone in town knows about Bridgette, and about Mom's difficulties since the accident.

"It really was special."

Ella Mae's smile hits me in the middle of the chest like a defibrillator. Her happiness over Mom seems to magnify the whole experience.

I'm beyond questioning this. I've gone three days without seeing Ella Mae. Right now, we're together, and I'm soaking up the effect she has on me.

She must sense it because she tips her head to the side just a little and studies me.

Then she says, "You look pretty happy yourself, Big Boy."

"Yeah. I guess I am. How are you?"

"I'm great."

She turns into the living room. I haven't taken my eyes off her since I got here. She's wearing jeans with some intentional rips in them and a crisp white T-shirt that says the words, *Ooh La La* on it. And she's barefoot again, those hot pink toenails on display.

"Hi, to you too," Meg says.

I look up from staring at Ella Mae's feet. Next to my yoga fart, this may be the second most embarrassing moment of my life. I was definitely checking out her feet. And they both know it. It was that post with all those sandals and shoes. It got me thinking about her feet. I'm sure not admitting that to them. *Uh, yeah. I've been stalking Ella Mae's posts. I especially like the summer shoe selection reel.* Nope. I'm taking that info to my grave.

"Hey, Meg. How are you doing?" I ask, trying to move past the whole staring at feet thing.

"Great. I'm officially your photographer today."

I look at Ella Mae for any clue as to what we're doing.

Ella Mae explains, "Some shots can be taken with the tripod, but action shots are better with an actual photographer behind the lens. Today, we're doing action shots."

She's taken this whole Instagram couple thing to the next level. I'd expect nothing less. Come to think of it, her followers would expect this.

"Okay. Just tell me what to do, and I'll do it."

Ella Mae cocks a brow at me and makes a face. "You're just going to do whatever I say today? Did you hit your head?"

"No. I'm just feeling extra agreeable, so maybe take advantage of that while it lasts."

Truth is, I probably would do anything she asks today,

and that's nothing she needs to know. I already feel like I'm playing poker with a bunch of mismatched cards and no hope of the dealer cutting me a break.

"Let's get this party started!" Ella Mae says, waving her hands over her head and shimmying her hips as she walks out of the living room and into the kitchen. Meg and I follow her out the back door.

Once we're in the back yard, she's got all sorts of poses in mind. She's even pulled up photos from a site called Pinterest of other couples doing romantic things together.

If you had told me even three weeks ago that I'd be in Ella Mae's back yard, giving her a piggyback ride while Meg tried to capture the best angle of the two of us, well, I'd have shaken my head and sent you to see a specialist for help. But here I am, Ella Mae's legs wrapped through my arms and around my waist, her arms around my neck, and her laughter vibrating across my back.

"You make me feel like I don't weigh anything!" she says from up there.

"You don't," I assure her.

"Awww, Soldier. That's the sweetest."

She leans down and rests her head on top of mine. I wish I could freeze time to keep her there.

Meg shouts, "Oh my gosh! That was the best shot yet! Ella Mae, you are going to love that one."

We lay on the grass with our legs going in opposite directions and our heads touching. Then we slowly walk toward the front of the house, holding hands while Meg shoots us from behind.

It should be nothing, holding Ella Mae's hand, but it's something I don't usually do with women. For some reason, hand holding feels like a commitment. I could hold Ella Mae's hand all day. It's so small in mine, and soft, and warm.

"You've got beefy bear paws for hands," she says, looking up at me.

I look down at her, giving her hand a little squeeze. "They fit the rest of me."

"Well, I guess they do, don't they?"

Meg snaps more pictures. Once Ella Mae is satisfied, we head back inside for some iced drinks and a look at the photos.

Just like last time, we look like a couple in love. Ella Mae and Meg gush over all of them. I let them pick which ones I'll post and which ones she will. I search the photos for evidence that Ella Mae feels anything like I do, but I can't tell if she's feeling anything or if she's just a good actress.

CHAPTER 30

Chris

"WE REALLY SHOULD HAVE HAD another kissing shot," Meg says to Ella Mae, as if it's no big deal.

"Yeah. You're probably right. We can do one right here in the kitchen. Right, Chris?"

"Uh. Yeah. Sure. Whatever you think."

"I think you need to kiss me, is what I think."

Kissing her for show is one thing. Kissing her when all these confusing feelings are constantly throwing me off kilter is another.

"So, why don't you stand on one side of the island, Ella Mae. And Chris, you stand on the other, and then both of you lean on your forearms and meet in the middle with a kiss?" Meg suggests.

"Oooh. I love that!" Ella Mae says, totally into the concept of getting the best shot, and obviously completely unaffected by the idea of kissing me.

Ella Mae walks to one side of the island. I stand across from her. She props herself up on her arms.

"You know what? I'm going to need a boost. Get me the kitchen stool."

Meg brings the stool over, and Ella Mae stands on it, bringing her more than halfway in my direction.

"Okay, Chris. You lean in now," Meg coaches, like I've never kissed a woman before. I'm sure that's how I'm acting.

I lean in, letting my weight fall onto my forearms until my forehead is resting right against Ella Mae's. Her eyes are right there, and they're not shut like most women's when they're about to be kissed. She's looking at me.

We stare at one another like that for a few moments. I forget everything except the scent of her, and the way she makes me laugh, and the fact that she was happy about my Mom's happiness. I forget the room, the date, the time of day. All I see is her. And, I think she might sense this isn't a game to me anymore. I hope she does, because this kiss means something. At least, to me it does.

I lean in, and her eyes flutter shut. I move so my mouth is hovering over hers and then I brush her lips with mine, softly, lightly. But that's not nearly enough. At least that's what my lips say, so I move back again, brushing another gentle kiss across her lips. And then, a third time, but this time I linger. Ella Mae's hand comes up behind my neck, holding me in place. Our mouths connect and we deepen the kiss. Tingles erupt across my body. I want more. More of this. More of her.

I'm about to tug Ella Mae toward me when Meg's voice cuts through and reminds me where we are and what we're doing.

"Okay! Okie Dokie, guys. That's great! Good kissing. Great. Yep. I think we got some shots that will really work there."

Ella Mae pulls away like she's been shot out of a cannon. I blink. Then I stand up and concentrate on making my face neutral. My lips hum with a memory of our kiss. I can't even look at Ella Mae yet. What we shared felt mutual. But maybe it wasn't.

Neither of us says anything. Meg breaks the awkward tension by saying. "Let's look at what we've got."

Only, that doesn't help much because the photos of our kiss look like nothing I've ever seen between me and a woman. They're sweet, but also filled with chemistry. Maybe Ella Mae and Meg can't see it, but I do. Everything I was feeling is captured right there in those photos.

Ella Mae moves on pretty quickly, getting right down to business.

"Grab your phone, Chris. We can upload everything right now."

I pull my cell out of my pocket. Meg airdrops the pictures from the camera to each of us, and we compose our posts.

Within a few moments, Ella Mae's getting responses from followers. She reads one out loud.

"It's from him. ImSOBeefy. He says, *This is looking serious. You're breaking my heart Ella Mae. But I'm still here. I'll catch you when he lets you down.*"

"Gross," Meg says.

I nearly growl. But I hold back from acting overly affected. I know how it upsets Ella Mae when I go into bossy caveman mode.

"At least he's accepting that we're together," she says.

"True. He's just going to have to see us stay together, from the sound of things."

"Agreed," Meg says. "Once he sees you're really sticking it out with Mr. Shoulders over here, he'll tuck his tail and run."

"I hope so," Ella Mae says.

It's the first time she showed any sign of irritation or concern about this guy instead of getting defensive.

"If not, we'll figure something out," I promise her.

She smiles up at me. It's the first eye contact we've had

since the kiss. I smile back at her and every potential wrinkle between us seems to iron out.

"I have to run," I say, looking at my phone to check the time. "I've got a haircut."

Ella Mae walks me to the door.

"Thanks. For everything."

"No problem. That's what boyfriends do, right?"

"Yeah. It is. But seriously, Soldier. I'm grateful for your help with this."

I smile.

"And you're not a half-bad kisser either. Lucky me!"

She winks at me, and then she turns and walks back into her house. Leave it to Ella Mae to lighten any tension with an over-the-top comment.

And, wait a second. Not half bad? That was a great kiss. What is she even talking about? She thinks that kiss wasn't good enough? Just wait until our next fake kiss. She's going to need me to hold her up. I'm going to rock Ella Mae's world —just like she's been rocking mine.

~

We really need a barber shop around here. If I didn't have a government job that gave me a sense of purpose and guaranteed benefits, and if I didn't have one weekend a month committed to the National Guard Reserves, I'd consider opening a shop.

The Dippity Do is one of those salons that makes you feel like you stepped back in time. The decor is current enough, but it's all hot pinks and blacks. The back wall sports a graphic illustrated mural of a bunch of women from the shoulders up. As if that didn't make this whole place scream of estrogen, the clientele is eighty percent women most days.

Usually, I'm the only guy in the shop when I come in for my monthly cut.

I've given up the army look, but I can't quite shake the need to keep things looking somewhat high and tight. This beard is the exception. I wasn't planning on growing it in. I just let it happen one week, and once Ella Mae reacted the way she did, well, that was that.

I've been dying to touch your beard.

Trust me, I know the feeling.

Not that I'm dying to touch anyone's beard. I'm just dying. Mostly dying to touch her, to be with her, to laugh with her, to call off this charade and make something real out of what's been tugging between us for ... well, a long time, if I'm honest. Huh.

When I walk into the salon, Laura ushers me over to her chair. Most of the guys in our friend group go to her. Angie's fine. And most of the stylists here are decent. But Laura's the best, and everyone in town knows it.

"Same ol', same ol'?" she asks, taunting me with a bored look in the mirror.

"I like consistency," I tell her.

Maybe I actually don't. If there's anything Ella Mae is, it's definitely not consistent.

"I'm liking the beard, though. It gives you a more rugged look. Are you keeping it?"

"Yeah. Just trim it up for me, if you would."

Laura and I chat about life and the adoption process she and Rob are going through. Then the conversation turns to the reception for Brooks and Gabriela in Cincinnati.

Our conversation is cut short by the arrival of three of our seniors: Mabel, Esther, and a woman we all call Memaw, even though she's only officially Lexi and Felicia's grandma.

"Oh! Chris!" Mabel shouts as the door shuts behind them. "I've been hoping to run into you!"

Mabel walks over to Laura's chair and Laura spins me so I can face Mabel.

And then, in a voice that can probably be heard two shops down in each direction, Mabel asks, "When did you and Ella Mae start dating?"

Laura drops her scissors. Her mouth flies open and she stands there, staring at me like I just grew a second head. Not only Laura. The whole shop goes still. Every eye is trained on me. I'm cornered, and I'm caught off guard, which isn't a usual experience for me. I've been going soft with Ella Mae filling my thoughts and time.

I take a breath. Assess the situation.

Never react. Always respond.

When I finally speak, my voice is calm and steady. "It's new."

"I know!" Mabel exclaims. "I see everything Ella Mae does online. She's my guru, or whatever you want to call her. She helps me so much with my dance tutorials. She even bought me a ring light!"

"You need more than a ring light," Esther mumbles under her breath.

Mabel ignores Esther and continues talking to me. "And isn't it exciting?"

"What?" I take the bait.

"Ella Mae going to California to attend that party with DrakesDaMan?"

"How do you know about DrakesDaMan?"

"He's huge on the YouTube. Ella Mae did the cutest little stunt with him a few weeks ago on her page. Well, that was after her dinner out with you," Mabel pauses, and then with emphasis, she says, "Big Boy."

Did Mabel just call me Big Boy?

"You saw our dinner?"

"Of course I did. Ella Mae helps me with my TikTok channel. I watch all her videos and posts just so I can learn how to gain traction on my socials."

"Traction on your socials," I echo.

"You know it. I've got four thousand followers now. And I'm growing all the time."

This online life is like a cult.

Next thing I know, my dad's going to want to be on TikTok to spread the word about his accounting business. Take me back to the days when phones were connected to the walls. Everything was so much simpler.

Memaw walks over to Angie's chair. "I think it's wonderful you and Ella Mae are gettin' together. Let bygones be bygones, I always say."

"When did you ever say that?" Esther asks.

"All the time. And you'd know it if you'd give in and get yourself some hearing aids. Half the time you think I'm saying something that sounds so absurd. Why would I say, *Bill and I got an outhouse?* What would we need an outhouse for when our toilets work just fine? Can you imagine me strutting into the back yard in the middle of the night just to relieve myself? I'm tellin' you Esther. It's time. Trust an old friend and take the plunge. Get yourself some hearing aids."

"I'm sorry," Esther replies calmly. "I couldn't hear a thing you just said."

She gives Memaw a meaningful glance and Memaw rolls her eyes heavenward and purses her lips.

I'm relieved they've gone off on one of their usual tangents. There's nothing like a distraction to take the focus off a conversation that should never have happened. I chide myself for being unprepared. After Duke confronted me, it was obvious people had seen me in Ella Mae's home. And that means the rumor mill is already flowing like a marble run.

But my relief is premature, because Esther loops back around to address me.

"Chris, I agree with Virginia." Esther refers to Memaw by her given name. "I think it's great you're seeing Ella Mae. Put family feuds to death. And besides, someone ought to have mercy on that girl, after all. Otherwise she'd never find herself a husband."

Mercy on her? This town. I think I see red. Why can't anyone appreciate Ella Mae's special qualities that are so obvious to me? I get it. Sure, she's been over-the-top—annoying even. She even irritated me, so I understand how off putting her behavior has been at times, but she's never been unkind.

This whole conversation is one that would gut Ella Mae if she happened to overhear it. And yet, no one's feeling the least bit guilty for acting like she's a charity case when it comes to romance.

"What's wrong with Ella Mae?" I defend.

Laura has already picked up her scissors and shut her gaping mouth by now, but her brow raises like she wants to take my temperature.

I can't help myself. Even if all Ella Mae and I ever are is friends, I can't just sit by and let this pass.

"Isn't she the one who dropped everything to help Jayme get her publishing deal?" I ask, looking each woman in the eye. "And like Mabel just said, doesn't Ella Mae take time out of her week to coach Mabel in everything she wants to know about being online? And what has she ever done besides being a little bit loud and over-the-top? She volunteered her time to take the photos of the firemen last year, just so the town could get a new popcorn machine. If you think about it, she's constantly giving to others without any thought of return. And this is the thanks she gets. People talking behind her back."

I finish my speech, close my eyes for a moment, and then I look at Laura who has a stunned expression on her face.

"Cut my hair."

"Yes, sir."

CHAPTER 31

Ella Mae

I'M NURSING my nighttime tea. It's one of those evenings I feel like simply doing nothing at all. Meg's out with Joe, and I have the house all to myself. Being an influencer means I call my own hours. It also means I work late into the night most nights, and I am on the job over weekends and holidays.

So, yes. I'm sitting here, already in my fuzzy socks and a pair of pink pj's with sloths all over them, with my warm mug of tea in my hands. I'm so on brand right now, and the theme is: Unplug, girly.

My hand almost itches to reach for my phone to check my notifications, and okay, I'll admit it, to check out those pictures from our photo shoot today—especially that kitchen kiss. That's the stuff dreams are made of. But not my dreams. I learned a long time ago that dreams are for girls like Lexi, Shannon, and Em. Maybe Jayme and Laura had a harder go of things, but even they ended up with their prince at the end of their fairy tale.

I'm not a princess, and I'm not checking the driveway for white knights on horses. I'm my own white knight. Knightess? Knighterina? Knightella? Whatever. I've got my own back.

A sigh escapes my lips. Seriously. A sigh? The thought of what Chris' mouth felt like on mine has been on an infinite loop ever since he left. What.a.kiss. I've been kissed before. I'm nearly thirty. But I've never been kissed like *that*.

Thank goodness Meg had the sense to blurt something out. I was about to climb across the island and scale Chris like one of those guys who climb for coconuts in Polynesia.

Okay. One peek at our photos won't kill me. I can just scan my camera roll. I don't have to go online. I set my tea on the coffee table in front of me and open my phone.

There we are—piggyback riding, walking and holding hands, and kissing. Whew. It's a little much to take in. In a different world, I'd say I'm falling for the soldier. But this is Bordeaux. And lines are drawn. Besides, I'm Ella Mae. And that alone means no man from this town would dare tarnish their reputation by dating me.

It's okay. I'm having more fun than I hoped to have doing this charade with Chris. And if it means a few more kisses, and a few more laughs, I'll take what I can get. At least at the end of all this we'll still be friends. I think that's what we've become. Even that development is basically a miracle.

There's a knock at the door. Did Meg forget her keys? It's only seven forty-five. She wouldn't be back so soon.

I stand up, shouting out, "Who's there?" as I walk toward the front door.

"It's me," comes the all too familiar voice, that also happens to send goosebumps across my skin.

"Wait a second. I'm not decent." I say.

I hear Chris clear his throat. I don't know what he's thinking, so I clarify. "I'm in my baby sloth pjs. Let me get some sweats on."

I hear his rumbly chuckle through the door and I want

to throw it open. Just once, I'd have him come in, we'd cuddle on the couch, make out a little, talk, laugh. Just be together. No faking, no worrying about tomorrow, or this town, or stalkers. Just Chris and me and an evening together.

I scurry upstairs and change and then I come down and let him in.

He looks a little distraught. His hair's cut shorter and his beard's been trimmed. Thank you, Laura. Who knew it was possible for Chris to look even yummier than he did when he left today?

"Come in. Did you eat?"

"Yeah. I ate. Then I went by Aiden's to get his opinion. Then I came here."

"Aiden's opinion?" I step out of the way so Chris can pass by me. He smells like a workshop—like fresh cut wood. But also like something almost minty.

"I'm liking the haircut, Soldier."

"Yeah. Laura took care of me. She even put this stuff in my beard."

"Beard oil?"

"Yeah. How'd you know?"

I point to myself. "Influencer. I know all the beauty and self-care stuff."

"Huh."

I lean in and sniff his beard.

He chuckles, and looks down at me with warmth in his eyes. "Did you just sniff me?"

"Sort of. You said beard oil. I wanted to smell it. It's yummy. Sandalwood, Cedar and Eucalyptus. I thought I smelled mint."

"I brushed my teeth."

I laugh. It's this laugh that only Chris seems to elicit from me. I love this laugh. I feel like I can be a complete dork and he'll just wait my little dorkfest out until it passes. Maybe it even entertains him.

"What? What's wrong with brushing my teeth?"

"Nothing. It's just, usually when a guy comes by a woman's house in the evening and he brushed his teeth, he's counting on her being so close to his mouth that his breath would matter. It just made me laugh. It's a good thing. I like when you make me laugh."

"Yeah. Me too."

I can't dwell on that fact. So, friends like making one another laugh. It's all good.

Chris follows me back to the living room. Thankfully, my screen on my phone went dead so he can't tell I was sitting here reminiscing over our romantic photo shoot this afternoon.

"Have a seat. Want some tea?"

"No. I'm here for a reason."

"I figured. It's not like you're actually my boyfriend, so you'd just show up here with your teeth brushed and your beard oiled all ready for a night together on my couch."

I glance over at Chris. He's blushing. That's for sure a blush.

He clears his throat and takes a seat in one of our living room chairs. I plop back down on the couch.

I'll never decipher this man. Maybe that's part of the allure. He's so mysterious. At first, he comes across almost pompous, definitely steely and reserved. Then he softens and you surprisingly encounter this tender heart.

Yes, he's a hero. But underneath his acts of heroism, he genuinely cares. And he's got a layer of radical guilt in there. Of course, I know about Bridgette and his mom. And I can only assume his time in the military wasn't all unicorns pooping marshmallow rainbows, so I'm sure he's got some stuff he's hanging onto deep down. It should make him less appealing—this wounded side—but somehow it just makes him more relatable. And maybe I want to rescue him a bit too. After all, it's only fair if I return the favor.

But more than all that, Chris is funny, and serious, and thoughtful, and he's really intelligent. Yep. Chris St. James is the whole package.

"So, spill. What brings you here on my unplugged night?"

"Unplugged?"

"Yeah. Sometimes—maybe about once a week—I just feel like turning the phone off and sitting still. I curl up with a book, or I just sit. It's a nice break from all the posting, and commenting, and people always wanting a piece of me."

"Sounds nice."

"It is. Sometimes it's a little lonely, but you know how that goes."

"I do."

I think of Chris, night after night, alone in his house. I wonder what he does with himself. Most of his friends here in town are married, some have kids. I'm pretty sure they're with their families or wives every night.

"Well," he says, leaning forward and bracing his elbows on his knees. "I got my haircut today."

"I know."

"Yeah. Well, while I was there, Mabel, Memaw, and Esther came in."

"Do they go there daily, or what?"

"I think it's once a week for a wash and curl. It's an old-fashioned tradition."

"Leave it to them to keep that up."

"Yeah, well, like I said, they came in and Mabel … Well, she asked how long we'd been dating."

I should have thought of that. Mabel follows my every online movement. She's so dedicated to her channel, and she treats me like I walk on virtual water.

Of course she saw our posts.

"What did you tell her?"

"I said, 'It's new.' There was no use denying it. She saw the posts."

"Sorry about that. About all this. You didn't sign up for this level of crazy."

"I'm here for it now."

"You are?"

"Yeah. But you know what this means, don't you?"

"It means we've got to act like we're dating here. In Bordeaux."

He just looks at me, not saying a word. If anyone could win a staring match, or go a whole day without saying a word, it's Chris.

"What do you want to do?" I ask him.

"Whatever you want to do."

"Really?"

"Yeah. Really. That Beefy guy still isn't backing down, so we ought to keep this farce up online. The way I see it, now that Mabel knows, we have to fake it here too.

"Laura nearly had a heart attack when Mabel asked me about you. You should have seen her. She dropped her scissors, and her mouth popped open. She didn't even have the wherewithal to try to act like she wasn't shocked."

I laugh. "Man, I wish I had been there to see that!"

"Nah. You don't. But anyway, I'm up for whatever you want to do. I'm in this, Ella Mae. I'm here for you."

He's here for me?

"You realize how weird this is," I say.

"I do."

"And you realize our parents are going to go bat-spitting bonkers about this, and not in a good way."

"I do."

We could just admit this is a farce. At least locally, we

could. And then we would just maintain the online impression that we're dating.

I tried to get this town on social media back when I was helping Jayme get her book deal. Most of those accounts are as dry and dusty as cyber deserts, but enough of Bordeaux remained active online. They're bound to trip across my account eventually and see these photos. I hadn't thought about it when I agreed to this ridiculousness, but if we're going to pull off faking it, we're going to have to convince the people of Bordeaux that we're a couple.

"You're still willing to take this to the next level," I ask.

"I'm willing to go to the next level with you, Ella Mae. For you, I'm all in."

If I didn't know better, I'd take that as some sort of sign that Chris St. James had romantic feelings for me. Instead, I'll take it for what it obviously is. He's crossed a line. We have. He's officially my friend. And, as a woman with only a handful of friends, I feel like I just won the lottery.

CHAPTER 32

Ella Mae

"I'VE GOT one more thing to ask you before I leave you to get back to your unplugged night."

Chris actually looks a little nervous. Doesn't he know I'd pretty much say yes to anything he needs from me? It's not like I'm known for turning people down when they ask for help. Well, I'm not known for most of my good qualities, but he should know me well enough to know I pitch in whenever I can.

"You remember Brooks?"

"Of course I remember Brooks. What kind of question is that? I probably could recite our town's population in alphabetical order, you goof."

He shakes his head as though no one's ever called him a goof before. Maybe no one has.

"Okay. Well, he and Gabriela had their wedding in Boston. I went. I didn't tell anyone here that I went, because a lot of them weren't going, and ... Anyway, Brooks and Gabriela are having a second reception in Cincinnati, where he grew up. It's next weekend."

"That's nice."

"It's … yeah. I guess. Anyway, I'm invited."

"Well, you should go."

"I am."

"Okay?"

"I want you to go with me."

"Me? You want *me* to go with *you* to Cincinnati? For a reception?"

"Yeah. If you were my girlfriend, you'd go. Everyone's bringing their wife or girlfriend. And, you're my girlfriend, so I want you to come."

"You really know how to woo a woman. Don't you, Big Boy?"

"Honestly? I think I used to have those skills, and I'm starting to wonder if they atrophied from lack of use."

"You're good. Don't worry. I'm sure when the right one comes along, you'll be inspired, and it will all come rushing back just like riding a bicycle."

"You think?"

"Yeah. And another thing. It won't matter. When it's the right one, you won't need the moves. She'll be so swept up into you, and all this—" I gesture to him from his head to his feet and back up again. "You won't need any extra moves."

"So you think I've got what it takes to win a woman over?

"I know you do. And I think you know it too."

Chris stares at me. I stare back. These stare-offs used to be more contentious. Now, they're more like a silent conversation. We've got this hard-earned ease between us.

How'd we even get here?

I chuckle to myself.

"So, will you go with me?"

"Yeah. I'll go. Despite my better judgment, I'll go. It's the least I can do for you after all you've done for me."

"You don't have to go. I just thought it would be a good way to make what we're doing look legit."

"It'll be fun. I haven't been out of Bordeaux in a while. Not unless you count my two trips to Columbus for work."

"I don't count those. You deserve a weekend away."

I smile over at him. He smiles back.

I know Chris is about to leave. There's no reason for him to hang out. I'm trying to think of things that might keep him here, which is ridiculous. The man obviously has a life. He's doing me a favor—one that's getting more and more out of control each day.

"Do you want to stick around and watch a movie?"

His brows draw together.

"I mean, you probably don't want to. And I know you've got things to do, obviously. I just thought if you wanted to. But obviously you have friends, and work, and probably hobbies. No worries. Thanks for coming by to tell me about Mabel. And to ask me to the reception. I'll see you in a few days to film more content."

"Ella Mae?"

"Yeah?"

"I'd love to. But isn't this your unplugged night?"

"It is, but a movie sounded better than a rousing game of Monopoly."

"I guess it does, considering I'd take you down in Monopoly."

"You tell yourself that, Soldier. But I'm the queen of Monopoly. You'd walk out with your head hung low. And that's no way to end a night between friends."

"Is that what we are?"

"I'd like to think so."

"Yeah, Okay. We're friends. Now, show me where you keep that Monopoly board."

"You are going to regret this, Soldier, because you are going down in a blazing ball of loser shame."

He chuckles as I walk to the cabinet where Meg and I keep

our inner-nerd supplies: Chess, Monopoly, RummiKub, and a whole bunch of jigsaw puzzles.

I look at him before opening the cabinet door. "You may never, and I mean never, repeat what you are about to see here to anyone. This is classified. Capiche?"

He chuckles and then he holds up his left hand as if he's taking an oath. "Your secret's safe with me."

"It would ruin me if people found out someone who is supposedly superficial actually geeks out over board games."

"I won't tarnish your bad reputation."

He's got that smile. I'm appreciating it—as a friend. I wonder if friends are allowed to rub their friends' beards, just a teensie weensie bit. Not anything crazy. Just a little stroke or two. I bet it's softer with that oil Laura put in there today.

"I appreciate you keeping my bad repute in good standing."

He shakes his head—still smiling. This must be a record. I wonder if his face is starting to cramp since he's so unaccustomed to having a smile going for this long.

We play Monopoly for the next hour, laughing, talking, and hanging out like real friends. I whoop his tooshie. Not literally, of course, but I *am* the queen of Monopoly, and I especially gloat over those dark blue properties: Park Place and Boardwalk. They are full of hotels. I'm basically a real estate mogul, and I stripped the soldier of all his cash every time he landed on my sweet holdings.

When I win, I stand and do a celebration dance, waving my arms overhead and doing hand rolls while I chant, "Uh huh! Uh huh! Who's the winner? That's this girl!"

Chris cracks up at my antics. I plop back down on the floor, smiling. I should feel embarrassed, but I don't. Not even a little. Somehow, in the strangest and most unexpected turn of events ever, Chris has become one of the people I trust most in the world.

"You play a mean game, Ella Mae."

"I play to win, Soldier."

"Me too," he says, and I can't help the tingle that courses through me at his words.

We're cross legged on the floor. Well, he's not. He's laying down on his side with his legs extended, and his head propped in his hand.

He stretches his arms overhead. "I'd better get a move on. I've got a lot of work to do tomorrow. I'll see you in a few days for our next photo shoot."

"Let's switch things up and go out in town, since we're trying to sell this thing locally."

"Sounds good," he agrees. "I'll pick you up for dinner. We can go grab Mad River burgers and then get some ice cream. We can stroll down Main with our cones. That should give everyone something to talk about."

"Are you ready for the backlash of this?"

"I fought overseas. I can handle pretty much anything."

A cloud of memories crosses in front of his eyes. It's so poignant I almost feel like I can see them too.

I don't know what makes me say the next words out of my mouth, but I know him, and maybe that's enough.

"Whatever went on, I'm sure of one thing. You did your best. And you did what you were trained to do. You don't slouch, Soldier. You're honorable and you have people's backs. Things happen that are out of our control. We have to accept that whatever went down in life wasn't always our fault."

Chris stares at me. His eyes are stormy and serious, but his face is soft. He's not mad, but my words struck a chord.

"Thanks," he says. "That means a lot. More than you know."

I smile at him. He's shaking his head like he can't believe something.

"What's up?"

"This," he waves his pointer finger back and forth between us. "It's kind of crazy, right?"

"Yeah. It is. But a good kind of crazy, like when you think you're going to owe taxes, but somehow you get a return."

"Yeah." He nods. "Exactly like that."

Chris stands. I walk him out.

We stand facing one another, unsure how to actually say goodbye. Finally I reach out and give him a hug. I step forward and wrap my arms around his massive body. He stands there for a moment, not responding, and I rethink my life choices. But then, a beautiful thing happens. Chris lifts his arms, and he pulls me near. He wraps his big arms behind my back and holds me. I lean my head on his chest. Neither of us moves. But he gently rubs my lower back with his hand.

"Thanks for asking me to stay," he murmurs into the top of my head.

I look up at him, his face is so close.

"Best unplugged night ever," I tell him.

It's the truth.

"I'm a fan of unplugged night," he says.

He releases me, and I step back. Then he turns and walks out of my home, saying, "Have a good rest of your night, Boots."

"Boots?"

"It's your winning Monopoly piece. I think it fits you."

Huh. I don't know if I've ever had a nickname. God knows I love me some boots. And yes, I'm always that boot when I play Monopoly. Everyone wants to be the dog. I'm all about the boot.

And, yes, in case you're wondering, I stand at the window watching him drive away. In a different world … we'd be more. So. Much. More.

My phone is buzzing on the coffee table when I walk back

into the living room. I hold it up to see who's trying to message me. It's Drake, so I break my little hiatus from social media to see what he wants.

@DrakesDaMan

I'll cut to the chase. How serious is it with this ex-military dude?

Wow. Okay. Well, that makes sense, Drake sees my posts. I guess. Okay. Yes. He's watching my posts! That's pretty awesome. But, why does he care how serious I am with Chris? I take a page out of Chris' book and use the same answer he gave Mabel.

@Fab-U-lous_EllaMae

We're still new.

@DrakesDaMan

Good. Good. My offer still stands for you to come out. Let me know about staying here. I'm sure you and I will have plenty to talk about, and I'm looking forward to helping you get a leg up. I think about you, you know. We made a good team.

@Fab-U-lous_EllaMae

Thanks for reaching out. I'll keep you posted. I really appreciate your support.

Chris' adamant declaration echoes in my mind. *You're not going out to see him.* If only he'd give me a real reason to turn Drake down. But he's not, so I'm a free agent, and I'm pretty sure this party will be just the ticket to secure my place as a much larger influencer than I've been up until now.

CHAPTER 33

Chris

THE PAST WEEK, Ella Mae and I have continued posting on social media, in addition to faking around town. We went to Mad River Burgers and then out to ice cream last Friday. And as we had planned, we strolled down Main Street eating our cones. I even tipped mine over to Ella Mae to give her a bite off it.

She licked that cone so slowly, just to make a show—so everyone around us could see we were clearly out on a date. And also, to torture me, I'm sure. She ran her hand over my beard at dinner. And we held hands.

Since she was being so touchy and affectionate, I reciprocated. I put my hand on the small of her back when I held the door open for her, rubbed my thumb across her knuckles while we held hands, and leaned in to place a soft kiss on her temple a few times throughout the night.

I know I was pushing my luck, but I figured, there she was, and we were trying to look convincing, so I went all in. Of course, I have ulterior motives. I'm starving for time with her, for any touch, look, laugh, smile. Faking gives me a certain ticket to show her affection, and I'm cashing that ticket in at every.single.opportunity.

Things between us feel easy, and half the time I forget we're faking. Well, I'm not faking, but Ella Mae doesn't know that yet.

Yes. Our situation is getting beyond complicated. And it's not merely the added element of having to act like we are dating here in town now. Constantly being around Ella Mae makes me feel so many things. Keeping those feelings and longings in check is becoming increasingly challenging. All the lines are running together and blurring like a fresh watercolor.

I'm on my way to pick her up for our weekend in Cincinnati. There's a little gathering with just our friends tonight, and then the reception with extended friends and family is tomorrow night. We all got Airbnbs to split the cost of staying overnight. Grant and Jayme, Duke and Shannon, and Ella Mae and I are all sharing a four bedroom house. Ella Mae and I will have our own separate rooms, and the married couples will take the other two bedrooms.

Ella Mae has two full suitcases and a hot pink bedazzled backpack sitting on the porch when I drive up—for our two and a half day weekend away. I chuckle and run my hand over my beard as I walk up to greet her.

"We're going for two days, not two weeks," I say with a taunting tone.

I really don't care how many bags she packs, but I love poking fun at her, and I think she enjoys it as much as I do.

"I have to accessorize, Soldier. And stop running your hand over your beard. It's too much of a tease. If you don't want me touching it, you don't get to touch it either."

I look straight in her eyes, and lift one brow as a slow smile spreads across my face. Then I hold my right hand a few inches from my jawline. Slowly—oh, so slowly—I cup my chin and drag my hand down my facial hair. All the while, my eyes never leave hers.

Her pupils might dilate, or I might be dreaming that they do. Either way, I can tell my taunting got to her. Maybe it's just because we love playing cat and mouse almost more than we enjoy anything else we do together. But maybe, just maybe, she's starting to feel a fraction of what I'm feeling for her.

"Okay," she says, not missing a beat. "I warned you."

Ella Mae reaches over and runs her hand over my beard. And she's not just getting it over with so we can get in the car and hit the road. Oh, no. She's retaliating. And I am here for all of it. If this is her way of getting even, I say bring on the revenge.

She is basically petting my beard, and she hums while she runs her palm across my jaw.

"Mmmmm, that's so nice."

She has the audacity to look me straight in the eyes while she caresses my beard and coos out her appreciative comments.

I resist (1) purring like an overgrown cat, (2) leaning into her hand like a lovesick puppy, and (3) grabbing her face and kissing her senseless. Basically, I deserve a medal for self-control.

"Have you had your fill of fondling my beard?" My voice is raspy and intense.

"Hmmm … maybe. For now, yes."

I shake my head.

I grab both her suitcases and walk toward my truck, hoisting them into the back and securing them. Then I walk toward the passenger door and open it for Ella Mae.

"Why, thank you, Soldier. I'm not sure we have an audience, but I appreciate the gesture anyway."

I give her my hand and she hops up onto the bench seat of

my truck, pulling that beacon of a backpack behind her. If we need to flag someone down for roadside assistance, all we'll have to do is wave that thing around.

I've barely started the engine when Ella Mae announces, "I brought snacks! And I have the playlist all queued up on my Spotify. Do you have bluetooth in this thing?"

I chuckle. "I've got bluetooth. And I just had my protein shake, so I'm good for now. Do you need me to drive through anywhere to get you breakfast?"

"Nope. I had my smoothie too. It's not all Pop-Tarts and Lucky Charms over here. A girl's gotta watch her figure."

I'm trying not to watch her figure now that she mentions it.

She promptly kicks off her sandals and puts her feet up on the dash, her hot pink toenails on full display.

"I just love a road trip! Don't you, Big Boy?"

"Usually."

"When don't you? Now?"

"No. I like this fine. I just sometimes would rather not drive anywhere."

"Not me. I love getting out of this town and seeing the world. I don't do it near enough. I mean, maybe I'm a creature of habit. But I also love seeing new sights, meeting new people. Just shaking things up a bit, you know?"

"Yeah. I do."

Some people might want a drive to be quiet and peaceful. Maybe there were times I would have preferred that. Today, all I want is to listen to Ella Mae rattle on, her exuberant personality filling the cab with a sense of hope and anticipation. It's been a while since I've felt either of those emotions.

The drive from Bordeaux to Cincinnati takes us an hour and a half. In that time, Ella Mae breaks out the Cheetos, then Red Vines, a bottled Frappucino (I turn one down while she cracks hers open and hums after she sips it), Ritz Bits, and finally, M&Ms.

"Where do you put all that?" I joke.

"It's a magical thing called metabolism. I've got one that I think belonged to a horse in a previous life. Not that I was a horse in a previous life. As crazy as I am, I don't buy into that whole past life stuff. Sorry, Shirley MacLaine. I just think we're here once and we need to make the best of it. Plus, I work out daily."

"Me too."

"Obviously. I mean, look at you. You're quite a specimen. I know I always joke with you about it, but you're pretty impressive." She reaches over and squeezes my bicep. "Gosh. You're like a rock, Soldier."

She's killing me. Kill-ing. Me.

"We should workout together sometime. It would make a great photo shoot. We've done the whole yoga thing. You could even bench press me. My peeps would *love* that."

I laugh out loud. "I'm not bench pressing you."

"You could, though. Right?"

"Here's a concept. Just because you *can* do something, doesn't mean you *should* do it."

"How about you tell me what you can bench."

I pause. I know I'm in shape. I work hard to maintain my level of fitness.

"Around 385."

"Pounds?!"

"Yeah."

"Oh, my word."

She mocks fanning herself.

"You could bench Duke!"

"Like he'd sit still for that."

We both laugh.

"Anyway, we should workout together. Don't you think?"

"We could," I agree. "I'll ask Davis if it would be okay for you to come by the firehouse sometime when I'm going to lift."

She smiles big, like a kid waiting for the family trip to Disney.

Our conversation shifts from exercise to the events of the weekend. Turns out, Ella Mae's a little nervous about the people we're going to be around—aka my friend group. After all, we're fake dating and most of the people from Bordeaux at this reception are not her biggest fans.

"I think I'm going to catch some shade being thrown my way for dating you," she says.

Her brow furrows and I want to drag her right next to me and keep her tucked under my arm so she'll never feel that vulnerable again.

"I've got you, Boots. I won't stand for anyone treating you with anything less than complete respect."

"Boots," she says with a giggle. "I've never had a nickname before."

"Never?" She sure dishes out the nicknames. I'm surprised no one ever gave her one. "Do you like it?"

"Truth?"

"Always," I say.

Insisting on truth feels a little ironic since we're colluding to pull off a farce online and in person right now. But I always want nothing but complete honesty between us.

Ella Mae's voice is soft when she answers me. "I love it." She says the nickname under her breath. "Boots."

I glance over at her. "Good. I'm glad. It fits you."

"Has your family said anything about us?" she asks.

"I've been dodging their calls."

"Me too." she admits. "My mom called a few times and then resorted to texting. I'm just like la, la, la, la."

She covers her ears and squeezes her eyes shut.

"I know I have to face the music at some point," she says. "I'm just postponing the inevitable."

"I am too. I will face them. And they better be careful how they handle the conversation. That's all I know."

"I love when you get all tough and protective like that."

"No you don't. You usually hate it."

"No. I hate when you're all bossy and try to tell me how to live my adult life, as if I don't have the sense of a common garden slug." She spears me with a look for emphasis.

"But the way you go all protective, like you'd never let anyone near enough to hurt me? That is my kryptonite."

Okay. That's very good to know.

We pull in front of the house where we'll be staying. The event this weekend is at the Anderson Pavilion, right on the river. The home we rented is a two-story, white brick house in a residential neighborhood. It has a broad front porch with a colonial front door. The photos showed a nice-sized deck off the back of the house.

I put the truck in park just as Jayme and Grant step out onto the front porch.

"Okay," Ella Mae says, taking a deep breath. "Here goes nothing."

CHAPTER 34

Ella Mae

"HEY YOU TWO," Grant hollers down to us from the porch. "Need help carrying anything in?"

"Got a forklift?" Chris says under his breath so only I can hear him.

Then he shouts up to Grant. "We've got it. Thanks."

"Ha ha, Soldier. You'll appreciate the outcome of my over-packing. I've got all the things to make heads turn as your fake girlfriend right there in those two bags."

"You don't need all that to make heads turn, Ella Mae."

The words seem to slip out of his mouth without a second thought. I wonder if he realizes how much he's complimented me today. It's like all this faking is making him soft.

And he called me Ella Mae. As much as I love that new nickname, there's something about the sound of my name coming out of Chris' mouth that does things to me. It's so intimate—caring, even.

I'll take it—all of it. Most of the compliments I get are either from Meg, who is biased as all get out, or from my followers, who don't really know me. Chris knows me. It's a whole different story when he says something nice.

He lifts his duffel, and then my two suitcases, and heads up the path toward the front door with all three bags like it's no big deal, leaving me to follow him carrying only my backpack.

Jayme pulls me into an unexpected hug when we reach the porch.

"Welcome to Chez Cincinnati! We just got here about an hour ago. We left Fiona with Hazel, so it's just me and Grant here."

She pulls me near after Chris and Grant walk into the house and nearly whispers, "When did this development start? I'm so intrigued—and happy, for both of you."

"You are?" I can't help but sound skeptical.

"Of course. I love romance—especially when the two people are the least likely candidates to fall for one another. But on second glance, you two make so much sense."

"We do?"

This I have to hear.

"Of course. Think about it. You're both insanely independent. You have intense personalities. I mean that in the best of ways. You're private about the things that matter most. And you both easily and willingly drop whatever you've got going on to help anyone when they're in need."

Wow. Of course Jayme would see my generous side. I did drop everything to help her achieve her life's dream. I just never realized how much she actually acknowledged my role in her success until now.

"So, yeah," she continues. "I think you two have the perfect blend of opposite traits and compatibility to make things highly interesting—and the chemistry between you two must be off the charts. Right?"

"I mean, it's Chris." That's all I can say. I'm sort of stunned into a type of wordlessness.

"Right? He can seem so broody, but he's really a big softie

under all that tough exterior. Kind of like Grant, only Grant is actually a genuine grump, but he's got a heart of gold."

She's confiding in me like we're best friends. I came here prepared to be excluded. I don't even know what to do with this interaction. There's no place where it fits in my repertoire of *How to handle a weekend with Chris' best friends and a bunch of strangers*.

"You and Grant make such a good match."

It's true, but that's not why I'm bringing it up. I remember an influencer saying something years ago when I was much smaller and trying so hard to be relevant. She said, *If you're ever at a loss as to what to say in a social setting, turn the tables and ask the other person about themselves, or find an opportunity to compliment them. People love to talk about themselves. Voilà, problem solved*.

"Awww, thanks. Well, we have you partially to thank for helping us get back together."

Yeah. I did that too. I just smile.

You know when you dump one too many sweeteners into your tea? That's how I feel right now. Like I want to pucker from the extra sweetness.

I stand on the porch, looking at the door like I wish it were a portal to another world, or like it could summon Chris to my rescue. From what? From being befriended? Maybe. I just don't trust this. It's unlike anything I've experienced with people from our town. And, yes, Jayme's nice. Super-nice. But she's never given me the time of day outside the usual cordial greeting when we see one another around town. And now it's like we're bffs. It's a bit too much to swallow.

"Let's go in. I'll show you to your room and you can get settled."

"Sounds good," I say.

While I'm unpacking alone in my room, getting some much needed space, I hear the volume in the living room ramp up. Duke is here. Only that man can make an entrance like he does. I hear Shannon too. I should go out and get this over with. But a huge part of me wonders if anyone would notice if I stayed sequestered in this room all weekend.

Nope. No. Chris invited me. We've got a charade to pull off, and besides, I miss him.

I know. It's pathetic. But lately, when he's not around, my mind drifts to memories of our interactions, or thoughts of his touches. He actually kissed me on the temple a few times when we were on our fake date, and it was one of the sweetest gestures ever. Not to mention the way my body lit up like a fireworks show. Just a brush of that man's lips and facial hair across my forehead, and I'm officially softer than a fresh container of playdough.

I take a deep breath. Recite a few affirmations.

I've got this.

It's only a weekend.

Everything goes back to normal Sunday.

Chris is here.

Chris has my back.

I've got my own back.

I don't need a man.

That last one leaves a different taste in my mouth than it usually does. Sure, I don't need a man. But I'm kind-of enjoying having one. Not that I have one. Whatever. Leaning on Chris has been nice. And he hasn't let me down.

Okay. Time to bite the bullet and come out of hiding.

As soon as I step into the living room, Chris stands and walks over to me. "Hey, babe, you all settled in?"

Babe?

I shoot him a look that says, *Babe? Really?*

He sends me a look that says, *What? You don't like it?*

I shake my head and smile at him.

"Yeah. I'm settled in."

He puts his hand on my lower back and guides me toward the couch. And, yes, it occurs to me to tell him I didn't break my leg and I can make my way across a room on my own. But then again, considering the level of social tension filling the air right now, maybe I do need an escort and a crutch.

After Shannon and Duke both greet me, conversation picks up where it must have left off before I came out of my room. I'm silent, sitting on the couch next to Chris. He's all casual and relaxed, his arm outstretched behind me. I'm uptight, but trying to relax. Everyone else is carrying on without me, which is more like what I had anticipated.

We end up grabbing lunch at a local deli, picking up some groceries to keep on hand, and then coming back to the house to hang out. I haven't said much all day, but I'm not as uncomfortable as I was at first.

Chris keeps checking in with me. It's sweet, really. He doesn't leave my side, as if he knows his presence is a buffer between me and everyone else. It's not like they don't like me. It's just that we're bending lines that have been set in something more firm than concrete for as long as I can remember.

Evening comes and we all retreat to our respective rooms to prepare for our night out with Aiden, Em, Rob, Laura, Lexi, and Trevor. I put on the special outfit I chose to give myself an extra boost of confidence. I'm wearing a matching jumpsuit that consists of a white, clingy crop top and wide-leg pants in a flowing fabric. I pair that with some hot pink stacked sandals. Then I pull my hair into a high ponytail and put on my makeup.

When I exit my bedroom, Chris lets out a low whistle. His eyes track from my feet up to my face.

"You look amazing," he says.

"I know," I tease back.

He chuckles. Then he walks across the living room and stands close enough that I can smell his cologne.

He leans in and places a soft kiss on my cheek.

"I'm glad you know. You're stunning. I won't be able to keep my eyes off you."

No one else is in the living room, so I'm not sure if he's hoping they are listening, or he's just playing the part, or if, by some off chance, he actually means what he's saying. I barely let my heart hope for the last possibility. It's too fragile a thing—hope.

Instead, I wink at him and say, "You look pretty scrumptious yourself. We'll have to get a ton of photos tonight to post online."

Chris' smile fades for the slightest moment, and then he says, "Yep. Let's get lots of photos to post online."

CHAPTER 35

Chris

I'M SIPPING my coffee out on the back porch of the house we're renting. Yesterday's gathering with all my friends was … Well, it was a complete and utter dumpster fire. Maybe no one noticed. They were all enjoying one another, laughing at Duke, talking about Shannon's pregnancy, Laura and Rob's adoption, and how the Mighty Fireflies are doing in summer little league.

But every time I looked over at Ella Mae, she looked like Westley in *The Princess Bride* when he's being tortured in the Pit of Despair—barely veiled agony. I'd give her a comforting touch, or try to send a non-verbal message of assurance her way, but nothing I did could make up for the invisible wall between her and everyone else in the room.

That's why I decided she and I are getting out and doing some sightseeing today in Cincinnati—alone. We've got the reception this evening, but a day out on the town together will be the least I can do to give Ella Mae a break from the odd mixture of scrutiny and neglect she's been having to endure.

The glass door to the deck slides open. I look over my

shoulder to catch a glimpse of Ella Mae walking toward me in a fuzzy tracksuit. She's cupping a mug of coffee with both hands.

"Have a seat," I offer.

"How'd you sleep?"

"Okay. You?"

"It was fine. I had weird dreams," she says, scrunching up her nose in this adorable way.

"Any you want to share?"

"With you? No."

"Now that's just mean. You tell a person you have weird dreams and then you refuse to share the storyline."

She gives me a playfully wicked look. "Yep."

"Was I in them?"

"Don't you wish you knew." She takes a long sip of coffee, her eyes sparkling with mirth over the edge of her cup.

I just shake my head and smile. She's so much fun. Even after living through a night I wouldn't wish on anyone, she just bounces back. No complaints. No bashing the people who treated her poorly. She'd have every right to say a few things right now, but she's not.

I have mad respect for the woman sitting across from me. It still blows my mind to think that she's won my heart, but from where I'm sitting, how could she not?

She's not bringing up yesterday, so I will.

"So, last night …"

She just nods, continuing to sip her coffee and stare at me with those blue eyes. Not a bit of makeup this morning. She's exposed and natural. It's all I can do to stay in my chair right now. I want to pull her into my lap, or at least reach over and hold hands.

"It was not cool," I say.

"What?"

I give her a look with my lips twisted and my brows

raised. Seriously? She's not even going to acknowledge how poorly everyone treated her?

"Didn't you feel left out?"

"By you? Not at all. You were the perfect fake boyfriend." She's quiet for a beat. Her face shifts from dismissive to serious. "And, in all seriousness, you were the perfect friend. I wouldn't have been able to sit through a night like that without your little glances, and the way you kept silently checking in with me."

I can feel my molars connect and my face grow taut. I've never been short on testosterone, which is usually a benefit in my line of work. But right now it's making me feel like punching something.

"Down, Big Boy. It's all good. This is my life. You're just getting on board the Ella Mae train. I've been riding it for years. None of those people hate me. They just don't know me well enough to like me."

"That's crap," I spit out. "They've known you your whole life. You've helped each one of them at some point or another."

She reaches over and places her hand on my forearm. Skin to skin. And I feel her touch everywhere. I'm going out of my mind for more than one reason.

"At ease, Soldier. I'm fine. Would it have been nice to have a better night, to be treated like I belong, to be included? Yeah. It would. But I'm not living out my best Disney princess life over here. I'm me. I'm not everyone's fave flavor, you know? I may be over-the-top, but my feet are firmly planted in reality. Those aren't my friends. They're yours. I didn't expect anything other than what I got. So, I'm good."

Her hand is still on my arm, making light, comforting strokes.

"Are *you* good?" she asks.

She gets rejected and she asks if *I'm* good?

"I'll get over it."

"Good, since it's not your cross to bear."

She looks out over the yard and takes another sip of coffee. "What's the plan for today?"

"I thought you and I could get away together. Just hang out and do some Cincinnati things until we have to come get ready for tonight."

"Sounds fun! Should I change?"

"Not a bit."

I mean it, too. I hope she never changes. But man, do I wish the people in our hometown would.

While Ella Mae goes back to her room to grab her things, Duke comes to ask me if I want to hang out with everyone today. I explain to him that I'm taking Ella Mae out alone. Duke's the one person who truly tried to include Ella Mae last night, but it was a losing battle, so he gave up and just enjoyed himself—as he always does. When I explain today's plan, he nods and a knowing smile crosses his face.

"Moving in for the kill?" Duke asks.

"She doesn't know how I feel yet, if that's what you're asking."

"Sort of. But I get it. She's a little skittish. You have to pace yourself. A day alone is a good call. And tonight will be all kinds of romantic. You'll be able to play off that. Maybe you'll get your moment."

"Maybe. I'm a patient man, though. And she's worth waiting for."

Duke grins. "You can outlast the best of them. I have a good feeling about this for both of you."

"Thanks, man."

Ella Mae comes back onto the porch. We say goodbye to Duke. Once we're in my truck, I tell her I'm leaving the decision as to what we'll do with our day up to her. We start by grabbing bagels at a shop Ella Mae finds on Yelp. Then she decides we're going to the zoo for the morning. She insisted she had to feed a giraffe. So, I made sure that happened. And, yes, I took photos for her to post.

After the zoo, we were pretty hungry, so we took the Connector, a local public streetcar, to Findlay Market in the historic Over-the-Rhine district. We grabbed lunch at the market. We got back on the Connector and rode to Fountain Square where they have roller skating.

By the time we arrive back at the rental house, it's late afternoon, and we are happily wiped out. We laughed, talked, and sat in comfortable silence throughout the day, and I feel more convinced than ever that I want to pursue something real with Ella Mae. She seems content to stay in the friend zone, or whatever zone we are in. She used the word *friend* no less than ten times today.

We are friends. But if I have anything to say about it, we will be much more than that, and soon.

We shower and change into our outfits and Ella Mae meets me in the living room. We're driving over with the other couples in the house to the Anderson Pavilion, an impressive glass two-story building that faces the river. The upstairs houses a carousel. Downstairs has rooms for events.

Ella Mae has on a long red dress with thin straps. Her hair is pulled up with tendrils of curls falling down and framing her face. I have on dress slacks, wingtips, and my white cotton dress shirt. My tie is black to match my pants.

When Grant parks his SUV, I help Ella Mae out of the backseat and loop her arm in the crook of my elbow.

I lean in, and in a low, private voice, intended just for her, I say, "You are beautiful."

In a conspiratorial voice, she answers me. "You say the sweetest things, Soldier. And you're looking so dapper. I have to say, you clean up nice."

I smile. I'm still talking so only the two of us can hear.

"Well, if things go well, maybe I'll even let you touch my beard before the night's out. I put some of that oil Laura gave me in it."

"I can smell it from here," she nearly whispers, looking up into my eyes.

She reaches over and places her palm on my face and slowly runs her hand along my jawline. "See, I don't have to behave to touch your beard. And I don't have to wait either."

I'm speechless. No words form. I have no witty comeback on the tip of my tongue, no clever thing to say to her. Somehow, I manage to walk the two of us into the reception. Heads turn when we enter. Ella Mae catches the eye of nearly every man in the room.

Needless to say, the night goes far better than yesterday evening did. My friends are all busy with their spouses, we eat around two large tables, but the conversation includes everyone. Ella Mae makes an effort to include herself. She tells everyone what we did all day, and they smile at both of us. A few people ask her questions. It's not great, but it's a start.

It's good to see Brooks and Gabriela so happy together. They do a first dance, just like they would at a wedding, and then the dance floor opens up.

"Want to dance?" I lean in and ask Ella Mae.

"Only if you promise I get cake afterward."

"You can have both our slices," I say as I pull her chair out and extend my hand.

She takes it and we make our way to the dance floor. The DJ plays *If I Ain't Got You* by Alicia Keys. I couldn't have ordered up a more perfect song. I pull Ella Mae into my arms and she slips right in place. Her hand in mine, the other looped up around my neck.

Maybe it's the mood of the evening. It could be the faking. I couldn't care less what it is that makes Ella Mae do the next thing she does. She takes her fingers and toys with the edges of my hair near my neck. Then she leans in and kisses my jaw, right on top of my beard. I'm watching her. She won't look at me. Instead, she nestles her head under my chin, right next to my heart, and we dance smoothly and slowly until the song ends.

When the music changes to an uptempo song, Ella Mae brings it. I've seen her feed. I've even checked out her dance videos with Mabel. And I knew she could dance, but knowing it and seeing it are two different things. We dance every fast and slow song for over an hour.

Finally, Ella Mae says, "Time for me to collect on that offer of cake, Soldier."

"Let's grab two slices and take them outside," I suggest.

"I like how you think."

I actually grab three slices, since I promised Ella Mae two and I know she'll hold me to it. We walk out front, right along the river. The lights of the city sparkle on the water. We eat our cake and talk about our day.

When Ella Mae finishes, I take her plate away from her and set it off to the side on a concrete half-wall that runs along the river.

She shivers a little. It's not cold out here, but there's an occasional breeze coming in over the water.

"Are you cold?" I ask, moving closer and looping my arm around her shoulder.

"Not cold, but that feels nice anyway."

I need to kiss her. I can't go one more minute looking at her in that dress, holding her in my arms, smelling her sweet citrus-cinnamon scent and not kiss her.

I look around. A man's gotta do what a man's gotta do.

"I think we're being watched," I say.

I don't know if anyone's watching us, and I don't care. I

also don't give Ella Mae any time to confirm or deny my suspicions.

I bend in, twirling one of the tendrils of hair in my fingers. She looks up at me, anticipation written all over her face. I move closer.

"I'm going to kiss you, Ella Mae."

"Yes, please," she breathes out softly.

Never one to turn down a reasonable request, I move my mouth closer to hers. This may be a fake kiss, but my brain is not computing that fact. For my heart, this is the most real kiss of my life.

I put my hand behind Ella Mae's neck and hold her to me while my lips move with hers. She lets out the softest sound from somewhere in her throat and I wonder how I'm still standing upright. She's my undoing. Always has been, and with any luck, she always will be.

She places a hand on my chest, and for the briefest moment, I think she's going to push me away, but she fists my tie and drags me toward herself. I put my other hand around her and pull her near, running my fingers in soft caresses over her lower back. She loops her other hand behind my head and runs her fingers through my hair.

We kiss for far longer than would be necessary to convince anyone we were dating. When Ella Mae pulls away, she has a bewildered look on her face. I'm not sure what I look like, but I feel my smile tugging at my cheeks.

"Okay. Well," she says.

"Yeah," I say, my voice husky from our kiss. "I'm pretty sure that convinced everyone we're not faking."

CHAPTER 36

Ella Mae

"DID YOU HAVE A NICE WEEKEND?" Chris asks me.

We're a half-hour outside Cincinnati, on our way back to Bordeaux. My head's been buried in my phone. It's the third time he asked the question, but I'm partially acting oblivious. It's true, I'm focused on my post. But I'm also trying to sort through my thoughts and feelings—which is not an easy task with Chris sitting less than three feet away from me in the cab of his truck.

That was the best kiss of my life.

It was probably the best kiss of anyone's life. I mean, no offense to Liam Hemsworth and Miley Cyrus, Kim Kardashian and Kayne West, Angelina and Brad, or any other famous smoochers. Their kisses might have been special, hot, even newsworthy, but they weren't life-changing, earth-shattering kisses. And that one last night—it was.

I think I'm having a hot flash just remembering the way Chris held me, the feel of our lips meeting, and the way he gently rubbed his fingers on my back.

I know we were putting on a show. And believe me, I'm all about giving people what they want to see. But I'm not a fool, and that kiss was for more than show. I think. And if it was more, what does that even mean?

Chris asks the question again. Bless him. I don't want to make him mad by ignoring him. I just don't know if there's enough room in this truck for him, me, and the memory of that kiss.

"Did you have a nice weekend?"

I nod and hum, "Mm hmm," while keeping my eyes super-duper focused on my phone.

Yep. I am one busy social media influencer.

"What was your favorite part?"

"You sound like my kindergarten teacher after spring break."

"Yeah? Did you have Mrs. Goodwin?"

"Yep."

"I had her too," he says. "I loved the way she read to us—always using all the different voices for each character."

"Me too," I say.

Well now. Look at us, talking all civilized and avoiding touching the subject of the big kissy elephant in the truck.

"So?"

"So, what?"

"What was your favorite part of the weekend?"

That hot as tamales kiss. And it was my favorite part of my week, month, year, and possibly life … But I'm not telling the soldier that. Second fave: dancing. Being held while we swayed on the dance floor. Let's go with the third favorite thing.

"Feeding the giraffes."

"Yeah. That was pretty cool."

"What was your favorite part of the weekend?"

No. No. No. Why? I need a delete button. Rewind. Reverse. I didn't just ask him that! He's going to say it. I can see the smirk forming on his smug face. Don't say it, Chris. Don't.

"Oh, I think you know what my favorite part of the weekend was, Boots."

"Bagels?"

"Nope."

"Zoo."

"Not the zoo."

"Skating?"

"I haven't skated in years. I loved that. But still not my favorite part of the weekend."

I drop it, hoping he'll drop it.

Chris looks over at me, wags his eyebrows. Then he returns his eyes to the road.

"What are you posting?" he mercifully asks.

"Just putting a string of photos from this weekend into a carousel post."

"Seriously, though, Ella Mae. Besides the harder parts of the weekend, I hope you had a good time. I'm grateful you came with me."

"I am too."

"There's somewhere I'd like to take you next Wednesday."

"Frisch's Big Boy?" I joke.

"Ha! No. I have a friend in Columbus. I think you'd like him and his wife. They're special to me. I'd like them to meet you. Courtney, the wife, well … she's sort of a fan."

"A fan of mine?"

"Yeah." He looks over and smiles at me. "But that's not why I want you to meet them. I just want you to come. If you want."

"I'd love to."

"Great."

Invited to dinner with his friends. What is even going on here? First the kiss, now this.

Hope, you are a relentless beast.

I turn my focus back to my phone. Comments are coming in on the pictures I just posted.

I scan down and see one from Drake telling me to check my personal messages. I click the message icon at the top of my page and see this message from Drake.

@DrakesDaMan

Saw your post. This is looking serious between you and that guy, EllaMae. Touch base about our plans when you can. I've got lots of leads lined up for you. You can contact Genesis, or even reach out to me directly.

I don't offer that to everyone, but after our collab, I feel like we've got a connection, so you get special access to me.

I don't say anything to Chris. He's not a fan of Drake's, and I know how Chris feels about me traveling out to L.A. to attend the bash. I return to the post and scroll more comments.

People comment on how cute we are, how beautiful I look in my dress, some are raving about Cincinnati. Then I see it. A comment from ImSOBeefy.

@ImSOBeefy:

> Babe, you look beautiful. You need to call it quits with that guy. I'd treat you so much better.

"What's wrong?" Chris asks.

"What?"

"What's wrong? You look troubled."

"How do you know how I look? You're driving."

"I was watching you for a second. And you look like something upset you. Did it?"

"That guy, ImSOBeefy, left a comment on my post from our weekend."

"What did he say?"

I read Chris the comment. He's quiet. An eerie silence hangs in the air while he grinds his molars and grips the steering wheel with white knuckles.

"Hang on," Chris finally says.

Then he takes the next off ramp and pulls over onto the dirt that runs alongside this country road that seems to lead nowhere.

Chris pulls out his cell. I watch him scroll and then type.

"What are you doing?"

"I'm commenting on your post."

"You pulled over to comment on my post?"

I look at my phone. Sure enough, Chris commented.

@got.your.six.now.:

> Dude. She's taken and happy, as the photos show. Show some respect and leave her alone.

. . .

"You commented on his comment?"

"Yeah. You can block him. But we both know he'll come back under another name. Plus, keeping him here gives us a way to monitor him. I figured it was time for decisive action. I let him know you are happily taken. Hopefully he takes the clue and backs off."

Happily taken. If only it were that simple.

~

Mom's been nearly pestering me to death ever since rumors of Chris and me dating started circulating through town. I neatly avoided her calls and texts for long enough. She's not going to cave. I finally decide to bite the bullet and make a visit out to her place. It's Monday. My head's still swirling from this weekend.

When I open the screen door to Mom's house, I shout, "I'm here! Are you home?"

"Well, now. You finally decided to show your face?"

"I have a busy life, Mom. I know it seems like I do whatever I want, but I have a lot to do to keep my business going, and I went out of town Friday and just got back yesterday."

"Oh, I know you were out of town. Nice to hear that from people at the grocery instead of my own daughter."

"Am I on trial here? I popped in for a visit."

"A trial, no. But Ella Mae …" she pauses and lifts a stack of magazines and coupons she clipped out of the newspaper from off a sofa cushion. "Here. Sit. Sit."

I take a seat, knowing this is like getting a filling. You can put it off, but the pain only gets worse. Better to muscle through.

"You know how much I've warned you about putting

your eggs in one basket. Men are fun. But they can't all be relied on. And yes, I know I sound jaded."

"Maybe, because you are slightly jaded."

I say it. I'm not one to mince words and beat around the bush. I say what comes to mind unless it really shouldn't be said.

"Maybe I am. I'll give you that. But, sweet baby girl, you cannot date that man."

There. She said it.

"I can, and I am."

I know. I know. I'm not.

Mom has zero capacity to keep a secret. If I tell her Chris and I are faking, that news will fly around town like a flock of sparrows in springtime.

Besides, after that kiss and him inviting me to his friends' house, I don't even know what we're doing. And Mom won't only object to Chris and me dating. She wouldn't want us to be friends, or even share the same air, if she could help it.

"I told you not to date him. He's off limits."

"Off limits because of you and your past, not me and mine. Do you find that a little unreasonable?"

"Ella Mae." Mom sighs a weary sigh.

"I know. I know. I don't need another history lesson about how Dad and Mrs. St. James were high school sweethearts, and how you lost him to a woman he can't even have."

Yeah. You heard that right. My dad dated Chris' mom. They were even homecoming king and queen—as in, their photo is in a glass case in the hallway of Bordeaux High, on display for every student to walk by for a daily reminder of the bad blood between our families.

So, to make matters worse—hang with me here—as soon as Chris' mom broke things off with my dad before Christmas their senior year, Chris' dad made his move.

My mom had always had a giant crush on my dad, but of

course, he had been seriously committed to Chris' mom. So, when the breakup happened in high school, my mom brought on the flirt (yes, I came by that talent honestly). And my dad fell for her efforts. He probably didn't actually fall for *her*, in retrospect.

So, if you're following the soap opera that is my family history, we've got Chris' mom being loved by two men, and my mom being the consolation prize for my dad, who still pined away for Chris' mom. He probably still pines away for her to this day.

It's pathetic, but I can't hold it against him. My dad fell in love. He lost the one woman he wanted. He tried to make it work with his second choice. He left us when he realized a marriage to a woman you don't really love isn't something that works long-term.

I'm a symbol of his lack of backbone, or something like that. He's pleasant to me, like some uncle you never met, but when you finally meet, you realize you're related. But he's not a dad in any real meaning of the word. Thankfully, in my line of work, I rarely need to pick up a nut and bolt, so I can stay out of his way for the most part.

Fast forward to four years after our parents graduated from high school. Chris' parents had gone away to college—together. Mine did not. My parents stayed here and dated. Dad worked at his dad's hardware store until he moved up to managing, and then owning the shop. Maybe it was a case of loneliness, or just doing what was easy at the time, but Dad never let go of Mom when he should have.

Chris' parents came home after college and promptly got married. The St. James' wedding sealed the deal. Mrs. St. James was officially off the market for life. So, my dad, being the romantic that he is, proposed to Mom. They were married six months later.

"I can recite the rest of your love life by heart," I remind Mom. "And it's got nothing to do with me."

It's taken years to realize that. This town, as sweet as it can be, is also brutal when there's any sign of a feud. People pick sides. The rumor mill flows like the Mad River in spring after a snow melt. No one cares too deeply about the truth. And no one acknowledges that in all disputes, every side is at least partially right.

Upshot? My mom has been viewed as pitiable. My dad has been labeled as a homewrecker. And the St. James and Lindstrom families do not mix—at all. Not until that handsome soldier waltzed into the Big Boy and saved my hide by being on that live with me. And now—so much more. I'm not sure what, but I've got some big feelings where the Big Boy is concerned. I haven't even had time to sort through all of that yet.

My mom sighs again. She looks weary, concerned, and beaten down. She's not mad.

"Look, Mom. I love you. I really do. But I can't live my life fighting your battles. I can't help that this town is so small-minded that they never fully included you after what you went through in high school. It was *high school,* for goodness sakes. If it weren't so painful, it would be laughable."

She lets out a laugh that sounds more like the verge of tears.

"I love you and I'm not picking the other team, or anything like that. You and I are the dynamic duo. You'll never shake me. I'm like a bright pink, fluffy, well-dressed burr you can't ever get out of your side."

She smiles.

"My beautiful burr." The words come out so softly it's like she almost didn't say them. "I don't deserve you, baby girl."

"Maybe I don't deserve you. You've been my cheerleader.

I wouldn't have pushed myself to do all I've done without you."

"Don't make this sound like a farewell speech."

"Not on your life."

It's not a farewell speech, but for the first time in my life, I'm drawing some lines. I'm nearly thirty. It's taken me this long to see that certain battles aren't mine to fight.

"Whatever happens between me and Chris needs to be between the two of us. He's not off limits. He's been the most kind, supportive, caring, thoughtful person to enter my life in years—maybe ever. He's fun and he's funny. And we get one another. There's this ease when I'm with him. I can't even put words to it. But he's become very important to me. He sort of snuck in with this stealth attack, and in the process, I think he won my heart."

I sit on the couch, stunned at the words that just flowed out of my mouth.

Mom beats me to the punchline.

"You're in love."

She smiles the first genuine smile of the day.

"Yeah. I think I might be."

"Oh my goodness. You're in love with Chris St. James."

She doesn't say it with anger or condemnation. She's actually in awe. No one is as shocked as I am.

Not quite sure what I'm going to do with this revelation. One thing I'm not going to do is hash it out with my mom right now.

"So, we're good?" I ask her.

"We're good."

She gets out of her chair and walks toward me. I stand and we hug.

Mom rubs her hand down my hair and then she whispers into my ear, "I'm sorry, baby girl. So sorry."

"It's all water under the bridge, Mom."

Between us, it is. I'm not telling her how much living in this town with all the judgment and rejection is getting to me. I think I've held it together for so long, using my online community, who love me well, to buffer the reality of where I live. Being more open to life here—spending time with Chris—has cracked something inside of me. Now I feel like I'm a bunch of exposed nerve endings. I can't stop feeling all my emotions. That man has wrecked me.

CHAPTER 37

Chris

MY HANDS TAP out a rhythm on the steering wheel as I drive to pick up Ella Mae to take her with me to meet Alex and Courtney. No one in my life has met them before, which seems wrong, now that I think about it.

I guess keeping my two worlds separate felt like one way to cope with everything I've endured in each of them.

But Ella Mae makes me want to merge everything, to take risks, to start fresh. More than that, she makes me want to buck the rigid lines that have constrained us our whole lives. I'm going to burn those lines to the ground if it means actually having something real with her.

Ella Mae has been blatantly avoiding me since our kiss Saturday night. We had returned to the party inside the pavilion, but she didn't dance another slow dance with me the rest of the night. She was pleasant on the surface, but I picked up on her body language. She kept her distance, barely holding eye contact with me for more than a beat.

On the drive home, she kept our conversation playful. She tried to act like our kiss didn't rock her world. But that kiss told me everything I need to know about what Ella Mae really wants. Our situation is beyond complicated, so I won't push her.

The Army taught me strategies for offensive attacks. Granted, Ella Mae's not my enemy, and we're not at war, but I can use what I learned in the military to our advantage. And yes, I said *our*. It's in Ella Mae's best interest that we pursue a relationship. She may not know that yet, but I do.

We're good for one another. If I didn't think so, I'd abandon this whole pursuit. But since I know it's only a matter of time until she gives in to what she really wants, I'll patiently outwait her resistance. Then I'll make my move when she's optimally ready.

Ella Mae answers the door wearing a pair of stretchy pants and a loose top. She's got on sandals, and her hair's in a ponytail. She's wearing makeup, but not too much. I've concluded that her level of makeup reflects how much she intends to put on a persona over her real personality.

When she's got fake eyelashes and sparkly dust around her eyes, she's in full-on influencer mode. Her voice even changes, like an actress going onto stage. But when she's bare-faced, that's when her heart is on her sleeve. She's vulnerable and relaxed. Very few people have the privilege of seeing this side of Ella Mae. I'm one of them, and I treasure the fact that she trusts me enough to let me that close.

Our drive to Columbus is less awkward than the drive home from Cincinnati was. She seems to have resolved something. There's a lightness to her that wasn't there after our weekend.

We pull up in front of Alex and Courtney's around five. I skipped working at the office today so I could bring Ella Mae with me. Kassie's out front kicking a soccer ball and Alex is in his chair cheering her on. I didn't tell Ella Mae that Alex uses a wheelchair before we got here.

"How do you know Alex?" she asks before we get out of the truck.

"We served together. He was my best friend overseas. He's like a brother to me."

"So," Ella Mae says, her eyes trained on Alex through the truck window. "That happened over there?"

"Yeah. It did."

"Okay."

She opens the door and steps out.

"Mommy!" Kassie shouts. "Chris is here with his girlfriend, and she's really, really pretty!"

Kassie runs into the house.

Alex watches her and then turns to us, still chuckling. "Hi, I'm Alex. You must be Ella Mae."

He sticks out his hand and Ella Mae shakes it.

"Yeah. That's me. Nice to meet you."

"Chris has told me a lot about you," Alex says, wagging his eyebrows at me.

"Well, lucky you," Ella Mae says, spearing me with a playfully accusing look. "He hasn't told me anything about you until the moment we parked in front of your house."

"Typical," Alex says with a smile.

"Right?!" Ella Mae says. She laughs and gives me a playful shove in the arm.

"I already like her," Alex says to me.

"Yeah, me too," I say, peering over at Ella Mae to gauge her reaction.

She doesn't flinch, so that's probably a good sign.

Kassie comes out of the house, dragging Courtney by the hand. "See, Mommy! She's really pretty."

"She is," Courtney says to Kassie.

Then she looks at Ella Mae and says, "Welcome. I'm so glad you could come. I'm Courtney. This is our daughter

Kassie. I follow you on Instagram, so I feel like I already know you. That's weird, right?"

"It's totally normal. I just met one of my online heroes this month. He's always been larger than life in my eyes. I felt like I've known him forever. But he's different in person. We all are."

"I'm sure of that," Courtney says.

Ella Mae's talking about Drake. Larger than life? A guy who stood her up? His ego is larger than life. That's what I know.

"We're making homemade pizzas and salad. I hope that's okay."

"Sounds good. May I help?" Ella Mae offers without a second thought.

"You could help us!" Kassie says. "Mommy has a stool I stand on when I put the toppings. You could do that with me."

"Sounds fun," Ella Mae says.

And just like that, the three women disappear into the house and leave me with Alex and his cocky grin.

"Oh man," he says. "This is awesome."

"Shut it."

"No, seriously, Cap. Seeing you like this, I could die a happy man tonight. I never thought I'd meet the woman who was your match. This one, though. She's got your number. I am loving this."

I just chuckle. "She's pretty special."

"She ought to know you feel that way."

I told Alex about the whole fake dating thing before I asked if I could bring Ella Mae with me tonight. He understands. He told me then, like he's telling me now, *Life's too short to waste your time when you care about a woman. Tell her how you feel.*

He doesn't realize how complicated things are in Bordeaux for us—especially for her.

"Well, enough sitting around looking at your face," Alex says. "Let's go join the women inside."

"Try not to embarrass me too much," I say.

Alex spins his chair. "Your days of telling me what to do are long past, Cap. I plan to see how many times I can make you blush before you take your girl home tonight."

My girl.

I like the sound of that.

"Does she know how I got my new set of wheels?" Alex asks before we make it in the front door.

"She knows it happened on duty."

He nods. "Does she know you think it's your fault?"

I shake my head. Discomfort seeps through me, but it's not as much of a gut punch as it has been in the past.

Alex's lips draw into a thin line and he stares at me like he's looking into my soul. "Gotta let that go, Cap."

"I know."

I haven't gotten over what happened yet, but I feel something shifting. I think back to the night Ella Mae told me not to feel so responsible for everyone and everything. She probably doesn't even remember saying it. People have been telling me that same thing for years—ever since we lost Bridgette. Yet, that one night with Ella Mae cracked through something I thought was impenetrable. My guilt doesn't feel as ominous as it had before then. It's still here, just less intense.

Ella Mae fits in with Alex, Courtney and Kassie so seamlessly. We eat our pizzas around their dining table, laughing and sharing stories until Courtney announces it's Kassie's bedtime.

"I want Miss Ella Mae to read me my story," Kassie says with the whine of a child who's ready for bed.

I'm about to jump in to spare Ella Mae having to say no to a near stranger, when Ella Mae says, "I'd be glad to read to you, if it's okay with your mom."

"Can she, Mommy?"

"Sure. That would be fine."

Kassie makes the rounds, giving me a big hug, then hugging her dad, and then Ella Mae and Courtney walk with Kassie down the hall to her bedroom.

"... and she reads bedtime stories," Alex says with a smirk. "You should see your face right now. Wipe that drool off your chin."

He laughs. I don't deny it at all.

I'm gone for this woman. Completely gone.

"Ahhhh. I see it now. You didn't know she liked kids, did you?"

I have nothing to say. He's right. Ella Mae never struck me as the maternal type. I don't know why. She's cared for me more than most people. When she sees someone in need, she jumps in without a second thought. She looks out for Meg. She's far more responsible than most people give her credit for—than I ever gave her credit for before I got to know her better.

She'd make a fun and creative mom—if motherhood's something she wants for herself. I don't know if it is. I wouldn't push a family on her. I'd be happy being the best uncle in the world if she were by my side, sharing life with me. Those thoughts should send me reeling. They don't. I'm thirty-two—and I had all but given up on the idea of actually settling down with someone. I don't know when it happened, but I can easily envision a future with Ella Mae, and it's a future I'm willing to work to pursue.

CHAPTER 38

Chris

SATURDAY MORNING, I'm turning the corner onto my street from a run. I see the car before I see the man leaning back against it. My dad's Audi S3 sits parked squarely in front of my home. It's an ambush.

Yes. I've been avoiding him. I don't usually take that tack with confrontation. I'm a soldier to my core. But this is one battle I hoped to evade or postpone. Welp. Now the time of reckoning has arrived.

I jog up to my dad, who is casually scrolling on his phone.

"Hey, Dad."

"Hey, Chris. Thought we might have a chat. You free for about a half-hour?"

"I'm free. Wanna come in?"

"I do."

I turn and jog up to my front door. Dad follows me in.

"Let me just hop in a quick shower so you don't have to deal with me post-workout. I'll be out in three. Help yourself to anything to drink in the fridge."

Dad nods. I turn to shower and change. Another perk of military life is the ability to be ready in a split second when needed. I'm back out with dad in under three minutes. He's sitting on my couch, a glass of water on the side table next to him.

I sit on the chair opposite him. "Okay. Let's get this over with."

"Son," Dad starts.

It's never good when he says, son. It's a warm term of endearment, but in our family it's always been used as a lead in for a lecture.

"I'm not one to give heed to rumors. This town has had its way with our family in the past. Even when the hearsay is true, it's often not anyone's business. But you know how it goes. People with nothing better to do find entertainment in discussing the comings and goings of others."

I nod. I don't really need a lesson on Bordeaux gossip. But he's my dad. I'll respect him enough to let him say his piece.

"But," he continues. "When the gossip pertains to one of my children, that's another matter. I want to go to the source and straighten out whatever I heard so I know the truth."

"Okay."

"And what I heard is that you and Ella Mae Lindstrom are in a romantic relationship. I'm pretty sure I heard wrong, but then the next thing I heard is that you traveled out of town for the weekend last weekend, and then you took her out of town Wednesday night. That's leading me to believe these rumors are grounded in some facts. Add to that the detail that you've been avoiding my calls and your sister's calls, and I think we've got ourselves a concerning situation."

"Concerning situation?" I echo.

"She's a Lindstrom."

"That she is."

I'm not about to make this easy on him. If he wants to come after Ella Mae, he's going to have to go through me.

And that's pretty much a wall of defense he doesn't realize he'd rather avoid. He will realize it, though.

"And we're St. James."

"Right again."

"And she's …"

I sit quietly, my arms loosely folded over my chest, a kind, but firm expression on my face.

Dig your ditch, Dad. I'm right here watching you.

"The history between our families is something well-known by everyone. And she's … so different from the type of woman I'd expect you to pursue."

"How so?"

I'm making him spell it out.

Say it all, Dad. I'm not going to save you from your prejudice or your misguided perceptions.

"Well, you know how … eccentric she is. Loud. Outspoken. Flashy. Materialistic."

My arms fall from my body and I grip the armrests of my chair, reminding myself to keep a cool head. No battle is ever won by a strict show of force. Battles are won by the clear-headed.

The silence in the room thrums with tension.

"Do you know her well?" I finally ask.

"I've known her her whole life."

"Known her? Or known of her? Have you had any real conversations with her? Do you know what she does with her free time? Have you talked with her about her dreams, or discovered what makes her tick?"

He stares at me, obviously not having expected this response from me.

"Because, I have. I've spent hours with her. I've seen her vulnerable. I've watched her persevere against odds. I've gotten to know her creative, spunky side. I've laughed hard with her. I've been changed by her, Dad. By Ella Mae. She's the one who has made me realize how much guilt I've been carrying around that isn't mine to bear. Not the therapist you hired. Not the VA people. Not my best friends. Her."

Dad looks incapable of forming a thought, so I continue.

"She's got an image she portrays. And believe me, I thought that was all she had to offer for years. Though, I always suspected there was more beneath the surface. It seemed a waste for her to live in this shell of an image when there was so much more to who she could be.

"But through the strangest of circumstances, we started hanging out, and then we became friends, and now, as you have heard, I'm dating her."

"Chris, are you sure?"

That's all he says.

"Sure of what?"

"That this is the direction you want to go. Our families have been at odds since high school."

"That's on you, Dad. Not me. And it's for sure not on Ella Mae. I think if you gave her a chance, you'd get to know her like I have, and you'd sing a different tune."

Dad looks baffled.

I know it's hard to change a life-long assumption about someone. It's hard to drop your weapons and enter a truce and a ceasefire.

"Right now, if I'm being honest with you, I'm offended on her behalf. She's done nothing to you. Nothing. And you've condemned her unfairly. And if you did have a hunch that I was dating her when you got here, the way you spoke about her was offensive to me. Don't you think I have a head on my shoulders? Aren't I capable of judging someone's character? Would I be so blinded by a woman that I couldn't see who she is beneath the beauty?"

Dad sits back. His eyes roam the pictures on my walls. Then his gaze meets mine again.

"It's hard for me to see what you see," he admits.

"I understand that."

"So, you really like her?"

I pause. Then I look directly at my dad.

"I think I love her."

Dad's eyes go wide. I'm sure, being the accountant he is, he's doing some sort of analysis right now. And that includes factoring in the long-term impact of me loving Ella Mae. It would mean our two families would be bound in a way no one could fathom.

I couldn't care less. They need to handle that crap and get over it—or not. Ella Mae and I aren't responsible for their mess, and if I have anything to say about it, we'll find a way to be together despite the unspoken and spoken taboos surrounding us.

Even though my dad stays another twenty minutes, nothing is resolved. He leaves me with a mild apology for offending me. He doesn't even apologize for what he said about Ella Mae.

He just says, "I'm sorry, Chris. I shouldn't have doubted you."

He's not ready to move forward. On one hand, I understand him being confused and stuck in his ways. Beliefs are ruts. They can guide us along a path, or they can keep us woefully entrenched, heading the wrong direction.

My dad is a kind man with a good heart. Maybe in time he'll come around. But that's not my circus, and these people are not my monkeys. Whether he comes around or not, I'm pursuing something deeper and long-term with Ella Mae.

CHAPTER 39

Ella Mae

"YOU GO AHEAD WITHOUT ME," I shout down the stairs to Meg. "Chris is coming to pick me up in an hour. We'll meet you and Joe there."

Meg appears in my bedroom doorway.

"I thought you were downstairs," I tell her.

"I was. I came up here to grab my lipstick. I left it on the bathroom counter."

She crosses her arms across her chest and sizes me up. I'm in my underwear with clothes spread across my bed in three configurations of red, white, and blue outfits.

"What? I'm getting dressed. I just need to decide on the best outfit."

"That one," she says definitively, pointing to a pair of cut-off white denim shorts and a red eyelet lace top with puff sleeves.

I'll wear my navy espadrilles if I choose that one. I look over the three outfits one more time and decide she's right. That one is casual, but sexy, and somewhat playful. It's borderline Daisy Duke without putting too much out there. I'll be keeping Chris on his toes—maybe pushing him just a little to notice me. I don't know where we stand, and the uncertainty is making me slightly crazy.

"So, Chris is picking you up?" Meg asks as I slip into my shorts.

"Yep. He is."

"This is getting a little serious between you two. Don't you think?"

"Serious how?"

"I mean, a lot of what you do goes beyond faking. Pulling the charade off happens in public. But he stops by, or he calls. You call him, or you two, oh, I don't know, go out of town for the night with no one else around. That seems serious."

"He invited me to meet some friends of his. We're friends now. All this faking has led to a friendship between us. I like him."

"I can tell."

I pop my head through my shirt and look over at her. She's waiting for me to spill everything.

"Okay. Yes. I like him a lot. And, also yes. He and I have a lot going against us here. Besides, I don't know how he feels."

I still haven't told Meg about the kiss in Cincinnati.

"I know how he feels. It's pretty obvious he's into you."

"Well, until he makes that obvious to me, we're friends."

"Okay. But you know, you could make it obvious to him. The guy doesn't always have to be the one to make the first move."

I consider Meg's words. I know she's right. I've made the first move before—when it didn't matter so much. But with Chris, it's different. He matters—a lot. I don't know if I could take putting my heart out there and having him turn me down, even if he let me down gently.

"I think I need him to make the first move."

"Okay, well. Here's hoping he does that soon."

Joe's knock on our front door carries upstairs.

"I'd better get going. I'll see you there," Meg says.

"Yep. See you."

I finish dressing and put my hair up in two pigtails, styling them so they fall in big curls. Then I look in the full-length mirror. This top is all wrong. I take it off and head to my closet.

My phone buzzes with a notification. I pick it up off the bed and carry it into my walk-in closet while reading the message.

@DrakesDaMan

Thinking of you. What do you do on the 4th of July? I'm heading to the beach to watch fireworks over the water. Have you talked to Genesis yet? I'm looking forward to introducing you to people when you're out here.

Drake's pretty presumptuous, but then again, it's flattering that he still wants me to come to the bash—and that he wants me there so badly that he keeps reaching out. I shoot him a quick response.

@Fab-U-lous_EllaMae

I used to be Miss Corn Husk every 4th of July. Don't ask. It's like being the queen of our parade. But I've passed that honor on this year. So, I'm just going to the local street fair and fireworks with friends. I'll get a hold of Genesis this week.

I need to reach out to Genesis. I should make this trip out west happen. It sounds like a great opportunity to connect with a lot of influential people and to network. Besides, I'm feeling so sick of this town. Ever since Chris and I extended our fake dating into Bordeaux, I've been the recipient of more judgmental stares than ever, and I've even gotten some unsolicited comments from people.

Not to mention that confrontation with my mom. It went better than I'd hoped, but it still drained me. Getting away might be just the thing to give me a break from being under the local spotlight. I haven't faced my dad yet. I won't even touch that hornets' nest unless Chris and I actually start dating.

I put the phone down on a closet shelf and begin hunting for a different shirt. I'm walking back and forth in my walk-in closet, pulling shirts down, looking at them, and putting them back. I want to make the kind of impression on Chris that leaves him wondering why he hasn't asked me out for real. And that means looking my very best.

"Ella Mae?"

Who is that? It sounds like Chris, but on a recording or something.

"Ella Mae? Hello? Are you there? Did you call me?"

I glance over at my phone screen.

It's on a video chat!

Holy toadstools!

Faster than you can say, "corn cobs," I drop down low and crouch at the bottom of my closet, leaving my phone on the shelf overhead. I think I scream "Aggggh!" on my way down, but everything happens so quickly, I can't be sure.

"Um, yeah. That was a butt-dial," I say, carefully staying out of view from the screen which is perched two feet above me.

I don't think Chris hears that part because he asks, "Where are you?"

I answer him from my hunkered position, "On the floor of my closet."

"What are you doing on the floor of your closet?" He sounds bewildered.

Trust me, no one is more caught off guard than me in this scenario.

"I'm picking my outfit! I'll see you in a bit! Bye!"

"Ella Mae?"

"Hang up, please!"

"Are you okay?"

"Chris, please do what I say, and hang up this call. I'll explain later."

Silence.

"Chris? Did you hang up?"

"No."

I'm lying on my belly now, as if getting lower than I already was would do a better job of keeping him from seeing me.

He can't see me, I know that. But just to be sure, I'm apparently trying to become one with the carpet.

"Hang up!" I shout.

"Okay. I'll see you in about forty-five minutes."

"Okay."

I wait a few moments. Then I say, "Chris?"

No one answers.

"Chris, if you're still there, I'll kill you."

Nothing.

"Chris, I mean it! I'll go all banzai kamikaze on your butt, and you will regret being born. Tell me you hung up!"

Silence.

I guess I'm going to have to take my chances.

I move back to a squatting position, grapple for my phone overhead, and grab a T-shirt from the bottom rung of my closet. Keeping the phone so the screen faces away from me, I throw the T-shirt over my cell. Once the phone is securely wrapped in the T-shirt, I peek my face in through the neck hole so I can see my cell. I push my hand up under the hem of the shirt and power the phone off.

Whew.

Oh. My. Lanta.

I nearly flashed Chris!

And I told him I'd explain more later.

I won't. No way I'm ever telling him that story. I can see it now, "So, what happened in your closet?"

... Yep. I'm not telling.

Chris shows up forty-five minutes later. After that whole closet fiasco, I decided the red eyelet shirt really was the best option after all. And his reaction to my outfit does not disappoint.

I do a twirl in the foyer when I open the door. "I'm ready to go all Red, White, and Blue, and Corn Too!"

"Looking good," Chris says. "And what was that Face-Time call all about?"

"Nothing. Just a classic butt-dial. Are you ready?"

"I am now."

He holds the door open for me and we walk side by side to his truck. He's wearing a red T-shirt and blue jeans, and looking all patriotic and scrumptious.

"Let's snap a selfie," I suggest before we get in the truck.

"Sounds good," he agrees.

I almost chuckle. He's gotten so used to this process. A few weeks ago he would have been all grumbly. Before that, well, we all know how he was. He actually turned my phone off mid-livestream. That seems like a lifetime ago.

Chris loops his arm around my waist. I lean into him and I extend my phone. He has to tip his head down to get closer to me, and his woodsy, orange, campfire scent wraps around me when he does.

It's all I can do not to turn and plant a kiss on his face. I could—under the guise of it being for social media, but something in me holds back. I'm tired of faking things with Chris. I want our next kiss to be real, something we both want for the right reasons, and only between the two of us, not for show.

On the drive downtown, I tell Chris about the trip to LA and my plans to go.

"I still don't think you should go out there," he says.

"Why not?"

"I don't trust Drake."

"You don't even know him."

"Neither do you."

"I know him well enough. He wants to help my career. Besides, what's it to you, Chris? You're my friend, and I appreciate that, but why do you care what I do?"

"I care. Okay?"

That's not enough. I go silent. I don't want to fight with Chris. My mind reels thinking of everything that's been bugging me for the past month. Meg's moving out in less than a year. I'm chronically disliked in my own hometown. I swim upstream daily just to exist here. I'm aging, which puts my position as an influencer on thin ice. This "Beefy" guy seems obsessed with me in an unhealthy way. And, as much as I've loved faking things with Chris, putting on a charade has drained me. I'm just tired of fighting to fit in.

CHAPTER 40

Ella Mae

WE MAKE it downtown and find parking behind the hardware store. It's too close for comfort, but Dad's always closed for the holiday, so I take a breath and step out onto the hot pavement.

Chris meets me before I even round the back of the truck. His hands come up and frame my shoulders.

"You look good, Ella Mae. Better than good."

"Why, thank you kindly, Soldier," I say in a feigned southern accent.

He shakes his head lightly. "What I'm trying to say is …"

I pop my hand on my hip, daring him to say what I think he's about to say—what I hope he's trying to find the words to tell me.

"All this faking …" he stares down at me.

Whether he knows it or not, his hands are making soothing strokes up and down the exposed skin on my shoulders.

"All this faking," he repeats. "Well, it's not. It's not for me."

"It's not what, Big Boy?"

"I don't want to fake it anymore."

"You don't want to fake being my boyfriend?"

Call me a sadist, but I need him to spell this one out.

He looks beyond frustrated, and then I see a shift in him. His jaw is set, his eyes steely with resolve, his grip on my shoulders is steady.

"I don't want to fake it with you. No. I don't. And I'm not. I haven't been faking for a long time now. You mean so much to me. I don't really know how it happened, or when, but I know this. When I tell you I care about you, I'm being honest. When you make me laugh, it's genuine. And when I kiss you, it's very, very real."

That's all I needed. His words echo in my ears: *I haven't been faking for a long time now.* I reach up, loop my hand behind Chris' neck and pull him down to me. Our lips collide like two magnets, north to south. Home. He feels like home.

I may have started the kiss, but he takes charge and pulls me toward himself, keeping one hand on my shoulder and bringing the other around behind me. I hum into his mouth as his hand makes leisurely strokes across my lower back. He teases my lips and drags his mouth across my jawline. Then he nips at my earlobe, and kisses a trail down my neck.

I think my eyes roll to the back of my head. Tingles explode across my body. Chris says the sweetest things on a whispered breath into my ear, punctuating his comments with kisses and the tickle of his beard.

It's you, Ella Mae.

You're it for me.

No one else.

I need you.

I want you.

You mean everything to me.

He's just shy of saying he loves me. And I'm right there

with him, though he's rendered me speechless, boneless, mindless. I'm putty in his arms. Deliriously giddy putty.

I find words, somehow.

But I want to look in his eyes when I say this.

"Chris?" I say, pushing back a little so his arms are still looped behind me, but my hand is flat on his chest and our faces are just inches apart.

"Yeah?"

"You …"

I stare at him. There aren't any words. His beautiful, ocean-blue eyes search mine. His mouth turns up in a smirky smile.

Something about that challenges me enough to press on and speak my mind.

"I feel all that. For you. I feel it too. You and I … we weren't supposed to be like this. But I don't know how to say this, except to say I can't imagine it not being you. What did you do to me?"

He chuckles.

"Somehow you went from being so very annoying, to being one of my closest friends, to being my person."

"I'm your person?"

"Yeah," I say. "You are."

A tear surprises me, coming to my eye and leaking down my face.

"You're crying," Chris says, wiping my cheek gently with the pad of his thumb.

"I'm just not used to having anyone in my corner. And I couldn't ask for a better person."

"I've got you, Boots. Always. I've got you."

He tugs me close and I fall into him, nestling my head under his chin. I grip him like a life ring, allowing myself to feel how much he means to me. It's scary—these feelings, and having someone matter the way he's come to matter to me.

"So," he murmurs into the top of my head. "No more faking?"

"I haven't been faking for a while either," I confess.

I look up and he's smiling down at me with that smile—the one I love most.

"For the record, you were way more annoying than I ever was," he has the nerve to say.

"Oh, yeah?"

"So annoying," he says, leaning in to kiss me.

His lips brush across mine. "Completely aggravating," he says in a husky voice. "Drove me insane." He kisses me again. "I was completely wild with frustration." His lips land on mine, and this time he holds me to him, and our kiss deepens. I'm smiling, even though we're kissing. This man. He's tough as nails, a genuine hero, funny, deep, tender—and he feels all this for me. It's almost more than I can believe.

I kiss him. It's the only way to say everything I feel for him without using the actual words that are pressing to come out. Not yet. I will tell him. Just not yet. So, I kiss him with everything I have, running my fingers through his hair, across his jaw, down his chest, over his arms. He's savoring me in return. It's like a dam has broken between us.

Something tugs at my attention, reminding me where we are—behind Dad's store, on the Fourth of July.

I pull back, smiling up at Chris. "We should go find everyone and try to celebrate the holiday. I'm pretty sure Riley would want me to see her in the parade."

Chris twists one of my pigtails in his fingers. He holds my gaze. "Let's go then."

We don't move. I cling to him, and he towers above me, looking down into my eyes.

"Yep. Let's go," I reiterate.

But we still don't move. Neither of us wants to break this moment. Once we walk away, it's over. Something new will take its place. But this is the spot—of all the places—where Chris took the risk and told me how he feels about me. It's the spot where I let my guard down and told him what he means to me. I feel like staying here, in this place—in this moment—forever.

That is until the whir of lawnmowers and clang of cymbals sound on the street in front of the shop.

"The parade!" I shout.

Chris chuckles. "Let's go."

We walk around the row of stores just in time to catch the start of the parade. It's a group of dads on riding mowers, and some with push mowers, walking in formation. They're all wearing sock sandals, white tank undershirts, and khaki shorts. The guys with push mowers do a slow synchronized spin, and then they continue to march forward.

Some of the men on riding mowers have someone seated with them, holding cymbals and clashing them at random, unpredictable intervals. There's no rhyme or reason to the presence of the cymbal players. But hey, this is Bordeaux.

On the final John Deere, bringing up the rear of the *Dad Squad with Dad Bods*, as they're called, is Duke's dad, Walt Satterson. He's got a boom box perched on his mower, belting out quasi-patriotic tunes like *Born in the USA, Yankee Doodle Dandy*, and *Party in the USA.*

Just behind the Dad Squad comes a series of floats all decorated to pay homage to corn. In front of those is the Miss Corn Husk convertible. Riley is perched on the top of the back seat and she's waving at everyone as she passes. I send her a thumbs up, and she mouths, *I'm so itchy*! back to me. I give her a sympathetic shrug.

Chris reaches down and slips my hand into his, and we stand there holding hands, watching the rest of the parade. Later, we find his friends and lay out a blanket from the back of Chris' truck so we can watch the fireworks. I settle in between his legs and lean back on him. Our heads tilt upward so we can watch the colorful explosions overhead.

Every so often, Chris plants a soft kiss on my temple. We get all sorts of side-eye looks from people. Tonight, I'm setting all that aside. Nothing can taint the elated feeling of knowing Chris and I are actually together. I can barely allow myself to accept the reality, but every time I look in his eyes, it's all right there—the way he feels for me, written all over his face.

Right when the grand finale erupts with repeated bursts of spiraling, swirling, starry light, the sound of a cow fills the town square.

"Oh, no," Chris says, laughing through his words. "Is that Lulabelle?"

People abandon the rest of the fireworks show as mayhem breaks out.

Apparently, Lulabelle found the floats, which are covered in corn, wheat, and hay, and she's going to town—literally—helping herself to the cow version of an all you can eat buffet.

One person shouts, "We've got to surround her."

Another says, "She's eating the floats!"

"Someone get a trailer!"

"Where's Jed? We need Jed!"

Lulabelle looks up, realizing she's now the center of attention. A group of men have organized and are trying to hem her in from six points, like a human cinch.

Lulabelle's smarter than that. She heads straight through the gap between two of the men, and runs through the town square, trampling picnic blankets as she goes.

People start shouting and waving their arms.

Cooter's voice is louder than the rest. "Would you'uns pipe down! Yer all agitatin' her like nobody's business. Everyone needs to get a hold of themselves!"

No one listens, so he puts his two fingers in his mouth and

lets out a long whistle. People stop. Lulabelle, who has been running in circles, dodging people, and slightly bucking at times, also stops.

Cooter shouts again. "What we need here is some organization. Listen up."

Surprisingly, everyone does. Except Lulabelle, who is now drinking out of the base of the town fountain.

Under Cooter's direction, a few men gather some wheat and corn from one of the floats. He sends Bubba to get the trailer. Then he selects a group to slowly cajole Lulabelle toward the spot where the trailer is parked.

I lean back into Chris. He wraps his arms around me as we watch our townspeople capture the cow so she can be taken back to her farm.

"This town sure can band together when it matters," I mutter.

"Yeah. They sure can," Chris agrees.

Fab-U-lous_EllaMae

Happy 4th to each of you!
Are you shooting off fireworks or barbecuing or in a parade? I want to know.

This year, I wasn't in the parade, but there were definitely fireworks – see photos of me and @got.your.six.now. Mmmm. Snap, crackle, pop! Independence is overrated, girlies! Lean on a man—a good man. And let the star-spangled sparks fly between you.

Add to that a runaway cow #smalltownproblems and a #buttdial which shall not be mentioned or talked about ever again, and the day was a well-rounded tribute to our nation's fave holiday.

Leave a comment with what you did for the 4th this year. And if it wasn't your fave, don't worry, I've had plenty of those. Puh-len-ty. But one day, you just might meet a soldier, or whoever you meet, and have your own private fireworks show. I'm believing it for you.

He's so #rippedandshipped
Yes, we're #ChellaMaeBae
He's #myguy #hesthebest #stilllovingthebeard #kissmenow #ticklemyfacewiththosewhiskers #mysoldier #bigboy

#fireworkswhewbaby #cowsontheloose #smalltownholiday #celebratethe4th #foundingfathers #lawnmowerparade

Comments:
942 Comments

@lifes_a_beach123: Awww 🩶 So happy for you and your hottie! We went to the beach for the evening. Picnic dinner with the kids. They probably ate more sand than food, but they went to bed happy.

> **@Fab-U-lous_EllaMae:** That's just the best! Fun memories!

@midwestcutiepie: Local parade and fireworks here. Nothing fancy. Love those pics of you and Mr. Shoulders!

@fashion_beauty_lifey: Wore the ultimate red-white-blue outfit #trending #holidayfashion #showyourspirit … Love you two … and you're using my hashtags! That's a total win for me! Happy 4th gurrrl!

@ImSOBeefy: Spent the holiday wishing we were together. These pics are just wrong. I love your smile and those pigtails. It should be me holding you, Ella Mae.

CHAPTER 41

Ella Mae

"… BLAH BLAH BLAH … IMSOBEEFY?" Meg asks me at breakfast the morning after Chris rocked my world with his declaration.

We're standing at the island in our pjs. I still haven't told Meg about the latest with Chris. She got home late. Well, I got home late too, but she was still out with Joe when I got here.

"Hmmm?" I ask.

I only half heard what she said.

Okay, yes. I'm in a complete haze of puffy pink sweetness where every thought circles back to Chris kissing me, or the words he softly whispered in my ears, or how it felt leaning back on him and watching the fireworks together.

"I said, did you see the comment from ImSOBeefy on your Fourth of July post? And I have to say, those photos of you and Chris make me almost jealous. You two should get an Academy Award for faking."

"We're not."

"Obviously. I mean, I think that goes to Tom Hanks or someone. I was kidding."

"No, I don't mean we're not getting an award. I mean, we're not faking."

Meg's eyes snap up to mine and she stops filling her coffee cup mid-pour.

"You're not faking, as in, he told you he likes you and you told him you can't stop thinking about those arm muscles, and that chest, and those thighs?"

"Enough on the muscles. He's mine," I practically growl.

My reaction nearly throws Meg into a fit of laughter.

"Okay. Okay. But is that what you're telling me? You called off faking so you can actually date one another."

"Yeah. That's what I'm saying."

My voice has this airiness to it—dreamy, floaty, happiness. Gah. I'm so happy it's scary. Things like this don't happen to me. And if they do, they don't last.

"Now what's that face?" Meg asks.

"What face?"

"The one that looks like you just saw Pennywise scream, *Egg Boy!* in the movie *It*."

"You know I don't watch thrillers."

"Well, you look like you saw a killer clown."

"Shouting about eggs?" I ask.

"Back to you. What's that face?"

I take a sip of my smoothie. Do I really want to share my overthinking spiral? It's probably best if I do.

"It's just … things like this don't happen to me. And they don't last."

"Things like a man falling for you?"

"Online, maybe. In real life, yeah. They don't."

"Well, I don't know why they haven't happened to you. But I'm here to testify that Chris looks at you with something like heart-eye emoji eyes."

I think of Chris. The way he looks at me has all the warmth rising up in my body again.

"There you go," Meg says, obviously satisfied that she's banished my fears—at least for now. "Much better. Stay in that dreamy place. And squeeze those biceps for me when you can. Just once. Grab hold of those giant arms and think to yourself, *This one's for Meg*."

"Not happening."

"Awww."

"But thanks," I say. "I needed that pep talk."

I walk around the island and give her a hug.

After Meg leaves for work, I check my comments and see the one from ImSOBeefy. Gross. That guy is really out of line. I want to block him, but Chris assures me they're watching him. He says keeping ImSOBeefy in my feed gives him and Aiden a better way to track him.

I run out to the grocery after filming two live videos: one of me doing yoga, and another of me sharing my top five beauty hacks.

Heads turn at every aisle. People whisper. When I get to the cash register, the middle-aged checkout woman says, "You and Chris St. James, huh?"

"Yep," I say.

I'm being friendly, even though my nerves are frayed from being the not-so-subtle subject of town gossip.

"I thought he'd find himself someone more …"

I wait.

She doesn't finish.

I cross my arms.

She just says, "Well, congrats. Whatever you did to catch him, you obviously have him under your charms."

I don't dignify her with an answer. At least she said it to my face. Most people don't even have the decency to do that.

I load my groceries and head home like the troll needing to curl up under his bridge. Only, I think trolls are mean. Maybe they aren't. It could be they're just misunderstood and mistreated. Maybe that troll was the brunt of one too many whispered insults, or was left out of yet another social function. Poor troll. No wonder he resorted to eating anyone who crossed his bridge. A person can only take so much.

I'm putting away groceries when my cell rings.

Chris.

Can I help my face lighting up like last night's firework show? Everything in me starts jumping up and down. I take a breath. We may be officially dating, but I don't need to overwhelm the man with my swoon-induced euphoria.

Chill. I'm so so chill.

"Hey, Soldier."

"Hi, Boots."

Okay. You can know this, even though I can't tell him. I have to grab the counter for a second when I hear his voice call me that nickname. He literally makes me weak in the knees.

"What's up?" I ask, all casual like the super-casual, not head-over-heels-in-love woman I am.

Chillin' like a villain. I'm so easy-breezy.

"Not much. Thinking of you, if you want to know."

Okay. Yes. I do. I do want to know.

"Really? What would you be thinking about?"

"Maybe I should come show you."

Fan. Ice. Cold water in my face. I'm definitely overheating.

"Um. Yeah. Sure. That would be great."

Gah. I lost my game. See what this man does to me?

He chuckles. "Are you okay?"

"I'm good. I just got groceries. And gave the town something to talk about—again."

"What do you mean?"

Oh, to be a golden boy in Bordeaux. I think back to the party the town threw for him when he was discharged a few years back. The *whole town* threw *him* a party. Wanna guess if this town ever threw me a party? If they did, it would be my going away party—sort of like in *The Wizard of Oz* where everyone sings *Ding dong, the witch is dead,* or in *A Christmas Carol* where Scrooge's funeral is the cause of a spontaneous town parade.

"Nothing. It was nothing. Just some whispers and a comment that got under my skin. I'm fine."

"You're not fine. I can hear it. And you shouldn't be fine with this kind of crap. It's uncalled for."

"Thanks, Soldier. I appreciate it. Really. Knowing you're in my corner helps."

"I'm not just in your corner," he says. Then I hear the knock at my front door. "I'm at your house."

I run from the kitchen, then slow to a trot, so I don't seem so overeager. By the time I reach the door, I take one deep breath, and open it.

Yep. There he is, wearing a white T-shirt and jeans and looking good enough to eat in that backwards ballcap. It's his eyes that get me, though. They're full of concern and care.

"Come 'mere," he says, opening his arms and stepping inside my house.

I fall into his arms and collapse. I've never had this—a man who gave me comfort. If my dad did something like this, I don't remember it. After I was five, he sure didn't. It's beyond amazing to have a man hold me when I'm feeling so fragile. And, it's not just any man, it's Chris.

My thoughts spill out in the safety of his arms. "I'm just tired. You know? I'm tired of not fitting in, of the rejection, of having people think the worst of me. I'm tired of this feud between everyone over things we can't change."

"I hear you, Boots. It sucks."

"But you're making it better."

"That's what I'm here for. I'll kiss it and make it better."

Even though I can't see his face right now, I know he's wagging his eyebrows playfully.

I chuckle and smack his chest. My hand lightly stings from the impact. He really is a behemoth of a man. My fingers slide over to his biceps and I squeeze. Yeah, Meg. One for you.

Chris tilts his head toward mine and gives me this soft, gentle kiss that barely brushes my lips and then lingers.

"You're not in this alone. I'm here."

"Thank you."

"In the army, we learn not to fight alone. It's a surefire way to bring on defeat. Don't fight alone, Ella Mae. Not when you've got people who want to fight with you—for you."

I tuck my head into Chris' chest and soak up the feeling of being held by him.

"I've got a spot where I go when the walls feel like they're closing in. Let's take a little drive. Grab your swimsuit and a towel, and I'll help you forget this town and their busybody ways for a while."

I dash upstairs fast enough to leave Chris chuckling in my entryway. I don't spend too much time deciding on the right suit. Whatever. I lay out every suit I own and hold them up to myself in the mirror. That stops when Chris shouts up asking if I'm sewing my suit from scratch.

I finally land on a yellow two-piece. I put it on under my clothes and throw a change into my floppy bag along with my big fluffy towel and some sunscreen. Then I hustle down the stairs.

"Ready! Take me away, Soldier!"

Chris leans in and kisses my cheek, like a genuine, honest-to-goodness boyfriend.

We haven't used those labels. Maybe we won't. We're in our early thirties. Do you even say boyfriend-girlfriend at that point in life? All I know is Chris makes me feel like I'm in high school, dating the most popular guy in class.

We're only on the road for ten minutes when I get a hunch where we're going.

"You're taking me to the reservoir?"

The scenery is familiar. And this is not a private spot. The whole town heads out here in the heat. Even on a late afternoon on a weekday, the moms will be bringing their kids out here to get out of the house and cool off. It's summer, so that goes double. Some families come here for a picnic lunch and stay until dinnertime.

"I'm not taking you to the part everyone knows about. I've got a spot."

Chris keeps driving past the main turnoff. He drives around to the other side of the lake. We veer off onto this unpaved road that looks almost overgrown. Grass grows high along the edges of the dirt. The ride gets bumpy as we pass under natural arches of trees, and then we emerge into a clearing with a bunch of cattails on one side of the water and a cluster of bushes behind them on land. There's a spot right up at the edge of the lake that's cleared, like a beach.

Chris turns the truck in a one-eighty, and parks so the bed of the truck is pointing toward the water.

"This is it," Chris says, waving his hand toward the scene in front of us. "No one can see us from over on the other side because we're tucked away in a cove. And basically no one seems to know this spot exists."

"This is amazing."

"I've never brought anyone here," he says, looking suddenly bashful.

It's a good look on him, but honestly, what isn't a good look on him, am I right?

"Want to swim?" Chris asks. "Or we could sit and chat, or just ..."

"Let's swim," I say, shucking my shirt and shorts and tossing them into my bag.

Chris' eyes heat and his gaze rakes over me. It would almost be overwhelming, except it's like an unspoken compliment. He doesn't take his gaze off mine as he slowly lifts his shirt, peeling it off with one hand as he lifts his hat with the other.

Oh, sweet honey on a corn cake.

Abs. First it's the abs. Then the pecs. And those arms. His face pops through and I'm so, so busted.

"Objectifying me, Boots?"

"I'm completely objectifying you, Soldier. It's not your kind heart or your great sense of humor. I don't give a rip about your bright mind and the way getting to know you is like a trip through a labyrinth. Nope. It's all about this."

I step closer to him, placing my hand on his chest and trailing my fingers over his abs. I look up into his eyes as I cup his jaw in my palm.

I want to say something funny—to keep joking. But I can't. Not when he's staring down at me with that look in his eyes.

He leans in and kisses me, pulling me close. Our skin touches and I feel every spot. My hands don't even know where to go. I run my fingers through his hair, down his shoulders, onto his back. He's being so careful with me. Kissing, gently stroking my hair, touching my shoulders and arms with the lightest caresses.

He pulls back. "Let's get in the water. I think I'm going to overheat."

I already beat you to that, Big Boy.

CHAPTER 42

Ella Mae

CHRIS TAKES OFF HIS JEANS. He's got on board shorts. Then he offers to rub sunscreen on me. I return the favor.

We run toward the edge of the water and splash in. Then we make our way out to a spot where the water comes up to just below my shoulders. We swim and laugh all afternoon, floating on our backs, racing to a log further out and back, and letting go of everything that isn't right here in this cove.

When the sun starts to dip low, Chris suggests we eat a little something.

"I don't want to leave," I say, trying not to whine.

"We don't have to. I brought stuff."

"Of course you did," I tease.

He hauls out a mini barbecue and cooler. We eat hot dogs and chips on paper plates. And then he pulls out a box of Pop-Tarts.

We're leaned on the back of his truck, up in the bed, a bunch of blankets under us to make things cozy.

"Is that what I think it is?" I say, laughing.

"To show you I know how to have fun."

I lean over and trace his bottom lip with my finger. He nips at it. We smile into one another's eyes.

"I know you know how to have fun, Chris."

I don't use any nicknames. This moment feels far too raw and real for anything but his actual name.

"I wasn't fun before. I haven't been fun in years, really," he says. "You taught me how to have fun again."

"I'm glad."

I want to tell him all the things buzzing inside my head. Most of all, I want to tell him how much he means to me and the scary big feelings I'm having for him. I think he knows, but he deserves to be sure. Only, when I go to say everything, my tongue feels stuck, my throat thick with emotion.

"I really like you," I tell him.

The air between us is languid and effortless. We're leaning on one another, no agenda, not a care in the world. The comfortable weariness of a day spent in the water has relaxed us, and now the setting sun only adds to this unhurried ease. I'd trade my Jimmy Choos for a hundred more days together like this—or even one day.

"I don't know what that means, but it sounds good."

"Did I say that out loud?"

"You sort of mumbled it. It sounded like a compliment. Anytime someone says they'd trade something, it's usually something they cherish."

"Trust me, it's good. I love my shoes—but I extra-love those Jimmy Choos. But seriously, Chris. I honestly have never felt like this before for anyone."

"I know. I feel it too."

"You're the bright spot in the middle of a whole lot of not-so-bright things right now."

I pause, tilting my head up to see if I just freaked him out. He's steady as ever, looking down at me.

"No pressure," I joke.

"I thrive under pressure," he assures me. "Bring it."

Then he asks, "What if I have something big to say to you?"

"Are you moving?" I ask, mostly joking, but secretly freaking out when the thought occurs to me.

"No. Not moving."

"Pregnant?"

"That would be Shannon."

"You got a promotion?"

"Boots … Ella Mae …"

He shifts, sitting up and taking me up with him. He makes sure I can see his face, cupping my jaw and flicking his eyes between mine like he's searching for something—I sure hope he finds it.

"I love you," he says.

Then he leans in and kisses me before I get a chance to answer him. His kiss is tender and warm. But it ramps up in no time. Oh, yeah. He loves me alright. I kiss him with my mouth, but more so with my heart. My kiss says, *I love you too. You're everything. How can you be so good and be mine? I want to keep you forever.* We lay there kissing until the darkness closes in around us and the stars start to smatter the sky overhead.

When we come up for air, I look at his muted features in the darkness. "I love you too, Chris."

"You do?"

"Yes. I love you so much it hurts."

"It's not the love that hurts," he says, running his hand up and down my back in soothing strokes.

"It's not?"

"No. It's the fear. And I feel it too. This is so good. What if we don't get to keep it?"

"Are you a psychic?"

"Nope. Just a man who watches people and pays attention. And I know when you're freaking out. But you don't have to. I'm not going anywhere."

But I might. How do I tell him I can't take this town much longer? Even with him in it, I can't be the pariah. It's like every day I'm trying to climb up a hill, while people at the top kick dirt down toward me. I need to be able to live where people don't think of me as *that* Ella Mae.

So many things feel uncertain right now. If I'm honest, even creating online content feels flat. I need a boost, or maybe a complete change of pace. But what?

Chris settles back onto the truck bed, then he pulls me down with him, so my head is on his chest and his arm is wrapped around me. We stare up at the stars, his heartbeat steady beneath me.

"Can I tell you something?" I ask.

"Anything."

"I'm afraid of losing my fame." He's silent, so I spill the rest. "I mean, what am I if I'm not Fab-U-lous Ella Mae?"

Chris takes his time answering me. It's one of the things about him that drives me nuts, but also makes me respect him deeply.

Finally, he says, "You are …"

And then he pauses.

Impatient woman that I can be, I ask, "What am I?"

"You're still fabulous."

"That's so cheesy, Soldier."

"No, seriously. You are. You've got so much going for you. And you don't need an online platform to prove that. You can keep doing your social media gig, or you could do something else."

"What else is there? I've put everything I am into becoming Fab-U-lous Ella Mae."

"I don't know, but let's dream. What would you be or do if the whole internet crashed tomorrow?"

I sit up, looking down at him in horror.

"First of all, blasphemy. Never utter that sentence again in my presence, Soldier."

He chuckles, pulling me back down onto him. I feel the vibrations of his laughter rumble through me. It's beyond delicious. I snuggle back into him like a cat in the sunshine.

"Second of all," I say, "Isn't that a little touchy-feely for a big guy like you? You're not the *let's dream* type."

"Maybe you make me want to be all touchy-feely." He accentuates that comment with a gentle stroke of his hand across my cheek while his other hand brushes down my back and lands on my hip with a possessive squeeze.

Oh, I want to be all touchy-feely with you too, Soldier. You better believe it. I clear my throat and tip my head back and to the side so I can look up into his eyes. He's got this sweet, protective expression. His whole face is soft and open. He's giving me space to find my answer.

I think for a bit, staring into the night with Chris' protective embrace infusing me with courage.

"I guess, photography?" I finally say. "I love taking photos. But also, maybe helping other entrepreneurs and creatives get their businesses off the ground. I know people think I'm a spaz, but this spaz has made a lot of money and a name for herself starting with nothing but a phone and a strong will."

"You've got a lot more than that going for you," he says with such earnestness I feel my cheeks heat and my eyes well with unshed tears.

"Could you loan me the glasses you use when you look at me?"

"I don't need glasses. I see what's there—maybe you cover it up at times, but you're brilliant, quick on your feet, unafraid, persistent, and you look out for others. You don't hold grudges, and you're one of the most fun people I've ever hung out with."

"You didn't even mention how ravishingly beautiful I am," I tease.

"You already know that. But, yeah. Sometimes I can barely look at you. That's how beautiful you are."

"What a way with words." I roll my eyes even though he probably can't see me do it from his position lying next to me in the dark.

"I hope you know what I mean. I can't look at you because I will lose all self-control. You make me want to do things … to say things … and I'm not a man who acts without thinking."

"Tell me about it," I breathe out a laugh.

It takes a minute after my knee-jerk joking reaction to let his words hit me. And then they do—like a shot of adrenaline. Having that kind of effect on a man like Chris is a heady experience.

"You know, you're a lot softer than you let on," I say.

"Don't tell anyone. I've got a reputation to uphold. Only Duke and Alex really know what a big softy I am. Maybe Duke knows most of all. Well, Shannon does, but she's all but forgotten I exist now that she's married and expecting."

"I highly doubt that. I'm sure she knows you exist. Think about how much you mean to her. She put off dating Duke just for you."

"Huh. Yeah. I never saw it that way."

"She's lucky to have you."

"How about you?" he asks.

"What about me?"

I flip on my side, so my arm splays across Chris' chest and my bent leg is propped slightly over his. It makes it easier to see his face from this position—to look into his eyes.

"Are you feeling lucky to have me?" he asks.

"I'm feeling something," I say with a note of mischief in my voice.

I reach up and stroke Chris' beard.

His eyes heat with the touch. In an instant, I'm flipped onto the blanket and he's the one half-hovering over me.

I squeal and smile up at Chris.

His eyes roam over my features and a predatory smile takes over that gorgeous face. The skin around his eyes crinkles with his grin. Then his mouth descends to mine. I expect a fierce kiss, full of hunger and passion. Instead, this is the most reverent, tender, careful caress of lips. His beard tickles my face just the slightest.

Our mouths connect, and Chris runs his hand through my hair and then cups his palm behind my head. I run my hands along his back, cataloging the muscles beneath his shirt. My fingers roam to his arm. More muscles ripple beneath my touch. We're deepening the kiss, and like a fire that started as only a smolder, the intensity builds between us with licks of flames now. We lie there kissing, saying things we haven't dared to speak aloud. Making promises we intend to keep. Sharing a secret meant only for the two of us.

When Chris pulls back, he runs his fingers through my hair, smoothing the wild strands that went haywire from our kiss. Then he gently runs his palm down my cheek, brushes his pointer finger along my hairline, rubs the pad of his thumb across my still sensitive lower lip.

He looks like he has so much to say to me. His eyes are full of thoughts. Maybe he's as dumbfounded as I am. How did the two of us end up here—willingly?

I giggle.

"What's so funny?"

"Us. We're funny. You and me. The least likely pairing in all of Bordeaux. Probably all of Ohio."

"Yeah." He chuckles. "But then again, no. You just have to look a little deeper to see we're meant to be. We just fit."

Just when I think my heart can't take anymore, he says something like that, and I feel like someone pumped me full of helium. I could float up and mingle with the stars if he weren't hovering over me, leaning on his elbow, keeping me grounded in this truck bed.

CHAPTER 43

Chris

"SO, you sent the message and made it seem like it was from her?" I ask Aiden.

We're standing around Aiden's kitchen island. I'm looking over his shoulder at his laptop. Em's with the kids on a play-date at Aiden's sister's. It's just me and Aiden here—and their dog, goats, and that crazy llama.

"Yeah. I made it look like Ella Mae invited him to meet her at the Big Boy in Columbus. He jumped on that invite way too quickly. He's eager. So, then I sent him a message." Aiden pauses and opens the app on his computer. "Here. See it? I made it look like she's asking him for a photo so she can identify him when he comes into the restaurant."

Duke walks in Aiden's front door. "Hey, broskis! What's up? What are we working on here?"

He walks right up to us, and peers over Aiden's other shoulder.

"Is that Ella Mae's account?"

Confusion rightfully clouds his features. Why would Aiden and I be sitting alone in the kitchen looking at Ella Mae's Instagram?

"Yeah," I say.

Aiden gives me a questioning glance. I nod. We're going to have to let Duke in on everything.

"So," I say. "You know that guy who's been lightly stalking Ella Mae for a few months?"

"That Beefy guy?" Duke asks.

"How do you know his account name?" Aiden asks.

"I follow Ella Mae, of course. She's got awesome tips."

"On how to paint your nails?" Aiden asks.

"Right?!" Duke laughs. "No. Her other stuff. Like keeping a positive outlook. Great smoothie recipes. She's even got me trying yoga. Shannon and I do it together, but we do it with some YouTube teacher. Ella Mae was the one who got me started with it, though."

I shake my head. "You think you know a guy."

"Tell me about it," he answers. "I thought I knew you, and then before I knew it, I was seeing pictures of you and Ella Mae online. Next thing I know, you're in love with her."

"Love?" Aiden asks, his face serious and strictly inquisitive.

"Yeah," I confirm. "Big time. I'm in love with her. Like a Mack truck hit me. Like, I'd take a bullet for her. I love her."

Aiden smiles over at me. "Good for you, man."

"You tell her yet?" Duke asks.

It's obvious he thinks I'm going to tell him I chickened out again, even though he saw us at the Fourth. But these two have known we're faking, so they could have thought all our cuddling and affection was still part of the charade. Man, I'm glad that's over.

"Yeah, Duke. I told her. On the Fourth I told her I didn't want to fake anymore, and then yesterday I took her out to this spot I know about, and we spent the afternoon and evening there. I told her then."

"The big three?" Duke asks.

Aiden looks confused. I know what Duke's trying to say.

"You know." He ticks each word off on a finger when he says it. "I … love … you. The big three."

"Yeah. I said it."

Duke shakes his head. "Chris St. James. In love. It's a momentous day for our boy, Aiden."

"A real milestone," Aiden agrees.

"Can we get back to this?" I ask.

"Yeah," Aiden agrees. "So, basically it's set. We just have to show up."

"What's set?" Duke asks.

Aiden pivots on his barstool. "Chris and I sent a message to that Beefy guy asking him to meet Ella Mae at the Big Boy."

"You sent the message," I correct him. "I know nothing. I'm not a part of this."

"Right. Right. I sent the message. The guy thinks it's from Ella Mae. He agreed to meet her. He's sending her a photo so she can identify him in person. But the photo will actually come to us. When this guy shows up to meet Ella Mae, we'll see him and have a little chat."

"I wanna come," Duke says, like a kid who's begging to stay up past his bedtime.

"Can't hurt," Aiden says. "Strength in numbers."

"It can hurt," I say. "No offense, Duke. But you can be a loose cannon at times, and we're not playing around here. This guy could be a danger to Ella Mae. We want to let him know his time is up."

"Yeah. That wasn't offensive at all," Duke deadpans. "What do you think I'm going to do? I'm here for you, man. Let me come. That way there's three of us. He'll see three strong men instead of Ella Mae, and he'll know we're onto him. Like Aiden said, strength in numbers."

I think it over.

"Okay. Yeah," I agree.

"This is so cool," Duke says, rubbing his hands.

I shoot him a look. He calms down, but he still wags his eyebrows once. If Ella Mae weren't being hassled, this actually would be totally cool. The three of us haven't done anything like this in years. It feels like old times.

Two days later, Aiden, Duke, and I pull into the Big Boy parking lot in Aiden's family vehicle. Nothing that would identify me can be involved in this meeting, so I left my truck in Bordeaux and Aiden drove. Of course, this Beefy guy's seen me online in the photos. If he scrolls back through some of Ella Mae's reels, he'll hear her use my name, but I don't know if he's got the sense of a ground squirrel, so he may not think to track me down.

I'm prepared to take this to authorities if things get worse. The reality is, most online harassment cases get ignored or disregarded. Nothing of consequence happens unless the harassment escalates to some type of real-life threat. And I'm not willing to sit by and watch that happen to Ella Mae.

"You ready?" Aiden asks, looking over at me.

"Yeah. As ready as I'll be. I'm more than ready to send this guy a message."

"Oh yeah, baby. We're sending him a message alright," Duke says from the back seat.

"Don't make me regret bringing you," I tell him.

"Moi? Never. You are going to be thanking your lucky stars I was here. Trust."

I look over at Aiden. We share a knowing look.

"Okay. Showtime," Aiden says.

We get out of Aiden's minivan. Yeah. Minivan. We're cool like that. Out on a stealth mission with goldfish crackers scattered in the back seat. We're three big dudes, exiting a momvan at a Frisch's Big Boy. Nothing says, *Your military days are over,* like this moment.

I walk around to Duke and Aiden's side of the car and—no kidding—Duke is sipping out of a juice box.

"What are you doing?" I ask.

"What?"

"Where did you even get that?"

"Aiden had it in the pocket on the door for me. Like a snack for the ride out here."

"Sorry to disappoint," Aiden says. "But Em puts those in the doors for the kids on long trips. I think that was Paisley's."

Duke looks down at the juice box, back up at Aiden, and shrugs. Then he puts that tiny straw back in his mouth and slurps the rest of the juice until it makes that obnoxious noise from him sucking air at the end.

I shake my head and walk ahead of Duke and Aiden, asking over my shoulder, "Do you both remember what he looks like?"

"Yeah. You showed us the picture at least ten times," Duke says.

I walk into the restaurant, sizing up the whole situation. I make note of where people are sitting, and check to see if Beefy is here.

His real name is Raymond. He told us that when he sent the photo of himself lifting weights. What a dipstick. Of course, he thought he was sending all that to Ella Mae.

I'm looking around when Amber greets me.

She smiles eagerly and says, "Hey, Chris! I haven't seen you in so long."

Aiden and Duke exchange a glance.

I haven't come here since that night with Ella Mae. I'm not sure why.

"I'm here with friends, Amber. We're expecting a fourth to join us."

"Right this way," she says, grabbing four menus and making sure to exaggerate her hip movements as she walks.

"Old friend?" Duke asks once we're seated.

"She'd like to be. I ate here pretty regularly over the past few years."

"Wait! Is this where you filmed your social media debut?" Duke asks.

"The night I walked in and Ella Mae had been stood up? Yeah. That was here. Right over at that table."

"The restaurant that changed your life. Iconic."

"I guess so," I say.

We're not here to eat, but of course, when the waitress comes by, Duke orders food. Aiden and I just order sodas.

"What?" Duke asks. "I'm hungry. That juice box didn't really do it for me."

I shake my head.

Then I see him—Raymond—ImSOBeefy. He walks in and looks around the room, obviously searching for Ella Mae. Aiden sees Raymond right after I do. He nudges Duke, and Duke looks up. Duke tips his chin at me and lifts his brows to let me know he's aware Raymond's here.

We're actually doing this thing.

I stand up, like we planned, and walk toward Raymond.

When I'm only a few feet away from him, I address him.

"Raymond?"

"Uh, yeah?"

Good. He's caught off guard. And he's a little confused as to why I'd know his name.

"You're here to meet Ella Mae?"

"How do you know that?"

"Because I'm her boyfriend."

I cross my arms across my chest and stand with my feet a little wider than usual.

"Oh, uh ... well, she agreed to meet me here. She wanted to come here. I'm here because she wants to meet with me."

"Actually, I'm here because she *didn't* want to be here. Do you understand what I'm telling you? I'm here instead of her."

Raymond screws up his face.

"Hey," he says. "I know you. You're that guy in her posts."

"Yeah. That's me. Like I said, I'm her boyfriend."

He looks me over, maybe trying to decide whether we're evenly matched.

I tip my head toward Aiden and Duke. "You see those two guys?" They wave in unison from our table. "They're here with me. They're friends of Ella Mae's. She doesn't want you bothering her anymore. As a matter of fact, she wants you to stop following her on Instagram."

He doesn't miss a beat. "That can't be true. She'd block me if she didn't want me. She keeps me on her account. She must want me there."

"Raymond, I'm going to spell it out for you. Ella Mae is in love with me. I'm in love with her. She and I are together. She's not interested in anyone but me."

"Are you sure?"

This guy. Is he for real?

"Yeah. I'm sure."

When I say those words, something clicks in me. It's like I'm finally hearing the facts myself. Ella Mae loves me. She's not interested in anyone else. She's mine.

"So, I know you recognized me," I tell Raymond. "But I recognize you too. Did you have another account? BeefyDude or something."

"beefitupfitnessdude?"

"Yeah. That's the one."

"How'd you know about that?"

"Because you kept coming on to my girlfriend with both those accounts, and when she blocked you on one account you started following her on another. That's not cool. And it shows me you know Ella Mae actually asked you to leave her alone in her own way once already. If you had listened, we wouldn't be here right now. Do you hear what I'm saying, Raymond?"

Aiden and I discussed what I would say when I confronted Raymond. The pattern between the way beefitup-fitnessdude and ImSOBeefy approached Ella Mae is consistent. We decided I could confront him based on the similarities between those two accounts and never have to reveal Aiden's hacking.

Raymond is staring at me, obviously rattled, but not yet giving me the definitive answer I will get before I leave this city tonight. One way or the other, Raymond is going to agree to back off Ella Mae.

Amber walks over to us. "Is your friend going to join you, Chris?"

"I'll let you know in a minute, Amber. Thanks."

She walks away, and I look over my shoulder and give a small nod to Aiden and Duke. Just as we planned, they stand and walk toward the entryway where I'm talking with Raymond. They flank me from behind, both crossing their arms over their chests.

"What I want you to do, Raymond, is stop following Ella Mae. You're not going to unfollow her and make another account. You're not going to private message her. You're just going to unfollow her—right here, while I watch you, and then you're going to leave her completely alone. Do you understand me, Raymond?"

This time, Raymond looks at me, then at Duke and Aiden. Then he nods.

"So, why don't you get your phone out and unfollow my

girl, Raymond. And then we'll let you get on with your evening."

He doesn't say anything. He glances back at Duke and Aiden. Then he pulls his phone out of his pocket and he opens the Instagram app. I watch as he searches for Ella Mae's account, and then I watch as he clicks, *Unfollow*.

"That wasn't so hard, Raymond. Was it?"

He shakes his head.

"I just want to assure you that this was the friendly way to go about this. We like doing things the friendly way. But, Raymond, if my friends and I have to come out here again to deal with you harassing my girlfriend, there will be authorities involved and things won't be so friendly. Do we understand each other?"

"Yes, sir," he says.

I haven't been called "sir" in a while. When I go to my weekends for National Guard Reserves all the usual military protocol is in place. But in a setting like this, it almost makes me laugh. I won't lie. Hearing Raymond use the word *sir* is slightly gratifying.

I don't say goodbye to Raymond. I actually don't say another word to him. My self-control feels like it's on a parking meter timer and the meter's almost up. I turn and walk back to our table. Duke and Aiden follow me. Duke immediately digs back into his dinner.

"He left," Aiden announces, glancing at the door of the restaurant.

"I know."

"Capiche?" Duke says with a chuckle. "You were so brilliant, man. *Do you understand me, Raymond?* You're like the Godfather. Or Tony Soprano."

He starts laughing at his own joke.

I laugh along with him.

Relief floods me. We sliced the Beef out of Ella Mae's life.

CHAPTER 44

Chris

MY PHONE RINGS. I look down. It's Ella Mae.

I put my finger up to let the guys know I'll be right back, then I walk out of the restaurant to take Ella Mae's call.

"Hey, Boots. What's up?"

"I hope nothing," she says.

"You okay?"

"Yeah. I just thought you should know I got a message from ImSOBeefy this afternoon saying he was looking forward to seeing me this evening for dinner. I didn't answer him, of course. I had some errands to run, so I figured I'd tell you about it later. But then he just unfollowed me. It's kind of freaking me out."

"That he unfollowed you?"

"The whole thing. Why would he say he was seeing me this evening? And then why, right after that, would he unfollow me?"

Maybe I should have told Ella Mae about our plan and what we were doing. I didn't want her to worry—or worse, insist on coming and end up having to be face to face with

Raymond. Who knows what he would have done if he saw her in person.

I never thought Ella Mae would get a message from him saying he was looking forward to meeting her.

"We set him up."

"Who set him up? ImSOBeefy?"

"Yeah. Aiden and I sent him a message that led him to believe he was meeting you out here at the Big Boy. We came instead of you. I told him you were my girlfriend, and then I asked him nicely to unfollow you."

"You did what?!"

"We met the guy. I told him to unfollow you and leave you alone from now on. He unfollowed you. He's out of your hair now."

I expect a thank you.

"Chris." She sighs a long, loud sigh, like she's at the end of her rope. "I told you I don't need you to be my bodyguard, or to go out on some vigilante mission to defend my honor."

"He was escalating again. You saw his most recent comments."

"I know. I did see those."

"I thought you'd be grateful. We handled this guy."

She sighs so loudly I feel like she's going to hyperventilate.

"You are so unnerving, Soldier. I mean, yes. On one hand, I'm grateful."

She's quiet, but I know she's not finished talking. No one says, on the one hand, without having something to say about the other hand.

And, just as I thought, she continues. "On the other hand, no. Just no. I told you not to get involved. You don't listen to me. This is my life. I get to choose my followers and how I handle them when they get out of hand."

"I know you said that. And, believe me, I think you are

the baddest, most impressive influencer. I know you know how to handle yourself and your business."

I run my hand through my hair. I get that I shouldn't have overstepped, but then again, she's my girlfriend. Don't I get to protect her?

"I just want you to be safe," I explain.

She's quiet. I don't know if she's mad, or sad, or plotting my death.

"Thank you," she finally says. "I wish you would have come to me first, but I do appreciate you looking out for me."

"And Aiden and Duke. They're here too."

"Oh my gosh! That poor guy. He had to be shaking in his boots."

"We were mellow—this time. But, yeah. He knew he was outnumbered."

She giggles a little and my chest loosens.

"Are we good?" I ask her.

"Yeah. We're good. Where are you?"

"Still in Columbus. We literally just got rid of that guy when you called. Want me to stop by when I get back?"

"Yeah. I have some things to tell you."

"Good things?" I ask.

"Yeah. I think so. Yes. Good things."

"Okay. I'll be there in about an hour and a half at the latest."

"And, Chris?"

"Yeah?"

"Next time, talk to me first. I deserve to get to make the call on things like this."

"Okay. Next time, I'll come to you. You have my word."

I walk back to the table. The waitress shows up and asks Duke if he wants to look at a dessert menu. He instantly says, "Sure!" Then he looks over at me and Aiden who have identical expressions on our faces. "What? It looks like good pie."

Aiden and I end up splitting a sandwich while Duke eats his dessert. Then we load up in Aiden's van and head back to Bordeaux. The van barely stops, and I hop out and trot to my truck to drive straight to Ella Mae's—beyond eager to see her.

Ella Mae answers the door in a pair of loose gray sweats with some designer name running up one leg. She's got on a thin white T-shirt, and she's barefoot. No makeup. She's looking good.

"Hey," I say, trying to keep from reaching out to touch her too soon.

"Heya, Big Boy. Come on in."

As she walks toward the back of the house, she says, "Meg's home. She's upstairs getting ready for bed."

"Okay."

"Can I get you anything?"

Is a kiss out of the question? A hug?

"I'm good."

She walks to the far side of the couch and plops down. I glance between the other corner cushion and the middle one.

"Where do you want me?"

Ella Mae smiles. "Your choice."

I take the middle cushion. It feels like ages since I've seen her. I place my hand between us, palm up in an unspoken invitation.

She loops her fingers through mine.

"Thank you, again," she says. "I still don't condone you doing something like what you did today without my knowledge or consent, but the more I thought about it, the more grateful I am. You took care of a big situation for me. No one has done anything like that before."

"I'll always take care of you—with permission."

Ella Mae smiles.

Something feels heavy, and not necessarily in a good way.

"Are you okay? You seem like there's something on your mind."

"I went into the Seed and Feed today. Just needed some potting soil for the back garden beds. I got more stares. I don't know why it's getting to me now so much more than ever. Maybe it's ramped up since we started dating."

I want to go to that Feed and Seed and … I don't know what. But I sit still, my eyes on Ella Mae. She's hurting, but she's trying to power through. I'm a problem solver. This is one problem I don't know how to fix. The high I was riding from slicing the Beef evaporates in light of Ella Mae's pain from being blacklisted here in town.

"I already didn't fit in here, but now, with us dating, I can't go anywhere without people treating me awfully. It's like our dating has thrown a match on the smoldering fire between our families. I just need space to figure my life out. I don't know how I can stay in this town with everyone treating me like I'm public enemy number one."

Her eyes plead with me. I would give anything to fix this for her. My heart thrums with a need to protect her. This is my hometown. They've always cheered me on—in football, when Bridgette died, even when Mom took a turn for the worse. When I left for the military, they had a send-off. When I came home, they threw a party.

Now, when the most important and best thing in my life happens, they turn on the woman I love?

I wish I could whisk Ella Mae away—start fresh in Columbus. Maybe we could live near Alex and Courtney. But we're so newly dating, and my family needs me near them. All my lifelong friends are here. I don't know what to do to make this better for Ella Mae. It's eating me up knowing I'm powerless to do anything.

"I don't know what to tell you."

"I don't expect you to tell me anything, or do anything. Not all problems are yours to solve, Chris."

"What are you thinking?"

"I need to get away for a while. Put some space between me and the whispers and stares."

I try to put myself in her position. I'd want that too. Only, I could barely wait to get to her tonight. If she goes away, it will mean an even longer separation. Is this so easy for her—being apart? Doesn't she miss me the way I miss her?

"I'd miss you a lot," I tell her.

"I'm not moving—at least not yet. I just need to get some space. I don't think you'll ever know what it's like for me. You've got really great friends who would do anything for you. Your family loves you. You are wanted here. I've never been wanted here."

"I wanted you—I want you."

Doesn't that matter? I know I'm being partly selfish—maybe I'm being really selfish. I reach my arm behind Ella Mae and pull her in toward me. She rests her head on my chest.

"You're basically the only one," she says. "You and Meg. And now Meg's getting married, so I won't have her. Put yourself in my shoes."

"I am, Boots. And it sucks. You're one of the best people I know. It makes me angry knowing how people have treated you. I guess in some ways, I was one of them."

"You weren't like that. You said everything right to my face. And you never really disliked me. You just tried to boss me around and make me stop being so over-the-top."

"I didn't dislike you. You just got under my skin."

"Yeah?"

She tilts her head up.

"Yeah. You got so far under my skin, I'll never get you out. Not that I'd want to."

She smiles and settles back into me.

We sit like that for a little while. Silence stretches between us. We're both holding one another like we're going to lose something precious if we let go. My hand runs up and down Ella Mae's back, then I stroke her hair.

She's right. This is not my problem to solve. That doesn't make it an easier pill to swallow.

"I wish you could put those people out of your mind."

"Me too. But if it helps, I forget them when I'm with you."

"That does help. I want to be your safe place."

I kiss the top of her head.

She tilts her face up and kisses me lightly. I return the kiss. But it's not a kiss full of passion. We're not making out. This is so much deeper. We're connecting and comforting one another. Even when I dated women for longer stretches of time, I never had someone who felt like she belonged with me at such a deep level the way Ella Mae does.

I kiss her forehead, run my hand down her hair, kiss her cheeks. She closes her eyes and lets me soothe her with my kisses and touch. She cups my face, leaning in to kiss my cheek, my lips, the tip of my nose. She brushes her hand along my jawline.

When we slowly break apart, Ella Mae looks up at me.

"Drake reached out again today—about the bash," she says.

His name feels like an intrusion.

"Yeah?"

"Yeah. He wants me to come out so he can introduce me around. He wants to help me get more connected."

I wonder about the things she said at the lake about her dreams, and what she'd do if the internet broke. I remember her saying social media feels flat right now. Why does she want to grow if she doesn't even know if she wants to keep doing what she's doing?

I'd ask her, but it feels wrong to push her after all she's been through today and this week. She needs my support. I don't think I can support her going to see Drake, though. Something about that guy rubs me very wrong.

Ella Mae continues to tout the benefits of going to Drake's bash. "All the important people will be there. I would have never been invited even a year ago. It's kind of a miracle that I was included this year. This is really a once-in-a-lifetime opportunity. If I'm bigger next year, I might be on the A-list. But if I don't go this year, Drake might never include me again. Invites are coveted. Turning him down would be a slap in the face."

The words, *So what,* sit on my tongue like the shell of a sunflower seed, ready to be spit out. I obviously don't say them. This is Ella Mae's life. She's already had to scold me once today for sticking my nose too far into her business uninvited.

"I'm not telling you what to do," I say by way of a caveat. "But I'm concerned about Drake and the inconsistent way he's been with you."

Ella Mae doesn't chew me out, so I keep talking. "Plus, I think he just wants to see if he can get together with you. I think he's got a thing for you, Ella Mae."

"Who cares? I don't have a thing for him. Besides, that's ridiculous. He's Drake! He could have so many women. He doesn't want me. I'm not in his league. He's genuinely trying to help me. You don't have to get all caveman-jealous, Soldier."

"You really think that highly of him?" I ask.

The guy strikes me as a grade-A jerk. Selfish, full of himself, inconsiderate, and unreliable.

"Hey," Ella Mae says, twisting so she's sitting on my lap and cupping my jaw. "You're it for me. I don't want Drake. And, he for sure doesn't want me, you big goofball. So stop worrying about that. I need to get away. The trip to LA will give me that chance. And it will provide me the opportunity to build my business with a lot of really influential people. I'll come back with my head cleared, a little tan … And, bonus! Absence makes the heart grow fonder, so I'll be itching to see you."

She leans up and kisses me. I melt into her, wrapping my arms behind her and holding her to me. Our mouths dance and she runs her hands through my hair. She fists my shirt and kisses me with a fierceness that I know is meant to quell my fears. It only serves to stoke the fire constantly burning inside me for her.

CHAPTER 45

Ella Mae

I'M PACKING my most fierce, fashtastic power outfits—sexy, but subtle; trendy, but not try-hard. There will be plenty of people at the bash who have actual Jimmy Choos, in multiple colors. It's a way bigger pond out there and I'm acutely aware of my guppy status. But I'm going to be a knock-out, boss babe of a guppy if I have anything to say about it.

I chant some affirmations while I lay outfits on my bed. I'm looking at mixed-patterns on silk scarf tops and silk pants. I choose one combo that slays.

I'm as talented as any of these people.

I built my own business from scratch.

Picking up a pair of red flair capri pants and a chevron crop top, I hear Chris' voice saying what he thinks of me.

You're one of the best people I know.

You're brilliant, quick on your feet, unafraid, persistent.

You look out for others.

You don't hold grudges.

You're one of the most fun people I've ever hung out with.

Yes. I memorized every word he said to me. Those impressions have traveled deep into my heart and touched dusty places, long neglected. If I didn't believe them just a little bit, they would have rattled around and bounced back out. But I know, at some level, he's right, even if he's one of four people in this zip code who think so.

The thing is, I can't let Chris be my anchor. As far off base as Mom has been about men and relationships, she got that part right. A person can't count on anyone to be their everything. I need to find my own way and place in the world, and then I will more than happily share all that with the soldier who has won my heart for good.

Chris will hopefully be a huge part of my future, whatever it ends up looking like—if he chooses me. But I need to lean on something more than him alone.

I know one thing for certain. I can't stay in a town where I'm scorned and mocked daily.

After a few hours of outfit selection, packing my makeup and skin care products, and wheeling my suitcases downstairs and parking them next to the front door, I'm ready.

It's only lunchtime. My flight to LA leaves Columbus at 6:08 pm. Chris insisted he'd drive me. It's not that I don't want him to, I'm just so scattered and worn down. My brain feels like an old jigsaw puzzle that spilled out of the box. Some of the pieces are upside down. I don't even know where they fit. The only corner piece I see is Chris. It's tempting to fit the rest of my life around what's building between us. But I know better.

I sit in the front room, staring out the window. Chris is getting some work done today. I have two-and-a-half hours to kill before he gets here.

I call Meg in my boredom.

"St. James Accounting, may I help you?"

"Meg, it's me."

"Oh, hey, Ella Mae. How's the packing going?"

"I'm finished. And I'm sitting in our empty house watching the grass grow from the front room."

"I hate those last few hours before a trip. I'm either scurrying around like a chicken with its head cut off, or I'm like you, ready and antsy. I wish I could offer you a lunch date to distract you."

"I know you're busy."

"I'm working through lunch so Joe and I can go scout out some venues for the wedding this afternoon."

"You mean you're not going to get married out on the MacIntyre farm?"

"Ha! Like Aiden wants to offer his farm to his brother's ex-girlfriend for her wedding. You know how that goes."

"Better than most people around here."

"True."

"I'm so sick of the ridiculous lines and the sideways glances and the judgmental attitudes, Meg."

"It can wear on a girl, I'm here to testify."

She starts singing *Can I get a witness?* like she's in the front pew of a southern church. I crack up. It feels good to laugh with Meg.

"Don't do anything crazy, like relocate to LA, okay? I don't know what I'd do without you here."

I sigh so loudly I'm surprised Meg doesn't comment on it.

"I won't," I promise, even though I'm not sure I won't.

I'm pretty certain I'd never move my life to Los Angeles. When it comes to what I won't do, everything seems so obviously a definite no. I only wish the next steps as to what I will do were as clear cut.

I end up editing a few reels and preparing content for the coming week. Working on my page makes the hours between calling Meg and Chris knocking on the front door melt away. Social media always does that for me. It's a productive distraction, and the one place I know I'll find appreciation for my brand of personality.

Haters? Yes. I have plenty, but they are far outnumbered by the people who wait for my next post with baited breath. My peeps. What would I do without them?

Chris knocks and then lets himself right into my home. I love the ease with which he enters my world these days—like he's this missing piece that always belonged here. My corner piece.

"You ready?" His face is a combination of care and reserved dissatisfaction.

He's not happy I'm going. But he's not abandoning me or making me suffer for our disagreement. Look at us, being all grown up about things where we can't find a common ground.

"I'd actually love to remember you with a smile on your face in the event this plane goes down."

That comment does not earn me a smile. Instead, I'm face-to-face with the glorious scowl that makes me want to cancel my flight and go away with Chris for a weekend.

"How do you get cuter when you're mad?"

He nearly grumbles out his response. "I'm not cute. Nothing about me is *cute*."

I walk toward him, ready to soothe the beast. "Oh, Soldier. You're so wrong about that. You're the absolute cutest thing I've ever seen."

I place my palm flat on his chest and go up on tiptoes to kiss the skin on his cheek right above his beard. His face morphs into a sort of pout. Still cute.

"Chris," I say, stepping back only a few inches. "I know you don't want me to go. I get it. And I know there's a lot up in the air right now. But one thing that is not confusing, not uncertain, and not going to change one bit is how I feel about you."

He smiles a little. It's a begrudging smile.

"There's nothing to say that I haven't already said. Your bags are packed. You've got your mind made up. You know I'm dead set against you going. And for good reason. I just don't want to see you hurt."

"I've been hurting," I remind him. "And I think this trip will help with some of that."

"You'll call me if you need anything?"

"I'll call you even if I don't need anything."

He smiles bigger this time, and then he tugs me to himself and kisses me for real.

Cancel my tickets, people! This kiss.

His hand holds me close to him while his other palm cups my cheek. He kisses me, then he pulls back and stares into my eyes like he's memorizing me. Then he leans in again like he can't get enough of us—enough of me. I wrap my arms around his neck, holding his head in place so I can show him everything he means to me.

When we break apart, he says, "I'm going to miss you, Boots. And I wish I could do something to change this town and their hurtful ways."

"Not your circus. Not your monkeys."

"I know. I really do."

He brushes a hand down my face. Our eyes lock. I lean my cheek into his palm.

Then he says, "Okay. We'd better go."

The drive isn't silent. I fill it with talk of all I'll be doing and what I'm looking forward to. He asks if I want to stop by Alex and Courtney's on our way back from Columbus when I get home. I think it's his way of mentally fast-forwarding ahead of this trip he doesn't want me to take.

"Of course I want to see them. I love them!"

He smiles at that. "I think they're pretty far gone for you too."

Chris drops me at the curb. I insist he doesn't come in with me. It's a madhouse inside and we'll just clog things up standing there kissing and looking all madly-in-love. It still blows my mind. I'm deliriously in love with Christopher St. James. And what's an even bigger shocker? He's fiercely in love with me.

Chris takes all my bags from the trunk and then we stand there kissing until the airport employee tells Chris this is a loading and unloading zone and he needs to move his car.

I stand on the curb, watching Chris drive away, and then I go through the whole process of checking my bag and walking through TSA. My flight's running on time and I'm at the gate sitting across from a family of three. Dad, Mom, and daughter who looks to be around five or six.

The little girl is leaning on her dad's arm. He's reading something, but he's got his other arm around her and he's rubbing her back absentmindedly while he reads. The mom has her kindle out. They look happy—whole. I keep glancing around, trying to focus on anything but them. My eyes drift back to them regularly.

Our flight is called to board. The little girl gathers her backpack and walks to the gate between her parents. They enter the gangway before me. When we take our seats, it turns out they are in the two seats next to mine, and the dad is across the aisle from us. I asked for a window seat since I never fly. I think the last flight I took was maybe seven or eight years ago when I went to visit Meg in Pennsylvania.

"Mommy, I'm hungry," the girl says with a little whine to her voice.

The mom leans in. "We've got snacks. Let's wait until take off and we can see what we brought. Okay?"

The little girl scrunches her forehead, but she nods.

She looks over at her dad. He smiles so warmly. Then he looks up at the mom and they exchange this glance that's conspiratorial in the best of ways—like they're in this together. A parenting team.

I try not to be so blatant as I watch them.

Once we're in the air, the mom produces a snack and a coloring book. The girl lowers her tray and colors happily while she eats. She holds her picture up occasionally to her dad. He beams like she's the next Michelangelo. She tells him about every detail of her drawing, and his eyes stay fixed on her the whole time. She's his delight, you can tell.

The mom reads her Kindle, but occasionally says something softly to her daughter.

I eventually lose interest in snooping on this family, so I turn my attention to putting together a post with a picture of me on the plane along with a few I snapped in the terminal before takeoff. I paid the extra ten dollars for in-flight wifi. I mean, duh. That's a no-brainer. If I can be online while I fly, win!

Once my post is live, I scroll through pictures of me and Chris on my feed. There we are kissing across my island, sitting on the curb after the porch fire, holding hands in my back yard, doing yoga, at the reservoir, out to eat … I reread comments about us. I can feel the soft smile on my face. It makes my eyes feel misty. No one has ever stepped up for me like Chris has.

He's one of a kind.

CHAPTER 46

Ella Mae

WE LAND after eight California time. Dusk obscures my view through the airplane window. The entire city of Los Angeles sprawls out in every direction until it hits the shoreline, and my eyes are drawn out over the ocean where the sun dips at the horizon.

While I'm standing at baggage claim, I notice two younger women, probably college-age, whispering to one another and watching me. This is the good kind of whispering. Finally, they walk over.

"Are you …" one starts in and then she blushes.

The other one takes over. "Are you Fab-U-lous Ella Mae?"

"That's me!" I strike a little pose even though I'm travel-weary.

"OH MY GOSH!" the shy one gushes. "Can we … would you … can we get a selfie with you? I'm dying." She fans her face. "I can't believe it's really you. I'm such a fan. Oh my word." She turns to her friend. "I'm freaking out. Stop me from freaking out. I'm making a complete fool of myself."

"You're adorable. Don't worry," I assure her.

"I've followed you since I was sixteen," she says. "You taught me so much about fashion, beauty—and just life."

She's got stars in her eyes when she looks at me.

"We're both hugely devoted superfans," the other girl says. She rattles off their insta-handles just so I'll know who they are.

We huddle up and the girls take selfies. We do duck lips and peace signs, and then they stand gawking at me a little longer. In a city where nearly six out of every hundred people are famous, I can't believe I've just been treated like a celebrity. I'll take it. Considering the stress of what I'm about to walk into this weekend, a little extra fan-crushing is just the boost I needed.

I pick up my rental car and drive the twenty-five minutes to my hotel in Santa Monica. Drake continued to offer me the room at his house in Malibu right up until a few days ago. The man is certainly persistent.

Even though I think Chris is being overly cautious about Drake, I'm not throwing prudence to the wind and staying with a near stranger when I'm traveling alone over two thousand miles from my hometown. I may have spent an afternoon with Drake in Columbus, but I don't know him well enough to be his houseguest.

I fall back onto the hotel queen bed. The view out my window contains the whole skyline, littered with lights. I'm one of millions here. A dot. A speck. Easily forgotten or overlooked. But to those two girls at the airport, I'm someone. And, most of all, I matter to Chris. He'd notice if something happened to me. I picture him going all *Die Hard* on whoever did something to hurt me, and I smile.

Despite the overwhelming urge to crawl under the covers and let sleep overtake me, I send Meg, Mom, and Chris quick texts to let them know I made it and I'm settling in for the night. They each answer separately, telling me to have fun, be careful, and best of all, from Chris, *I love you, Boots*.

I tell him I love him too and then I head to bed. Tomorrow's the big day. I'll start with pilates here in the hotel and then I'll put my game face on and head to Drake's. I know @ariapilatesgoddess lives somewhere near LA. It's too bad I don't have time to visit her in person on this trip. Maybe next time.

~

The drive down Pacific Coast Highway takes about a half-hour from my hotel to Drake's impressive mansion facing the sand. The cliffs rise up on my right and the Pacific ocean fills my view to the left. I scold myself for not renting a convertible, but then again, good hair is everything. And I'm styled in beach waves that would ironically be wrecked by the wind coming in off the beach. Who actually maintains beach waves on the beach? No one. That's who.

Parking is scarce, but then I catch sight of the attendant out front of Drake's house. Drake told me there was a pre-party this afternoon before things get into full swing tomorrow night. The whole bash lasts several days with various bands, and even a fashion show in the middle of it all. Rumor has it, Drake spends somewhere around twenty thousand dollars on this extravaganza.

Who knows what he really spends.

Gossip.

You should never fully believe it. Am I right?

I hand the valet my keys and walk toward the front door. Houses are built with barely five feet of space between them on this section of the coast, but they all face a restricted road that runs parallel to the freeway, and then the back of their homes sit directly on this private section of the beach.

My heart feels like it's in my throat when I ring the doorbell. A few moments later, Drake's standing there wearing only swim trunks. His aviator glasses are perched on top of his head, keeping his wild, wavy hair away from his face. He looks good—really good. But I feel nothing.

Chris is it for me.

"Ella Mae!" he shouts when he sees me. "You made it. I wish you would have let me put you up here. You can see it's a far cry from wherever you stayed last night. My bed is custom-made, and the sheets are one thousand thread count Pima cotton."

His bed? Maybe that was a slip. I'm pretty sure he's just sharing about his bed so I'd know all the beds in the house are high quality.

"I reserved a nice room in Santa Monica with a view of the city. It's comfortable."

"Well, no worries. You can always crash here anyway. Mi casa es su casa, and all that. Come in, come in."

He waves me inside and then he surprises me by pulling me into a hug. His hand moves up and down my back. I'm wearing a top that ties at my neck and wraps around my waist. My whole back is exposed. And I'm not going into the magical details of how I keep everything tucked where it needs to be. A girl's got her secrets. All I know is Drake's hands are on my bare skin. I give him a quick squeeze and step back.

"Where's everyone else?" I ask.

The house is quiet except for the sound of an Ed Sheeran song playing through the home audio system and the noise of the surf crashing in the distance out through the huge sliding glass panels at the back of the great room.

"Ah, yeah. They'll all be here in a while. I thought we could hang out first. Just the two of us, you know?"

"Okay."

I'm a little wary, but I know Drake's been talking about connecting me with big influencers. He may want to talk shop before they all get here. Once the house fills with guests, we won't have as much of an opportunity to catch up.

Drake walks further into the house. He looks down at the bag at my side.

"Did you bring a suit?"

I did, but I honestly don't want to mess up my hair before everyone gets here.

"Yeah. For later."

"Later. Yeah," he agrees. "Well, let's go out back. I've got a full kitchen out there. I'll get us drinks and we can catch up. Did you eat?"

"Yeah. I'm good."

He walks ahead of me, out through the floor to ceiling opening, past the glass panels that are pushed open to create a seamless indoor-outdoor feel. He walks over to a bar area where there's a pizza oven, a stovetop, and two low refrigerators all set in stacked stone. Everything looks like it's straight out of a magazine.

He opens one of the refrigerators. "Wine spritzer? IPA? I could mix you a drink."

"Seltzer water?" I ask.

"Sure. I've got that. Once things get under full swing, the bartender will be here—and the servers, of course."

"Of course."

I'm smiling past this awkward feeling. He's just welcoming me ahead of the other guests. I should feel honored. But I've got a spidey-sense when it comes to people, and I'm starting to feel like the fly in that old nursery rhyme, *The Spider and the Fly*. I'll play along with Drake for now, but I'm not telling my gut to shush.

I picture Chris. He would not be happy about me being

here alone. I'm not doing anything wrong, but something's not right either.

"What time did you say everyone else is coming?" I ask.

"Relax, Ella Mae. We're just getting to know one another. I want to hear all you've been up to. And maybe we can take some pics together to drum up some action on social media. Don't worry. I've got you covered. Plenty of big names will be here tonight and the rest of the weekend. @Miss-charity-thang is coming. @Slay-Dawggytown and even @The.Shannon.Price.Is.So.Right."

Wow. Huge doesn't begin to describe the people he just listed. It's worth a little awkward pre-party if I'm going to mingle with that level of influencers.

"Come over here. Make yourself comfortable," Drake says.

He points to an outdoor couch that faces the pool with a view over the railing to the sand and the ocean stretching beyond the patio.

I take a seat on the far cushion. Drake sits in the middle one and tilts his body so he's facing me.

"So, tell me all about your latest projects," he says, casually lifting his glasses, putting them on, and running a hand through his hair. "What are you focusing on in the coming months? Any big plans?"

I wish. If I'm perfectly honest, I've been treading water with my account ever since Chris and I started faking our relationship online. When he and I really began dating, it only got worse. I've been more focused on Chris than my work. And I've been less energized for creative endeavors while I've been fending off the reactions around Bordeaux. But I can't tell Drake all that.

"I've got some secret projects I'm cooking up," I tell him. "You know, a little this and that."

"Oh, I do. I love secrets," he says, leaning in a little closer.

In a slightly husky voice, he says, "You want to know one of my secrets?"

The hum of concern in my gut is waving around a caution flag like a city worker in front of a manhole.

"No. You don't have to tell me your secrets. I'll wait to find out with the rest of your fans."

"Oh, Ella Mae." He glances down at my lips and then back up into my eyes. "This secret isn't for our fans. It's just between us."

I stand quickly. "Do you have a restroom?"

He chuckles. "I've got six. Closest one is just past the kitchen."

Drake leans back, spreading both arms out along the back of the couch.

I smile my best confident smile. "I'll be right back."

"Take your time. I'm here."

Yeah. I know.

CHAPTER 47

Ella Mae

I MAKE every effort not to sprint to Drake's restroom. Instead, I stroll slowly, looking over my shoulder at Drake whose back is to me while he sips his drink and looks out at his amazing view.

Am I crazy?

No. I'm not crazy.

I make my way through the huge, dreamy designer kitchen, and find the bathroom immediately past it, just as Drake said. I step inside and flick the lock. Then I collapse back against the door.

I consider texting Chris. Nope. Not unless I want a special ops helicopter hovering over this building in a split second. I'm joking, mostly. But I imagine Chris could probably rustle up someone local in a pinch, knowing him. I'll call him if things get out of hand. So far, I don't even know what's going on.

Nothing really happened out on the patio.

Drake wants to tell me a secret. So what?

Is he coming on to me, or am I reading into things?

Yeah, he's acting flirty. But maybe that's just his way of

interacting with everyone. He's probably used to snapping his fingers or just looking at a woman, and having her pant at the sight of him. I can easily see why. He's famous, wealthy, and gorgeous. It's the male trifecta.

But really, it doesn't matter what he's used to. I'm getting full-blown creeper vibes from Drake.

I decide on the best course of action: calling Meg.

"Hey, beach bunny! How's it going?" Meg squeals into the line when she answers.

I whisper my answer. I figure Drake's out on his patio, but I don't know if he came inside after me.

"I'm at Drake's," I say in such a soft voice, Meg has to ask me to repeat myself.

When she makes out what I'm saying, she asks, "Why are you whispering?"

I explain the whole situation from the valet greeting me—even though I'm the only guest so far—to the hug, to the whole conversation on the couch.

"You need to get out of there," Meg says. "And, are you sure that was a valet? Maybe someone just stole your rental!"

"It's the valet. Drake waved to him before he shut the door behind me," I whisper.

"Here's your clue," Meg says. "You're locked in a bathroom, whispering. Does that scream, *I'm feeling super safe right now*? No. No, it does not. I don't think he's about to attack you, but who knows what he's going to try.

"You need an exit plan, and pronto. Come back tomorrow when the party's in full swing. Tell him you forgot you scheduled a quick meeting with someone there in LA today, and your time is full right up until the party. Then hightail it away from that house until you have some people there to buffer you from that guy."

I keep my voice soft and private. "That's not a half-bad idea. Thanks."

"No problem. I'm so glad you called."

"Me too."

"And, Ella Mae?"

"Yeah?"

"Nothing is worth letting him treat you badly or push himself on you. You know that, right?"

"Of course I do. This all came out of left field. I really think he still wants to help me get connected. He probably just wants to press his luck with me if he can."

"Welp. His luck just ran out."

"Sure did."

I hang up with Meg, flush the toilet and run the faucet for effect, and then I head back through the kitchen out onto the patio.

"I just got a call," I tell Drake. "I'm so sorry. I totally forgot a meeting I had set up while I'm out here. I'll be back tomorrow night for the bash. How do I get my keys back?"

"Seriously? You're leaving? What meeting could be more important than hanging here for the afternoon? I thought we'd get to know one another a little better."

"I appreciate all that, Drake. But," I wave my hand around in some sort of gesture, trying not to look just shy of hysterics. Who knows what I look like. "I've gotta run."

I start to walk toward the front door to emphasize my words.

"Keys?"

"Yeah. I'll get Serge."

Serge. Okay.

Drake presses a button on a panel near the front door. A voice comes through. "Yes, sir?"

"Ella Mae is ready to leave. Bring her car."

"Yes, sir."

Drake turns toward me. I step closer to the door and turn the handle.

"I'll see you tomorrow night, Drake. Thanks for having me over."

He leans onto the wall in a pose that would look awesome if I were someone else and my heart weren't threatening to jump out of my chest and do a little impromptu berserk dance of dread around the foyer.

"I have to tell you, Ella Mae. I'm a bit disappointed."

"I hear you. Life's full of disappointments," I blurt. "But we have all weekend to catch up and what not."

I don't even know what I'm saying.

My car pulls up and I turn and walk out the door.

I don't think I take a full breath until I'm about ten miles away from Drake's house and halfway back to my hotel. It's then that it dawns on me—I'm in LA. The ocean is literally right there. I pull into this smaller parking lot right off Pacific Coast Highway. Sand has blown onto the pavement. It's all so California. I fish around my purse for some coins to feed the meter, and then I take my shoes off and allow my feet to touch the beach for the first time since I got here.

Ahhhh. Something loosens in my chest the moment the warmth of the sun-baked sand shifts between my toes. I take a deep breath in and out. Then I walk down along the shore, letting the tide lap over my feet and up my ankles while I stroll without purpose. I head south for about a half-hour, then I turn around and walk back.

My mind flashes to the interaction with Drake at times, but I send those thoughts out on the waves. I need this time to decompress. I partly came on this trip to get perspective. I deserve to take this afternoon to myself without letting thoughts of Drake and his seemingly misguided intentions filter into what I so desperately need.

After an hour on the beach, I grab a smoothie at a spot closer to my hotel. Then I drive back and take a nap. When I wake, it's still light out, but obviously evening. I'm sure the people who were coming over today are at Drake's by now, but I'm in for the night. I do a live with the view out my hotel balcony as a backdrop. Then I change into my Kardashian-inspired loungewear and order room service.

When Chris texts later that night, I text back that I'm exhausted from a long day and I'll touch base with him tomorrow if I get a minute between events. I just can't face him yet. What's worse? I know I might crack once I hear his voice, and I don't want to get into any of the details until I'm back home—if ever.

Does Chris need to know Drake might have maybe flirted with me? Probably not. No good can come of confirming his suspicions. It's not like I flirted back. Nope, I called my bestie and hightailed it out of there. What's done is done. I just need time to put the whole situation fully behind me before I face Chris.

I spend the next day sightseeing and getting completely styled to the hilt for tonight.

This time, when I drive up the private road leading to Drake's, I'm sure I'm not the only partygoer here. The music is loud enough to hear from out front. Couples and well-dressed individuals walk toward the door. My heart beats faster with excitement instead of nervousness this time.

I knock, but no one answers, so I push the door open. Elegant people fill the foyer and the great room. The crowd spills out toward the patio. Who knows where Drake even is in the middle of all this.

I walk in, making eye contact and smiling with anyone who looks at me. Guests are drinking, taking selfies together, leaning on furniture in poses that feel so iconic and borderline cliché. The atmosphere vibrates with the energy of all the who's who mingling and chatting. There's this feeling that this is the place to be and these are the people to be with.

"Ella Mae!" I hear Drake's voice from the patio area.

I walk out toward him. Once again, he moves in for a hug. Then he loops his arm around my waist like it belongs there. It doesn't, so I sidestep and give him a winning smile in exchange for my personal space.

I'm still riding the calm of my day alone and drawing from the high of being recognized at the airport and at a bistro in Santa Monica today. I've let any feelings and thoughts about my time yesterday with Drake go. We're starting from scratch.

"Come with me," he says. "I want to hook you up. You've been on my mind ever since you took off."

I smile at the people watching us. I think I recognize a few of them. If he wants to hook me up, he could just start right here, with these people. But he's already headed in toward the kitchen, so I take off after him.

The light over the stove is on in here, and a few built-in cabinet lights give a soft glow to the opposite side of the room, but otherwise, the kitchen's surprisingly dark and empty compared to the rest of the house.

I step in further, wondering where Drake went. I thought he came this way. The din of conversation in the next room filters through the wall. Music thrums throughout the house.

Suddenly, he's right there, coming around the door of the open pantry. He steps up to me and nearly cages me in against the island. His breath smells a little fermented. He may have had a few drinks tonight.

I try to move out of the spot where he's enclosing me with his arms outstretched on either side of me with his hands gripping the island, but he protests.

"Ella Mae. Ella Mae. You've been driving me crazy since that day we drove around Columbus together. The way you ate bites of food from my hand … that was so hot. I knew you were beautiful before I met you in person, but when I saw you, I could tell we'd be good together."

"I've got a boyfriend," I say. "We're serious."

I try not to look in Drake's eyes. He's right there, not touching me, but keeping me pinned in place. "I'm flattered, but I'm also taken. Drake, please back up."

Instead of backing up, he lifts one of his hands and brushes it down my cheek. I shudder, and not in the good way.

"Come on, Ella Mae. What's some guy in a small midwestern town going to give you? I can give you all this—connections, a sweet life … and think of the shopping sprees. You know I'm a better choice."

I duck under Drake's arm, and thankfully he doesn't stop me. I was prepared to use the self-defense moves I learned years ago when that was a trending topic. Thank goodness for trends like that, otherwise I probably never would have made the effort to learn how to protect myself in a threatening situation.

"So," Drake says, dragging his hand through his hair and eyeing me like I haven't just given him the clear brush-off. "Are you sure about this? You aren't interested in me?"

"I'm sure," I say. "No offense. I'm already dating someone, like I said. But we can still be …"

I'm about to say *friends*. Why?

Drake's not my friend.

As a matter of fact, I can't wait to put a whole lot of distance between me and him—for good.

Meg's words run through my mind.

Am I that desperate to fit in? Has the constant rejection of my hometown—my own dad—made me willing to give up my dignity in exchange for more likes and more followers?

When will it be enough?

When will *I* be enough?

I thought getting one million followers was the apex. Now I have over eight million people who willingly follow me, and it still never feels like I've made it. There's always another benchmark. Another person to impress. Another like or follow to garner.

Drake's words snap me out of my internal spiral.

"You led me on, Ella Mae. You flirted that day in Columbus. But you were just trying to get something from me. You made me think you were interested."

He shakes his head and hardens his features. Gone is the man who tried to charm me. Drake no longer looks like a casual surfer who's made something of himself. His eyes are steely, despite the haze from whatever he had to drink.

"I'm done with you." He squints at me. "You could have had all of this, but you threw it away for some midwestern nobody. You need to stop riding my coattails."

I open my mouth to defend myself, but I know it's not worth it. Besides, his words feel like darts, piercing holes in my confidence, all the air feels like it's seeping out of me.

He continues to berate me as I turn to leave the kitchen and walk toward the front door.

"You're a poser, Ella Mae. You'll never be more than a wannabe. Insignificant influencers like you are a dime a dozen."

CHAPTER 48

Ella Mae

EVEN THE STRONGEST people have their breaking point. And I just hit mine. I run out of Drake's home, unsure whether I even shut the door behind me. People watch me go, too. It's not exactly a scene, but it's not a subtle exit where I simply slip into the night either.

I don't even have the energy to think about the ramifications of me leaving the way I did, being witnessed by the types of people who live for a juicy tidbit and don't hesitate to capitalize on someone else's drama.

As soon as I reach the valet, I tell Serge which car is mine. He retrieves it for me.

There's this certain kind of sadness that dries you up from the inside. You'd give anything to be able to cry a river, but nothing will come. Right now, climbing into the front of this Altima sedan, I'm grateful my tear ducts are twin deserts.

I put the car in drive and pull away, watching Drake's house disappear in my rearview mirror. He didn't chase after me, thankfully. Not that he'd stoop to come after an insignificant influencer like me.

What was I thinking?

I nearly bang my head on the steering wheel.

Everything feels numb and pointless. I'm supposed to be at that party—the party I flew here to attend—mingling with the famous and influential people who would skyrocket my platform to another level.

Drake's words start to reverberate through my mind. I know he was partly drunk. And he had such a misguided idea about what was going to happen between us. Did I lead him on? If I did, it was unintentional. I've been beyond clear that I'm in a relationship.

Either way, he never should have cornered me in that kitchen and made me feel so paralyzed.

The further I get from his house, the more my emotions start to swell until I'm crying so hard I have to pull over. It's not merely Drake causing this meltdown—though it's definitely him and the demeaning things he said to me.

I thought coming here would give me some sort of get out of jail free card, only it would be a get out of Bordeaux ticket that gave me an excuse to leave that town and the constant condemnation behind me.

If Chris weren't in the picture, I think I'd never go back.

My sobs fill the interior of the car.

Chris.

I'd call him, but two things stop me. One: Chris warned me against Drake, and I insisted he was wrong. And two: He'll want to kill Drake if he hears what he did and said to me.

I look out my window at the pitch black ocean with only a visible edge of whitewater defining where the foam hits the shore. Tide rolling in and out, in and out, as if my whole world didn't just crumble around me.

I've got nowhere to go. Nowhere I belong. My online life

just took a hit, and my real life is rooted in a town that can't stand me.

The tears subside enough that I'm able to drive. I'm still softly sobbing when I turn onto the street for my hotel, but my heart feels bled out. I'm so very weary and sick of trying. A soft voice from somewhere inside me urges me to call it a night and not attempt to solve the world's problems in a day. All this confusion and pain will be here to wrestle through in the morning.

I pull into the hotel parking structure and park my car. When I walk into the lobby, my heart literally skips a beat. I must be conjuring up a dream because I could swear I see Chris standing off to the side of the main desk, casually leaning against the wall, scanning the room.

When his eyes land on me, I know he's real—and he's here. I don't stop to ask why. I run straight into his outstretched arms and I collapse. We're in public, but that doesn't stop my tears from streaming down my face.

"You're here," I mumble through my sobs into his shirt.

"I'm here. Let's get you upstairs and you can tell me everything. I should have come with you to start with."

His voice is strong and certain, with an edge of gruffness that I know is him beating himself up for not being here for me.

So many words flood my mind. I want to say everything, but I say nothing. I simply allow Chris to lace our fingers together and walk me to the elevator. The touch of his hand feels like a lifeline. As long as he's holding me, I'm not going to completely self-implode.

Once we're inside and I push the fifth floor button, Chris pulls me to himself and holds me. I rest my head on his chest and grip him with everything I am.

The elevator dings and we step out into the empty hall. I pull my keycard out of my purse and let us into my room.

Chris looks around, taking in the furnishings and the view.

"Why don't you change into something more comfortable? I'll wait here. Then you can tell me everything."

That sounds beyond wonderful. But I have to know.

"How did you know to come here? Why? How?"

"When I dropped you off at the airport, I drove away with an unsettled feeling that wouldn't quit. I kept telling you I didn't trust that Drake guy, and yet I let you take off to come here alone. It ate at me all night. Then, yesterday, Meg called me."

I could possibly kill her. Or kiss her. Maybe both. Whatever, she got me what I needed when I didn't have the sense or strength to call Chris on my own.

Chris takes a seat in the corner chair. He's watching me. I know he can read my thoughts right now.

"Meg was concerned about Drake—worried for you."

Chris shakes his head and his jaw clenches. *Die Hard*. But way, way sexier. He's in military mode, ready to eliminate whatever threatened me.

"Basically, I had some things to wrap up yesterday, but I got a ticket and made sure I was here as soon as I could be. Now, go change and get comfortable. I'll order us some pizza. We can catch up over pepperoni."

I rifle through the dresser drawers and pull out something infinitely more comfortable than this fashion-statement I'm wearing. Then I kick off my shoes and walk to the bathroom.

"... and onions!" I shout just before I shut the door.

I hear Chris mumble something like, "You and Duke and your onions."

Once I'm changed, and I've cleaned my face and held a warm cloth to it while I take deep breaths to calm myself from this whole night, I rejoin Chris in my room. He's sitting in the same chair, looking out at the lights that seem to spread out forever outside my window.

"I can't believe you came," I say, plopping down on the hotel bed near the headboard and fluffing a pillow behind myself to lean back on.

"I can't believe you didn't call me."

His lips are in a thin line and he's staring at me with a piercing gaze that holds me in place.

"I didn't want you to go all Rambo. And I didn't know how bad it was going to get."

"What do you mean, how bad it was going to get?"

"Yesterday, Drake asked me to come over under the guise that there was a pre-party. I thought there would be other people there—influencers he wanted to introduce me to.

"But we were alone. And he gave me the creeps, so I called Meg, and we made an exit plan, and I skedaddled out of there."

"So she told me."

Chris is none too happy that this had to come from Meg. I get it. Maybe I should have told him. But in my defense, he's one to call in the artillery. Literally. And I had a lot of sorting to do.

"So, I waited until tonight, knowing there would be a houseful of people there. When I showed up, he cornered me in the kitchen."

Chris' jaw looks like it's about to pop. The skin on his neck is slightly red with light white splotches. That dent over his one eyebrow is back.

I get up off the bed and walk over to him, nestling myself on his lap. I brush my thumb over his brow, trying to soothe away that telltale sign of stress and concern.

"I took self-defense. I could have given him something to remember me by, don't worry, Soldier."

Sure, I'm still freaking out inside, but Chris is here. And

something about the way he's distraught over this makes me want to lessen his worry. He doesn't have to know how I really felt—my tears in the lobby probably told him all he needed to know about that anyway.

"You think you could have defended yourself?"

"Yeah. I could even take you down if I needed to."

I so couldn't.

"Right. We'll have to see that one day. We can use the high school wrestling gym."

"Bring it, Big Boy."

He chuckles, his face relaxing a little.

"Tell me the rest, Boots. I promise not to drive to that jerk's house and hang him off his back patio."

"That's an awfully specific promise."

"It's one of the plans I considered on the flight. And that was when I only knew about yesterday."

"Okay." I take a deep breath. Then I look into Chris' eyes. There aren't words for the way he's looking at me. I lean in and hug him. Yes. I want to tell him the story—at least in a general way. But more than that, I just want him.

"Thank you," I whisper into his ear.

His warm, strong arms encircle me.

"I've got you, Ella Mae. I told you that, and I mean it. I don't say that to everyone. When I tell you I've got you, I've got you."

"Okay," I murmur into his neck.

My head is resting on his shoulder and he's still holding me.

"I'll trust you," I promise him.

His neck is right there. And his skin is so warm. His beard tickles my cheek like an invitation. So I plant a soft kiss on the skin below his ear. Then I trail my lips up toward his earlobe and give it a soft nip.

"Story time is over?" he asks in a very raspy, definitely affected voice.

"For now. We'll resume stories over pizza."

I say the words with my mouth right against his neck, and he shivers. Then he shifts me so my face is right in front of his.

"I love you, Ella Mae."

He says the words with such intensity, I almost start crying again. And then his mouth is on mine, releasing all the feelings of this day—telling me the things I needed to hear, but didn't even know I needed.

I'm here for you.

I'll always come for you.

You're more than enough for me.

I kiss him back, cupping his face in my hands. Tears start to fall and I don't stop them. This beautiful giant of a man, strong and so privately tender came all the way across the country to make sure I was okay.

Our kiss is wild and sweet and full of too much and not enough. I feel him everywhere. Tingles course through my body, I grasp at his hair, his shirt, his arms. He caresses my back, my shoulders, my hair.

A knock at the door brings us back to the moment.

"Pizza delivery!"

I chuckle and stand, straightening my shirt and running a hand across my hair.

"Coming!" I shout to the delivery guy.

Chris stands and takes his wallet out of his pants. He collects the pizza, and then he gives the guy a tip. I have a flashback to a trip we went on with our town last year. Chris insisted on tipping our driver on behalf of the whole town.

Why didn't I see it then—see beyond the muscles and the sometimes stern expressions to one of the kindest, most steadfast hearts in the world?

Chris places the pizza on the comforter and we take up opposite sides of the bed. I fill him in on the rest of what happened with Drake tonight. It honestly feels like a week ago and so far away.

With Chris here beside me, everything else fades into insignificance.

CHAPTER 49

Chris

I LEFT Ella Mae to get some sleep after we had stayed up eating pizza on her bed, and then kissing goodnight. And kissing goodnight a little more at the door.

When I had talked Meg into telling me where Ella Mae was staying, I booked a room in the same hotel. Last night, once the pizza box had been set onto the desk, Ella Mae snuggled up beside me. I pulled up the airline website on her laptop. For a small fee, I was able to switch her onto my return flight, and I even finagled a window seat next to mine so we can sit together. Ella Mae's flight home was scheduled for two days from now. After the stunt Drake pulled, we're leaving today.

I couldn't sleep—probably only got four hours after leaving Ella Mae's room around one. I spent the night tossing and turning while agitated thoughts about what she endured battered my mind.

Once the sun came up, I hit the hotel gym. The fitness room here isn't as decked out as the one I'm used to using at the fire station back home, but it will do. I need to blow off some steam this morning before we head to LAX to catch our plane.

Ella Mae might be acting tough, but I saw her face when she came into that lobby last night. It's a sight I'll never forget. And when she crumbled into my arms … well, it took everything in me not to get in my car and exact revenge. But I knew she needed me with her. I wanted to be there for her, more than anything I've ever wanted.

I am relatively sure Ella Mae toned the story down as to what happened with Drake. Every time I think of him cornering her, coming on to her, and then demeaning her when she didn't respond to his advances, I want to get in my car and … well, prison isn't my end game, so I'm here pumping iron instead.

I load as many weights onto the bar as I can and squat. The burn in my thighs is just what I need. There's nothing like squats to focus my mind and engage my whole body. For a nanosecond, I forget about Drake. I finish a set of reps and my phone buzzes with a text from Ella Mae.

Ella Mae:

Where are you, Soldier? I'm hungry and we have to hit the road soon to make the flight.

I shoot her a quick answer.

Chris:

I was letting you catch up on your sleep. I'm in the fitness room. I can shower and dress in less than five minutes. I'm packed.

Ella Mae:

You don't want to know how long it takes me to shower and get ready. But I'm packed. And hungry. Did I mention I'm hungry?

I chuckle. Even with all she went through, she's the same resilient woman I've come to know and love.

Chris:

I promise to feed you. I'll meet you in the lobby in fifteen minutes. 😚

Ella Mae:

Did you just send me a kissy face emoji?

Chris:

What? No. That must have been a typo.

Ella Mae:

Sure, Soldier. You tell yourself that. 😘

Once we return both rental cars and check our bags, we head to our gate with time to spare. Our plane boards on time—ten o'clock California time. We'll be in Columbus at five, and then we'll head straight to Bordeaux just in time for what I've got planned. And, yes. I'm not foolish. I got Ella Mae a very nice breakfast at one of the cafes in the terminal before we took off.

Ella Mae looped our hands together as soon as we were seated. She hasn't let go of me the whole flight. Mostly, she's dozing on and off. I'm running through details for tonight, hoping I didn't leave anything out.

She stirs, looking up into my eyes.

"You know, I didn't really want to go back to Bordeaux. Before you showed up, I didn't know what I was going to do."

Her eyes look drowsy, but there's a sadness in her features.

"You would have just skipped town?"

I know things have been hard on her, but I had no idea it had gotten that unbearable.

"If you weren't living in Bordeaux … yeah. Maybe. I don't know. Last night when everything went south, on the drive back to the hotel, I started crying so hard I had to pull over. At that moment, I wasn't sure what to do. Everything seemed so bleak."

"How are you doing now?"

I rub my thumb along her index finger. She burrows her head into my shoulder.

"I'm better. Trying not to think too much about any of it. I haven't even been on social media today. I'm a little scared to check."

I steel my features and tell her, "Maybe you ought to check. Just to know what you're dealing with."

Ella Mae lets out a long sigh. "Yeah. You're probably right."

"And, I've given it a lot of thought," I say. "If you want to leave Bordeaux after this week, we can start making plans. The main DOD office is in Columbus. Alex and Courtney are there. Maybe we can make a fresh start. We'd still be close enough so you could visit Meg and Mabel every week, or whenever you wanted. And I could travel to see my family and friends."

"You'd do that for me?"

"There's not much I wouldn't do for you, Boots."

"I'm starting to believe you."

I watch closely as Ella Mae pulls away from my shoulder and reaches down into her carry-on to bring out her phone. She powers it on and clicks on the Instagram icon. I don't know if I'm even breathing. She taps her feed and starts scrolling. Her forehead scrunches. She keeps scrolling. I'm sitting still, waiting for her to say something—anything.

"Chris?"

"Yeah?"

"What is all this?"

"All what?" I ask.

"These posts in my feed. I'm tagged in all of them."

"What kind of posts?"

She looks over at me with a skeptical side eye. "Do you know about this?"

I take her phone and scroll, allowing a small smile to cross my face as I see each post, one after the other. I hand the phone back to her. She looks down at it again, and then up at me.

"This hashtag. It's got to be you who did this."

"What's the hashtag?"

"Chris! Tell me you did this. I know it's you."

"What's the hashtag, Ella Mae?"

Her eyes are misty with unshed tears when she looks up at me, and in a voice barely above a whisper, she says, "#ComeHomeEllaMae."

She shakes her head in disbelief. Or maybe she's overwhelmed by the gesture. It's not enough, in my opinion. But it's a start.

"Come home. Me. They want me to come home."

"Looks like it," I say.

She shakes her head, turning to look out the window. Her body is so still. I wait. If she thinks this was all me, she's so dead wrong. Maybe I set the ball rolling, went around town knocking sense into people, but this was all them. The hashtag was Jayme's idea. She said, *We have to find a way to tell Ella Mae she's a part of this town, and it has to be a way that matters to her.*

"I feel like one raw nerve ending," Ella Mae says. "After all the hope I put into this trip … All the scorn before I left … I thought I'd get clarity while I was out here. I'm going home more confused than ever."

I nod. "Been there."

She looks at me with a questioning expression.

"Coming home after I discharged from the Army. Life had gone on over the four years I was in college, naturally. But everyone scattered then. Most of them came back, but I enlisted right out of college. Officer Candidate because of my ROTC. Then I was in the Army for seven years. I came back home here and there for short visits, but for the most part, I spent eleven years away from Bordeaux. And …"

I look out the window past Ella Mae.

"I saw a lot. What happened to Alex was the worst of it, but there was just … so much."

Ella Mae nods, placing her hand on my knee.

"Then I came home, naively thinking I could seamlessly blend right back into my friend group. Brooks was there. I had never met him. People had gotten married. I mean, Trevor and Lexi had a baby. Trevor and Lexi. That blew my mind. And Shannon and Duke were together behind my back. It took me a long time to feel like Bordeaux was home again."

Ella Mae's lips draw into a thin line. Her eyes soften with

compassion. She doesn't say anything, leaving me room to say whatever else I need to get off my chest.

I only have one more thing to say, and it's the most important thing for her to hear.

"I guess I didn't really feel like I had truly come home until we started faking. And that feeling kept growing over the past few months. Once we told one another how we really felt—that was it. That was the moment I truly came home."

The smallest smile starts to emerge on Ella Mae's face. Her brows draw up and her eyes meet mine with such compassion and understanding. We're two misfits, strong-willed, difficult at times, but somehow, we fit with one another.

"You're my home too, Chris," she says.

I turn my head toward her and she leans up and places a soft kiss on my lips.

When she pulls away, she says, "Now fess up, Soldier. You started that hashtag, didn't you?"

"No. I really didn't."

Ella Mae's mouth drops open.

"Then, who?"

"Jayme."

"Jayme?"

"Yep. Jayme."

CHAPTER 50

Ella Mae

"CHRIS, why are you pulling into Aiden's driveway?"

Our flight here was four and half hours, but with the time change and the hour drive from Columbus, it's nearly dinnertime. I just want to get home, shower, and fall into bed. I'll figure out my life a little more tomorrow. Maybe.

I look around. Cars are scattered everywhere, up and down the driveway and on the gravel near the goat enclosure.

"Chris, whatever this is, it's a bad idea. I just need to go home, wash up, and have a little time to decompress in my own house."

He looks over at me, obviously too stubborn to give up whatever he's got in mind to do.

"Do you trust me?"

It's a simple question. In context right now, I'm inclined to say no. But do I trust this man? That's a no-brainer.

"You might be one of three people in the world I trust. Yes. I trust you."

He puts the car in park and looks over at me.

"Then, just follow me."

Before I can argue, Chris hops out of the driver's side of his truck and comes around to help me out. He extends his hand and I take it. Chris weaves our fingers together. He pauses, smiling down at me. Then he bends in and kisses me softly.

"What you're about to hear … I want you to know it's not me. I've got plenty I want to say to you, but this … well, it's not me."

"Okaaayyy." I draw out the word, feeling even more uneasy than when we first turned up the driveway and I saw the cars of half the town here.

Chris leads me toward Aiden's barn. The doors are open, and the closer we get, the more the sound of conversation drifts out to us.

When we're standing right in the middle of the barn entrance, heads start to turn. Slowly, the conversation lulls and Chris says, "She's here."

A whoop goes up from one side of the barn. That's Duke.

He shouts, "Welcome home, Ella Mae!"

I look over at Chris and whisper, "I don't know if I'm strong enough for this right now."

He whispers back, "You're the strongest person I know. And I'm right here. I'm not going anywhere."

Jayme walks up to us. "Ella Mae, we've got a seat for you right up here. How was your flight?"

"Um. Good. It was fine."

She smiles at me and leads the way toward the front of the barn. A microphone is set up with a free-standing speaker. Two chairs are off to the side, facing toward the back of the barn with a view of the mic.

Once we're seated, Jayme steps toward the microphone and starts talking, her eyes trained on me.

"Ella Mae, we owe you an apology. And that's what this is. A good friend taught me years ago that sorry is as sorry does. Words are cheap. Action is what really matters. So, this is a little bit of both. But it's just a beginning."

Jayme looks at me intently. "I'm sorry."

Then she pauses and wipes a tear from her eye. I feel my eyes threaten to leak as I watch her.

"I'm sorry I haven't been a good friend to you. If it weren't for you and your brilliant scheming, I wouldn't have the publishing deal that put my books on the map. You dropped everything and took on my dream as if it was your own. And then when Grant and I were struggling and our relationship was hanging on by a thread, you pulled off one of the biggest grand gestures in the history of this town to get us back together.

"I never thanked you enough. And I never treated you like the friend you are."

She looks over at me with such remorse written across her face.

I mouth the words, "It's okay."

She shakes her head and mouths, "No. It's not. But it will be."

Chris grasps my hand and places our enjoined hands on his thigh.

The rest of the women from that group of friends get up one by one: Laura, Lexi, Em. And they each tell me they're sorry they've ignored me and excluded me.

Lexi says, "You're welcome to come to girls' night, Ella Mae."

I lean over to Chris and say, "I'd rather hang with you."

He chuckles and says, "Me too."

Shannon gets up and tells me how good I am for Chris, and how she wants to treat me more like a sister. I can't believe my ears. She tells Chris she's sorry too.

People get up, one by one, and each one shares something I've done or said to them over the years that blessed them or made a difference. I can barely sit still through it all.

I left on Thursday feeling like I wore the scarlet letter and I was one situation shy of being burned at the stake. Coming back to this radical of an about face only four days later feels like more than I can absorb in one sitting.

Cherry Blanchard stands up in her spiky red heels and a pair of red shorts to match. She's got on a white bandeau top. She stands out, as usual.

"Ella Mae, you give the best fashion and makeup advice. I don't know where I'd be without your tutorials."

Chris chuckles and I elbow him in the ribs.

Then Mabel gets up there. She pulls the mic too close to her face and it squeals a little.

"Sorry, people. Technical difficulties! Am I right, Ella Mae?"

I nod. Having Mabel up there feels more comfortable somehow. She doesn't owe me an apology. She's been a real friend and always saw the best in me.

"I don't reckon I owe you an apology, Ella Mae, but if I do, I'm quite sure you'll tell me. But I didn't want to be left out when I found out what they were planning for you."

Mabel turns and addresses the group. "Ella Mae here taught me how to get on social media and then she taught me all them TikTok dances, and she even comes by once a week to help me out. I bet most of you'uns didn't even know that." She gives the group a scolding look which makes me smile.

"For a special treat, I've asked Memaw and Esther to join me up here."

Memaw and Esther stand up and take their places on either side of Mabel.

The song *I Like Big Butts* comes on, and the three of them start dancing along to the music, doing all the motions, and turning so their rear ends face the audience at the moment the lyrics say, *I like big butts.* They shake their hips from side to side and the room erupts in laughter.

This town.

I've always said we're a dysfunctional family of twenty-five hundred. If these three seniors doing that dance doesn't prove it, I don't know what does.

When the dance is over, Mabel takes the mic and says, "And if you want to follow me on TikTok, I'm at Bordeaux Granny's Got Back."

She gives me a thumbs up.

I give one back to her.

As she passes by me and Chris, she leans in and stage whispers, "Just like you taught me, Ella Mae. I didn't pass up the opportunity to give 'em my handle."

"Well done," I say.

People continue to filter up to the mic, and then there's a little commotion at the back of the barn.

I turn with everyone else to see what's going on, and my hand grips Chris' knee when I see who's standing between the barn doors.

My dad.

He makes his way up to me. I'm unable to move. He doesn't take the mic. Instead, he stands right in front of me, glancing over at Chris, and then meeting my eyes. "Ella Mae, I'm a private man—and a man who's seen the worst this town has to offer. If it weren't for the store, I might've moved years ago. And that's an awful thing to know about myself—that I'd stick around a town that looks down on me just for the sake of a store. Especially when I didn't have it in me to stand by my daughter. I don't know what to say to you, except I'm proud of you and all you've done. And I wish I had more of whatever you have in you, in me. I'm sorry my mistakes made your life hard. I'd like to think they helped make you into the kind of woman who doesn't let the opinions of others determine her life.

"I am truly sorry. I don't know what I can promise you, but I wanted you to know all that."

He turns to leave, obviously intending to walk out of the barn and go home now that he said his piece.

I stand up. "Dad?"

He slowly turns around. "Yeah?"

"Thanks."

I want to run to him and give him a hug, even with everyone standing here witnessing one of the most vulnerable moments in my life.

I can't, though. Maybe I'll just go by the shop more often. Or maybe …

I'm in the middle of trying to figure out how I can show my dad I accepted his warped apology—the best one he was capable of making, when he does the most unexpected thing. He takes a hesitant step, and then he walks back toward me. When he's right in front of me, he reaches out his arms and draws me into a hug—the hug I've apparently been waiting to experience for nearly twenty-five years. I melt into him and he holds me.

The barn is silent.

My tears fall onto my dad's shirt.

He steps back and looks me in the eyes. I smile at him. He gives me a soft nod and then he turns and walks out of the barn.

Chris must sense that I've had all I can take.

He stands up, and without even needing a mic, he addresses the crowd. "It's been a long day. Ella Mae's heard all you had to say. I'm thanking you on her behalf. And now I'm going to take her home so she can rest. I liked what Jayme said. Sorry is as sorry does. I'm counting on this town to put their money where their mouths are by treating one of the best people I know with a little more respect from here on out."

Chris turns to me and asks, "You good?"

"Yeah. I'm good."

I turn to the town I've called home for my whole life, looking across the sea of faces gathered here for me.

"I've only got one thing to say."

Chris looks confused. I smile at him and wink.

"Let's take a group selfie!"

The crowd erupts in laughter, but we do end up snapping some photos together. I doubt I'll post them on social media. Some things are meant to be cherished in your own heart, not shared with the world.

Chris backs down Aiden's driveway, but he turns the opposite direction than what I expect.

"What now, Soldier? I thought you were taking me home."

"I'll take you home if you want. But I thought you might want to go hang out at our spot by the lake before you call it a night."

"Oh, *our* spot is it?"

"Definitely."

Chris looks over at me. "I know I sprung that whole thing at the barn on you. I hope you know why I kept it a secret."

"Because I never would have let you take me there?"

"Pretty much. Do you forgive me?"

"If I'm dishing out forgiveness to just about everyone in town, I'm pretty sure your name is on the list."

"Whew. Well, I'll just have to let my actions match my words."

"Sounds good to me. I'm all about you groveling and making it up to me, Soldier."

Chris chuckles low and deep.

We pull up to the secluded beach—the spot where Chris

first told me he loves me. He kills the engine and then he leads me to the back of his truck. After he rearranges our suitcases so they're out of the way, Chris spreads out some blankets to cushion the bed of the truck.

"A girl might think you planned this, Big Boy."

"Planning is one of my strengths," he says.

I see the smirk on his face, despite the darkness starting to close in around us.

We lean back on the wall of the truck bed and Chris puts his arm around me.

"Was it too overwhelming?" he asks.

"A little. I don't know. I think it's going to take a while to feel real. I've lived here my whole life. Everyone's always treated me one way. It will be an adjustment getting used to being accepted and included."

"You adjusted to me," Chris says.

"Easy."

I run my hand through his hair and down his beard. "You made it so easy."

Chris leans in so his face is next to mine, his mouth tickling my ear, and then he whispers, "I like making things easy for you, Boots."

I shudder from the feel of his breath on my neck.

He kisses me in the very spot that's already feeling sensitive. Then he kisses his way around to my mouth. When our lips meet, I feel sparks erupt everywhere. Maybe it's the aftermath of so much emotion. Maybe it's just us, together.

Chris pulls back and looks down at me.

"I've never felt like this for anyone else."

I smile up at him, feeling more content than I've felt in days.

"Felt like what?"

"Love."

I think he's done, but he runs his hand along my face, his

blue eyes gazing into mine with such intensity of emotion, I hardly know how to keep looking at him.

"The kind of love I feel for you is like nothing I've ever felt."

He's talking so carefully, like he needs me to absorb every word.

"It's this love that makes me take stock. The kind of love that makes me fly to LA to chase you down—not because I didn't think you could handle yourself, but because I always want to be there when the world doesn't perceive how amazing you are."

He cups my face and leans down to press a gentle kiss to my forehead.

When he pulls back, he says, "Ella Mae, I'm not pulling out a ring quite yet, but I want you to know how serious I am about you. You're the one I want to do everything with.

"I want to feed one another dessert, to share our secrets, and to be the one to hold you when you cry. I want to watch you take over the world with your passion for positivity. I want to be the one person who gets to see the girl behind the camera—as she really is, vulnerable, tender, beautiful. And I've never felt like that before."

I smile at him. Wondering if I can even find the words to tell him what he means to me.

"You've been what no one ever has to me, Chris. I've had friendship—especially with Meg. And I've dated guys here and there. But I've never had a man see me so clearly and love me despite all my flaws. The way you believe in me is overwhelming.

"But even if you weren't all that. I'd still love you. I used to think you were this tough guy who never knew how to have fun. I was so wrong. You're the most kind hearted, caring, selfless man. And you make me laugh. I've never wanted any man as much as I want you. And I don't want you to save me. I just want to share my life with you—to be the one who goes to our secret place by the lake with you. I want to be the one who cheers you on, and who makes you feel like you can take on the world, and also reminds you that you don't have to. I'm so madly in love with you, Soldier."

Chris smooths my hair back and leans in to take my mouth in another kiss. It starts slow and tender, but we're both too wound up with all the emotions we've just expressed to one another. Chris kisses me like a man in love. And I kiss him with all the passion I feel for him. I run my fingers along the edge of his hairline across the back of his neck. A deep rumble comes up his throat. I giggle. He leans back, smiling down at me. This is us. Able to move from a moment of deep intimacy into a fit of laughter together. When our laughter dies down, I snuggle closer to Chris. We lay there holding one another, looking up at the stars overhead.

Bordeaux may have welcomed me back tonight, but this—being held in Chris' arms—this is home.

The End

But wait! There's more …

Epilogue

Ella Mae

"YOU LOOK BEAUTIFUL, like a bride out of a magazine," Meg's mom coos over her.

"I one hundred percent agree," I say from across the bridal suite.

I finish swiping the last coat of waterproof mascara on my lashes and stand to walk over toward Meg.

Meg and Joe chose a venue in Dayton, only a half-hour from Bordeaux. It's a historic home with a sprawling back yard with beautiful gardens. So far, the weatherman is on our side. Having an outdoor May wedding in southwest Ohio is like putting all your chips on black. You'll either win or you'll lose.

It's been nearly ten months since the overwhelming evening on Aiden's farm when the townspeople declared their love and admiration for all things Fab-U-lous. At first, no one really knew how to treat me after that night. It would have been comical if it weren't so completely awkward. Okay. Okay. It was pretty comical.

I'd walk into Bean There Done That, and Riley and Madeline would be their usual perky selves. That was fine. But the patrons around tables would look up as though someone tolled a bell announcing my arrival.

"Oh! Heya, Ella Mae!" someone would shout.

"Ella Mae, do you want to join us?" another person would offer, even though it was obvious they were here on a special coffee date.

"Hiiii! Ella Mae!" would come from somewhere across the other side of the shop. More greetings would follow that one.

"Ella Mae's here, everyone!" someone would announce, a little too late, but with gusto.

I wanted to wear a paper bag over my head, and trust me, even with the recent fashion of upside down dresses, that paper bag's never a good look on anyone. I can't blame the townspeople. We all could have used a manual with the title: *How to Include the Town Outcast After Your Grand Gesture.* I teased Chris that I just might take him up on his offer to move to Columbus if the weird vibes continued.

But they didn't.

Eventually, people went back to ignoring me, just in a much friendlier way, or they'd say hello without such pomp and circumstance. The girl group tried to invite me to girls' night—an event I always secretly wanted to attend. We all tried. And I give us an A+ for effort, but halfway through, I told them I was missing Chris—because I was. And they all commiserated about their early months of dating and excused me to go find my man.

Meg does a slow turn in the middle of the room and when she finishes, she looks me over.

"You're the prettiest Maid of Honor ever. People won't even notice me with you standing next to me."

I smile. "That's silliness. It's all about the babe in the white dress. Even Joe is just your accessory today. No one will be able to take their eyes off you."

Meg giggles. Her friends from Pennsylvania walk into the room. Two of them are in the wedding. I guess Meg made a ton of friends when she worked out on the east coast after college. Joe's sister, who lives somewhere else in Ohio, is also in the wedding. On his side are his best friend, who Meg tells me is a mortician, two cousins, and Chris.

The four of us started going on more double dates after Chris and I came back from Los Angeles. Joe and Chris have formed a friendship. Chris still hangs out with his lifelong friends regularly, and they have their guys' nights the same nights their wives have girls' nights. When there's a co-ed event, I tag along. Everyone does their best to be friendly. I'm probably the most comfortable with Jayme. Always was. But the rest of them are trying, and so am I.

The wedding coordinator knocks on the bridal suite door and announces, "It's showtime, Meg. May I come in?"

Meg's mom opens the door and we're all ushered downstairs to a spot just inside the french doors at the back of the house. There's a brick patio with three steps leading down to the yard where Meg will walk to Joe.

I peek through the glass to see the groomsmen. Well, I'm not interested in the mortician and the cousins, obviously. It's Chris who catches my eye, looking so scrumptious in a tux. His beard is trimmed short and his hair has a little product in it. I can barely focus on the instructions the wedding coordinator is giving us. He's just so distracting.

I finally look around at the guests in white wooden folding chairs, the string quartet set off to the side of the arbor, and then the groom. Joe looks a combination of nervous and overjoyed.

My eyes drift back to Chris. He's scanning the back of the house. I can tell the moment he sees me through the glass panes of the french doors. His face slowly breaks into that smile I love, and then he winks and his tongue darts out to wet his lips. I think my knees might buckle and give out. It's been a year since that night he saved me at the Big Boy and he still has the same effect on me —probably even more so now that I know the heart under all those muscles and rugged good looks.

Weddings make people dream, and I'm definitely dreaming of the day I'll be the one in the white dress, walking toward my man to say, "I do" to whatever it takes to make him my forever.

The music starts and the first two bridesmaids walk onto the patio, down the steps, and onto the runner, one right after the other. Joe's sister follows them. Then it's my turn. I step out of the house and my eyes immediately lock onto my soldier. He's the same calm, steady presence as always. And the way he's looking at me makes me feel like I could take over the world—a goal I've left in the dust this past year.

No more world domination for this boss babe. Though, I still have my social media. I post about three times a week these days, giving most of my time to a photography business I started a few months after our trip to LA.

I make my way down the runner, never taking my eyes off Chris. Is this what it will feel like on our wedding day? I know I'm here for Meg, and I'm all about being the best Maid of Honor ever for her. But at this moment I'm giving myself permission to dream, something I'm doing a lot more of lately. Hope had her way with me, and now I seem to be addicted to hoping and believing in my own sweet ending.

I used to strive for success and notoriety, like a dying

woman gasping for her very breath. But something shifted, and now I just know. It's gonna be so, so good, this life of mine. And I'm allowed to have my own happily ever after just as much as anyone else.

I reach the back of the garden and join the rest of the wedding party. Chris leans over just a touch so we can see one another, and mouths, "You look beautiful." He puts his hand over his heart, and I think I blush. I mouth back to him, "You look pretty beautiful yourself." I lightly lift my eyebrows with a promise of showing him just how beautiful I think he is after this ceremony is over.

The music shifts and Meg steps out through the french doors. The guests rise from their seats and turn to watch her walk toward Joe. I glance over at Joe for a split-second. He's beaming and a tear tracks down his cheek as he watches Meg walk toward him. I turn my eyes back to Meg who has a smile on her face like none I've ever seen.

The ceremony goes as usual. Some words from the pastor, vows, the exchanging of rings, and finally, the kiss. Joe lifts Meg's and his enjoined hands into the air and says, "We did it!" The crowd bursts into laughter.

Meg and Joe run down the aisle toward the house and we all follow, my arm looped in Chris'. Guests file out of their chairs and mingle while the staff at the venue do their magic, changing the setting from wedding to reception. Large tables are wheeled out, chairs are rearranged around the tables, and a dance floor is set up right near where the ceremony took place. The whole transformation takes under five minutes.

We're already taking photos in the living room. We'll take more outside shortly. I look out the windows. The sky has a few more clouds than it did this morning. Nothing unusual for this time of year. I'm sure we're good. I just worry for Meg. She put so much into planning every detail of her wedding. I want it to go perfectly for her.

Meg and I hug, and I hear the click of the photographer's camera. I pull back, "You are married!"

"I am!" she beams and her eyes dart away, looking for Joe. He sees her searching for him and walks over to put his arm around her waist.

"Congrats, you two," I say.

"You're next," Meg whispers.

"Not yet, I'm not."

"I bet it's soon," she says. "I've never seen a man more in love than Chris is with you."

"Hey," Joe says, smiling. "What am I over here?"

Meg giggles. "Okay. Chris is the second most in-love man ever."

"That's more like it," Joe says, leaning in to place a kiss on Meg's forehead.

He can think that. I know better. Chris is the most in-love man ever—and he's in love with me. It still blows my mind on a regular basis.

We're ushered back outside for more pictures while the guests mingle and eat tray-passed appetizers, and help themselves to drinks from the portable bar.

Since the reception area isn't divided at this venue, some guests stand around watching the wedding party take pictures. Then the DJ announces the couple. They step out onto the dance floor together. Chris stands at my side, his arm around my waist. Our eyes are on Meg and Joe. The air feels a little chillier, so I snuggle up next to Chris and he pulls me closer—like I need an excuse to be nearer to him. I don't.

Joe takes the microphone and greets the guests, thanking all of us for being here for Meg's and his special day. Then they have their first dance while we all look on. Christina Perri's *A Thousand Years* plays through the speakers set around the garden. It seems like it's telling our story—Chris' and mine. I pull him near and give him a squeeze. He looks down at me and our eyes say everything we need to say.

My opportunity to dance with Chris is next, during the wedding party dance. My arms are looped around his neck like a junior high student and his arms are laced behind my lower back.

Calum Scott's *You Are the Reason* plays, and Chris softly sings it into my ear as we sway. As if I needed any more persuading to fall for this man, he can sing. His resonant voice vibrates through me, telling me I'm his reason. Declaring all the things he'd do just to be with me.

He pauses his singing and says, "What a day," in his only-for-me voice.

He's looking at me with an expression I want to memorize.

"It's amazing. My bestie is married."

"You doing okay with all that?"

Ever the protector. He's got to check in on me, take my pulse, make sure I'm good. It used to unnerve me. But now I cherish it.

"I'm fine. I'm so happy for her, I've put the move completely out of my head."

"Obviously," he teases.

"Mostly," I admit.

Laura's aunt and uncle have a studio apartment over their garage. Laura mentioned it to me a few months ago, when I was getting my hair done. *That* would never have happened a year ago. So, for the time being, in a few weeks, I'll be moving up over the garage. It's not ideal for my yoga shoots, but it's a place to live for now, and the rent is dirt cheap. I nearly had to beg Laura's aunt and uncle to let me pay them.

The song stops, and Joe walks over to me and Chris, holding out the microphone in Chris' direction. It should be time for the meal now. Toasts come later.

I can feel my face scrunch in confusion until Chris drops down on one knee. I don't flinch like I thought I would. I've imagined this scene hundreds of times over the past six months, at least. Every meal out, every drive to Columbus to visit Alex and Courtney, every time he showed up at my door looking a little preoccupied, I'd ask myself, *Is this the time?* I've been so ready for this. So very ready.

Chris looks up at me and starts speaking into the microphone. "A year ago, I happened to be walking into a Frisch's Big Boy near Columbus. And, as fate would have it, Ella Mae was there."

People hush and now we're the center of everyone's attention. All eyes are on us—on Meg's big day. I glance over at her and she's beaming. Obviously, they're all in cahoots about this. I look back down at Chris.

"As you all know, Ella Mae and I didn't run in the same circles around Bordeaux, and to be honest, we sort of grated on one another's nerves half the time."

I whisper, "All the time, Big Boy. All.the.time."

He chuckles. "Yeah, more like all the time."

"Anyway, she had been stood up by a man I hope I never see in person. And I offered to step in. It wasn't like me to go on social media, but something about her that night made me bend my rules."

Duke shouts out, "We've got the footage if anyone wants to see it later! It's better on the big screen!"

Chris and I laugh along with everyone else in the crowd.

A lightning bolt cracks in the distance. Chris looks in that direction and his brow furrows. No thunder follows. It's a distant storm. We're good.

He keeps on relaying our history from his kneeling position. My whole body is humming with a light vibration of excitement. I know where this is headed. I mean, that's what happens when a man bends his knee in front of the woman he loves, right?

"Back then there was another guy—one I ended up meeting in person—who was saying inappropriate things to Ella Mae on her posts. Being the hero I am …" he laughs, and then he beams up at me. "I offered to put on a front like we were dating, just to give the guy a clear message to back off.

"But then people around town found out we were dating from what they saw online—even though we weren't—and we had to decide to either call it off, or carry it off. As you know, we kept it going. And I can't tell you the day or time, but I started falling hard for Ella Mae."

His eyes are fixed on mine, fierce and tender, the blue is more deep today, like a sky in spring. Not this sky, though. Another lightning bolt cracks, and this time a few seconds later, there's thunder. The crowd murmurs. We're midwesterners. Most of us are amateur meteorologists.

"Eh, Bob. Looks like rain." "Yeah, Sam. I reckon it's gonna be coming for a few days after this." "My knee agrees with your prediction. Reminds me of that storm we had back in '90." "Oh, yessir, that was a doozie. Got my tractor stuck in a ditch during that one."

Even those of us not living the agrarian life tend to scan the horizon and decide if the weatherman's right or not. What does he know? We can see the sky and feel the air.

And right now, this sky and this air does not bode well for an outdoor reception.

Chris soldiers on, but this time, even though he's holding the mic, his words are all for me. "I fell so hard for you, Boots. You came out of nowhere—the last woman I'd expect to fall for. I wasn't looking for a relationship, and here you were, stealing my heart, and changing me in the process. I'm a different man because of you. Still the same in the ways that matter, but you've helped me grow."

I never used to cry this much. Chris changed me too. I'm more confident in the deepest places, and I feel everything these days—especially how much I love him.

The lightning cracks, thunder sounds almost immediately, and before we can think about it, the rain comes down like a firehose. There's no slow build, we're at the heart of the storm. People start jumping up, screaming and yelling, running in all directions. Someone must have unplugged the mic, because it's dead now. Chris is still on his knee, and I'm still standing in front of him, one hand in his outstretched one, the rain rapidly soaking through my bridesmaid's dress.

"Ella Mae," Chris says, in a voice that sounds like we're basking on the beach and have all the time in the world to soak up the sun and relax. "You're it for me. I love you. Will you be my wife?"

Rain is coming in sheets, the sky has darkened. People continue to scramble all around us. The grass is pooling with puddles already. Guests are running to their cars, since we can't all fit into the house. I feel my makeup streaking down my face. My hair is a flattened mess on my head. Drenched. We're drenched. And I couldn't care less.

I shout through the rain to Chris. "Yes! Yes! I will be your wife! I promise to drive you crazy the rest of our lives."

Chris stands and pulls a ring box out of his pocket. He pulls me into his embrace and murmurs into my soaking wet hair, "I'd expect nothing less. And I promise to return the favor." Then he looks around and, as if he just noticed it's raining, he asks, "Um, do you want to do this somewhere else?"

"Nah," I answer with a huge smile.

"Yeah," he agrees. "I love this. We're going to have such a story to tell our grandkids."

I think I nearly pass out on the spot.

Grandkids.

That means kids. And then growing old. And then more kids that came from those kids. And me being the grandma.

But when I look at Chris, his face so focused and concentrated as he slips the ring on my finger, my heart settles.

Yes. I'll have all that.

If it's with this man, I'll have it all.

What's Next?

Share the book love ...

Something you can do really quickly:
If you loved ***Ripped & Shipped,*** you can help other readers find this story by leaving a review on Amazon.

~

If you've missed any of the Getting Shipped Series, you can find all the books on Amazon.

Join Savannah Scott in the NEXT SERIES!
Love Trippin' will take place on th fictional Marbella island off the coast of California ... picture *Gilmore Girls* meets *55 First Dates*. Book one, *Are We There Yet,* releases summer 2023.

To be the first to hear about release dates, sales, sneak peeks behind the scenes sign up for Savannah's weekly email.

Sign up at
https://www.subscribepage.com/savannahscottromcom

A little backstory …

I grew up in a small college town in southwest Ohio with farmland all around the outskirts, rivers and gorges to play in, and plenty of woods to hike in.

People stopped to chat when they ran into one another in the grocery (while impatient kids watched the ice cream melt in the cart). Neighbor children ran in and out of one another's homes all day long until supper time.

We caught fireflies on summer nights, sledded down snowy hills on campus, chatted around bonfires on our friends' farms, and drove the tractors before we ever drove cars. (*Shhh. Don't tell.*)

I adore the small-town Ohio culture. It really is down-home goodness, set in a beautiful landscape with rich history.

I love writing books that make people laugh, with a little life lesson tucked away in them somewhere. I always end with a happily ever after that gives us all a smile in our hearts.

Thank you for letting me share my stories with you.

And my heart is beyond full having finished this last book in the precious Getting Shipped series. Thankfully, we can all return to Bordeaux whenever we want — just pick up a story and revisit old friends.

Savannah Scott

All the Thanks ...

A story is birthed in one imagination, but it is raised by many hands and hearts.

I want to thank **Gila,** for walking alongside me through this story and for believing in me. Your eye for story has blessed me deeply.

Tricia Anson, thank you for being one of the best proofreaders and personal assistants out there, and for being a dear personal friend. Thanks too, **Kari Cheney**. You two are the keepers of my sanity. Here's to the snort laughs we share, answered prayers, and all the goodness we share nearly daily. You two are a gift to me.

A special thanks to **Tom A**. for helping me with the government aspect of Chris' life. You were such a valuable resource as I worked through what was realistic for his job and his internet involvement.

Kirsten (Kiki) Oliphant, you helped me find my wings. You believed in me. You taught me. Our friendship is a treasure. I'm so grateful to be doing author life with you.

To my **Awesome Advanced Readers** and the **AMAZING Bookstagram and Bookish Community** on Instagram and Facebook. You people bless my socks off—as evidenced by my nearly-constant bare feet.

Thank you to my oh-so-talented sister**, Mary Hessler Goad** for the cover design. This cover the best yet. You have outdone yourself!

Jessica Gobble, My first and best cheerleader, my ride-or-die, my pie-hoarding secret-keeper, the one I laugh most with and cry with first. You are the sister of my heart, and my soft place to land. You believed in me before I believed in myself. And now we all can thank you. I may have never stepped out to write like this if it weren't for you.

Jon, my not-book boyfriend, Thank you for believing in me and supporting me. There aren't words for the way you have made it possible for me to pursue my lifelong dream of becoming a full-time author. Special thanks for all the private stand-up comedy I get to have on the daily with you.

And the biggest thanks to God for making me a storyteller and giving me the gifts I've received on this journey.

And to the readers who faithfully read Savannah Scott romcom books — that's **YOU**. Thank you for believing in me and loving the stories I weave.

You are the best!

Made in the USA
Middletown, DE
02 November 2024

63304522R00257